"You miserable arrogant excuse for a gentleman,"

she all but snarled, punctuating her epithet with another swipe from the whip.

Gilen dodged the whirling thong and backed away, his initial astonishment giving way to incredulous delight. By heaven, she was magnificent! This girl still garbed like a proper ton maiden had changed before his eyes from demure virgin into the passionate creature who had told his fortune, teased his wits and tantalized him with a dance.

"You find this *amusing?*" she choked out. And lashed the whip at him again.

He ducked as the leather tip nearly caught his left ear. "If you can't control yourself, I'll have to disarm you."

Ah, that she might compel him to do it! With her body bound closely to his was exactly where this astonishing, intoxicating, intemperate vixen belonged.

He couldn't wait to see how her passionate nature played out in his bed…!

JULIA JUSTISS

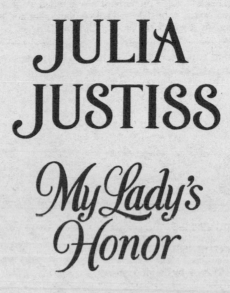

My Lady's Honor

HARLEQUIN®

TORONTO • NEW YORK • LONDON
AMSTERDAM • PARIS • SYDNEY • HAMBURG
STOCKHOLM • ATHENS • TOKYO • MILAN • MADRID
PRAGUE • WARSAW • BUDAPEST • AUCKLAND

ISBN 0-373-29229-5

MY LADY'S HONOR

Copyright © 2002 by Janet Justiss

Visit us at www.eHarlequin.com

Printed in U.S.A.

Please address questions and book requests to:
Harlequin Reader Service
U.S.: 3010 Walden Ave., P.O. Box 1325, Buffalo, NY 14269
Canadian: P.O. Box 609, Fort Erie, Ont. L2A 5X3

To my mother,
Beatrice Ruth Langley,
who taught me a woman can do anything.
For your love and support,
thanks, Mom.

Chapter One

"Your cousin Nigel—that is, the new Baron Southford, be awaitin' ye in the library," the maid informed her with a curtsey.

Gwennor Southford sighed and removed the apron with which she'd covered her mourning gown while she helped Jenny and the staff clear away the remains of the breakfast they'd served after her father's interment. "Thank you, Jenny. Tell him I will join him shortly."

While the maid departed, Gwen stopped to check her hair in the black-draped hall mirror, making sure no unruly strands had escaped her coiffeur to catch the eye of her punctilious cousin. A London dandy of the first stare, Nigel never failed to look at her without a slightly pained expression, as if she offended him by sporting soot on her nose or a spot on her gown. Which most of the time, she allowed, she probably did.

Or perhaps it was just that, not being able to peer down at her from a superior height, cousin Nigel tried to intimidate her with his faintly contemptuous gazes. Though they did not succeed in leaving her in awe of him, she did often feel like a large, ugly and not very interesting beetle being inspected under a glass.

Finding that her thick black hair, which had a tendency to curl wildly despite her efforts to subdue it, was still neatly braided, Gwen walked on to the library. She couldn't imagine what cousin Nigel needed to say to her that could not have been expressed in front of a roomful of other guests.

Perhaps he merely wished to complain—again—about the meals or accommodations. Which, she had no doubt, he would soon be "improving" by the addition of a foreign chef to create dishes more suitable to his cultured palate, followed by an army of workmen to update the century-old rooms to a more fashionable mien.

She grimaced at the idea of her beloved home being transformed under his ruthless hand. Pray God she could convince him to send her to London for the upcoming Season, so she might find a husband and Parry and herself a new home.

Damping down a niggle of unease, she knocked on the library door then entered.

She had to suppress a pang at seeing her cousin lounging in her father's favorite chair behind the massive desk. Wrenching her thoughts from reflections that could only bring on another wave of useless grief, she curtseyed and forced herself to focus on Nigel.

Once again he subjected her to a lengthy, critical inspection. "Well, cousin Gwennor, I'm afraid the years have not much improved you, but at least you've the sense to keep that peasant's hair tightly braided, and your other features are not unpleasant. I suppose, with the addition of a small dowry, you will do well enough."

"Thank you, cousin," Gwen said sweetly with a clenched-teeth smile, "for your kind condolences on my father's death. And I am...gratified to earn your approval."

"Your tendency to indulge in levity at inappropriate moments does not become you, Gwennor," he replied loftily. "I'm quite certain I offered you my sympathies upon my arrival yesterday. However, it does no good to linger in the past. Changes will be taking place at Southford now that I am baron, and you must adapt to them."

"Naturally, cousin." She would not refer to him as "my lord," she thought mutinously, no matter that she was no longer the daughter of the house but merely a female relation dependent on his charity. "Does your reference to my dowry mean that you intend sending me to London for the Season, as I've requested? I shall be ready to leave as soon as my bags can be packed."

She cast her eyes down and clasped her hands in such a picture of maidenly humility that Nigel, no fool despite his affectations, gave her a sharp look.

"I have given thought to your eventual settlement, yes. I think we both agree that it is in neither of our interests that you remain at Southford. After all, the quality of establishment you maintained for your papa, though adequate enough, I suppose, for a Welsh baron of rural tastes, will not do for me."

"No, cousin, my sort of household—" which, she added silently, would be notable for simplicity, kindness and courtesy to all "—would definitely not suit you."

"I'm glad we agree on that score. And since with the alterations necessary to bring the manor and outbuildings up to the standards worthy of my stewardship, the estate is likely to suffer some heavy financial demands, I see no reason to throw away money on a London season. You're well past the age of presentation, no great beauty and your dowry is merely adequate. I do not wish to be unkind, but a dispassionate assessment must conclude that your chances of attracting the eye of a gentleman wealthy and influential enough to make a connection with his family worth the heavy expense of sending you to London are, I regret to say, remote. In this, you must trust my far greater knowledge of the sensibilities of ton gentlemen.''

So used to his disparagement that his strictures scarcely made her wince, Gwen's active mind considered instead the implications. Not London. Would he send her to Bath, perhaps? Or to the Assembly in Gloucester?

''It was to announce my solution to this delicate dilemma that I summoned you. Of course, I am fully sensible that as a Southford and my cousin, you must wed a man of good reputation and standing, if not one as discriminating in his requirements as I am myself. I have chosen such a husband for you, cousin. You may congratulate yourself on soon becoming the bride of Lord Edgerton.''

Shock riveted her to the spot. ''Edgar Edgerton, B-Baron Edgerton?'' she stuttered, hoping there might be some misunderstanding.

''Indeed,'' the new Lord Southford replied, smiling benevolently. ''I can see how overwhelmed you are by my choice. Lord Edgerton may be a trifle older than you, but he is still a fine figure of a man, and his six motherless sons, poor lads, will give you ample opportunity to practice your preferences for frugality and a rustic outdoor life.''

Gwen swallowed hard. Edgar Edgerton, a hunting crony of Nigel's, was pushing fifty, with a short, stout figure and high coloring that indicated a probable tendency to gout. He resided all year on his estates in Lincolnshire, having, as far as Gwen knew, few interests beyond his stables and his kennels. There would certainly be no need to expend Southford estate money on modish gowns for her trousseau, she thought acidly.

''I...I have heard by all reports that Lord Edgerton is a most...amiable gentleman,'' she said with only a slight quaver in her voice. ''But I am somewhat concerned about

his sons, whom rumor would hold to be a bit…spirited."
In truth, the alarming escapades indulged in by the baron's
energetic offspring, descriptions of which had been brought
back to Southford by her father when he hunted with the
baron's pack the previous year, had made even as indulgent
a gentleman as her papa shake his head in dismay. "I hope
they will not be too rough with Parry."

Her cousin had been listening idly, his attention focused
on removing a barely visible speck of lint from the sleeve
of his immaculate coat of black superfine, but at this his
fingers stilled. "Parry?" he said with a frown. "What has
that half-wit to do with this?"

"Well, naturally I assumed that since you do not…get
on with Parry, he would go with me when I married."

"Whatever would cause you to believe such nonsense as
that?" her cousin demanded, his tone aggrieved. "Use
what little wit you possess, Gwennor. For one thing, your
father long ago designated me as the boy's guardian after
his death. Even though he's not a blood relative, I am not
one to shirk a duty, no matter how distasteful. Besides,
Lord Edgerton, who prides himself upon the bloodlines of
his breeding stock, could never abide having that degenerate about, no more than would any other person of sensibility."

"Parry is no degenerate," Gwen replied hotly, "and he
possessed more wit than you until that stallion kicked
him!"

Nigel looked at her with cold eyes. "I shall forgive you
that remark only because I know you still harbor some ridiculous conviction that, since Parry was injured going to
your defense, you are obligated now to defend him. But do
not trespass too far upon my goodwill. I grant you, so devastating an accident occurring to a child of his tender age
was tragic, but 'tis long past time to be done with such sen-

timentality. He's now—eighteen, is he not? He should have been confined years ago, instead of being allowed to wander the woods and fields of Southford, an embarrassment to the family and a threat to the countryside.''

"Parry is no threat to anyone!" Gwen protested. "He treats every fellow creature with consideration! And he's not an embarrassment—everyone at Southford knows and appreciates him.'' *Save you,* she thought furiously.

"Not an embarrassment?" Nigel retorted. "And what would you call it when he interrupted the solemnity of your father's obsequies, stumbling into the church in dirty boots and a torn jacket, his pocket full of wild creatures!" He made a grimace of repulsion.

"Baby rabbits," Gwen replied, trying to hold back the tears that threatened. "Papa was developing a new domestic strain, you'll remember, and interbreeding them with the darker-colored wild rabbits from the mountains. Parry brought him those as a parting gift.''

"Gift—bah!" Nigel said contemptuously. "That drooling simpleton had no idea the man who'd died was his stepfather—nor any conception of what death means. Although he's soon to get a lesson in the latter.''

"You're wrong, cousin Nigel. He knew it was his *papa,*" she emphasized the word, "and he understands about death." True, Parry might not have comprehended the threat to his own position implicit in his stepfather's demise, a threat that—with good reason, it turned out— Gwen had so feared, but he knew the elderly man who'd treated him with love and gentleness had gone away forever.

"Well, I find him offensive, so something shall certainly be done about it. Edgerton wishes to have you settled in at the Hall between the last of the hunting season and the beginning of spring planting, so the wedding is to be at week's end, here at Southford. Given the groom's age and the shortness of time to prepare, I see no need for anything elaborate. A simple ceremony with a small reception immediately after should be sufficient.''

Cheese-paring nip-squeeze, Gwen thought, too furious to respond. The will had not even been read yet, and already the new baron was determined to expend as few funds as possible on the former daughter of the house.

''Congratulations on your good fortune, Gwennor. You may go now to begin the preparations.'' He waved an imperious hand toward the door—dismissing her from her own library like a lackey.

Too shocked and angry to reply with a remark her cousin would consider suitable for a gentlewoman, in icy silence she pivoted toward the door.

''By the way,'' her cousin's voice halted her before she reached the doorway, ''since I expect your bridegroom sometime tomorrow, I intend to have your stepbrother...taken care of before his arrival. Parry shall be confined to the attics, where he can be restrained but kindly treated, at minimal expense. Oh, and should you suffer from some maidenly excess of nerves before the wedding and attempt to call off your nuptials, remember that I have the power to confine *you* as well, should you take a sudden notion not to acquiesce willingly in my plans.''

He paused, regarding her thoughtfully. She stared back at him, defiantly mute, not caring that he could probably read on her face the intensity of her dislike.

''I shall warn you only once,'' he said softly. ''Growing up, you had a deplorable tendency to obstinacy and disobedience, traits I doubt your weak-willed papa ever succeeded in rooting out of you. I am not a man who can be manipulated by a shrewish spinster entirely too accustomed to running things her own way. I am master here now, and the servants will obey me." He nodded. "That is all." And looked down to peruse a ledger on the desk.

Her head and heart teeming with a volatile mix of grief, anguish, worry over her brother, fury at her cousin's threats and fear for the future, Gwen picked up her skirts and half ran through the hall, down the servants' stairs to the deserted stillroom and out the back door.

Shivering in the late-winter cold, she continued on behind the gardens to the barn surrounded by a collection of sheds and pens where her brother carried out his father's breeding experiments. She spied Parry's dark head bent over one of the cages and walked in his direction. His sharp ears no doubt picking up the soft pad of her footsteps, he looked up and smiled at her.

As she drew closer, his smile turned to a frown. "You have no shawl! You'll be cold, Gwen." Before she could stop him, he shucked his tattered wool jacket and wrapped it around her shoulders.

She reached up to hug him fiercely, tears seeping now from the corners of her eyes. How she loved her gentle, serene brother. Even did she not, as Nigel had alleged, feel responsible for his injuries, Parry was so unspoiled and utterly pure a soul she must love him, as nearly everyone in the county did, for his healing hands and sweet-tempered kindness.

He had a special touch with animals and young people. Both seemed to respond to his straightforward nature and both seemed to sense how competently he could soothe and help them. Not only had Parry directed her papa's rabbit-breeding operations, he was sought by neighbors from all over to treat their ailing livestock, providing, despite Nigel's dismissal of his usefulness, a small income to Southford's coffers.

The whole county knew if Parry Wakefield could not

cure an animal's ills, the owner might as well prepare to bury it.

What was she to do? Gwen wondered as she held her brother close. She might detest Nigel, but she wouldn't make the mistake of underestimating him. If he'd said he would put Parry under restraint, he would do it. And he would have no compunction about locking her up too if she tried to stop him. Nor did she wish to put the servants in the untenable position of opposing their new master.

At last she released Parry. He held her at arm's length, his guileless face studying hers. "You're sad, aren't you, Gwen? Are you missing Papa? I am, too. Look at these babies." He opened a wicker cage and indicated some tiny balls of fluff. "Misty had them Sunday past—and they are all browns. Just what he wanted. I think he's happy, looking down at them from heaven."

"I'm sure he is." Happier than any of us this side of heaven are likely to be again, she thought bitterly.

Her brother had been wholly content since his physical recovery from his injuries, wandering the estate at Southford, watched over by family and neighbors who cared for him, collecting and succoring the animals he loved.

He would pine away and die without them, locked up in the attics at Southford Manor.

Well on the shelf at five-and-twenty, Gwennor had no illusions about her beauty or her prospects. She'd taken over the management of the household at age fifteen, upon the death of her stepmother—the only mother she remembered, her own having died at her birth. In her concern for her stepbrother and her grieving papa, she'd easily withstood the baron's half-hearted attempts to send her away for a Season several years later. If Lord Edgerton were prepared to accept Parry, she would give herself to him, if not enthusiastically, at least with resignation.

But would he?

She'd have little time to plead with him, and no leverage to bargain with. Besides, Nigel was probably correct. Most people shied away from anyone with an impairment, which was often looked upon as God's judgment upon the unhappy individual and his family. Being Nigel's friend—indictment enough in Gwen's opinion—as well as a fanatic on the purity of the bloodlines of his horses and dogs, Edgerton would doubtless agree with Nigel's solution for dispensing with the embarrassment of his bride's mentally deficient brother. No, she concluded, Parry would find no champion in Edgerton.

And if he would not accept Parry, she had no reason to wed the man, despite Nigel's threats. She'd not spent the last ten years, as he'd described her, an obstinate spinster growing accustomed to running things her own way, to meekly succumb to her detestable cousin's plans for either herself or her beloved stepbrother.

"I must feed the others," Parry said. "Can you help?"

"No, I must get back to the house. Here, take your jacket back before you catch a chill."

She held it out. With a smile he waved it away. "I'll get it later. I have these—" he scooped up a handful of soft rabbit babies "—to keep me warm."

She turned to walk to the house, her anxiety sharpening. Tomorrow morning was terrifyingly close. She would have to think of some way to rescue them both before then, but to be safe, 'twas better for her brother to remain well away from the house until she decided how she was going to do it.

"Parry!" she called back to him. "Nigel will be down for dinner."

Her brother's smile faded. The only person her friendly

step-sibling did not like was their father's cousin. "Must I come eat with him?"

"No. Stay with the animals. I'll bring you a tray later. No sense both of us having to deal with him." She made an exaggerated grimace of distaste that set her brother laughing.

"Thank you, Gwen. I'll find you a surprise for tonight."

A lovely surprise it would be, too, she knew—a bird's nest he'd rescued, or a rock crystal of unusual shape and color, or an intricately woven spider's web as complex and beautiful as a master engraving.

Unlike the surprise his cousin had in mind for Parry tomorrow.

A fate he will never suffer while I draw breath, Gwennor vowed, and walked purposefully back to the house.

Chapter Two

Her mind working furiously, Gwennor paced across the stableyard. They would have to leave tonight, secretly, after her cousin and the rest of the household had retired. She would tell Jenny and Cook when they prepared Parry's tray that she planned to work with him well into the evening, so not to wait up for her—a fairly frequent occurrence that should protect the servants from potential dismissal for not alerting their new master that she'd left the house. Since her cousin slept until noon, it was quite possible he'd not discover their disappearance until rather late tomorrow. Perhaps not even, she thought with a savage grin of satisfaction, until his dear friend Lord Edgerton arrived and he summoned the blushing bride to greet her eager bridegroom.

She'd need to pack a small bag—something that could be easily and surreptitiously transported. She'd better bring all her mother's jewelry; she would not put it past her cousin, once he discovered she'd fled, to sell it and keep the money. She'd also need to sneak into the office while cousin Nigel took his nap before dinner. Considering that she'd be saving the estate the expense of her wedding breakfast, she felt justified in removing all the coins currently in the estate's strongbox.

She would also have to go through the motions of planning a wedding. Though she didn't need to seem enthusiastic—that would certainly be suspect—Nigel might well inquire about the progress of her preparations at dinner and would find it suspicious if she had not set the servants to beginning the arrangements. They would have to be warned of Lord Edgerton's imminent arrival in any event.

Having dispensed with the details of getting away, she turned her thoughts to the thornier problem of where they would go and how they would get there.

By now she'd reached the house. Gwennor paused before the stillroom door. 'Twas still too early to risk entering the estate office. Best to slip unnoticed up to her chamber and finish planning.

She crept up the servants' stairs to her room and paced to the window. Hands clasped in concentration, she stared unseeing over the rose and herb gardens.

If only her first cousin Harry weren't away with Wellington in the Peninsula! First in each other's affections, they'd always joked. They'd been boon companions throughout the time she was growing up. Were he at home, Gwennor knew he would assist her escape. But though his mama, her aunt Frances, resided an easy two days' ride from Southford, that widowed lady would be no match for a determined cousin Nigel, should he decide to pursue his disobedient kinswoman.

Would he pursue her? Or simply wash his hands of her, glad to be rid of the burden of a cousin he'd never liked?

Were it not for the plans he'd set in train to marry her off to his crony, she might well think the latter. But she did not believe his kindly-elder-cousin talk of arranging her marriage to insure she had a permanent position worthy of her breeding. She suspected there was far more to the agreement, and given her cousin's proclivities, probably something involving money.

Ever since her father had declined to remarry after her stepmother's death, her cousin had been living on the expectation of one day taking control of Southford and all its resources. His self-professed "refined" tastes in clothes and furnishings were expensive, as were his gaming habits, and she would not be at all surprised to learn he was heavily in debt. Perhaps he owed Edgerton, and had decided to use Gwen and her dowry as a means to repay the baron, at no cost to himself.

Yes, that would appeal to Nigel: not only getting rid of his detested cousin, but using *her* money to pay off *his* obligations.

If her suspicions were correct, he would not view with equanimity the double insult of being embarrassed in front of his friend and losing his free means of repayment. She'd also had a glimpse this afternoon of Nigel's relish for exercising his power as Baron Southford. Even were there in actuality no financial considerations involved, having Gwennor flout his new authority before his friend and her former household was certain to enrage him. He'd probably be angry enough to pursue her, if only to drag her back and impose an equally public punishment.

So, how to make a swift and clean break? Were they to make haste to the nearest posting inn, Nigel would likely catch them either while they awaited the next mail coach or once they'd transferred to that slower conveyance. If they traveled by horseback and she used precious coin to hire new mounts at each stage, as a single lady traveling with no maid in attendance, she would be singular enough that most innkeepers or stablemasters would remember her, making them all too easy to trace.

It was imperative they get far enough away for Nigel's anger to cool and to make further pursuit sufficiently expensive and bothersome that he might choose to simply let them go. Of equal importance was finding a haven that offered some unimpeachable reason for her to withstand his efforts to force her back to Southford, if he did succeed in tracking her.

Harrogate! the answer suddenly occurred to her. They could make their way to her stepmother's Aunt Alice in Harrogate. Gwen had not seen the lady since her step-mama's funeral a number of years previously, but they still corresponded, and she had no doubt the sweet, frivolous Lady Alice would be delighted to receive her.

Not only was the mineral spa in which she resided fortuitously distant, many of its residents and visitors were elderly widowers come to take the waters. Among them, perhaps Gwennor could find a kindly gentleman who'd be willing to wed a young, strong, hardworking lady of good family prepared to run his household and care for him in his declining years—at the negligible cost of also housing her brother.

She could claim Aunt Alice's assistance in her matrimonial quest—what lady could resist the chance to play matchmaker? With luck, she might find an acceptable candidate quickly, perhaps even be wed before Nigel could trace her.

If the new baron found her still single and insisted she marry the suitor he'd chosen, Lord Edgerton could just as easily travel to Harrogate to claim her.

Gwen would wager her mother's entire collection of jewelry that Edgerton would not.

So she now had a destination, but there remained the problem of how to traverse that long distance undetected.

She had reviewed the alternatives over and over, unable

to decide which one offered the best chance of successfully evading pursuit, when suddenly another idea occurred, so far-fetched and outrageous she nearly rejected it out of hand.

But, she decided, the advantage lay in its very outrageousness. Cousin Nigel might scour the roads, make a sweep of the posting inns, and question every innkeeper and livery stableman within a hundred miles of Southford and never locate them.

She scrambled to her desk, jerked open the top drawer, and began tossing out the objects in a disordered heap on the desktop. After rooting through each of the drawers in turn, she'd accumulated a trove of small coins and one golden guinea.

Hardly a fortune, but, she hoped, enough to tempt a king.

Quickly she changed into her riding habit and stuffed her findings into a small leather pouch. Tying the strings around her wrist, she tucked it under her sleeve and summoned her maid.

Jenny arrived so speedily Gwennor suspected the woman had been anxiously awaiting a chance to learn the results of Gwen's interview. Sure enough, with the familiarity of one who had been first her nurse and then her maid practically since Gwen's birth, as soon as she hurried in, Jenny asked, "So what was it the new master be wantin'?"

"Cousin Nigel feels it is time for me to marry."

"Saints be praised!" Jenny replied. "'Tis the very thing I've wished for ever since your papa took so sick. Now that the new baron's here, and being how he is, 'tis best ye git a household of yer own, with a husband to protect you. So, when be we goin' to London?"

"We are not going to London. Cousin Nigel has already chosen my husband. In fact, he arrives tomorrow."

Jenny's enthusiasm chilled abruptly. "Already chosen? Who…who is it to be, my lady?"

"Lord Edgerton."

Consternation extinguished the remaining traces of Jenny's gladness. "Lord Edgerton! Why, that gentleman is twice your age or more! With a pack of unruly brats as would try the patience of the Virgin Mother herself, so the story goes! Surely your cousin—"

"My cousin is fixed upon it, Jenny, and will brook no opposition. Indeed, he's threatened to lock me away if I resist. So there's no purpose to be served in repining. Lord Edgerton arrives tomorrow and the wedding is to be the end of the week. A simple affair, cousin Nigel said. Given the circumstances," she finished dryly, "you may dispense with the traditional wishes for my happiness."

"My poor chick," Jenny said, distress on her face. "'Tis a dastardly thing for the new baron to do, and I can't help if I think it!"

Gwennor gave the maid a quick hug. "Bless you, Jenny. But you and the rest of the staff must be circumspect in what you say. I'm not sure who among you, if any, I'll be able to take with me when I wed, and those who remain will have to work for my cousin."

"Probably turn us all off without a character and fetch in some jumped-up London toffs," Jenny muttered.

"I hope he will value you all as he ought. Now, would you tell Cook and Hopkins to make a room ready for Lord Edgerton and ask them to begin considering preparations for a wedding breakfast? I shall consult with them tomorrow about the details, but for now…" Gwen let her sentence trail off and tried to look mournful, not a difficult task. "I believe I shall ride."

"Well, and I don't wonder at it!" Jenny said. "Settin' you up with a man old enough to be your papa, and marryin' you off all havey-cavey, without even time to buy bride clothes! You go on, Miss Gwen. A ride will do your spirits good, and I'll get Hopkins movin' on the preparations.''

"Oh, and Parry will not be joining us for dinner. I told him I'd bring him a tray later...and I—I think I shall stay out late, helping him with the animals. I shall not be able to do so much longer, after all.''

"Bless me, Miss Gwen, whatever is to become of that poor boy with you gone? I worry about it, I do!''

"You know I would never allow anyone to harm Parry— no matter what I must do to prevent it. I shall think of something, Jenny.''

"You bein' so clever and all, I suppose you will. Now, get you off ridin', and leave the rest to Jenny.''

Gwennor gave one last hug to the woman who'd been more mother than servant to her for the last ten years. "Thank you, Jenny. You're an angel!''

"If'n I was, I'd be spreadin' out my wings and carryin' you off to London,'' the maid declared, still shaking her head in disapproval as she walked away.

Gwennor picked up her pace and sped to the stables. She must complete her mission and return with enough time to rifle the strongbox before cousin Nigel rose to dress for dinner.

Firefly, her ginger mare, whinnied a greeting as she approached the hay-fragrant stall, and Gwen felt a pang of regret and anger. Another dear friend, along with her home, she'd soon be forced to abandon.

Sending the stable boy back to his other chores, she saddled the mare and headed off at a trot, letting the horse stretch her legs in a gallop once they reached the open fields near the Home Woods, and then continuing on at a canter to the far south meadow.

"Please," she prayed. "Let them still be there."

When at last she saw the gaily-painted wagons beside the stream that formed the border of Southford land, she let out a gusty breath of relief.

Slowing Firefly to a walk, she proceeded to the end wagon. Before she'd even dismounted, a dark-eyed urchin with a thatch of black hair ran over to catch her bridle.

"A copper for you if you'll take her to drink at the stream—but not too much water, now!"

Gwennor smiled as the lad trotted off, Firefly in tow, and turned to the old woman who sat by her campfire regarding her gravely.

"So, you come to have your fortune read, now that the Evil One descends upon your home?"

"No, Jacquinita. I'm afraid I know what you'd find in my palm," Gwen replied with a grimace, not at all surprised the most revered of the gypsy soothsayers already knew of her cousin's arrival. "I came to ask a favor."

With a jangle of her many bracelets, the gypsy motioned her to sit. "What favor?"

"Parry and I must leave Southford immediately, but we must depart in a way that my cousin cannot trace. I want to ask Remolo to allow us to travel in your train, disguised as Rom. I will pay in coin and in jewels for this boon. Will you plead my case for me?"

The woman fingered a pleat of her full red skirt. "He means to harm you, your cousin, yes?"

"He wishes to marry me to his friend, but that is not why we flee. He intends to lock Parry in the attics and not allow him to roam free. The Rom, of all people, should understand what this would do to my brother."

The old woman nodded. "He has the gift, your brother. Such a spirit should not be caged. Your father was a good man, for a *gadjo*. Every year he allowed us to camp in his fields. That one—'' she spat in the direction of Southford Manor, then made a sign of protection against the evil eye ''—will call the magistrates on us soon, so have I warned the people. Therefore we leave at dusk. I will speak with Remolo.''

"Dusk!" Gwennor cried with alarm. "If I am to depart undetected, I cannot leave the manor until near on midnight. Please, tell Remolo I will pay him well if he will wait and take us!"

The old woman stood, adjusting her full skirts and the multicolored head scarf. "I will tell him. You follow."

Gwennor removed the small leather pouch and held it out. "Take him this. 'Tis a token and pledge. Tell him I will bring twenty more gold pieces when we come tonight."

The old woman snatched the leather pouch from her fingers. "So will I say."

Gwennor followed as instructed, praying a merciful God would intercede with the gypsy overlord. Swarthy, handsome, mercurial and unquestioned master over his band, Remolo's decision—like her cousin's, she thought with irony—would be final and irrevocable.

As she had only a very basic knowledge of the Romany language, Gwennor could not follow much of the conversation that ensued. The old woman offered the money pouch, which the gypsy lord accepted with a short bow in her direction. But after Jacquinita spoke for several minutes, with gestures and dark looks toward Southford Manor, Remolo's face creased in a frown and he shook his head in vehement negative.

Though it would avail her little to beg, Gwennor was on the point of throwing herself at the gypsy's knees when, after another rapid-fire speech by the soothsayer, Remolo paused, a thoughtful look crossing his face, and then gave a slight nod. After an elaborate curtsey, the old woman returned to Gwennor.

"He will take us?" Gwennor demanded.

The old woman smiled. "For your small gold, he thanks you. But he did not wish to bring along so heavy a burden. I told him you would work for us, playing cards and telling fortunes for the *gadjo* who come to the wagons where we stop. He said we have women and children enough for those things. Then I reminded him that Parry had cured his stallion—and that his favorite mare is due to foal soon. So, he will let you come for the sake of your brother's skill and the money you promise—but he will not wait until midnight."

Gwen's initial exhilaration faded rapidly. "We cannot go before then! Or rather, I cannot." A heart-wrenching choice that really was no choice confronted her. Deciding rapidly, she said, "Parry can. If I pay Remolo as promised, will he take Parry? And will you watch over my brother and keep him s-safe?" Her voice broke at the awful thought of sending Parry away alone.

The old woman came over to touch Gwen's face. "Child of my soul, you know I will. But you would send your brother from harm and not yourself?"

Gwennor nodded. "For myself I do not care, I will figure out something. But I cannot protect Parry from Nigel if he stays."

"You have the heart of the wildcat, my child," the woman said approvingly. "So have you been since I met you as a little girl—brave, strong and fierce. Ah, if you had been Rom, I would have made you my *mulkini*, that you might carry on after me. Do not think I, Jacquinita, *drabarni* of the Remali Rom, will leave you to that Evil One. Come to the clearing at midnight. My grandson Davi—" she nodded toward the boy holding Firefly by the stream

"—will wait for you and lead you to us. Go in the spirit, child."

Gwennor threw her arms around the old woman's neck. "Thank you, *dya!*"

Jacquinita released her, chuckling softly. "We will dress you in skirts and the *kishti,* with bracelets and earrings and a scarf in that dark hair. Ah, *leibling,* what a gypsy you will make!"

Chapter Three

Three weeks later, Gwennor dropped the last load of firewood beside Jacquinita's wagon and brushed off her hands. With a now-expert eye, she calculated she had another half hour's daylight to return to the stream, draw water and wash.

She flexed her tired shoulders as she trotted back to the small river near which Remolo had ordered them to make camp this afternoon. Jacquinita had promised the gypsy lord that Gwen and her brother would work, and work they had, Gwen carrying water, foraging for firewood, and assisting with the cooking, while Parry helped the men hunt for game and care for the horses. Though Gwennor had supervised her Southford staff in performing a wide variety of household tasks, she had done little of the physical labor herself. Most evenings, she was so exhausted that she fell asleep the moment she rolled into her blankets in a corner of Jacquinita's wagon.

During the day-long rides, the soothsayer instructed Gwennor in the reading of palms, the rolling of dice and the playing of the various card games with which the gypsy entourage would entertain—and win money from—the people of the towns who came to their encampment. Around the fire on several evenings she had even, at Jacquinita's urging and much to the amusement of the rest of Remolo's family, joined the women in dancing to the plaintive music the men coaxed from their violins.

Her escape from Southford Manor had been almost ridiculously easy. After returning from her interview with Remolo, while Nigel slept, she'd simply walked into the estate office and, without a qualm of conscience, removed from the strongbox a sack containing almost forty golden guineas.

When she explained at dinner that Parry had remained at the barn to tend his animals, her cousin merely shrugged his shoulders, as if to indicate that her brother's behavior proved he was the incompetent Nigel claimed him to be. The new baron also seemed satisfied with her terse assertion that everything was in train for the arrival of Lord Edgerton, and happily monopolized conversation for the rest of the meal, expanding on his plans for the modernization of Southford.

Leaving him to his brandy and cigars, Gwennor had been able to creep out of the manor several hours earlier than expected, to the delight of the waiting Davi, who informed her that Parry had departed with the rest of the family at dusk, as decreed by Remolo.

She'd feared at first that her brother might resist leaving Southford. But though he was sorrowful at abandoning his animals, he seemed to sense without her attempting to explain it that with the coming of their cousin, life as they knew it at Southford could not continue. With the sweet-natured trustfulness she found so endearing, he merely inquired where she wanted him to go, and seemed delighted to learn they'd be traveling with the gypsy band.

After much internal debate, Gwennor had decided against leaving Jenny a note. Though she hated to worry her dear friend, she was more concerned about the consequences should Nigel suspect the maid had abetted her flight. This way, Jenny's alarm and worry would be too genuine for the new baron to suspect her former nurse had any foreknowledge of her mistress's plans. As soon as it was safe to do so, she'd vowed, she would write to her.

Reaching the swiftly flowing river, Gwennor quickly performed her ablutions. Shivering against the chill and thinking longingly of the hip bath full of hot fragrant water back at Southford, she filled two buckets upstream to bring back to the encampment. She hoped the stew would be ready when she arrived, for Gwennor was starving, and eager to practice her card tricks for the night ahead.

By now she was quite skilled, and not nearly so nervous as she'd been the first night the gypsies had welcomed curious farmers and townspeople to their camp. She rather enjoyed leaving her curly hair long and free, unencumbered by pins or braids, she thought as she tied it back again with the multicolored scarf. Accustomed to long, straight gowns fitted only at the bosom, at first it had seemed shocking to don the low-cut peasant blouse and long skirt that hugged her waist. But now she was as comfortable in her gypsy clothes as she was with the telling of outrageous fortunes and the deft shell games at which she won farthings from gullible young farmers.

If her time with the gypsies had given her a new appreciation for the comforts of living in the Manor, still she had found appeal in their simpler life, the camaraderie of the band and the esteem with which Parry was treated for his skill.

Only one aspect of the experience made her uneasy, she thought as she hefted the buckets and trudged back to Jacquinita's wagon. Though she'd never tasted passion firsthand, she recognized the hungry look in the eyes of the visitors as they watched the gypsy girls tell fortunes or ply the dice, a look that intensified later when the girls danced. Their steady, openly appraising stares while Gwennor dealt them cards or read their palms had at first shocked her, and often still made her cheeks redden beneath the scarf with which she masked her face.

No matter how hot their glances grew, though, most visitors were wise enough not to try to touch where their eyes lingered. Remolo permitted no carnal transactions with the women of his family, and few wished to risk the wrath of the gypsy men who watched and waited, vicious curving blades tucked casually in waistbands or boot tops. Still, Gwennor could read in the attitude of their male customers the opinion that the gypsy women were merely an exotic variety of lightskirt. Should the society to which Gwennor belonged ever discover she had traveled in a gypsy caravan, worn gypsy dress and read the palms of clerks and farm boys, all Southford's wealth would not be sufficient to buy her a respectable husband.

Mercifully, the visitors she'd encountered seemed to accept Gwennor as the gypsy girl she appeared, for which she thanked heaven daily, grateful the Lord had created her dark rather than blond. After the first week, when she'd listened night and day for the pounding of approaching hooves, her fear of pursuit or discovery lessened, though she alone of the gypsy women still wore a scarf over her face when strangers came to the encampment.

She trudged back to Jacquinita's wagon and deposited her twin burdens, mouth watering at the spicy scent emanating from the cooking pot.

The fortune-teller had already spooned her out a large bowl. "Eat quickly, my heart," the old woman said. "Remolo has ridden into the town. We've camped here before, and many will come to have their fortunes told and bet at cards.'' She smiled at Gwen. ''You must help them leave their money behind when they depart.''

Gwennor laughed and took the bowl offered. ''I shall do my best,'' she replied.

''I think it's a terrible idea,'' Gilen de Mowbry, Viscount St. Abrams muttered to his brother, frowning at the noisy group of friends preparing to ride out.

Alden de Mowbry grinned at his sibling. ''Don't be a dead bore, Gil. Chase tells me the gypsies camp here every year, and 'tis very amusing to have one's fortune read, or dice with their pretty wenches. Half the town comes out, as well as nearly all Lord DeLacey's servants. The masculine contingent, anyway.''

''The females have more sense,'' Gilen retorted. ''Certainly, visit the gypsy camp—if you wish to have the watch nabbed from your pocket while some dark-eyed charmer tells lies about your future.''

''Come on, Gil!'' Alden coaxed. ''Remember, you're bound soon for Harrogate. No amusement to be had in that rubbishing town full of half-pay soldiers and octogenarians. Best find some enjoyment while you can.''

''Perhaps you're right,'' Gilen said with a sigh. ''Jeffrey nursing a broken heart is devilish grim, and dancing attendance on his sick grandfather will scarcely be more entertaining.''

Alden shuddered. ''Sounds appalling! Why go at all? Stay here a while longer. Between billiards and cards, Chase has gone down to you by nearly five hundred pounds. I'm sure our host's son would welcome the opportunity to win back some of his blunt.''

Gilen chuckled. ''Given his level of skill, he'd likely only lose more. And I really must go lend poor Jeff my support. Damn that Battersley chit! I tell you, Alden, there's

nothing so perfidious as a woman! Leading Jeffrey to a
declaration, when all the time what she really wanted was
to make the Earl of Farleigh's chinless cub jealous enough
to pop the question himself.''

"Abandon old Jeff after he did, eh?''

"As fast as it took to slip Farleigh's emerald on her
deceitful finger.''

"You know Jeffrey, though,'' Alden countered, "Ten to
one, by the time you arrive he'll have fallen for someone
else. Too easygoing by half, and always fancying himself
in love with some chit or other.''

"Who's he to fall in love with in *Harrogate?*''

Alden nodded. "Point taken. I suppose you shall have
to go cheer him up. Best friend since Eton, and such.
Which,'' he added, pushing his brother toward the door,
"is all the more reason for you to come along with us and
enjoy yourself tonight. Mayhap you'll catch the eye of
some fetching gypsy wench.''

"And then catch the edge of her father or brother's
blade? Thank you, no!'' he replied, laughing as he gave up
his resistance and followed Alden.

Lacey's Retreat was only a day's ride from Harrogate,
but Gilen had broken his journey here with the ostensible
excuse of spending time with his brother before Alden,
Chase and their Oxford classmates returned to school. He
had, he knew, been putting off the moment when he must
confront Jeffrey's sorrowful face—a sight which would
only further inflame his temper against Davinia Battersley
in particular and matchmaking females in general.

Thank heaven that, not yet ready himself to become a
tenant for life, Gilen confined his attentions to bits of mus-
lin who performed zealously for the high wages he paid
them. No fraudulent shows of devotion, no false sighing
over his wit, strength, masculinity—just an honest

exchange of mutual passion that left each party satisfied. And if the parting was sometimes a bit…tempestuous, he mused, recalling the shrieks and breaking of glass that had accompanied his giving that delectable but fiery-tempered opera singer her congé, such uproar occurred infrequently.

Perhaps the gypsies also provided a straightforward bargain, he thought as he rode his skittish stallion behind the others. After all, if a man wished to throw away his coins listening to a pretty lass spout nonsense, that was his affair. In any event, observing the interplay should prove more amusing than the alternative—challenging himself to a solitary game of billiards while the rest of the party went off to the gypsy camp.

His doubts about the excursion returned after they arrived, however. Chase, Alden and their other friends turned their mounts over to some gypsy youths, who herded them into a brushwork enclosure already containing a number of other horses. His temperamental stallion Raven, however, could not be closeted with other beasts and would have to be kept separately.

While he hesitated, a tall gypsy lad approached. Before Gilen could warn him away, he came to Raven's head, crooning softly. Instead of snorting, shying or baring his teeth at the intruder as Gilen expected, the stallion grew still, watching the boy, who continued to speak to him in a low, singsong voice. To Gilen's surprise, Raven nickered and allowed the boy to stroke his velvet muzzle.

"He'll come with me now, sir," the boy said.

"You mustn't put him in with the others," Gilen advised as he dismounted.

"I won't," the lad replied. Then, while Gilen watched in astonishment, instead of leading the stallion by the bridle, the boy merely walked away, still murmuring, Raven following him docilely like a chick after its mother hen.

Shaking his head in wonderment at the spectacle, Gilen wandered into the encampment.

Brightly dressed gypsy girls rolled dice, or shuffled cards, or traced their fingers along the palms of eagerly waiting men. A large bonfire burned in the center of the circle of wagons, and at its edge the gypsy men stood looking on, one of them idly playing on a violin.

Gilen's attention was drawn to the wagon closest to the bonfire, where a large crowd surrounded a slender figure seated in the wagon, dealing cards to three of the men.

A silky saffron scarf veiled all but the lady's eyes, and silver bangles glittered at her wrists as she laid out the cards. "Stakes in the pool, gentlemen," she said in a soft, lilting voice.

Not only was her accent oddly different from the tones of the other gypsies, she was the only lady veiled. Curious, he drew closer.

She looked up at his approach. A flash of something almost like...alarm registered briefly in her eyes before she lowered them back to the cards before her.

He stood frankly inspecting her. Perhaps the tallest girl he'd seen here, she was whipcord slender, just a hint of full breasts outlined beneath a woolen shawl that mostly obscured her narrow waist. She looked up again, as if conscious of his stare, and he realized with a start that her eyes were not brown, but an intriguing shade of violet. It must have been a trick of the firelight, but he would almost swear the pale sliver of cheek revealed above her veil had reddened at his survey.

As she met his gaze, an instantaneous and entirely physical energy surged between them. Her eyes widened, her hands stilled on the cards and for a moment she sat utterly motionless before once again dropping her eyes beneath a thick veil of lashes. Gilen inhaled sharply, his pulse racing, the rest of his anatomy stirring in turn.

No longer regretting his foray to the gypsy camp, with avid interest he watched her play out the hand. Silver loo was the game, he noted, enjoying the quick movements of her long fingers laying down cards and taking up wagers, the intimate gurgle of her laughter as she bantered in low tones with the men. Starlight flashing on her bangled wrist, she brushed off her forehead one errant lock from the wild tangle of black curls that cascaded out of her colorful kerchief and flowed down her back.

Thick hair a man could wrap his hands in while he drew that tempting body closer, crushed those teasingly camouflaged breasts to his chest and brought the saucy lips beneath that veil close enough to kiss, Gilen thought. Burgeoning desire and heightening anticipation broke a sweat out on his brow.

After the hand ended, Gilen pressed forward. "The next play must be mine, enchantress."

Muttered complaints of "wait yer turn, gov," and "I were next," faded as the local youths, recognizing from his voice and attire his status as the Quality, grudgingly gave way.

The gypsy flashed him an annoyed look, then gestured toward the men. "Abandoning me, my lords?"

"Let them go, lovely one," Gilen said. "Whatever stakes they offered, I will double."

"Too rich fer me," one said to her, while the others, after sidelong glances at Gilen, nodded reluctant agreement and drifted off.

The girl exhaled with exasperation, that slight movement lifting the breasts beneath her shawl. Gilen's fingers itched to remove the woolen wrap so he might view the bare skin of her shoulders and chest, see fully revealed beneath the thin cotton of the low-cut gypsy blouse the shape of those lovely mounds as they rose and fell with each breath.

"If you deprive me of my game and my winnings, milord," she said, "my master will likely beat me."

He dragged his attention back to her face—wishing he could snatch away the fine cloth veiling her countenance as well. "Then I must see that your winnings are bountiful," Gilen replied. "Shall we play piquet?"

"Your lordship has doubtless the superior skill. Better that I roll the dice."

Gilen pulled a fistful of coins from his pocket and tossed them on the wagon bed. "Name your stakes, my beauty, and I will pay."

Her eyes narrowed as she calculated the value of the gold and silver rolling across the scarred wood. "You must be drunk, milord."

"Not yet, my enchantress, but I should like to be—on the honeyed mead of your lips."

Her brows lifted in surprise at his boldness, the left one winging higher than the right. "My lord, where the honeypot lies, lurk bees to guard their bounty. Take care you are not stung for your efforts."

"To die in your arms, lady, would be worth the gravest sting," he replied, grinning.

"You are bawdy, sir," she reproved.

Surprised she'd apparently comprehended his Shakespearean allusion, he countered, "Nay, mistress, I do but give homage to your beauty."

"I would rather you give gold to my purse. Now, do you play or go?"

"Oh, most definitely, I wish to…play."

She arched again that delicate, high-flying brow. "Some games we do not entertain here, milord. I can offer but cards, or dice."

The wench was not only lovely, but needle-witted, Gilen concluded with delight. "Could you not also read my fortune?" Smiling, he stripped off his riding glove and extended his hand.

Ah, yes, he wanted her to rest his hand in her smaller one, feel those fingers tracing patterns on his naked palm. And on every other part of his body, he thought as hunger surged, thick and potent through his veins.

She studied him without reply, as if uncertain whether she wished to proceed. Gilen dug another handful of coins from his pocket and dropped them atop the others. "Have all those and more, for the future you would pledge me."

"I will read what the stars have written in your palm, milord, but pledge you nothing else," she parried.

"Then we shall agree on that—for now."

Once again he held out his hand, but at a slight distance, requiring her to move closer to the edge of the wagon if she meant to take his palm—closer to him. Her brows knitting as if she'd figured out his stratagem, she hesitated.

So intently was Gilen watching her, the sudden movement from behind startled him. A tall, powerfully built gypsy with an air of authority strode forward and swept up the coins. "Tell," he commanded the girl.

She dropped her eyes before the gypsy lord's glare. After he moved away, she reluctantly took Gilen's hand.

Shivers of delight ran through him as, with barely perceptible pressure, she traced a fingertip across his palm. "This is your head line, milord—see, it is long and straight. You are a man of much ability, born to do great deeds."

"My head tells me that you and I together would do great deeds," he murmured.

Ignoring the comment, she continued, "This is the life line, milord. It, too, is deep and straight. You will live long, have many sons, and watch grandchildren grow to bring you honor.''

"Come with me and share that life," he suggested, grinning as another exasperated exhalation briefly lifted the silken veil above her lips.

"And this," she said, jabbing her fingernail into his flesh, "is the heart line. You will know many women—"

"All I desire is you, my princess—"

"Whom you will bewitch and bedevil," she concluded with asperity. Dropping his palm, she jerked her hand away.

"Can you tell me nothing else, my Delilah?" he asked. "Surely you know more of my future than that."

Before she could reply, the melancholy cry of several violins filled the night, followed by the jangle of bracelets and a shout of acclamation from the crowd. Beside the fire, the other gypsy women had gathered and begun to dance.

Gilen seized his gypsy girl's hand. "Dance for me."

She backed away. "N-nay, sir. Dice I play, or cards. I do not dance."

He released her, pulled the purse from his pocket and tossed it on the wagon bed. "All this and more will I pledge, if you will but dance for me."

"S-sir, I cannot—"

Once again, as if conjured from firelight, the gypsy leader appeared behind them. With one quick stride he seized the purse. "Dance," he commanded the girl.

Her veil trembled as she swallowed hard, but her gypsy lord's stare did not falter. At last she nodded, and only then did her master walk away.

She jumped down from the wagon and took a step toward the other women. Gilen grabbed her elbow. "Stay," he said softly. "Dance here—just for me."

For a long moment he held her gaze. Then, pulling away from him, she began to dance.

Hands above her head, arms arched and gracefully swirling, she dipped and swayed to the wild call of the fiddles, the clamor of the crowd clapping. The shawl slipped from her shoulders and she shrugged it off and kicked it free. Gilen caught his breath as, eyes closed, breasts straining against the cotton of her blouse, hips undulating in sinuous rhythm, she became one with the passionate beat of the music.

He scarcely heard the roars and cheers of the men, the clink of the coins they tossed at the gypsy girls by the fire. His entire being focused on the violet-eyed temptress dancing for him alone.

At last the music ended. The girl finished with a final flourish of outstretched arms, her neck arched and her head back. Without thought or conscious volition, Gilen pulled her pliant body in his arms, brushed the gossamer veil aside and kissed her.

No doubt shock immobilized her for an instant, and then for the briefest moment her clenched fists pushed at his chest. But as he moved his mouth over hers, just nuzzling at first, then adding the gentle entreaty of lips and tongue, her resistance dissolved and she swayed against him, opening to his persistent advance.

Exhilaration flooded him when he captured her tongue and she moaned deep in her throat, her slack fingers clenching at his shoulders and her nipples peaking against his chest. He pulled her closer still, voracious, starving to taste every surface of her tongue and every contour of her mouth, his ears throbbing to the hammer of her heartbeat against his own.

So lost to reality was he, there was no predicting how much further he might have gone had not a sudden jerk at his shoulder loosened his grip on her. Before he could re-establish his hold, strong arms seized him and dragged him away.

"No! Forbidden!" the outraged gypsy lord screamed in his face.

Thrown off balance, Gilen staggered a little before righting himself. The blast of cool air rushing into the void left by the loss of her passionate body and the cold fury of the man before him finally doused his overheated senses, making Gilen realize where he was and what he'd been doing. The girl stood where he'd been forced to release her, one trembling hand holding the veil to her face.

For a moment, Gilen thought the gypsy lord would strike him. However, apparently deciding that attempting to mill down an aristocrat would bring him more trouble than satisfaction, the leader stepped back.

"Go!" he shouted at Gilen, gesturing out of the camp. "All, go!" He motioned again, encompassing this time the entire crowd. "Evening is over."

At a sweep of his arm, the gypsy women slipped back toward the wagons. A line of grim-faced gypsy men, hands poised over the knives at their waists, advanced to stand beside him.

With a few muttered oaths, the milling group retreated from the fire toward the enclosure that contained their horses. When Gilen turned from the leader to catch one last glimpse of his gypsy enchantress, she was gone.

He looked back at the gypsy lord, who stood with feet planted, his arms crossed over his chest, his eyes radiating menace.

Obviously he had overstepped the bounds. Giving the man a deep bow by way of apology, Gilen turned and walked away with the others.

"Well done, brother," Alden threw at him as Gilen caught up with their group.

"S-sorry if I put a premature end to the night's activities," Gilen replied, still rattled by the intensity of the reactions he had just experienced.

"'Twas the close of the evening anyway," Chase replied. "They always finish it with the wenches dancing. Though I must say, you're lucky you cut so commanding a figure. Had one of the farm lads touched a woman, I swear that heathen would have knocked him down and carved out his eyeballs."

"You were right after all, Gil," Alden said with a grin. "You nearly did end up with a gypsy's knife in your ribs. Next time, I shall be more careful what I wish for."

Though he'd gone back with Alden and his friends for a convivial evening of cards—winning yet more from his hapless host, as he took himself up to bed, Gilen still could not shake from his mind the image of the gypsy girl's veiled face...or the feel of her in his arms, her honeyed lips yielding to his.

With so enchanting a body wedded to so keen a wit, what a mistress she would make! His blood heated anew at the thought. He'd give a king's ransom indeed to claim her. Perhaps he should return to the gypsy encampment in the morning, make an attempt to discover the correct protocols so he might negotiate an agreement with the gypsy lord. Given the strength of the attraction between them, confirmed beyond doubt in her kiss, he felt sure if her leader approved, his gypsy enchantress would eagerly accept his offer.

Then he recalled something she'd said, something about being beaten by her master if he deprived her of her winnings. Had the gypsy leader been ready to turn the visitors out of camp, or had he thrown them out because of Gilen's rash action? If the latter, would the loss of revenue that might have been earned during the remainder of the evening be blamed on the girl?

Remorse with an uneasy layer of worry stabbed at him. What if the leader chastised an innocent maid for his transgression? Although he could not imagine ever striking a woman, apparently beating was not an uncommon punishment among the gypsy clan. And if that slender wisp of a girl were punished, it would be his fault.

The very thought of it made him ill.

He sat straight up in bed, but a moment's reflection was enough for him to realize he could do nothing further tonight. Tomorrow at first light, however, he would ride to the gypsy encampment to offer more gold, and his formal apologies.

Having made that resolve, he still found sleep elusive. What slumber he managed was disturbed alternately by heated dreams of a dark-haired vixen writhing under him and horrific images of her writhing under the lash. He awoke early and unrefreshed, his mind seized by a combination of eagerness and anxiety.

Gilen made short work of shaving and dressing, and after tossing down a mug of ale brought by his astonished valet, headed for the stable. The sleepy-eyed groom who wandered out goggled at him as he saddled Raven.

The stallion was happy enough to set off at a run. Gilen's spirits rose too, the exhilaration of a gallop heightening his anticipation.

Slowing the stallion as he rounded the last bend, Gilen rode into the clearing where the gypsy lads had corralled the horses and reined in, looking toward the river.

Where a semicircle of wagons had stood last night, a blazing fire at their center, there now remained only a pile of barely smoking embers. Consternation slammed him in the chest.

During the night as he slept, dreaming of a violet-eyed vixen, the gypsy band had departed.

Chapter Four

Next day, dressed in their own clothes and delivered by Davi to the edge of town at about the hour the mail coach would be arriving, Gwennor and Parry found a hackney to take them to the home of her stepmother's aunt, Lady Alice. After identifying themselves to her butler Mercer, they were led to a small back parlor to await the pleasure of their aunt, who, the butler frostily informed them, obviously skeptical of their unannounced arrival and suspicious lack of either baggage or retainers, had not yet left her chamber.

Although it had been more than ten years since Gwen had visited Harrogate, apparently Lady Alice's cook remembered her, for a short time later, the butler returned bearing a heavily laden tray, his manner now all gracious condescension. "Forgive me for not immediately recalling you, Miss Southford!" he said as he hastened to pour them tea. "I did not recognize in your elegant self the child who came with her lady mother. Cook reminded me, and also remembered you were particularly fond of her jam tarts. Allow me to offer you some fresh from the oven."

Knowing her aunt was not an early riser, Gwen feared they might spend most of the morning waiting in the parlor. However, the news that their mistress's niece from distant clear that the baron was as revolted by my brother as he is. I mean to keep Parry with me permanently, ma'am. Beyond that unconditional requirement, I am not at all particular about the attributes of my potential husband. A kind, decent man who will see Parry for his strengths and not find it embarrassing or uncomfortable to be around him is all I ask. Do…do you think I shall be able to find such a man?"

"I don't see why not. The dear boy appears perfectly normal to me. Indeed, if Nigel could be induced to agree to it, do you not think Parry could live on a small estate of his own?"

"'Tis a bit…complicated," Gwen returned, frowning. "At times his intellect seems not at all affected by his accident. But it's as if the blow from that stallion's hoof severed the link in his mind from the present to the past or future. You cannot tell him in the morning to do something at noon, for by noon he will not remember the request, nor can he envision what he needs to do tomorrow. He seems instinctively able to perform quite complicated tasks, but if he's given a list of duties to accomplish or a long series of sums to add, he will lose track of them in the middle, which upsets him dreadfully."

Lady Alice shrugged. "Computing a long series of sums has the same effect on me."

"You can see how difficult it would be for him to manage a household, however, and he is so innocent of evil, if a venal or crafty person should enter his employ, they might steal his last shilling or commit some dire mischief without his ever suspecting it. Occasionally he does realize something is…wrong with him, which upsets and alarms him, and requires the reassurance of someone he trusts to help him regain his equilibrium. Most importantly, I love him and I *want* him with me."

Lady Alice patted her hand. "Such a good sister you've been to him, for all that you're not really blood kin. Still, such a handsome young man, 'tis a shame he'll never—but no sense repining."

"Nor are *we* blood kin. But will you help me anyway? You know how I've counted on your wisdom and counsel ever since stepmama died."

"Well, of course I shall! You're a handsome, capable young woman, Gwennor, of excellent family. I have no doubt we can find you a suitable candidate—or several. My, to have beaux about the house again, coming to call and leaving bouquets and such! And the shopping…new gowns and pelisses and bonnets. Oh, 'twill be a delight! I shall begin a list of eligible gentlemen immediately."

"Thank you, Aunt Alice! I shall be forever indebted."

"Nonsense, child," Lady Alice replied. "'Tis I who am indebted to you for rescuing me from my ennui."

After making some discreet inquiries of the staff which confirmed her suspicions about the state of Lady Alice's finances, Gwen resolved to be as slight a burden on her aunt's household as possible. Therefore, after adamantly refusing to have her aunt purchase her a new wardrobe, she was forced to expend far too much of her slender resources in acquiring the minimum number of garments her aunt considered necessary for a lady about to make her bow in Harrogate society.

She had to admit, though, as a week later she exited their carriage and strolled on her aunt's arm toward the Pump Room, that facing the world in a stylish new gown of black silk, her hair artfully gathered in a topknot of curls fashioned by Lady Alice's deft-fingered maid Tilly, certainly gave one a welcome dose of confidence.

"Colonel Haversham should already be within," Lady

Alice confided. "I've asked him—quite discreetly of course!—to gather about him any of those gentlemen whom we've discussed. Such as his friend Colonel Howard…" She paused and looked over at Gwen.

"A fine army man who returned here from India to recover his shattered health—a widower of about forty possessed of a comfortable income," Gwen recited her aunt's coaching. "Likes dogs and billiards."

"Very good," Lady Alice nodded. "And Lord Sandstone…"

"Also a widower, tall, thin, suffers from gout but preserves great sweetness of manner despite his pain. Enjoys angling and gardening."

"Mr. Phillips…"

"Youngest son of an earl, a bit vain of his looks and lineage but quite affable; maintains a fine house in town between visits to his father's nearby estates."

"And still in his thirties!" Lady Alice prompted.

"Mustn't omit that important fact." Chuckling at the thought of the youngest of her prospects being nearly ten years her senior, Gwen looked back at Lady Alice, who was following her through the doorway—and was knocked nearly off her feet by a man who briskly shoved open the door they'd been about to enter.

She stumbled sideways, her arms flailing as she attempted to avoid the embarrassment of tumbling faceforward onto the flagstones in front of the Pump Room's main entrance.

"Gwen! Are you all right?"

Before she could reply to her aunt's cry, a pair of strong hands grabbed her from behind and steadied her. "Pray forgive me, ma'am!" said a deep, contrite masculine voice. "I trust you've suffered no harm?"

"I—I am quite unharmed, thank you, sir," she said, turning to face the gentleman, who, after insuring she'd recovered her balance, released her shoulders.

She looked up into a pair of clear green eyes set in a face attractive enough to make even her skeptical heart skip a beat. Firm masculine lips curved into a smile as he brushed a lock of blond hair off his brow, revealing a charming set of dimples.

"Thank heavens for that! I was opening the door for grandpapa's chair and did not pay sufficient attention to who might be approaching. Indeed, let me escort you in before some other ignorant oaf assaults you."

He made them a bow. "Lady Alice Winnerly, isn't it? I believe you are acquainted with my grandfather, Lord Masterson. Please, let me show you back in."

"What have you gotten yourself into now, boy?" an acerbic voice demanded as they entered.

The gentleman hastened back to a thin elderly man who sat in a wheeled chair, swathed in robes. "Nearly ran down these ladies on the sidewalk, I'm afraid, grandpapa."

"Lord Masterson!" Lady Alice said, a smile of delight breaking out on her face. "You look much improved! I trust the waters are proving beneficial, or perhaps it is the reviving presence of your grandson Mr.—"

"This jackanapes?" the old man said with a jerk of his chin toward the young man. "My grandson, Jeffrey Masterson, come to turn me up sweet enough to leave him some of my geld when I'm gone, no doubt—but he's tolerably amusing, so perhaps I shall," he said, ignoring the young man's strangled protest. "And the waters are as nasty as ever, my lady. I suggest you avoid them. Take me home, now, Jeffrey. These old bones are longing for their bed."

The embarrassment in the young man's eyes swiftly changed to concern. "At once, grandpapa. Lady Alice, will you be remaining at the Pump Room?" At her nod, he continued, "Then please give me leave, after I've gotten grandfather settled, to return and deliver my apologies to you and your charming companion at more length. Ladies."

After bowing, he pushed his grandfather's chair out.

Lady Alice gazed after them for a moment, her bright blue eyes shining. "What a fortuitous encounter! I'd heard Lord Masterson's grandson was visiting but had not yet had occasion to meet him. So attractive, and quite young! A bachelor possessing a large fortune from his mother's side, 'tis said he has no need of his grandfather's money. Most charming, did you not think?"

"Indeed, Aunt Alice," Gwen replied, impressed, but resisting the urge to succumb to the pleasant imaginings which Lady Alice was doubtless entertaining. "If he isn't hopeful of a bequest, it speaks well of him that he would come spend time with his grandfather." Especially a man who appeared as irascible as Lord Masterson.

Fool, she told herself, sternly damping down a niggle of hope as they walked from the entry into the Pump Room itself. Just because Mr. Masterson appeared to possess the kindness and tolerance of infirmity that might make him accept Parry did not mean he would be impressed enough with her to come courting.

She'd better not set her hopes higher than the infirm gentleman stricken in years and wishful of a handmaiden's assistance whom she'd originally envisioned for herself.

Perhaps then she might banish the disturbing memories that, once they'd been accepted under Lady Alice's roof and she'd stopped living in constant fear of pursuit from cousin Nigel, returned all too frequently to plague her.

Memories of a tall blond gentleman whose handsome face and broad shoulders had elicited an immediate, visceral pull of attraction. Whose clever banter had delighted her mind even as she knew she ought to deplore its fixation on the physical. Who, after their encounter and despite her shame over her unprecedented reaction to it, she could not help wishing she might have met instead under proper circumstances, so she might, with the same shivery agitation his presence had excited, look forward to his calling on her, riding with her, becoming a friend.

She suppressed a scornful chuckle at so naive a wish. 'Twas not platonic friendship he'd wanted from her. But given her inexplicable response to his audacious kiss, she could not very well condemn only the stranger's behavior.

Still, the very thought of that kiss refired within her a simmering urgency previously unimaginable in the bounds of her staid existence. A kiss unlike any she'd ever experienced, that within an instant had marshaled the vague longings that had often roiled within her and forged them into irresistible, all-compelling desire.

Instead of exhibiting the horror one would expect of a virtuous maiden suddenly assaulted by a man with whom she'd been acquainted for barely half an hour, her hands had ceased their protesting resistance to clasp about his neck. And her lips had not just yielded to his, but actively responded to the stranger's caress.

Just as bad, once compelled to it, she had to admit she'd enjoyed dancing for him—the erotic freedom of the wild music that matched the fire flaming through her blood. Such incredible behavior must have originated in some previously unsuspected but obviously deep vein of carnality of which she'd heretofore been completely unaware.

The whole experience had been shameful, appalling— and marvelous.

However, if she wished to contract a respectable alliance, she'd best thrust those rash and wanton responses back into the Pandora's box from which they'd sprung. Much as her body might protest, she was probably better off setting her matrimonial sights on a staid and possibly infirm gentleman many years her senior—or an obvious gentleman like Mr. Masterson, who would expect virtuous and restrained behavior from his bride.

And who would have no wish to evoke in her so exhilarating, intense—and frighteningly uncontrollable a reaction.

Chapter Five

"Oh, I see Colonel Haversham—with Colonel Howard!" Lady Alice exclaimed.

Jolted back to the present, Gwennor watched Aunt Alice wave across the room at the gentlemen. "Excellent!" she said as the men approached. "Two eligible suitors already this morning, and only our first day!"

Gwen's trepidation at meeting one of the prospects her aunt expected her to attract faded as soon as the two men arrived and she perceived the lines of suffering that marked Colonel Howard's too-thin face. Her ready sympathy immediately activated, as soon as the introductions had been performed and Lady Alice, with a wink at Gwen, sent the two off to procure a cup of the waters, Gwennor set about trying to put the colonel, who seemed rather shy and diffident for a military man, more at ease.

"My first cousin, Major Harry Hartwell, was in India before transferring with his unit to the Peninsula," Gwen said as she took the colonel's arm. "He wrote us there were any number of dreadful maladies that plagued Englishmen there. Did you happen to meet my cousin on the continent, Colonel?"

"'Heedless Harry' is your cousin? A fine lad, full of

enthusiasm, an exemplary rider and marksman besides. I fear he's correct—there are any number of diseases, each one more noxious than the last, as my pitiful frame can testify. I'm sure Wellington is glad to have your cousin with him in Spain!'' The colonel grimaced. ''How it grates me, knowing the import of the business going on there, and being forced to remain here so far from the action.''

They reached the basin, where a waterspout delivered a continuous stream of the heated, faintly sulfur-scented mineral water from a natural spring beneath the pump-house floor. ''Aunt Alice tells me you are much improved of late,'' Gwennor said as he filled two glasses. ''Perhaps before long you shall be able to rejoin your unit.''

''So I keep trying to tell myself! If I could just shake this curst fever…'' He sighed and, glasses brimming, turned back to her. ''Malaria, they tell me. But so young and lovely a lady cannot wish to hear of pills and potions. Nor is it comforting to a man's pride to demonstrate how thoroughly he's been defeated by his own constitution.''

Her sympathy increased a notch as they walked together back toward her waiting aunt. So much of a man's self-esteem, she knew from observing her father as he battled his final illness, derived from his sense of having mastery of the responsibilities given into his charge. For a military man accustomed to command, it must be especially galling to have been invalided out of his post. Perhaps here, too, was a man who could understand and exhibit a tolerance for infirmity.

''I should suppose a malady is no more discerning than a bullet in battle, nor any more avoidable,'' she replied.

Surprise lit the eyes that glanced over to her. ''I never thought of it in quite that way, but I imagine you are correct.'' His assessing gaze lingered on her face before he murmured, ''You are a perceptive young lady.''

She flushed a little. "Only a practical one, I fear."

"As lovely as she is practical, then. Though I understand that you are in mourning, I am happy to note you do not intend to completely shun society gatherings. I haven't previously visited the local assembly, but I'm told the affairs are quite enjoyable. Should...you and your aunt be planning to attend next Friday?"

"I shall have to inquire, but I would presume so."

"Good. You must save me a dance, then—or at least promise me a stroll about the room."

Before she could reply, they reached her aunt, and a few moments were occupied in the transferring of cups and a discussion of the benefits to be obtained from sipping the warm, heavily mineral-flavored water.

Just as, noses wrinkling against the taste, Colonel Haversham and Lady Alice finished sipping their glassfuls, Mr. Masterson hurried back in. After scanning the room to locate them, he walked over, the smile of delight mirrored by one on the beaming face of Lady Alice.

The men exchanged bows, and Gwennor sensed the colonel's warm manner chill abruptly.

"Colonels Haversham and Howard I know, Lady Alice," Mr. Masterson said. "Please, will you not present me to your charming companion?"

The introductions duly made, Mr. Masterson promptly requested Lady Alice to allow her charge to take a turn about the room with him. Her aunt's smile, if possible, grew even broader as, permission granted, she walked off on Jeffrey Masterson's arm.

Knowing her aunt was envisioning a courtship of rivals with competing offerings of flowers, books and invitations, Gwen was hard put not to smile, too. If either of these gentlemen came calling the next day, Lady Alice was going to be in alt.

"What brings you to the city?" Mr. Masterson asked. "Certainly not, given the bloom of health on your cheeks, a need to sip the waters. You are paying your aunt a visit?"

"Y-yes. Although seeing my aunt is always a pleasure, as you can tell by my dress, I've recently lost a kinsman—my father. With my cousin now taking charge of my old home, I wished a…change of scene."

"My condolences on your sad loss."

She nodded briskly, refusing to let her thoughts stray to such doleful ground. "I understand you are attending your ailing grandfather. How kind of you to leave the attractions of London to succor a sick relation."

He smiled slightly. "Much as I should like to boast that noble purpose was my sole reason for quitting the city, honesty forces me to confess that, though I was truly concerned about the recent decline in grandfather's health, there were…other considerations." His smile faded. "I, too, recently suffered a…disappointment, and felt the need for a change." With a shake of his head, he summoned back the smile. "But enough of that! Does your mourning permit you to attend the assemblies and the theater?"

"I expect we shall attend both."

"Would you permit me to call tomorrow? Perhaps we could arrange a theater party." His clear green eyes gazed into hers appealingly.

A shiver of both anticipation and trepidation rippled through her. Firmly suppressing the latter, she replied, "I should like that very much."

As it turned out, she saw him again sooner than expected. Early the next day as she and Parry took their morning walk, they encountered Mr. Masterson near the park, riding a handsome chestnut gelding. Drawing rein, he dismounted and came over to greet them.

Gwennor had a moment of satisfaction upon noting his obvious relief that she presented Parry as her *brother*.

He, of course, was more interested in the new four-legged arrival. "What a fine beast, Mr. Masterson."

"We were...not able to bring our horses with us," Gwennor said, "and have not as yet had time to hire any. Though the walk is pleasant, we miss our morning ride."

"I'm afraid Vulcan is a bit too spirited for a lady's mount, but until you've made other arrangements, you are welcome to borrow him, Mr. Wakefield," Mr. Masterson replied promptly. "I must warn you, he dislikes strangers. 'Tis the reason I ride early, before the streets are full..."

His words trailed off and his expression turned to amazement as Parry approached his horse, murmuring softly. Vulcan alerted, his ears pricking up, and extended his head to nuzzle Parry's outstretched hand.

"Why, 'tis amazing!" Mr. Masterson exclaimed. "Truly, I've never seen him react like that! In fact, he still nips at my groom if Nichols approaches unexpectedly."

"Parry has a special affinity for animals," Gwen replied. "They sense and respond to it."

Her brother turned from crooning to Vulcan, as if suddenly reminded. "Can we return by the stables, Gwen? I want to show you what I've found."

"Oh, not already!" Gwen said with a groan. "My brother also has a knack for discovering lost and injured creatures wherever he goes. At Southford we possessed an ever-changing menagerie of rabbits, fawns, ducks, even wolves he found and healed before setting free again."

"I have to help them, Gwen," Parry said.

"Of course you must," she agreed. "What is it now?"

"Only a kitten. Come see him! His coloring is almost exactly the shade papa was seeking in our rabbits."

"My father was attempting to produce a stronger strain

of domestic rabbit,'' Gwen explained. ''Parry was directing the breeding experiments.''

''We must go see what he's found then, mustn't we?''

Heartened by Mr. Masterson's congenial response to her brother, as they strolled back, Gwen tried to draw out her potential suitor.

''How do you occupy your time while your grandfather is resting, Mr. Masterson? I imagine there are rather few pursuits here for a gentleman accustomed to London. Though there is, my aunt tells me, a fine lending library.''

Mr. Masterson chuckled. ''A claim whose truth I'm not likely to discover! I'm an indifferent scholar, I must confess, and works of literature are more likely to put me to sleep than amuse me. Had it not been for my best friend Gilen—now there's scholar for you—I would never have survived Oxford.''

Books being one of her chiefest pleasures, Gwen felt a mild disappointment. But there were other interests they might share. ''My aunt tells me you came by way of your home at Wilton Park, where you maintain a large stable,'' she continued. ''Horses are your particular pursuit?''

During the rest of the walk, she coaxed Mr. Masterson to describe his stock and his estate, which he did with so much enthusiasm she concluded both must be extensive, well-maintained and lovely. Once they'd reached the mews and Parry had tied the docile Vulcan to a stall, he led them to a manger half full of fragrant hay.

He clucked softly and a small, malnourished kitten popped out from under the straw. The little creature ran to Parry, purring lustily.

''Isn't he lovely?'' Parry asked.

''Very pretty,'' Gwen agreed. But when she reached out to pet the animal's back, the kitten whirled around and bit Gwen's finger before burrowing back under the straw.

"Sorry, Gwen," Parry said. "I forgot he is still shy of strangers. I think he was mistreated."

"Why don't you get him some milk from the kitchen?" Gwen suggested. As her brother, after a bow to Mr. Masterson, trotted off in that direction, she turned to give Mr. Masterson a rueful smile. "Obviously, I haven't my brother's skill."

"No, he is quite special," Mr. Masterson replied.

Gwennor's eyes flew up to his. He returned her steady regard, his gaze open and friendly. In his tone and manner, she could discern neither mockery nor disdain.

He accepts Parry. The realization filled Gwennor with such a sense of joy and relief, she could have wed Mr. Masterson on the spot. Despite his dislike of scholarship, if further acquaintance confirmed her initial impression of Mr. Masterson as a kind, congenial, sympathetic gentleman of sufficient means, Gwen felt she might be able to develop for him not just a fond regard, but a lasting affection.

An affection that might be coupled with a more measured attraction than the frighteningly intense desire that had swept her for the stranger at the gypsy camp.

If Mr. Masterson found her as appealing as she was finding him, perhaps she'd not have to hunt for an enfeebled octogenarian after all.

Ten days later, grimy and out of sorts, Gilen de Mowbry gritted his teeth as he unpacked clothing from his equally dusty saddlebags.

Weary from six days spent nearly ceaselessly in the saddle, he did not want to hear about the lovely, fascinating creature Jeff had just met. As Alden had predicted, he thought with disgust, only half listening to Jeff's rapturous flow of rhetoric, it appeared the distraught friend whom he'd felt compelled to come support had already fallen in love again with some other chit.

Though how he'd found someone in Harrogate under the age of fifty to fall in love with, Gilen couldn't imagine. If he'd known, he concluded sourly, longing for a bath and a glass of strong ale, that he'd find his supposedly inconsolable friend so irritatingly cheerful, he wouldn't have prematurely called off his search.

After the shock of finding the gypsy encampment deserted, he'd ridden back to Lacey's Retreat and questioned the staff, trying to determine the band's normal route. He'd wasted three days riding west after them before learning that instead of proceeding as usual, they had wandered north. When he finally found them, their leader at first refused to speak with him, then kept him waiting a day while he considered the generous sum Gilen was offering in apology for his previous intrusion.

At last the gypsy lord agreed to meet him, an old woman serving as translator. But to Gilen's infuriated exasperation, the man denied any knowledge of the violet-eyed wench who'd danced for him. He was almost positive the man was lying, but as it was already nearly two weeks past the arrival time he'd indicated in his last letter to Jeffrey, he felt compelled to give up the search for the present and make for Harrogate with all speed.

Only to arrive and find his supposedly brokenhearted friend waxing eloquent about some new female.

"Despite your stops, 'tis a tedious journey and you must be longing for a bath," Jeffrey was saying. "I told grandpapa we'd dine with him—he retires quite early—after which we shall still have time to attend the assembly. There you can meet Miss Southford for yourself. I'm sure you'll find her a delight!"

"As delightful as Davinia?" Gilen shot back.

Jeffrey's genial face sobered, and Gilen immediately felt ashamed of his churlishness. "Sorry, Jeff, that was unkind. Been on the road so long, it's made me snappish."

Jeffrey mustered up a smile. "I deserved that, I suppose. She *is* delightful, but nothing like Davinia. Lovely, though not as striking, and—I'm not sure how to describe it—so forthright and appealing. The sort of lady who not only encourages a man to talk, as they all do, but truly listens to what he says, and offers some intelligent comments in return. I'm sure you'll like her."

"If she has intelligent conversation to offer, she *is* unusual!" Gilen declared, only half jesting.

Jeffrey took a swipe at him and Gilen ducked. "At least *I* have the discernment to develop tendres for well-bred ladies of sensibility," his friend declared. "If you spent less time among mercenary females out of London's Green Rooms, your opinion of the sex might be higher."

"Perhaps," Gilen acknowledged, "though I doubt it. At least a female from the Green Room gives you an honest return on your investment, rather than false devotion and flattering lies."

"I admit, my judgment on this score has not always been accurate, but I assure you Miss Southford's honor and integrity are beyond reproach," Jeffrey asserted.

Gilen raised a skeptical eyebrow. "We shall see. Let me get near some hot water and a warm dinner, and then I shall be most interested to meet your new paragon!"

While Tilly looked on, sighing her approval, Gwennor inspected herself in the pier glass. At Aunt Alice's urging, she'd expended a bit more of her precious reserves on a new ball gown that, with its expert cut and flattering fit, would equal in elegance and sophistication any of the more colorful gowns being worn to the assembly tonight.

"You be ready, Miss," Tilly said, reaching up to make a final adjustment in the curls she'd pinned in atop Gwennor's head. "Lucky for you that dusky gray goes so good with your pale skin and dark hair. Indeed, 'tis so pretty on you, folks might think you're wearing it not 'cause you is in mourning, but for it becomes you so well."

"Thank you, Tilly," Gwen said, gratified.

"And with two handsome gents awaiting you tonight, 'tis fitting that you're in looks! Mistress will be that pleased. Go on and dazzle them, now, Miss!"

Gwennor took her evening cape from the woman with a wry grin. As quietly as she'd been living, 'twas more likely the company would dazzle *her*.

Still, Gwennor felt a pulse of excitement as she descended to the parlor to meet her aunt. She was wearing the most stylish gown she'd ever owned, her tempestuous hair had been tamed by the fingers of an artist, and with her well-respected aunt here to introduce her to the society of this small resort community, Gwennor had every expectation of both enjoying herself and progressing one step closer to obtaining the safe haven she sought.

Suitably enthusiastic over Gwen's appearance, Lady Alice hastened her to the carriage. "So lovely you are, I'm sure your dance card will be filled to overflowing!"

"Surely it is too soon after Papa's death to dance."

Lady Alice patted her hand. "Ordinarily, I would agree. But I've made the sad facts of your circumstances known to the hostesses here, and all of them understand you need to attract a suitor as quickly as possible. Unless you find yourself unable to countenance dancing, which of course I could understand, even though I should be most disappointed, for there is nothing that can more quickly engage a gentleman's interest than holding a lady close in the shocking intimacy of a waltz! If you are not set against it, then, I should strongly advise you to indulge, and assure you that Society here will not think it unseemly, even given the recentness of your bereavement.''

Gwennor had to smile through that long speech. Her gentle father, loving of life and mostly indifferent to its social rules, would have considered the notion of her refraining from one of her favorite social activities in respect for his passing quite ridiculous. "No, aunt, I should be quite happy to dance, if you think it proper."

"Good. Oh, we shall have such a lovely evening!"

They arrived at the assembly rooms soon after, and once they'd proceeded through the reception line and her aunt had introduced her to several matrons whose approval was essential to her acceptance in Harrogate society, they walked on to the ballroom. As Lady Alice had hoped, they discovered all Gwen's potential suitors already present.

The gentlemen soon spotted them. After greetings all around, Mr. Masterson bowed to Gwennor's aunt.

"May I solicit your niece's hand for the first waltz?"

"Miss Southford has just agreed to sit out the waltz and dance the next set with me," Colonel Howard said.

"You do not think the waltz inappropriate, surely?" Mr. Masterson appealed to Lady Alice.

"Certainly not! Indeed, 'tis my hope—oh, but of course, Colonel Howard did—'' her aunt stuttered.

"Good," Mr. Masterson inserted with a grin. "To accommodate the colonel, I promise to return the lady before the next set begins." After a quick bow to her aunt, he took her arm and urged her onto the floor.

"Are you kidnapping me?" Gwennor protested, laughing.

"Nothing so violent. But there didn't seem a tactful way to suggest that though Colonel Howard may not feel up to a waltz, I am quite capable."

His delicacy in preserving the colonel's pride further impressed Gwen. "That was most kind."

Mr. Masterson's smile deepened and his green-eyed gaze fixed on her with notable warmth. "Besides, I've dreamed all week of waltzing with you in my arms."

Mercifully, the music began, since Gwen was too flustered to reply. Acutely aware of his hands at her waist and shoulder, she let him sweep her into the dance.

Her enthusiasm at the prospect of dancing soon soothed her agitation, and she gave herself up to the delight of swirling with the music.

As they came to a halt at the end of the dance, their position and proximity inevitably called up memories of an even closer embrace that had progressed to a much less proper activity...one in which she'd also participated with great enthusiasm. Her face heated guiltily.

She half stumbled in her eagerness to quit the dance floor, as if by leaving the spot that had invoked them she might banish the disturbing recollections.

"Miss Southford, are you quite all right? You seem fatigued," Colonel Howard said as they returned. He cast Mr. Masterson an aggrieved glance.

"'Twas a bit warm," she replied, seizing that excuse to explain her overheated cheeks.

"Let me get you a glass of wine," Mr. Masterson said.

"Colonel, if you do not mind, could we postpone our dance? I believe I would like a glass."

While the men squabbled over who would bring wine and who the lobster pattics and tea cakes, Gwennor took the colonel's arm, glad for the respite.

The interlude in the refreshment room did much to restore her calm. She was able to dance several sets, and even welcome engaging in a second waltz with Mr. Masterson. He really was a very pleasant gentleman, she concluded as she listened to him expound on his plans for enlarging the horse-breeding operations at his estate.

Horse breeding. Parry would love that.

Dreamily contemplating her brother passing his days crossing bloodlines to produce steeds of particular colors or attributes, at the termination of the waltz she followed Mr. Masterson off the dance floor. And nearly ran into him when her escort suddenly stopped.

"At last!" he exclaimed. "Miss Southford, you must allow me to retain you a few more moments. My good friend Gilen has just arrived and I wish to introduce you."

Gwennor murmured her assent, smiling a little to think how delighted Aunt Alice was going to be if this friend turned out to be another eligible gentleman. Curious, as Mr. Masterson led her forward, she scanned the people crowding the room beyond the dance floor, but out of the press of guests she could not discern which particular gentleman he seemed to be seeking.

As it happened, the man they approached had his back to them. Mr. Masterson reached out to touch his shoulder.

"Gilen! I was beginning to think you'd not attend after all! Miss Southford, allow me to present my dear friend, Viscount St. Abrams."

The tall blond man turned. "Ah, Miss Southford—how delightful to meet you at last."

Those dark blue eyes. That chiseled jaw. Gwennor's knees nearly buckled as she sank into a curtsey with more speed than grace. When Lord St. Abrams reached to grasp her suddenly nerveless fingers for the obligatory salute, a wave of dizziness swept her. For one awful moment she thought she might faint.

About to bow over her hand was the taunting, tempting stranger she'd kissed at the gypsy camp.

Chapter Six

So this is Jeffrey's new love, Gilen thought, despite his friend's description of her, still a bit surprised as he inspected the woman curtseying before him. This tall, slender lady, her bowed head displaying a luxurious tangle of thick ebony curls, her long dark lashes in sharp silhouette against the porcelain of her face, was not the sort of gazetted beauty to whom his friend had previously lost his heart.

Nor—mercifully—upon Jeffrey's announcing his name and rank, had she latched on to his arm with an effusion of ingratiating chatter, as had happened on several uncomfortable instances in the past when Jeffrey had presented him to his inamorata of the moment.

Lovely rather than stunning, and pretty-behaved besides, he concluded as he reached for her hand. Perhaps she might do for Jeff.

His favorable impression of genteel beauty did not prepare him for the jolt of awareness that hammered his nerves when his gloved hand touched hers. That lingered, pulsing through his veins, while he hastily brushed his lips to her fingertips and released them.

She'd felt it, too—his shocked mind noted her gasping intake of breath, the slight tremble of her hand. It, he concluded as he tried to reorder his scrambled thoughts, being an intense, immediate and entirely unwelcome attraction to the lady who'd won his best friend's admiration. *Damn and blast,* he cursed under his breath.

"Lord St. Abrams," she murmured, her face still demurely lowered.

"Isn't she splendid?" an exuberant Jeffrey mouthed to him over her head. Reclaiming the lady's hand with covetous zeal, he motioned Gilen to follow them. "Come along, St. Abrams. I'll present you to Miss Southford's aunt, Lady Alice, and some of her friends."

After spending a moment staring in befuddlement at his hand, as if that appendage had betrayed him, Gilen started off a few steps behind the couple. Which, as they crossed the floor, gave him a good view—all too good a view—of Miss Southford, her graceful glide of a walk, that temptation of thick curls balanced on the arched perfection of her neck, the shapely arms beneath the flutter of dark sleeves. Much as he tried to rein it in, to his disgust his body was as enthusiastic as Jeffrey in appreciating the lady's charms.

There was no question of proceeding down that path. His goal was only to protect, as much as it was possible to protect a man who'd reached his majority years ago, his vulnerable friend from unscrupulous husband hunters.

He dragged his eyes from watching for tantalizing hints of the trim posterior beneath her silk gown and fixed them firmly on his friend's back. The fact that she was making no attempt to flirt with Gilen, who wherever he traveled seemed to be instantly identified by every unmarried female in the vicinity as a prime matrimonial prize, was both a relief and a promising sign.

Or perhaps it was just that his reputation as being impervious to female wiles had also preceded him, and Miss

Southford realized Jeffrey's easy-going person and titleless wealth made for an easier target.

Uncharitable, he chided himself. He mustn't let Jeffrey's recent unhappy experiences cause him to suspect the motives of every unmarried lady his friend encountered.

Still, he thought as they reached the small group to whom his friend directed him, she was wearing a dark gray color that, despite how well it became her, could only mean she was in mourning. And if the dear departed responsible for that ritual show of grief was a father or older brother whose loss left the family in pecuniary difficulties, she might well be desperate to contract a speedy alliance.

Well, he would neither rush to judgment—nor allow her to rush Jeffrey to the altar.

Still, something about her needled at him, alerted nerves simmering with a residue of that most unwanted attraction. Though her family was unknown to him—from Wales, or some such outlandish place, Jeffrey had told him—and he was reasonably certain they'd never been introduced, she seemed somehow…familiar.

A more sobering concern banished that puzzle. From what he'd observed of Jeffrey's behavior tonight, his friend was even more smitten with Miss Southford than their discussions had led Gilen to believe. Given the disastrous results of Jeff's previous infatuation, it behooved Gilen to confirm the true character of this new lady quickly, before his friend fell any further under her spell.

Covertly he studied the group as Jeffrey introduced him. Her aunt, a fluttery female of uncertain age, who grew nearly incoherent with delight at his presence. Their friend Colonel Haversham, a distinguished military gentleman, he knew slightly from his club in London. Colonel Howard he had not previously encountered. But it was soon clear, by the way the soldier regarded Jeff as a hound might look at another beast trying to make off with the choicest bone, that the colonel considered Jeffrey an unwelcome rival for Miss Southford's favor.

The lady herself gave no evidence of her vaunted conversational skills. To his surprise—and somewhat to his annoyance—as he tried to draw her out before she went off to dance with the colonel, his most practiced compliments won from her only a slight blush and several brief replies.

Gilen's concern increased as he observed Jeffrey chat with Lady Alice. Though his friend conversed amiably, his eyes continually strayed to the lady on the dance floor, dipping and swaying on the arm of her scarlet-coated escort. Not only did his friend's fixation on the girl disturb him, the warmth and ease of Jeffrey's manners with the aunt demonstrated that an alarming degree of intimacy already existed between his friend and the lady's family.

Still, he thought as he scanned the room, it was hardly surprising that the susceptible Jeff had latched upon Miss Southford. Harrogate was visited mostly by the elderly and infirm. Since local residents of sufficient rank and fortune preferred to present their unmarried daughters in the larger venue of London's Marriage Mart, during the Season few young ladies graced the assemblies here.

His wandering gaze collided with that of a tall, heavyset woman wearing a monstrous turban of vibrant purple hue. Though he swiftly looked away, to his annoyance, he saw out of the corner of his eye that lady beginning to approach, dragging along a strikingly pretty, dark-haired young woman in a white gown liberally festooned with bows, ribbons and rosebuds. *Another hopeful debutante,* he thought with a groan.

"Mr. Masterson!" the woman cried, extending her hands to Jeff. "And Lady Alice and Colonel Haversham, of course. Is it not a charming assembly? And not often that we have so distinguished-looking a visitor. You must introduce him at once to me and dear Mary Anne!'' She grabbed the girl's arm and thrust her beneath Gilen's nose.

Though Lady Alice looked affronted and the colonel made a minute grimace, Jeffrey's smile was courtesy itself. ''You are looking very charming tonight, ladies, and of course I shall present you. Lord St. Abrams, Lady Aylesbury, the widow of one of grandpapa's friends, and her daughter, Miss Aylesbury.''

While Gilen bowed over the woman's outstretched fingers, Lady Aylesbury said, ''What a delight to meet you, my lord. Mary Anne, is he not a handsome devil? For shame, Mr. Masterson, to have brought your friend here to break the hearts of all the maidens in Harrogate.''

Gilen gritted his teeth. Before he could edge in a word, she continued, ''Mary Anne, you must claim Lord St. Abrams's arm for a stroll about the room.

''Now, she's a bit shy, but I vow once you get to know her better, my lord, you will pronounce my Mary Anne to be charming!''

''Mama!'' the daughter protested in an urgent undervoice, her face coloring in dismay.

''Lord St. Abrams,'' she continued, ignoring the girl, '''Tis your first visit to our city, I expect. How do you find Harrogate?''

''Pleasant.''

''You must come out driving with us. We should be happy to show you around, should we not, Mary Anne? There is an ancient abbey on the heights that is quite lovely. So romantic and…remote. My daughter could recite you its history. Though you mustn't be thinking her a bluestocking! My, no! She's equally accomplished in needlecraft, the pianoforte, and all the ladylike arts.''

The girl's face flushed deeper and she lowered her eyes.

Gilen could almost feel sorry for her, if he weren't so irritated by her mother's encroaching familiarity.

Colonel Haversham coughed, Lady Alice looked mortified, and even Jeffrey appeared disconcerted by so inappropriate a remark. Swiftly recovering, no doubt to head off the set-down Gilen would not have been able to suppress, Jeff inserted hastily, "I have had the pleasure of hearing Miss Aylesbury play, and can testify to the excellence of her performance."

Lady Aylesbury was certainly not a lady bred, Gilen concluded, which would explain the aloofness with which both Lady Alice and the colonel were treating her. While Jeffrey at least momentarily diverted the woman's attention, with narrowed eyes Gilen subjected the pair to a closer inspection.

If the delicate dark loveliness of the girl had bred true, the mother was probably a wealthy Cit's daughter whose face, now wreathed in plump lines, and stout but still-statuesque figure might once have been beauteous enough to snare a titled husband whose land or wits had been to let. And though the girl was indeed beautiful, with her pale oval face, tiny pert nose and enormous dark eyes—now glancing up with a mixture of humiliation and misery—he had no desire to pursue so vulgar an acquaintance.

That being the case, he wished Jeffrey would bring to an end the conversation that Lady Alice and Colonel Haversham's silence and his own monosyllabic replies had tried to discourage.

"Lady Aylesbury, I believe Lord Rumpsfeld is signaling," Lady Alice broke in. "Do not let us keep you." As that gentleman, a very stout man with a florid face and extremely tight coat, was in fact waving at their group, Lady Aylesbury was at last induced to depart, though not until both Jeff and Gilen had been pressed to sign her daughter's dance card.

As soon as the pair walked away, Lady Alice latched on to Gilen's arm and leaned close, distress on her face.

"Pray forgive us, Lord St. Abrams!" she said in a low voice. "I am so sorry you had to encounter that…creature your very first evening with us! I assure you, our society would not normally countenance the presence of an India nabob's daughter, however wealthy she might be, but Lord Aylesbury was a longtime resident, well-respected by all of Harrogate. Despite the lapse in judgment he displayed in tying himself to…that woman, we could not bring ourselves to dishonor his memory by excluding his poor daughter, who in spite of her mother is a lovely, pretty-behaved chit."

Since the girl, had she possessed a bit more confidence, might well be thought stunning, Gilen thanked heaven her undeniable beauty didn't seem to have cast Beauty's usual spell over Jeff. Given any encouragement whatever, Lady Aylesbury would doubtless prove a difficult burr to detach, and he certainly wouldn't wish his friend to be maneuvered into so disastrous a connection, no matter how pretty-behaved the daughter.

Indeed, Miss Aylesbury's mama made Miss Southford and her relations appear virtual paragons of perfection.

His grin at that conclusion rapidly faded when he realized its full implications. With the dearth of eligible females available—and with Jeffrey asserting he would not feel comfortable returning to London while his grandfather's health remained so uncertain—detaching his friend from Miss Southford, if such a necessity appeared warranted, was likely to be a trickier business than Gilen had imagined.

Which made determining whether such a course of action

was truly necessary even more imperative. Especially after Jeffrey confided, as they waited for the colonel to escort Miss Southford off the dance floor, that he meant to claim the lady for another waltz—their third of the evening.

Appalled, Gilen cast about for some reply. Such marked attentions would cause comment enough in London. But did his friend not realize that in the narrower confines of Harrogate, to waltz so often with the same lady was tantamount to a public declaration?

He was about to point out that fact to his impetuous friend when caution stilled his tongue. Given Jeffrey's enthusiasm for the young lady and the threat posed by the attentive Colonel Howard, calling attention to that social convention might make Jeff more, rather than less, inclined to dance with her. Gilen would have to find some other way to deflect him.

"Unfair for you to have another waltz," he declared, improvising as he spoke, "when I've not yet had the pleasure even once. Come, you must cede it to me. I'd like to become better acquainted with the lady."

"I'm not so sure I wish you to become better acquainted," Jeffrey returned with a rueful smile. "Your virile charm has a tendency to overwhelm most females."

"I don't think Miss Southford is likely to succumb," Gilen replied drily, recalling her lack of response to his overtures thus far this evening. "Nor, I should hope, do you honestly believe I would serve you such a turn."

"No, of course not," Jeff replied, flushing a little. "Very well—the waltz shall be yours."

Counting himself fortunate to have won that small victory, during the time he awaited that dance, he was obliged to endure witnessing Jeffrey's doting behavior toward Miss Southford. He was nearly ready to cheer when the musicians at last began to tune up for the waltz.

"Y-yes." Was that wariness he heard in her tone?

"You are recently bereaved, I see."

"Yes."

"A close relation?" he persisted.

"My father."

"My condolences, ma'am."

"Thank you."

She certainly wasn't making this any easier. Had he only dreamed that Jeff praised her conversational ability?

"Did your brother succeed to the…?"

"Barony," she replied after a moment. "No, a cousin."

"Ah. And so you visit your aunt."

"She wished to console me in my grief."

"You were that close to your father?"

For the first time, her voice held emotion. "V-very," she said so softly he almost could not hear her.

For some reason, the desolation in that small word pierced both lust and cynicism. Despite his suspicions, he felt a genuine sympathy.

"Then I am doubly sorry."

She inclined her head, but did not reply.

"Do you stay long in Harrogate?" he continued.

"I am not sure."

As the waltz offered gentlemen the opportunity to clasp one chosen lady so closely that many older matrons still considered the dance improper, the floor was crowded, and Gilen had been bumped several times. While Miss South ford was answering him, a couple behind them careened into Gilen with such force, he was knocked into his partner.

He scrambled to regain his balance, then yanked her against him to keep her from falling. The musicians struck and held the final chord.

He felt the pressure of her breasts, the vibration of her heartbeat against his chest as she steadied herself. His lungs seeming suddenly starved for air, he inhaled with a great shuddering gulp, taking in the heady scent of her.

Awareness of her body pressed into his almost intimately, not intimately enough, swamped his senses and froze him in place. Until he realized she was not leaning closer, but pushing away. Trying to push *him* away.

"The dance is over. We should return to my aunt."

Baggage, he thought, again torn between admiration and annoyance at her sangfroid in the face of his agitation. Was she truly as calm and detached as she sounded?

He should move away instantly and release her. For some perverse reason, he could not.

As if too proud to try to struggle out of his unyielding grip, she remained motionless against him. Despite her modestly lowered eyes, her rigid stance was almost militant in its resistance.

Not once during this entire evening had she looked at him directly, he realized. Suddenly he was possessed of the need to see into her eyes. Would those orbs—the windows to the soul, some poet had proclaimed—show her to be embarrassed, indifferent—or suppressing an attraction as great as his own?

Anchoring her with one hand at her waist, he used the other to gently but firmly tilt up her chin. Large, startled, dark-lashed violet eyes gazed back.

A powerful sense of déjà vu swept over him. While he held her motionless, her forehead creased in annoyance and her brows lifted, the left one winging skyward.

His smile faded and shock like an exploding cannonball blasted his brain as his gaze riveted on that elevated brow and those indignant violet eyes. Eyes like those had sparkled in the light of a blazing campfire above a silky swirl of saffron veil. Dark, entrancing eyes he'd gazed into before claiming the lips beneath them in a kiss that had rocked his world....

In that instant his world rocked again. Gilen took one lurching step backward, suddenly so dizzy he feared he might lose his balance and send them both sprawling to the floor, right in the middle of the Harrogate Assembly Room.

It couldn't be.

Chapter Seven

His grip must have gone slack as well, for Miss Southford hastily pulled away from him.

"Shall I send Mr. Masterson to assist you, my lord?"

She stepped back as she spoke, and fearing she meant to escape, he rapidly marshaled command of his limbs.

"N-no, I am fine," he stuttered and seized her elbow. Though he managed to keep his legs in motion, his brain remained too fogged with shock and bewilderment to dredge up conversation, and the short walk back to her party was accomplished in silence.

Once they rejoined the group, before his numb wits could invent some excuse to delay her, she announced to her aunt that she was fatigued and wished to return home. Colonel Howard quickly offered his arm, Colonel Haversham taking her aunt's. Lady Alice's effusive expression of thanks and goodbye barely gave Gilen space to insert a monosyllabic response before the two gentlemen led the ladies off, a persistent Jeffrey trailing in their wake.

Still stunned, he watched Miss Southford disappear, back ramrod straight while her figure swayed gracefully as she walked off—away from him and a body reawakened to her touch, clamoring to recapture it.

He shook his head to try to clear his muddled thoughts. It had been six weeks since he'd parted company with his tempestuous opera singer. His long-deprived body must be playing tricks on his mind. The tall brunette in the demure mourning gown couldn't be his gypsy enchantress.

And yet...the feel of her under his fingers and in his arms...the timbre of her voice, recalling echoes of a vaguely accented speech...the thick black tangle of tresses...the subtle scent of perfume and skin. Most telling, however, those violet eyes and that unique arch of eyebrow.

No, he belonged in Bedlam for even conceiving the thought. Violet eyes and arched eyebrows couldn't be that unusual. He knew for unquestioned fact that Miss South-ford sprang from a respectable Welsh-English family and was in Harrogate under the sponsorship of her eminently respectable aunt, a longtime resident of the city. No gypsy wench could have cozened herself into Lady Alice's house, nor would such a woman possess the requisite knowledge and breeding to pass herself off to the gimlet-eyed ton as a gently born maiden.

Despite those rational conclusions, Gilen decided not to hunt up Jeff and share a bottle of brandy, as they'd planned. He needed time and solitude to reexamine the disturbing events he'd just experienced.

Gilen slipped into the hubbub outside the assembly rooms and hailed a hackney. He'd send a footman to Jeff with a note pleading fatigue, he decided as the vehicle proceeded to his lodgings.

Arriving in his rooms, he flung himself into the comfortable armchair in front of the blazing hearth and poured himself a glass of brandy. Savoring the liquor's sweet-tinged bite, he stared into the flames.

What did he know for sure? The lady calling herself Miss Southford was accepted as such in Harrogate by both her aunt and society. In word and action, she appeared every inch a genteel lady.

But his sensory impressions remained strong. After reviewing them again, leisurely and at length, as impossible as it seemed, he felt nearly convinced that the enticing, whisky-voiced gypsy girl he'd crushed in passionate embrace and the tall, dark-haired lady he'd caught to his chest tonight were one and the same.

Same thick ebony hair. Same scent. Same low-pitched voice. Same height and shape. Exactly the same bewitching violet eyes beneath an arched, flyaway eyebrow.

The wench who'd danced for him in the gypsy camp was no longer traveling with them, the gypsy lord had claimed. Perhaps the man hadn't been lying.

Perhaps to find out the truth, Gilen would have to pull the pins from Miss Southford's neatly bound hair, bind her against him, and plunder her mouth with a kiss.

Would Miss Southford respond as the gypsy maid had?

Desire swamped him, leaving him both exhilarated and horrified at the thought.

Belated reason surfaced, chilling his overheated thoughts. Sensory impressions notwithstanding, it was nearly impossible for his crazy suspicion to be true.

But there was one simple way to settle the matter. He need only ascertain how long Miss Southford had been with her aunt. If she had resided in the city for more than three weeks, there would be no possibility the lady he'd met tonight could have been his winsome gypsy cardsharp.

Gilen swallowed the last of his brandy. He'd have a chat with Jeff the very next morning.

"Gwennor, dear, wasn't it the most exceptional evening?" Lady Alice said as they climbed in the carriage.

"Quite exceptional, Aunt Alice," Gwennor replied, dry

irony in her tone as she sank wearily against the padded squabs and closed her eyes.

She prayed heaven the evening had been singular. Smiling and chatting and dancing with every appearance of gaiety through the interminable last half of the assembly, her heart lodged in her throat and her chest tight with trepidation, was an experience she didn't ever wish to repeat.

"Colonel Howard was so distinguished in his dress uniform, did you not think? And Mr. Masterson *so* attentive! I do think you've captured his interest, which is excellent, my dear, excellent! How fortuitous that his friend Lord St. Abrams has arrived as well. A handsome, agreeable gentleman—quite sought-after in London."

Lady Alice paused for breath and Gwennor braced herself for the rebuke she knew was coming. "Though I must own I found your conduct toward him astounding! Whatever possessed you to treat him with so little civility?"

Why could that "agreeable" gentleman have not remained in the London that so prized him instead of popping up in Harrogate to threaten her security and her future? "I'm sorry, Aunt," she replied, pulling out the requisite apology. "I've had the headache all evening and am not feeling quite the thing." Which was a true, if incomplete, explanation for her behavior, she acknowledged, rubbing her throbbing temples.

Lady Alice took Gwen's hand and leaned over to touch her face. "Why, your cheeks are hot and your hands like ice! I'll grant the rooms were frightfully stuffy."

"They were indeed," Gwen replied, seizing on the excuse. "Nor am I accustomed to being in such a large crowd of people indoors—the noise, the closeness…"

"You poor soul!" Lady Alice exclaimed, rubbing Gwen's hands. "I'd forgotten how quietly you lived at Southford. For one unused to ton gatherings, the experience can be quite overwhelming! And here I go, no doubt making matters worse by chattering on like a magpie! Lean your head back, dear. Once we're home, I'll have Tilly tuck you up in bed and tell Cook to make you her special lemon posset. We'll talk in the morning, when you're feeling more the thing.''

''Thank you, Aunt Alice.'' Gwennor collapsed against the cushions, glad for the temporary reprieve from the cozy chat about the evening's events she'd been dreading.

Before she conversed with anyone, she needed to cure the pounding in her head so she might figure out what she was going to do about one overlarge, overconfident and overly intelligent nobleman. Who, by the end of that waltz she'd tried so hard to avoid, might well have recognized her as the card-dealing wench from the gypsy camp.

After the initial shock of encountering him, she'd thought if she could respond to Lord St. Abrams civilly and then avoid him, she would be safe. After all, people generally perceive what they expect to perceive, and her reading of his courteous but slightly bored response to their introduction told her he'd summed her up as merely one more rather unremarkable maiden in the no-doubt endless line of young females to whom he was continually being presented. Once that first impression solidified, the earl was unlikely ever to take a close enough second look to connect her with the gypsy camp.

Unfortunately, the powerful response he'd evoked in her that night had not been a fluke. Surprise and alarm had certainly pulsed through her when first he took her hand— but just as strong was a compelling undercurrent of attraction that tempted her to engage his quick wit in conversation, to linger in his heady but dangerous proximity.

Her well-meaning friends certainly hadn't helped. Still, though Jeffrey and her ambitious aunt had virtually forced her to waltz with him, she might well have escaped notice, had not St. Abrams, autocrat that he was, dared to seize her chin and force her to raise her eyes.

Eyes—the only feature of her face he'd been able to see and thus had doubtless closely scrutinized that evening at the encampment. Their collision of gazes in the ballroom tonight intensified the already simmering connection evoked by the dance itself—his hands at her waist and shoulder, holding her in a position all-too-similar to the embrace he'd stolen that star-studded night. Had it renewed and magnified the attraction arcing between them to the point that Lord St. Abrams's memory would manage the leap from the assembly rooms of Harrogate to a firelit forest clearing?

'Twas an enormous leap, connecting two radically different worlds. She should focus on how small that chance in fact was, and calm herself. The viscount was a sought-after gentleman who had probably indulged in any number of trysts. Surely a simple waltz would not recall their midnight interlude to him as vividly as it had to one as inexperienced in dalliance as she.

He had been disconcerted, though—surprised into a misstep and out of his polished, practiced courtesies. Which had been a blessing, since it enabled her to collect a reluctant Aunt Alice and make her escape before he could recover enough to perhaps pose questions her throbbing head would have made it very difficult to evade.

At the jerk of the halting carriage, that afflicted member gave a painful lurch, and she grimaced.

"Here we are at home, my dear," Aunt Alice said, gripping her arm. "Let Hawkins help you up the stairs, and I'll send Tilly at once. By the time she has you tucked up in bed, the posset should be ready."

"Thank you, aunt," Gwennor murmured, more than

happy to allow her solicitous relative to cosset her. Hopefully by morning, when her head no longer threatened to split and she'd had time to reflect, she would be able to construct a story clever enough to answer all Lady Alice's inquiries about her waltz with St. Abrams.

But an hour later, though comfortably ensconced in her bed, the posset having dulled the worst of her headache, she found she could not sleep.

What should she do about Lord St. Abrams?

What was Lord St. Abrams going to do about her?

Despite her soothing arguments, she was unable to shake the discomforting suspicion that the gentleman had recognized her. Perhaps not as the gypsy dancer, but as a lady he had indeed met before at some place and point. If the nagging uncertainty of it prompted him to question her, how was she to answer him?

Being naturally unsuited to duplicity, her first impulse was to seek an opportunity to relate to him in confidence the entire story of her leaving Southford, and call upon his sense of fairness and mercy to excuse—and conceal—her actions.

But aside from his friend Jeffrey's commendation, all she knew of Lord St. Abrams was that he was a handsome, stylishly dressed, well-born gentleman much beloved by London society.

The only other society gentleman with whom she was acquainted was cousin Nigel. An instant's reflection was enough to convince her what his opinion of her character and reputation would be were he to discover she'd sojourned in a gypsy caravan.

Surely a true gentleman would be more fair-minded. She had no doubt cousin Harry would believe her—but cousin Harry knew her well. And besides, he had always been different from his peers, going his own way as heedless of general opinion as his nickname proclaimed.

Uneasily she recalled the hungry gazes of the men who visited the gypsy camp. All of them—from farm boys to servants to gentlemen—watched the gypsy women with an accusation of wantonness in their eyes. Could she reasonably expect Lord St. Abrams—a man who had been there, with the same hungry look in his eyes—to hear her confession and judge her more fairly than any of those men?

A shiver, part fear, part thrill, ran though her at the memory of that gaze locked on her as she danced before him. Perhaps she should abandon Harrogate, take Parry and try her luck in one of the smaller spas farther north.

Her spirits rebounded from that dismal conclusion in a flash of anger. 'Twas ridiculous for her to bolt like a nervous yearling, forsake her most promising opportunity to secure for herself and Parry the best possible future, simply because Lord St. Abrams had inconveniently arrived in Harrogate. After all, she had done nothing wrong! She was exactly what society perceived her to be: an honorable lady of good birth who would make some fortunate older gentleman a hardworking, faithful, devoted wife.

Besides, the men's pejorative opinion of the gypsy women was, in her close observation, based solely on prejudice and ignorance. Although the gypsy customs allowed young women a freedom of action not permitted the closely scrutinized maidens of the ton, Gwen had seen no evidence of promiscuous or wanton behavior.

There was, however, the matter of that unfortunate kiss. She stirred uneasily, her righteous indignation fading. Even an open-minded gentleman prepared to give her the benefit of the doubt might have his faith in her honor shaken by her reaction to that.

But though shame heated her cheeks, her anger refired.

If she were guilty of breaking the code of virginal behavior by responding to him, surely Lord St. Abrams deserved even greater blame for having assaulted her in the first place. No one was likely to take him to task for *his* part in the evening's events. Why should she admit *her* fault, and risk forfeiting her whole future for behavior that, in him, was considered a mere trifle?

One single kiss—no matter how passionate—out of twenty-odd years of blameless living did not make her a wanton. It simply wasn't fair that the sole means she'd had available to extricate herself and Parry from their dire situation be allowed to tarnish her reputation.

If it were only her future at stake, she might chance telling St. Abrams the truth. But Parry would suffer, too, if she trusted that gentleman to act with compassion—and was wrong.

Reluctantly she reached the only reasonable conclusion. Uncomfortable as she was with deception, she would not confess.

Perhaps it was the release of tension and the easing of the throbbing in her head, but she began to feel more hopeful. No need to make a Cheltingham tragedy out of this. If St. Abrams did connect her to the gypsy caravan, he had no way to prove she had been there. The idea of a gently bred girl living and working among the gypsies was too preposterous to be believed. He'd be thought a Bedlamite were he to publicly lance such an accusation.

No, if he suspected it, he was more likely to confront her privately. And if he confronted her, she'd not have to lie, precisely. She need only avoid a direct answer, while expressing shock and dismay—or maidenly faintness—at the very notion.

She grinned ruefully—the idea of being confronted by St. Abrams made her faint enough in truth. And oh, so regretful that it would be much too risky to indulge her strong desire to become better acquainted with him.

Despite the urging of intuition that whispered that in him she might find a kindred spirit, prudence predicted that he'd never become a friend, and he was even less likely to become a suitor. She'd do best, in fact, to avoid him.

Despite that comforting summary of the situation, as she recalled the strength of the arms that had bound her to him and the arrogant confidence Lord St. Abrams exuded, a small but persistent knot of apprehension remained lodged in her chest. As if suddenly compelled to action, she sat up and punched her pillow into a more amenable shape.

If St. Abrams *had* recognized her, he would probably think her an impostor unworthy to mingle in polite society. She had the uneasy suspicion he would not be easily dissuaded from doing whatever he felt necessary to correct the matter.

Well, she thought, settling back again, with the welfare of her brother and their future at stake, neither would she.

Chapter Eight

When Gilen called the next morning at Lord Masterson's town house, he found Jeffrey still at the table.

"Help yourself to a tankard of ale and some of this fine beefsteak," Jeff invited as the butler ushered Gilen into the breakfast room. "If you, the man who won every steeple-chase we raced at Oxford, were so fatigued from your travels that you felt compelled to excuse yourself last night, you must be in urgent need of restoratives."

His subterfuge not permitting him to challenge that mortifying statement, Gilen stomached his chagrin. "The journey tired me more than I'd realized, but I'm feeling right as a trivet this morning."

"Good. As soon as 'tis late enough, I intend to call on Lady Alice. You should accompany me and pay your respects to your waltzing partner." Jeffrey paused, throwing Gilen a speculative look. "Sure you're not sickening with something? I saw you…well, it appeared to me that you *stumbled* on the dance floor last night. At the time, I was merely astonished to observe that the dashing viscount so beloved of London hostesses could actually make a misstep like a common mortal, but when I got your note, I had to wonder if—"

"Nonsense, I'm fully recovered," Gilen said, his cheeks heating a bit as he cut off any further speculation on the state of his health. "Recovered and anxious to renew my acquaintance with Lady Alice. You seemed to be on terms of some familiarity with her."

"Lady Alice is a longtime friend of grandpapa's who I've met often during my visits to Harrogate. A bit of a widgeon, perhaps, but a very kind and gracious lady."

"Has her niece resided with her long?" Gilen asked, and held his breath.

At the mention of the lady's name, Jeffrey's negligent posture alerted and his eyes grew bright. "Ah, the lovely Miss Southford! She's been with Lady Alice only a short time, else I assure you my visits to grandpapa would have been much more frequent. Indeed, I shall never forget my first meeting with her a week ago—when I nearly bowled her over at the entrance to the Pump Room!"

His beatific smile faded. "But I'll save that story for the hackney ride over. Miss Southford often walks in the morning, and if we don't arrive early, the presumptuous Colonel Howard might bear her off before us. Let me finish up this beef and we can depart forthwith."

Good humor apparently restored at this prospect, between bites his friend launched into a renewed paean to Miss Southford's charms that fortunately required from Gilen only an occasional monosyllabic reply.

More dismayed by Jeff's revelations than he wished to admit, as he listened with half an ear, Gilen realized how much he'd counted on being able to definitely rule out the possibility that Miss Southford might be his gypsy maid.

Jeffrey's information didn't necessarily mean that the two women's separate identities could not still be established, he told himself bracingly. After all, Miss Southford might well have resided at another, easily verifiable location prior to her arrival in Harrogate.

The prudent course of action would be for him to accompany Jeffrey this morning, pay his obligatory respects and then leave his friend to play court to Miss Southford while he saw what further facts he could ferret out of the feather-witted Lady Alice.

To his disgust, the notion of calling on Miss Southford sent a spark of heat and anticipation licking through his veins.

Scowling, he tried to squelch it. 'Twas probably her slight, coincidental resemblance to the dark-haired, violet-eyed gypsy that subconsciously drew him. Seeing her again in the prosaic light of day, rather than under the golden light of a dozen massed chandeliers that cast a glow all too reminiscent of the gypsy bonfire, would doubtless extinguish this unseemly attraction for good.

If Lady Alice could provide him satisfactory information, Gilen would probably have to remain only a few more days to make certain that the lady his friend now seemed set on making his wife was a perfectly acceptable candidate for that honor—if Jeffrey's often fickle affections didn't dissipate before he got to the point. Gilen could then leave Harrogate with a clear conscience, to pursue the elusive wench who had so ensorcelled him—and escape his disturbing response to Jeff's lady.

Jeffrey threw down his napkin, interrupting Gilen's thoughts. "Shall I have the footman summon us a hackney? 'Twill take but a moment to gather up my coat and cane."

If he were shortly to be riding hard again to pick up the gypsy's trail, he'd best insure that he kept his mount well-exercised. "No, I believe I shall ride over," Gilen replied. "I need to let Raven run, and could take him out after we call. I've no doubt you can outflank the colonel and secure Miss Southford's arm without my assistance.''

Jeff grinned. "That balding half-pay officer? I should hope so. I shall see you there, then.''

Some forty minutes later, having turned his restless stallion over to Lady Alice's groom, Gilen entered the drawing room to find his friend and Colonel Howard flanking Miss Southford on a dove-colored settee, like two bookends jealously guarding a prized volume. The hostility between the two gentlemen was nearly palpable.

Miss Southford looked up at his entry, and at the flash of light in those violet eyes, Gilen's pulses leaped. He took three steps toward her before belatedly remembering he should properly address himself first to her aunt.

A little shaken, he offered the obligatory compliments to Lady Alice, who sat beside her cisebo Colonel Haversham and gazed with an air of approval at her niece holding court with her two suitors. Offering a promise to return and converse further, Gilen excused himself to approach Miss Southford.

Though she continued to face Colonel Howard, her attention apparently given to the discourse he was now delivering, Gilen had the strongest sense that she was as intensely conscious of his presence as he was of hers.

All his senses, normally functioning at subconscious level, grew suddenly acute. He heard the muffled tread of his bootsteps, the faint pop and hiss of the fire, the low tones of Colonel Haversham below the more strident voice of Colonel Howard. Felt the warmth of the sun, the slight cool stir of draft from the window, the rapid thump of his heart. And saw...ah, how velvet plush was her thick glossy hair, wildly curling wisps of it escaping the braid into which she'd tried to subdue it. The porcelain fineness of her skin that, he noted with surprise, was not the milk-white hue preferred by fashionable ladies but slightly sun-bronzed, her nose and cheeks sporting a dusting of freckles. And her scent—that elusive blend of roses—seemed to surround and intoxicate him.

Though a runaway carriage couldn't have dragged him away, still he stood silent once he'd reached her group, content to gaze at her while he awaited a break in the conversation. She gave no sign to indicate her attention had strayed from the colonel, but Gilen was almost certain a slight blush deepened the delicate color of her cheeks.

When at last Colonel Howard paused for breath, Gilen bowed. "Miss Southford. Let me thank you for a delightful waltz last night."

She did not start with surprise at his address, confirming his impression that she'd been aware of his approach. Was he dreaming it, or did the turn of her head toward him seem deliberately slow and studied?

"'Twas my pleasure, Lord St. Abrams," she said softly, once more keeping those thick-lashed eyes downcast.

She didn't offer her fingers, so he reached to take them. A spark shot through his nerves at the moment of contact. He felt an answering jump in her pulse beneath his fingers, and his heart exulted. He tightened his grip and brought her hand to his lips.

She wasn't wearing gloves. Gilen had the strongest desire to slide his lips across her knuckles and suck the tip of her little finger into his mouth, savor the taste and scent of her. She pulled her hand away before he could act upon that madness.

He heard her ragged intake of breath and dropped his eyes to the breasts rising and falling in barely concealed agitation. Another savage wave of satisfaction filled him.

"Won't you have a seat in the wing chair beside the fire?" she murmured, her cool voice revealing none of the disturbance he sensed in her. She possessed admirable sangfroid, he had to admit.

Look at me, he willed her. After a few moments, while he remained standing there without reply, as if against her will, she slowly glanced up.

So much for the effects of daylight dulling her charm. The golden sparkle within the depths of her violet eyes was more brilliant even than he remembered, the hue richer, more compelling. Eyes a man could lose himself in.

No wonder Jeffrey was dazzled.

Jeffrey! The realization that he was engaged in a word-less and intensely physical struggle of wills with the woman his friend claimed to love belatedly crashed over him, splintering the sensual spell. Mumbling something, he backed away, his heartbeat racing.

Jeff and the colonel both greeted him. Not surprisingly, Miss Southford made no attempt to bring him into the conversation, dividing her attention between the two gentlemen flanking her.

"As I was saying," Colonel Howard said, throwing Gilen an aggrieved glance for having distracted the lady, "my sister engaged me to purchase a new mount for her. I've looked at several offerings and tentatively chosen the one I think will suit her best. Lady Alice told me you are accounted a bruising rider, as is Helena. Could I prevail upon you to try the paces of the mare and give me a lady's opinion?"

Miss Southford smiled with real enthusiasm. "I should be delighted. I was not able to bring my own mount with me, and have sorely missed a daily ride."

"Excellent," the colonel exclaimed. "I shall have her sent round this afternoon. Perhaps we could ride together in the morning. And if you like the mare, please feel free to accept the loan of her for the duration of your visit."

"It is generally preferable to ride quite early, before the Harrogate streets become crowded," Jeffrey broke in. "I would especially recommend that you do so the first time you take out an *untried* mount. The morning fog being, my grandfather tells me, considered injurious to the lungs, I should not wish Colonel Howard to put his recovering health at risk. I would be happy to accompany you at whatever hour you wish to set out."

Neatly done, Gilen thought, suppressing a grin. Buy time to consider a gift of your own while in the same sentence reminding her of your rival's infirmities.

It appeared Colonel Howard also understood the stratagem, for his pale face flushed. "Nonsense. As I'm neither in my dotage nor apt to suffer a relapse, I am perfectly capable of escorting the lady—whenever she chooses to ride."

"Gentlemen," Miss Southford intervened smoothly, "how kind you both are to offer. But such a munificent gift, Colonel! It is so vastly tempting to accept, I know I really must refuse."

"Nonsense, Miss Southford. 'Tis *you* who would be doing *me* a favor. One that, I assure you, my sister will very much appreciate."

"Then how can I decline?" she returned with a smile. "But, at least for the first ride, I must firmly rebuff both your offers of escort. While I get acquainted with the mare, I should prefer to be accompanied by Lady Alice's groom only. If I come to grief he can rescue me, and I will be spared embarrassing myself before an audience."

It appeared Miss Southford handled competing admirers with as much skill as she was reputed to have with horses. Under other circumstances, Gilen might have found that ability as admirable as it was entertaining. At present, however, he could only regret a talent that might manipulate

Jeff ever closer to the declaration that would be the only sure way to eliminate his rival and secure the lady for himself.

All the more reason for Gilen to decide what must be done as quickly as possible.

While Gilen was assessing her tactics, Miss Southford led the conversation back to the safer topic of the relative merits of the play now being enacted at the theater. Not once did she spare Gilen so much as a glance.

For a few more moments Gilen gazed at her determinedly averted profile, vaguely aware he'd had some other purpose for this visit. Finally it surfaced in his boggy brain. *Extract information from Lady Alice.*

Every nerve protesting his retreat from Miss Southford, he forced himself to walk back to her aunt.

"So kind of you to stop by, my lord," Lady Alice said.

"How could I not express my thanks to the ladies who so kindly entertained a stranger last night?" he replied.

Lady Alice dimpled. "We shall have to insure that you do not remain a stranger. Please, do stop by and take potluck with us some night while you are in town."

"I'd accept that invitation speedily," Colonel Haversham advised. "All Harrogate knows what a sumptuous table Lady Alice sets, and she's everywhere acknowledged for her warm hospitality."

'Twas a perfect opening, and Gilen leapt at it. "So I've already learned," he said. "Miss Southford confided to me that when she lost her father recently, you were kind enough to invite her here and offer comfort in her grief."

"Yes, poor child." Lady Alice shook her head and sighed. "Gwennor lost her stepmama, my niece, nearly ten years ago, and has been running the household for her father ever since. Having buried two wives, I believe her papa hadn't the heart to consider matrimony again, and transferred much of his tender affections to his surviving daughter. The respect and mutual affection that developed between them was far deeper than the often-distant familial obligations one generally finds between father and daughter. She was fearsomely cast down by his passing.''

Lady Alice was even more loquacious than he'd hoped. Now, to take advantage of that helpful trait.

"She mentioned her father's estate had been transferred to a cousin," he continued. "It must have been especially distressing to relinquish control over her home after having been mistress of it for some years. You brought her back after the funeral services?''

"No, unfortunately I was not able to attend—and was so surprised when she arrived here so soon afterward! Not that I wasn't delighted to see her, of course. And equally delighted to be able to offer the diversions of Harrogate to help turn her mind from her grief.''

"She showed up at your door?'' Gilen repeated, alarm and excitement pulsing through him.

"She…left home in some haste, and there wasn't time for a letter to reach me before she arrived on the mail coach. Although the idea of a lady of her birth traveling by common coach! 'Tis all the fault of her odious cousin Nigel!'' Lady Alice uttered a scornful harrumph. "But, being a Christian lady, I shall say no more on *that* score.''

If Miss Southford were at odds with the head of her family, she was probably most anxious to marry away from him, which meant she would likely try to angle Jeff into a declaration as quickly as possible. But that information shed no light on a possible connection with a gypsy encampment. Unless the lady claiming to be Miss Southford was an imposter. How well did Lady Alice know her niece?

"You must be very close, if she felt comfortable paying

you an unexpected visit,'' he said. ''Does she stay with you often?''

''No, not that I wouldn't love to have her, but with her papa's household to oversee she had little time, and Wales is so far, you know. We've written frequently since my niece Eleanor died. Which, now that I think of it, was the last time I saw them. She and Eleanor paid me a visit just before my niece contracted the putrid fever that killed her. Which was—ah, ten years ago this February.''

So Lady Alice had not seen her niece in a very long time. Long enough that another woman of similar appearance might succeed in usurping her place?

''She must have been little more than a girl then. Did you find her much changed?''

''Oh, lovelier than ever, and much more settled! She was quite a handful in her girlhood. But,'' Lady Alice gave him a roguish smile, ''and so you may tell Mr. Masterson, she has grown into a pretty-behaved lady, well-trained to manage a husband's household!'' Lady Alice glanced over to the settee where Jeff was in animated conversation with Miss Southford.

So Lady Alice thought Jeffrey had sent him to investigate her niece's suitability as a wife? Gilen could scarcely contain a grin. He'd been growing more anxious by the minute, having not yet extracted precisely the information he required and knowing that to continue such direct probing would surely arouse suspicion. Lady Alice's misperception had just given him freedom to probe a bit longer.

''When, exactly, did your niece arrive?''

''Let me see…ah, 'twas two weeks ago Wednesday.''

That would have been only a few days after he'd met the gypsy girl near Lacey's Retreat—on a more or less direct route from Wales to Harrogate.

"She didn't visit any other family en route?" he persisted, risking one further question.

Lady Alice gave him an odd look, warning him he'd reached the limits of acceptable curiosity. "Her father's sister lives not far from Southford, but I doubt she stopped there. Why do you ask?"

At the other side of the room, her niece and the two gentlemen rose, mercifully sparing him from replying.

"Aunt Alice, I shall be leaving on my walk now," Miss Southford said as she approached. "Mr. Masterson and Colonel Howard have both asked to accompany me, so I shall have willing hands to do your bidding. Can we bring you anything back from town?"

"No, my dear. Do wrap up warmly, though."

"I had best take my leave as well," Gilen said.

"Why don't you join the party?" Lady Alice suggested. "Walking is so beneficial for the health."

Apparently the chaperone couldn't resist the opportunity to add another eligible gentleman to her niece's escort. Before Gilen could decide whether or not such a scheme might fall in with his plans, Miss Southford said, "Lord St. Abrams has so recently arrived, I'm sure he's still occupied with settling in."

Though it appeared nearly incredible Miss Southford could be his gypsy dancer, she did seem suspiciously unwilling to bear his company. "Another time, perhaps, Miss Southford," he said, bowing.

She curtseyed in response. "Gentlemen, Aunt Alice, if you will excuse me, I must fetch my pelisse."

"Sure you won't reconsider, Gilen?" Jeffrey asked. He darted a dark look at Colonel Howard. "I should be glad of your company."

"No, I must run the jitters out of Raven," Gilen replied, anxious to get away and evaluate this new information.

"Perhaps I can catch up with you later." He bowed a final time and walked out.

An hour later, as refreshed by the mind-clearing gallop as his mount, Gilen pulled up his lathered stallion at the outskirts of the city and dismounted. He'd walk the horse to cool him before returning to his lodging—and perhaps catch a glimpse of Miss Southford and her party returning from the park.

He walked Raven once around the leafy expanse, but did not encounter Miss Southford's party. Which was perhaps just as well. Lady Alice not having provided him a verifiable location for Miss Southford during the time he'd visited the gypsy camp, he still wasn't perfectly sure how to proceed next.

He continued his solitary route around the park, once more mulling over the facts he'd just gathered. Only his extremely strong physical reaction to Miss Southford and the happenstance that both females possessed dark hair, violet eyes and winged brows argued for the possibility that the two women might be one and the same. Logic and common sense all argued the contrary.

Having closely observed Miss Southford on several occasions, he could not believe she was an imposter. Not only was it highly unlikely a gypsy girl would have known enough of Miss Southford's family situation to take advantage of it, the woman calling herself by that name was just too obviously gentry-bred. Gilen could not believe any gypsy lass, coming from so vastly different a world, would have succeeded in moving as impeccably in Society as Miss Southford had last night. And widgeon though she be, surely Lady Alice would have been able tell her own niece from a gypsy wench.

The only other possibility connecting Miss Southford to the gypsies was equally remote. Though Lady Alice said she had departed her home hurriedly, the idea of her traveling to Harrogate in a gypsy train was so ludicrous as to be laughable. Any well-brought-up girl would have to know that, however desperate to escape home she might be, to remain a single night in so libertine an environment—dancing girls, money-tossing patrons, hot-blooded gypsy men—would irretrievably ruin her reputation. Even were she cloistered well out of sight.

The wench who'd danced for him had hardly been cloistered. Merely recalling the wild abandon with which she'd swayed and clapped to the music, seduction incarnate, was enough to heat his blood and harden his body. No demure virginal ton miss could have danced—or kissed him—as she had. For a moment he indulged himself in the memory.

Relief made him grin as he pulled Raven's slack reins taut and prepared to remount. Clearly there could be no connection between the two women. If Miss Southford *were* trying to avoid him, 'twas probably because, having primed two eligible suitors to pop the question, she found the strong physical pull between them unsettling.

The attraction certainly unsettled him.

Yes, 'twas merely proper maidenly behavior to concentrate her attentions on gentlemen with honorable intentions and avoid entangling herself with a newcomer who was definitely not a candidate for husband.

Gilen felt the last vestiges of uncertainty lift its leaden weight from his chest, and the resulting lightness sent his spirits soaring. He'd remain a day or so longer to set his seal of approval on Miss Southford, and then go off once more in pursuit of his vixen.

Only this time, he *would* find her.

So heartened was he by that resolve, he determined to ride by Lady Alice's town house and try to catch up with

Jeffrey. He would bear his friend off for a lavish celebratory lunch.

After turning his stallion back over to a stable boy, Gilen hurried from the mews, to be informed by the butler that Mr. Masterson had already departed, and Lady Alice was laid down on her couch.

A little disappointed at having missed his friend, Gilen left the butler to convey his compliments to Lady Alice and returned to the stables.

Having dispatched a groom to retrieve Raven, Gilen stood idly waiting, a half smile on his face as he contemplated the delights to come the night he welcomed his gypsy back into his arms. A tall young man emerged from the stables, his singsong murmuring pulling Gilen from his pleasant imagining.

The lad spotted Gilen and headed toward him, still crooning. Behind him, without benefit of rope or bridle, trotted Raven.

The boy, his voice and the nearly unprecedented sight of the feisty stallion docilely following as if under some spell brought the memory crashing back just as the young man stopped beside him.

The same young man who'd induced Raven to follow him that night in the gypsy camp.

Chapter Nine

The dark-haired young man made a clicking noise. As if in perfect communion with him, Raven halted.

"A beautiful animal, my lord," the boy said as he turned back to snag Raven's bridle and offer it to Gilen. "May I give you a leg up?"

Shock iced Gilen's tongue and froze his brain. He simply stood, goggling at the boy and the stallion.

"Be more fittin' for me to do that." The groom who had assisted Gilen earlier hurried out of the stable.

"As you wish, Jem," the boy said. With a nod to Gilen and one last murmur to Raven, who whickered in response, he bowed and walked away.

"Got a right peculiar way with the stallion," the groom told Gilen as he made a stirrup with his hands. "Amazafied me at first, too. All the beasties seem to like 'im—horses, dogs, cats."

Pull your wits together, Gilen ordered himself as his gaze followed the disappearing boy. *Find out what you can.* "How long has he been here?" he asked.

"Just a few weeks," the groom replied. "Came here with—" As if suddenly recalling some previous instruction, he stopped abruptly, his face coloring. "Best be asking the mistress after 'im. Let me help you up, milord."

Before Gilen could reply, a soft voice wafted out from behind the shrubbery of the adjacent garden, sending a shock of recognition through Gilen's nerves.

"Parry! Where do you want—"

At that moment the lady herself popped through the small back gate, an armful of what appeared to be mewling kittens gathered to her chest. Seeing Gilen, she stopped short, the rest of her sentence dying on her lips.

She'd evidently been walking in some haste—no doubt to rid herself of the squirming burden even now trying to claw their way up her shoulder—for her cheeks were flushed and a number of curly dark wisps had escaped their braid to circle her face in a halo of feathery ringlets. The lavender of the mourning gown and the limpid sunlight of early afternoon emphasized the violet clarity of her eyes, the magnificent contrast of black brow and ebony lash against the paleness of her skin.

A wave of deep, gut-level attraction once more hammered him, trapped the breath in his throat, sped his pulse and made his hands lift of their own volition, as if to reach for her.

Stung to the quick by a violent and illogical sense of...betrayal, he struggled to surmount it, dragging in a gulp of air, clenching the offending hands into fists and jamming them back at his sides.

And to think, he'd just finished acquitting her of all complicity! There could be no further doubt about her true character. The woman before him might or might not be a gypsy, but having seen in her aunt's household the same young man who'd led Raven away that night at the encampment, he knew she must indeed be the woman who'd diced with him—and danced for him.

And who now, posing as an innocent young virgin, was attempting to trap his best friend into marriage.

"Lord St. Abrams," Miss Southford said warily, breaking the long tense silence.

"Miss Southford," he replied in clipped tones, wondering if that was in fact her true name. Whoever she was, she would do well to be wary. He'd see her transported before he'd allow Jeffrey to offer his heart and hand to a wanton from a gypsy wagon.

Her face pale but expressionless, she turned from his accusing gaze to address the groom, who'd been casting nervous glances between Lord St. Abrams and his mistress's houseguest. "Jem, did Colonel Howard's mare arrive?"

"Yes, ma'am. Right pretty she is."

"Good. Would you please check the tack room to ensure there is suitable gear to allow me to ride her tomorrow?"

"At once, ma'am," he said, bowing and then trotting off, obviously anxious to quit the scene.

"You have the kittens, Gwen? Bring them in here." The young man who'd tended Raven strode back out of the stable, nodding pleasantly to the passing groom before proceeding to Miss Southford's side.

The lady turned back to address Gilen. "We are rather occupied at present, as you can see," she said, once more readjusting the kittens. "Do you require something, my lord?" She looked up with guarded eyes, her chin at a defiant angle, her tone both cool…and hostile.

Not as hostile as he, Gilen thought furiously. The strumpet ought to be whipped on the town square.

"For the moment…" he let the sentence trail off, watching her face, "only my horse. Which this young man so skillfully provided. Mr.—?"

Miss Southford hesitated. Apparently deciding she could

not avoid an introduction, at last she said, "Lord St. Abrams, my stepbrother, Parry Wakefield. Parry, the viscount is a friend of Mr. Masterson."

The young man bowed gracefully. "An honor, my lord."

His words were cordial, practiced—and uncolored by any emotion stronger than polite interest. Gilen searched the boy's face, but could discern no flicker of recognition, no evasive shift in the clear blue eyes.

It did not appear that the young man remembered him. Well, it had been dark, and none of Alden's party had revealed their names. But Raven was an exceptionally fine stallion—surely he must recall the beast.

"You have quite a nice touch with horses, Mr. Wakefield," Gilen said, hoping to jog the boy's memory.

The lad reached over to pat the stallion's soft nose. "He's a joy to tend, sir."

Gilen recalled the numerous occasions on which the temperamental equine had attempted to nip his handler's fingers or shoulder. "My groom would likely not agree," he replied drily. "But you seem to have had no difficulties with him—on *either* occasion."

Gilen watched carefully, but that deliberate emphasis provoked no change in the young man's guileless expression. "Animals like me, sir," he said simply. "I left the cages open, Gwen, so I'd better get back to them. I'll take the kittens, if you like."

"That's all right, I'm coming right in," Miss Southford said quickly. "Lord St. Abrams is just leaving. Good day, my lord."

Small wonder she was eager to escape him. Gilen fixed her with a look perilously close to a glare. As he had intended, she once more stopped short, clutching the kittens to her bosom, her gaze trapped by his.

How could a woman look at once so sultry—and so innocent?

He had to remember that he now had irrefutable evidence that she was far from the latter. As if in confirmation, as he continued silently staring, her cheeks began to color and her chin rose another notch. Once again, that winged brow lifted.

Yes, Miss Southford had to be the girl from the gypsy encampment. The imperative beating in his blood, this explosive, irrepressible reaction to her affirmed that identity more forcefully than any mundane coincidence of time or place.

He ought to despise her as the worst sort of female deceiver. Disdain and fury certainly figured among the violent emotions roiling in his gut. Also in the mix, though, was a guilty exhilaration.

"I will take my leave of you—for now," he replied at last. "But rest assured, I shall call again…soon."

As soon as he figured out what to do about one duplicitous gypsy dancer.

Luckily the long run had tired Raven into an atypical state of docility, else the normally fractious animal would probably have thrown his rider or bolted, so little attention did Gilen spare for his mount during the transit back to his rooms. He rode by instinct, his emotions still in an uproar and his whole mind churning with unanswered questions and half-formulated plans.

First among the questions—who was she?

After once more subjecting her behavior to a rapid review, his conclusion on that score remained the same. Her flawless company manners and easy acceptance in Harrogate society argued that she must have been born a lady. Those facts added to her aunt's unquestioning sponsorship indicated she probably was Lady Alice's niece, as she claimed.

So how did Miss Southford, daughter of gentility, end up dealing cards in a gypsy camp?

Lady Alice had informed him that her niece had left her old home in some haste after the arrival of her cousin, the new baron—whom Lady Alice apparently did not hold in high regard. Was the man reprobate enough to have made advances, even seduced, his cousin?

Or knowing her home soon to be forfeit, perhaps in her grief and desperation after her father's loss, she had succumbed to the blandishments of some local young man who promised marriage only to have that individual stop short of an offer once the deed was done, and then been evicted from the house by her guardian after he learned of her ruination.

He could understand the girl being sent away in disgrace. He could even, he thought with a disdainful curl of his lip, believe that her guardian might have sent her to Harrogate, a minor backwater compared to the Marriage Mart in London, where her dishonor was less likely to be discovered and where Lady Alice, if she were indeed a party to the deception, might attempt to quietly marry the girl off to some to some elderly widower or decrepit peer.

He frowned. Plausible though those theories were, since they supported quite well the passionate nature she'd displayed in his arms, neither would explain how she came to be traveling with gypsies. Even if—especially if—disgraced, the girl would have been sent to Harrogate by coach with her maid in visible attendance, so as to present an appearance of virginal propriety when she arrived in that new community.

His frown deepened as he attempted to construct some plausible bridge between the incongruent worlds of a gently born lady and a card-dealing gypsy. Lady Alice said Miss Southford had been mistress of her father's household. Mayhap while riding out to tend the tenants, she had encountered the gypsy band near Southford land, camped as they had been by Lacey's Retreat. It was not beyond possibility that a romantic, passionate, impressionable young woman might have been seduced by the clever flattery and false promises of some darkly handsome gypsy lad.

The idea of her in the arms of a gypsy man—any other man—brought an immediate surge of jealous outrage. But in the more rational reflection that followed, Gilen had to conclude that scenario also appeared unlikely. Of course, he was not familiar with gypsy customs, so could not predict with any accuracy how a man acted toward the woman he claimed, but he'd not noticed any potential protectors hovering about her. The gypsy lord himself had seemed to hold her in dislike.

Still, if she had taken a gypsy lover, why had she determined to seek out her aunt in Harrogate? Had she come to her senses and realized she could not adapt to their lifestyle? Or had she been rejected and abandoned by her gypsy seducer?

Of course, in the end it really didn't matter how she had ended up with them, or what lies she'd told the gullible Lady Alice to explain her sudden, unexpected arrival. The promiscuous company she'd kept on the journey—he recalled once more the wild abandon of the gypsy dancers—and the overt carnality of her kiss both proved she was no innocent.

Which meant his initial conclusion was absolutely correct. He must not allow her to trap Jeff into matrimony.

Gilen recalled the besotted look on his friend's face, his gaze following Miss Southford whenever she left his side, and his lips narrowed. Detach her from Jeff he must, and quickly, before his tenderhearted friend sank any deeper under her spell.

By now he'd reached his lodgings. He left Raven at the mews and paced back into the main building, intending to order up a bottle of wine and start debating strategy.

But when he strode into his sitting room, he found Jeffrey comfortably ensconced in a wing chair by the fire, his wine already poured.

"Gil!" his friend exclaimed, rising at his entrance. "Your man let me in. I hope I wasn't presumptuous in making myself at home."

Gilen struggled for a gracious response. Though he was always glad to see Jeff, he suspected his friend meant to tax him about Miss Southford—a matter he was not yet prepared to discuss.

"Only if you've already drunk all my wine. No? Then pour me a glass."

He shrugged off his coat, hoping for a reprieve, but Jeffrey's next words dashed that vain wish.

"So, now that you've twice had an opportunity to observe her, what do you think of Miss Southford?"

Silently he cursed the troublesome chit while he tried to pick words that would not prematurely tip his hand.

"Lovely, in an understated way." *Taming that exuberant hair in a braid and masking her true nature with a show of downcast eyes,* he thought. When Jeffrey continued to watch him expectantly, Gilen added, "Her, ah, manners appear to be quite pleasing." *Hah! And how appearances deceive!*

Jeffrey's air of eager anticipation faded, and he took a sip of wine, giving Gilen time to lay another mental curse on Miss Southford's head. "From the scowl on your face, I'd say you don't like her very much," his friend said at last. "What fault do you find in her?"

Deceitful, dishonorable, wanton…but it wasn't time yet
to recite a litany of her sins to Jeff. Gilen tried to smooth
the annoyance from his face and cast about for some honest
but unexceptional objection. "She…she does seem to be
rather blatantly husband-hunting," he said at last.

"You can hardly blame her for that," Jeff countered.
"What else is an unmarried lady to do, pray? Especially
one in Miss Southford's position, who no longer has a father to protect her."

"Perhaps. But having just suffered a…disappointment, I
should not like to see you rush too soon into a new attachment. Especially not with someone about whom we know
so little."

Jeffrey shrugged. "She is the niece of grandpapa's old
friend, and quite obviously Quality. What else does one
need to know?"

Words hovered on the tip of Gilen's tongue to describe
to Jeffrey in pithy terms just what sort of quality Miss
Southford possessed, but he managed to bite them back.
His friend was already looking frustrated that Gilen had not
perceived in the lady he favored the same perfections he
saw himself. No sense getting his back up any further.

"I suppose I do need to become better acquainted. Then
her true nature will be apparent to all."

Gilen was pleased with that little speech, which succeeded in being honest while at the same time soothing the
vexed look from his friend's face.

"You're right, of course. A toast, then," Jeffrey held up
his wineglass. "To a better acquaintance."

Gilen raised his own glass. *Now to try another tack.*
"Sometimes in cases where matters appear to be…
progressing rather too swiftly, 'tis useful to distance oneself
for a time. See if, after a period of separation, the attachment remains as strong. Alden is still with Chase

DeLacey and his friends. The hunting is excellent, as I can attest, and they all pressed me to return and bring you with me. What do you say to a week or so at Lacey's Retreat, having a go at some of the best coverts in the North? 'Tis near enough that we could return speedily to Harrogate, should your grandfather take a turn for the worse.''

Jeffrey rubbed his finger against the side of his wine-glass. "N-no, go back if you wish, but I can't feel comfortable leaving Harrogate at present.'' He put the glass down, frowning. "Colonel Howard is said to be departing soon, and I've heard he means to make Miss Southford a declaration before he goes. If I abandon the field to ascertain the strength of my attachment, he may well steal a march on me. And I'm nearly sure that Miss Southford is the One.''

Dismay tightened Gilen's chest. "You are that sure?''

That faraway look Gilen was coming to detest came back into Jeff's eyes. "Yes, I think I am.''

His worst suspicions confirmed, Gilen pinched his mouth together to keep a curse from escaping. He would have to move quickly indeed if he meant to detach Miss Southford from his friend before it was too late.

For if the woman managed to induce Jeffrey to propose, his friend would not later withdraw his offer, no matter what he learned about the character of his betrothed. His sense of honor simply would not permit it.

As a younger son with a comfortable fortune in his own right, Jeffrey might not need to marry wealth and title, but he did deserve to wed a lady. Never while he drew breath would Gilen permit his friend's honor to trap him into wedlock with a woman who had none.

Before he could dredge up a reply, Jeffrey had drained the last of his wine and set the glass back down. "There is a favor you can do me, though, before you head out of town. You see, Lady Aylesbury more or less coerced me into calling this afternoon to take Miss Aylesbury driving.''

Gilen groaned. ''You are too good-natured by half. You should have cut her off and walked away.''

''I'm not nearly as top-lofty as you,'' Jeffrey said with a grin. ''Besides, Miss Aylesbury is such a sweet, gentle girl. Though she never utters a word of disparagement about her mother, one can see how mortified the woman makes her. After her mama had drawn such attention to us with that scene in the assembly rooms the other night, I simply couldn't embarrass Miss Aylesbury further by snubbing her.''

The chit was, in Gilen's opinion, a pretty peagoose without an ounce of gumption, though he had to admit her vulgar dragon of a mother would be a millstone about the neck of a girl of far more enterprising spirit.

''What is this favor I can do you while you are out playing knight errant to Miss Aylesbury?''

''Take Miss Southford driving this afternoon. 'Twill give you an opportunity to get to know her better, which we've both agreed will be a good thing. And I understand Howard is angling to get her alone, so that he may ask her something of…significance.''

''Did Miss Southford tell you that?'' Gilen asked, suspicion sharpening his tone.

''No, I overheard him whispering to Lady Alice that he'd appreciate her help in arranging some private time. He'll not get the opportunity if I have anything to do about it. So do promise, old friend, that you'll go by early and take her driving in my place.''

Gilen paused, considering. The idea of having Miss Southford seated beside him in the close confines of a curricle both excited and repulsed him. Still, it would keep both Jeffrey and the hapless Colonel Howard out of her clutches for another afternoon. And surely by afternoon he would have decided how to counteract the threat she posed.

Driving her might also afford him the opportunity to put his yet-to-be-determined plan into action.

"I should be delighted. What time should I call?"

"Just before four, to be sure of beating out the colonel." Jeffrey grinned and clapped him on the back. "Thanks, Gil! I knew you wouldn't fail me!"

Gilen tried to suppress a stirring of guilt. He had to remember his friend's future happiness depended on his remaining resolute, despite any short-term distress his intervention was likely to cause Jeff.

"Whatever it takes, I promise you, I shall not."

After his friend departed, Gilen poured himself another glass of claret. How *should* he proceed?

He might call on old Lord Masterson, warn him of the danger in which his grandson now stood, and request that he invent some business upon which to dispatch Jeffrey until Howard made Miss Southford a declaration or Gilen managed to somehow remove her from Harrogate.

After a few minutes' rumination, he discarded that idea. For one, after the conversation he'd just had with Jeff, it seemed unlikely Lord Masterson would be able to induce his grandson to depart on some trifling errand. Secondly, it seemed unfair to the colonel, of whom Gilen knew no ill save that he'd been taken in by the same scheming wench, to rescue Jeff by foisting the charlatan off on him.

He dispensed with the next option just as rapidly. With the imminent prospect of securing herself a lifetime in luxury by inducing one of her competing suitors to propose, Miss Southford was unlikely to accept even the largest sum of money Gilen could stomach offering her in exchange for relinquishing her pretensions to Jeff's hand.

He could demand that she leave Harrogate immediately,

or he would reveal her presence in the gypsy camp to all Society. But a rapid review of the events of that night brought the unwelcome conclusion that he alone of Alden's party had been close enough to the girl to be able with any certainty to identify her again. The gypsy lord had already disavowed all knowledge of her.

Which left him no way to prove to Jeff that she'd ever been with the gypsies.

As the wench undoubtedly knew. Impotent fury again sizzled through his veins. In the absence of outside confirmation, the best he could accomplish by denouncing her to Jeff would be to wound his friend by accusing the woman he loved of perpetrating a deception of which Jeff would never believe her capable. At worst, he might rip an irreparable breach in their long friendship.

He could let the news slip anonymously—an *on-dit* as salacious as that would be certain to rapidly make the rounds of the Harrogate ton. But though it might prevent an overt blow to their friendship, the end result would still not accomplish his aims.

It would harm Miss Southford, assuredly, but it would also humiliate the possibly innocent Lady Alice. Worse yet, it would almost certainly cause the chivalrous Jeffrey to stand in defense of his distraught lady, who would doubtless lose no time in prodding him to salvage her good name by tendering the very proposal Gilen wished to avoid. He'd then be in the infuriating position of having to lend his own not-insignificant social support to his friend's wanton of a bride, lest he permanently alienate Jeffrey.

Short of murder, a solution that appeared more and more appealing as he discarded other options, there seemed no swift and tidy solution to the dilemma. Impotent rage swelled his chest, and if Miss Southford had been present, he could cheerfully have throttled her with his bare hands.

And yet, despite his rage, the thought of trapping her body against his at quarters close enough to effect strangulation even now had the power to submerge anger in heat of another sort. If only he could put her where a woman like that truly belonged.

In the next moment, his volatile mix of lust and fury coalesced in one simple, eminently satisfying conclusion.

He not only could put her there—he must. And with Jeff having provided him the perfect opportunity to do so, this very afternoon, he would.

Chapter Ten

Several hours later, after Tilly finished doing up the tiny buttons on her carriage dress, Gwennor took a deep breath and steeled herself to descend to the salon. Colonel Howard had hinted he meant to take her driving today, and though he'd said he had another engagement, Mr. Masterson indicated he would also try to stop by, however briefly. She should go seat herself beside Aunt Alice and prepare to help entertain any callers.

None of whom, she devoutly hoped, would be Lord St. Abrams. Her pulse stampeded when she recalled that strange confrontation in the mews earlier today.

She looked down ruefully at the scratches on her hands. In her agitation, she'd clutched the kittens so tightly, 'twas a wonder she'd not squeezed the life out of the poor creatures, and no surprise at all that they'd raked their little claws across her fingers in protest.

The anger on his face and the veiled innuendo in his tone had removed any remaining doubt. The viscount now recognized her as the card dealer from the gypsy camp, and apparently had seen Parry among the company as well. At first she'd thought he meant to accuse her then and there, in front of her aunt's groom. But though he had spared her that humiliation, his parting words—that he would call again *soon*—had nothing to do with politeness and everything to do with intimidation.

She drew in another deep breath. Perhaps it would be better to have him call this afternoon, so she could attempt to discover what action he meant to take and plan her counteroffensive accordingly. She would prefer to face and deflect the menace he represented straightaway, rather than have the threat of his hostility looming near her like a smoking, as-yet-unexploded cannonball.

For a moment she felt a stirring of guilty regret. Whatever the viscount did, she hoped it wouldn't embarrass her innocent aunt, who knew nothing about her means of transport to Harrogate. She'd seen no need upon arriving to reveal to Lady Alice circumstances she had trusted, before the unfortunate advent of Lord St. Abrams, would remain forever secret and whose revelation would only have sent her aunt into palpitations.

Just to be safe, perhaps she should have a portmanteau packed and a reserve of cash available. Though she still believed, once he'd thought the matter through carefully, that Lord St. Abrams would see the futility of making wild accusations he could not prove and that would undoubtedly subject him to almost as much speculation and gossip as it would her, 'twas always best to be prepared.

One way or another, she would find a safe haven for herself and Parry. If Lord St. Abrams discovered a means to make that goal impossible of achievement in Harrogate, she would simply have to go elsewhere. Conceding defeat, returning to Southford and submitting to cousin Nigel's plans for Parry was simply unthinkable.

Cousin Nigel who himself remained a threat. Though she no longer started at every knock upon the door, she couldn't yet risk assuming that her detestable cousin had chosen to let her go and content himself with claiming whatever inheritance her father's will had left her. She still could not be sure he would not descend upon them, bent on dragging her back to Southford and forcing her to do his will.

Despite Lady Alice's brave words to the contrary, Gwennor doubted her aunt would have the strength of mind to withstand Nigel should he indeed track her down. Yet another compelling reason to keep available the means to escape him again, should the need arise.

And try to settle the matter of matrimony with either Col. Howard or Mr. Masterson as soon as possible.

Given the latter's close friendship with Lord St. Abrams, Gwen was definitely leaning in favor of the former.

Acting upon her prudent resolution, instead of exiting her chamber, Gwen crossed to the clothes press and extracted the worn leather bag that contained her mother's jewelry. Reverently she took the fine old pieces out, stifling emotion along with the surge of memories seeing them always evoked. Dispassionately she inspected them, trying to decide which ones she should sell in order to replenish her nearly exhausted store of coins.

A knock interrupted that task. "Enter," she called, stuffing the jewels back in their case.

The upstairs maid opened the door and curtseyed. "Lady Alice needs you in the salon, Miss."

Gwennor frowned. 'Twas still a bit early for afternoon callers. "Thank you, Sally, I'm on my way down."

She quelled the flickers of nervousness twitching in her stomach. Probably it was Mr. Masterson, stopping by for a few moments before proceeding to his other engagement. He might not possess a rapier wit or a gaze that compelled one's attention, but he was withal a most pleasant, handsome gentleman, she thought with a sigh. How unfortunate he was also close friend to her chief nemesis.

Reminding herself again of how kind he'd been to Parry, she summoned a smile as she entered the parlor. A smile that froze in place when the gentleman within rose to greet her. Lord St. Abrams.

"My lord, what a...surprise," she said faintly.

Gone was the air of suppressed fury, the almost palpable hostility he'd radiated toward her in front of the stable earlier this afternoon. In fact, he was smiling with such affability that she was immediately suspicious.

His smile deepened at her greeting. "A pleasant one, I hope, Miss Southford. Though it should not have surprised you. I told your niece earlier, Lady Alice, that I wished most particularly to call upon her again."

While Lady Alice uttered an "ooh" of appreciation at that little speech, the viscount reached out to seize the hands Gwennor had not offered him. Like the shock she sometimes felt after walking across an Aubusson carpet in winter, a sharp, nearly painful energy leapt between his fingers and hers.

At least it jolted him as well, she thought with grim satisfaction. His eyes widened momentarily and his smile wavered before he regained his composure and raised her purloined hands for the obligatory salute. Which he prolonged much longer than was seemly, brushing his lips slowly across her knuckles, that glancing contact sending a skitter of sparks in its wake.

Drat the man and damn the response he seemed able to evoke in her with the merest touch! She all but yanked her hands free.

Which only broadened the smile on his too-handsome face, confirming her suspicion that the blackguard knew very well his effect on her—and had every intention of using it to his advantage.

Vaguely she heard Lady Alice invite him to be seated

again. Gwennor took the chair farthest removed from his current position. Even separated by five feet of carpet, the tea service and a heaping tray of macaroons, she still felt the magnetic pull of his presence. Determinedly she accepted tea from her aunt and avoided looking at him.

Her bold intention of uncovering whatever devious designs he had in mind shaken by the unsettling aftermath of his greeting, Gwennor took as little part in the conversation as she dared and prayed for an early arrival by another—any other—visitor. Even Lady Alice's elderly neighbor Mrs. Maxwell, hard-of-hearing and prone to monopolize the conversation with a discussion of her many maladies, Gwennor would be prepared to greet with pleasure.

She was smiling inwardly, envisioning the viscount trying to make polite chat around Mrs. Maxwell's description of her bodily ailments, when the ominous words her aunt had just spoken penetrated her abstraction.

"...be delighted to drive with you, wouldn't you, Gwennor dear?"

Gwen jerked her attention back to St. Abrams, who was gazing at her with an air of what had to be entirely spurious admiration. His show of ardency seemed to have duped Lady Alice, who beamed her approval.

The conniving weasel, she thought, incensed. He might be able to pass off that Spanish coin on her aunt, but she was not so gullible. "How kind, my lord, but I've already half promised Colonel Howard—"

"Who is not present to hold you to that promise. A sad lack of enthusiasm, which deserves that he forfeit the prize of your company, do you not agree, Lady Alice? The afternoon is lovely, my curricle and horses impatiently waiting. Do say you will come, Miss Southford, or I shall be quite cast down." He ended those gallant words with a look so beguiling she could almost believe he meant them.

Almost. Just what sort of rig was he running, being suddenly so attentive and agreeable?

"How could you refuse so pretty an offer, Gwennor dear?" her aunt asked.

"It seems I have little choice," she said at last, still irritated both by the viscount's high-handedness and by how skillfully he was manipulating Lady Alice.

"Oh, I intend to leave very little to choice," he murmured.

After that rather alarming statement, he stared into her eyes with another of those soul-capturing gazes that made it nearly impossible for her to look away. It took her several moments to manage the feat, and afterward she was breathing as rapidly as if she'd just galloped a mile on Firefly.

Driving with him would provide her with the opportunity to uncover his plans—a task urgent enough for her to set aside, for the moment, her aggravation. Ignoring the fluttering in her belly—alarm and something else she'd rather not put a name to—she summoned what she hoped Lady Alice would consider a pleased smile and nodded. "I'll just get my wrap, Lord St. Abrams."

Lady Alice was so beside herself with pleasure at the marked attentions being paid her niece by this most distinguished of potential suitors, Gwennor almost expected her to clap her hands. "What a delightful excursion, my dear," she trilled. "Do enjoy yourselves."

"My thanks, Lady Alice, for the generous gift of your niece's company," the viscount said, bowing to her aunt and then holding out his arm to Gwennor.

At those courtly words, Lady Alice sighed again, and one corner of Lord St. Abrams's mouth twitched. Gwennor felt a violent desire to strike him.

Instead, she took his arm, gritting her teeth at the now-

familiar spurt of sensation that raced over her nerve end-
ings, and stalked out of the room.

She might *have* to drive out with him and discover what
mischief he was planning, but she most certainly did not
want to accompany him, she fumed silently. By her presence thereby pandering to that vanity of purse and person
all too many ladies—her own aunt included—seemed only
too eager to further inflate with their fawning regard. She
disliked his arrogance as much as she despised this maddening hold he seemed to exert over her senses.

Well, whatever dastardly plan he'd concocted, she would
foil it, she vowed, raising her chin. Just as she would overcome this annoyingly automatic physical response.

Liar, her body whispered.

Mercer arrived with her cape, but the viscount took it
from him. "Allow me," he said, holding it out as if to
wrap it around her shoulders. "Can't have you catching
your death from a chill."

Meaning he'd prefer to engineer her demise by other
means? she wondered, half angry, half alarmed. Suddenly
she was conscious of the massive bulk of him looming over
her. Uneasily she noted the tight fit of his jacket across the
breadth of his shoulders, a snugness attributable, she suspected, to muscles developed in the ring at Gentleman Jackson's rather than to the buckram padding used by Corinthians of less athletic prowess.

Should she fear more than a verbal assault?

Nonsense, she chided herself, snatching the cloak from
his hands and pulling it close. She would not let the dratted
man intimidate her. Even should he wish to do her some
physical harm—and despite his anger earlier, she simply
couldn't believe that he would—what opportunity would
he have with them seated in an open curricle, in full view
of his groom and any passing vehicle?

Though they could be readily seen, with the noise from the wind and the carriage wheels, they could not easily be overheard, even by that groom. Perhaps St. Abrams *had* engineered this drive so as to spring on her whatever means of coercion he intended.

So be it.

By now they'd reached the bottom of the entry stairs. Taking a deep breath and girding herself for battle, Gwennor accepted his assistance into the vehicle.

The viscount climbed up, seeming to occupy an alarming amount of the cramped space within the curricle. He seated himself on the narrow bench, so close she could feel the heat emanating from the muscled thighs a bare inch from her own. The force exerted by rounding even a gradual curve would doubtless slide her into him, or he into her.

A shuddery feeling invaded her stomach and she felt suddenly too warm under her heavy wool cloak. As the viscount gave the horses the office to start, she clutched at the rail with fingers grown damp within their gloves.

For a few moments St. Abrams said nothing, his attention focused on guiding the horses through the crowded residential streets. But when they reached the park on the outskirts of town, he pulled up the horses and nodded to his groom, who hopped down from his seat and trotted off.

Before she could demand what he intended, the viscount turned to her. "Mr. Masterson told me you enjoy driving at a spanking pace. The ostler where I hired this conveyance claimed his horses were extremely fast, with a very smooth action. Shall we give them a go on the open road?"

Without waiting for her answer, he set the horses in motion. "Jeffrey also said you accounted yourself a fair driver. If this pair turns out to be as sweet-going as claimed, perhaps I shall give you a turn at the ribbons."

Her mouth had been opened to protest the jettisoning of

their chaperone and the abandonment of the safety of town. Confronted with the temptation of possibly driving such a fancy curricle at full speed in open country, however, she hesitated.

She angled a glance at Lord St. Abrams, who stared over his horses' heads, as if absorbed in his driving. Was that a tiny quirk of amusement in his lips?

She really ought to refuse, insist that they restrict themselves to a safe—and boring—drive around the park. But only during her cousin Harry's brief visits did she get the opportunity to drive such a carriage and pair.

She bit her lip, fierce desire to claim the treat being dangled before her battling with prudence. Blast the man for guessing how much she thrilled to the speed and danger of a gallop!

With each stride of the horses, the comforting busyness of the Harrogate streets receded. Soon they would pass the last of the houses clustered at the outskirts of the city and reach countryside where the carriage route was bordered only by fields and orchards empty of any human observer save the occasional farm worker. 'Twas folly to allow him to isolate her far from any potential assistance, should assistance be necessary.

He probably wouldn't even make good on his offer to let her try the team.

But if he did... After a struggle, temptation outweighed caution. "I should enjoy that very much."

By now they'd mounted the heights above the city. Though the glance the viscount spared her was brief, the hungry intensity of the eyes that roved her face once more sent a shock humming through her. "I very much look forward to giving you enjoyment," he murmured.

Before her shaken mind could puzzle out a reply, he continued in a lighter tone, "I understand your family's estate at Southford is rather remote. After weeks of the closeness of town, I imagine you enjoy escaping into the country. I know I do.''

A London dandy such as he? ''Do you?'' she asked, unable to keep the skepticism from her voice.

''Yes, I do.'' He looked down at her, his all-too-engaging grin dissipating some of her wariness. ''There are many things you do not know about me, Miss Southford, but I hope today we can begin to remedy that. And before we go any further, I do wish to apologize.''

Instantly alerted again, she repeated, ''Apologize?''

''I fear I was not as courteous as I should have been earlier this afternoon. I was laboring under a…delusion so ludicrous I dare not confess it, but I'm quite convinced now that I was mistaken. I do hope you will be gracious enough to give me the opportunity to start over again. As friends, Miss Southford?''

His voice seemed totally sincere, the glance he threw her open and appealing. Was this chicanery—or had he truly pondered the matter and concluded that his suspicions were groundless? Oh, that such a comforting thought were true!

Better not to lower her defenses yet, however. ''Of course, friends, my lord,'' she replied.

''Good. I shall accept friends—as a start.'' Before she could attempt to decode that comment, he continued, ''Jeffrey tells me you ran the business of the estate while your father occupied himself with breeding experiments?''

''Yes,'' she replied, surprised by how much he'd learned about her. ''As you may know, much of the land in that region is too rocky and mountainous to make farming profitable. Papa long sought other avenues that would allow the estate, and our tenants, to augment agricultural earnings with a more consistent source of income.''

''Did you keep the estate books as well?''

"Yes." She had to smile. "For a gentleman of keen scientific mind, Papa had lamentably little talent for figures—nor any interest in them, either."

"A skillful household manager, a bruising rider and a whipster with the ribbons—or so Jeffrey tells me—and absolutely lovely besides. The gentleman who wins you will be fortunate indeed."

Gwennor looked up sharply, sure she must not have heard the viscount correctly. Surely he couldn't be—flirting with her!

But the gaze he fixed on her was curiously intent, and his eyes held a heat that couldn't be feigned.

Gwennor looked away, suddenly unsure. She could not suppress a surge of purely feminine satisfaction that such a bang-up-to-the-mark Corinthian might possibly be interested in her, even as she discounted that possibility as ludicrous. More likely the viscount was, for ulterior motives of his own, attempting to maneuver her as skillfully as he had Lady Alice.

But he'd said he was mistaken in his suspicions, that he'd dismissed his earlier "delusion." Fact or tactic?

Before she could decide, he unsettled her completely by moving one gloved hand and cupping it over her own where she gripped the carriage rail.

"A very lucky man indeed," he murmured.

Whatever his motives, the pressure of his hand instantly revived the shivery mix of attraction he conjured up like a wizard's magic every time he'd touched her, from that first night in the gypsy camp. The heat of his gaze ignited a smoldering urgency within her.

Her startled eyes dropped to his lips, her mind invaded by the memory of the feel and taste of him. Ah, how stirring and sweet it had been!

Stop this, the prudent part of her mind warned. Despite

his fine words, Viscount St. Abrams couldn't possibly be interested in courting her—could he? She was too honest to deny that a rush of joyous anticipation filled her chest at the idea. Indeed, the notion of actually being able to pursue friendship—and maybe more—with a man who so forcefully engaged her mind and stirred her senses appealed so strongly, 'twas difficult to hang on to either caution or objectivity.

Just when she thought he meant to lean down and brush his lips to hers, he straightened and drew his hand back. "We're well away from the city now," he said. "These beasts appear as good-tempered as the ostler claimed. Should you like to try them?"

Now that they were far from all observers, he invited her to drive his horses. So much for her idiotish fantasy that the viscount was about to kiss her. Her wayward thoughts still making her cheeks heat, Gwennor welcomed the bracing slap of reality. "Yes, indeed."

"All that is mine I would offer you," he said and handed over the ribbons.

Was her reading of his intentions accurate? Made once more uncertain by his response, she gladly transferred her attention to the team, and for the next several minutes gave herself up to the uncomplicated enjoyment of tooling the sleek racing carriage behind its swift horses. Not until the beasts showed signs of tiring did she pull them up, exhilarated.

"That was marvelous! Thank you so much for permitting me to drive them!" Once again in perfect charity with him, she offered back the reins.

"Excellent driving, Miss Southford!" he exclaimed. "I must admit, I was somewhat skeptical that a female might actually be able to handle such a vehicle as this, but you are every bit as skilled as Jeffrey claimed."

"Thank you, sir," she said, pleased by this compliment from an undoubted top sawyer.

He wrapped the reins around one gloved hand and took her fingers with the other. "Do you know how adorable you look, your cheeks flushed from the wind, that lovely hair in wisps around your face?"

The intimacy of his tone, the intensity in the eyes that met the startled gaze she raised to his, set her own simmering desire once more to a boil. 'Twas merely gallantry, she told herself, trying to stifle her response to his words. Wasn't it?

"My lord, I think your friend Mr. Masterson might accuse you of taking unfair advantage of our lack of a chaperone and my inexperience at dalliance."

"My dear Miss Southford, in love and war, all is fair," he murmured, and bent to brush her lips with his.

The horses sidestepped. Lord St. Abrams abruptly straightened and manipulated the reins to steady them.

The moment was over so fast she might have dreamed it, except that her lips burned where he'd touched them and her whole body hummed with an urgent need to press closer.

Instead, her cheeks flaming, she pushed him away. Should she slap his face—or kiss him back?

Chapter Eleven

Ah, yes, she wanted him as much as he wanted her, Gilen exulted, gazing into Miss Southford's flushed face. Pleased to have established that fact beyond doubt, he was tempted to seal the happy conclusion with another kiss.

Best save that for later, regrettably. He cheered himself with a promise of how satisfying "later" would be.

"Little as I wish to," he murmured, breaking the sensual spell that held them both motionless, "I suppose I had best be getting you back to your aunt. Shall we?"

Numbly she nodded. Giving her hand on the rail one last, lingering caress, he sorted out the reins and set the horses in motion.

His plan to relax her seemed to have worked perfectly, Gilen thought, narrowly observing the slender figure seated so alluringly close to his side. In fact, this whole outing was going splendidly. So splendidly he was having definite trouble remembering the objective of this whole charade was to rescue Jeff, when all his body could concentrate on was rewarding Gilen.

He had better concentrate on finishing the bargain, lest he arrive back in town with the matter not yet concluded

and have her somehow manage to alert Jeffrey to his maneuvering.

A momentary uncertainty troubled him, and he frowned.
Although he was reasonably certain of success, he did wish
he could take more time to wheedle his way further into
her confidence and deepen the bond desire had already created between them. Unfortunately, with two suitors competing for her favor and Jeffrey hovering on the verge of a
declaration, time was a luxury he did not have.

He shifted uneasily. Though the strength of that potent
desire did an effective job of keeping the uncomfortable
emotion from the forefront of his thoughts, deep down
Gilen felt a sense of shame that he was going behind his
friend's back. A shame made deeper by the undeniable fact
that he wanted the wench.

He'd feel a good deal better about it, he had to admit, if
the prospect of luring Miss Southford away were odious,
rather than tantalizing enough to heat his blood and fire his
imagination.

Still, fostering the honest passion that existed between
them, even if he had to do it on the sly, was infinitely more
honorable than allowing her to perpetrate her dishonest
sham on Jeffrey.

Jeffrey would likely not see it that way—at least not
now—but later, when the fullness of time and the coolness
of reason demonstrated that truth, surely Jeff would realize
how narrow had been his escape and how selfless Gilen
had been in risking the loss of Jeff's good opinion by intervening to save him.

A troubling niggle of doubt still shadowed the otherwise
pleasant prospect of his plan's success. What if, once he
discovered it, Jeffrey did not understand Gilen's interfer-
ence? What if he believed that Gilen, knowing full well the
depth of Jeffrey's attachment to Miss Southford, had none-

theless deliberately set out to seduce the woman his friend wanted?

'Twould probably deal a death blow to their long friendship. The conclusion sent a bolt of bleakness marrow-deep.

Resolutely he stifled it. Having already run the situation through his head over and over most of the afternoon, Gilen had been unable to devise any other alternative both as quick and as sure of its effect. With a little luck and some understanding from Jeff, soon everything he wished for—Jeffrey's deliverance and the devious Miss Southford in his arms—would come to pass.

Time to set it all in motion. "Miss Southford, may I tell you again how much your deft handling of the ribbons impressed me. I've never before allowed a lady to drive me, and would not previously have considered permitting one to do so in a vehicle as dangerous as a curricle."

She shifted, as if embarrassed. "You are too kind."

"Nonsense. I generally describe matters as I find them, without subterfuge or exaggeration. Indeed, I am very much looking forward to enjoying the display of your other talents."

"My lord, I fear I must disappoint. I am not so fearsomely talented as that."

"Ah, but I disagree! Already I can recite quite a paean of praise—for your graceful dancing, your skillful driving, your kindness to the wounded and infirm. But then, that beauty of conduct is only surpassed by your loveliness of form."

She cheeks pinked and she stole a glance at him. "Now I know you are merely being gallant."

"No gallantry, I assure you. Did I not just say I speak my views plainly? The gentleman who wins your favor will be a lucky man indeed."

She laughed uncertainly. "My lord, I could almost believe you yourself should like to enter the lists."

He gave her a quick, intense glance. "Believe it."

"Excuse me for asking, but would such a course of action not appear a trifle—odd—to Mr. Masterson?"

Gilen felt his neckcloth grow tight. He took a deep breath and made himself continue. "In ordinary circumstances, perhaps. But in delicate matters of the heart, I imagine Jeff would be the first to concede the strong effect sensibility has upon one's conduct. It compels me to speak here, when I would otherwise feel obliged to remain silent. But the—violence—of my emotions is such that I cannot leave you in ignorance of my feelings. Nor are you, I hope... indifferent to me."

A long, tense silence ensued, during which he heard only the clip-clop of the trotting horses over the pulse that pounded in his ears. "N-no," she said at last.

He looked down at her again. With her averted face, her downcast eyes, she appeared the picture of maidenly confusion. She really was very good at playing her role, he had to admit.

Now to tie up the bargain. "You do find me...attractive?" he persisted.

"What woman would not? You are intelligent, witty, and can be...very charming when you wish." Despite that avowal, still she kept her head averted while her fingers played nervously on the carriage rail.

He supposed he should find it irritating that she could dissemble a character so different from what the facts declared hers to be. Somewhat to his surprise, though, he found the contrast between her shy demeanor now and the passionate abandon of the gypsy maid arousing rather than disgusting. "For you," he said, his voice husky, "I could be very charming indeed, for a very long time. Will you let me show you?''

That startled her into raising her eyes. ''I…I'm not sure what you mean. Are you referring to a…a future between…*us?*'' Her voice rose on a note of incredulity.

''Indeed I am.'' He shifted the reins and reached over to cover the small hand gripping the rail with his larger one. ''You do feel it, don't you? This…force between us?''

She jumped when he touched her and a warm crimson tide flooded her cheeks. ''Y-yes, I…feel it.''

''Then how could you expect me to ignore this and let you go to Jeffrey, good friend though he be?''

''But my lord, we've—we've barely met!''

''One need not examine a gemstone at length to realize that it is priceless.''

Her flush deepened and she stared at him. In those oh-so-seemingly-innocent violet eyes he read uncertainty—and desire. ''Just what are your intentions, my lord?''

Warming to the task now, he gripped her hand more tightly. ''I intend that we yield to the call commanding us to be together. I'm proposing that we allow ourselves to make each other very happy. I'm proposing…''

Her lips parted in surprise at his hesitation, her face both incredulous—and radiant. Doubtless she was unable to believe her good luck in snaring so wealthy a protector, he thought, confident now of success.

''I'm proposing,'' he continued, flashing a grin, ''that we finish the dance we've already begun—my little gypsy.''

For a moment she stared at him, uncomprehending. Then as the meaning of words registered, she gasped, her hand beneath his clenching on the rail. Her lips parted as if she would speak.

He rushed on, not wanting her to interrupt until he'd

given the little speech he'd rehearsed all the way to Lady Alice's. "No, my dear, you needn't attempt to deny it, nor should you fear my intervention. I knew from the moment we met we were destined for each other. Even when I encountered you again in your maiden's disguise at the Harrogate Assembly, I felt that instantaneous pull. At first I didn't understand it, but once I held you in my arms again—I knew. And so did you! Don't be vexed, my lovely—you can't really have expected your little scheme to succeed. Besides, I'm prepared to make you a counteroffer even more attractive."

"A...counteroffer?" she repeated numbly.

"Give up your pretensions to Mr. Masterson, leave Harrogate—and come to me. I'll have a post chaise waiting to take you to a snug house in London. Gowns, jewels, your own carriage and pair to drive through Hyde Park—whatever you wish shall be yours. I pledge to fulfill your every desire." He shifted his attention from the horses long enough to give her a smoky glance. "From the very first moment...through the very last night."

Miss Southford was staring straight ahead, as if fascinated by the road. Vivid color came and went in her cheeks. Overwhelmed by his generosity, he imagined.

They were beginning to approach the outskirts of the city. Now, to seal the bargain with another kiss, he thought, his body exulting.

Once again he pulled up the horses. Looping the reins over the carriage rail, Gilen turned to Miss Southford. "So, sweeting, don't leave me in torment. Make me the happiest man in Christendom, and say 'yes.'"

Miss Southford gazed up at him, amazement and some deeper emotion in her eyes. "Y-you are truly offering *me* c-carte blanche?"

"Truly I am," he confirmed with a tender smile. "Ah, my sweet, I'm sure you will be worth every penny."

Miss Southford shuddered, her eyelids fluttering closed and her face paling. For a moment Gilen feared she might faint. Then she straightened and looked up. Her eyes sparkled with—surely that couldn't be anger?

"You miserable cur," she hissed. Before he could begin to imagine her intent, Miss Southford drew her arm back and dealt him a blow to the chin that would have done credit to Gentleman Jackson himself.

The force of it knocked him off balance. As he scrabbled to grab the rail, she batted his hands away. "Get out of my sight!" she cried, and shoved him hard.

Already unsteady of footing and denied the brace of the rail, the force of his weight and her momentum sent him tumbling sideways—straight out of the carriage.

In a miracle of catlike grace, Gilen managed to land on his feet instead of sprawling face-first in the dust of the road. Quickly he steadied himself and looked up —to find Miss Southford frantically unlooping the reins, attempting to persuade the nervous horses, agitated by the disturbance taking place behind them, not to bolt.

Within a few seconds she had them settled. Before Gilen could compliment her deft handing, she seized the carriage whip from its holder. Without sparing him so much as a glance, she lashed the horses into motion.

He waited a few seconds, but she made no move to pull up the team as he'd expected. Alarmed, he took a few running steps.

Before he embarrassed himself by shouting after her, the incredible realization hit home.

Miss Southford had forced him out of his own carriage and was running off with it.

* * *

Gwennor had reached the outskirts of Harrogate before her fury and humiliation abated enough for her to be fully conscious of what she was doing. She slowed the horses to a cooling walk and attempted to sort out her own agitation.

She had, she realized, absconded with a viscount's hired carriage and abandoned him some half mile behind in the countryside, on foot. Under the English code of justice that favored the mighty, she'd probably broken some sort of law. She couldn't feel a particle of regret.

Indeed not. It served the duplicitous bastard right. She hoped she'd left a bruise on his arrogant chin, too, after landing a punch Harry would have been proud of. Absently she rubbed her sore knuckles.

She still could hardly believe what that ignoble nobleman had had the consummate gall and deplorable breeding to propose. Carte blanche! Her cheeks heated anew at the very thought. Gentlemen might—and often did—make such offers to low-born actresses, opera singers or ladies of demi-monde, even, she'd been given to understand, to widows in straitened circumstances whose breeding did not permit their lovers to contemplate marriage.

But no man with any pretensions to the title *gentleman* would ever offer such a thing to a gently reared virgin.

Of course, she reminded herself with renewed chagrin, he didn't believe her to be one. What he did think she was, she couldn't imagine. Surely he wasn't such a nodcock that he imagined a true wagon-born gypsy could have hoodwinked Aunt Alice and comported herself within Harrogate society with the manners and breeding of a lady.

But his addled conjectures on her true identity were moot. Though she thought she'd considered all the various actions Lord St. Abrams might take in the aftermath of recognizing her, she had never expected *this*.

Chagrin heated her cheeks anew, along with a ridiculous sense of hurt that he could truly believe her the sort of unscrupulous female who would masquerade as something she was not in order to trap a wealthy husband.

She laughed without humor. Oh, she was angling to trap a husband. But it was the gypsy girl who'd been the masquerade, not the gently born maiden. Were the consequences not so dire, she might find it quite amusing that St. Abrams had confused the false with the true.

But now that she knew for certain he had recognized her, the situation was far too serious for humor.

It would not matter to St. Abrams or others of his ilk that she truly was a gently raised virgin. The mere fact of her having traveled with the gypsy clan would forever damn her in their eyes as unworthy of being offered marriage.

Despite the fact that she'd known it probable from the first, still she felt an irrational disappointment at the fact that, beguiling and attractive as he'd seemed, Viscount St. Abrams was really no better than cousin Nigel.

She supposed she ought to take his disgraceful offer as a sort of underhanded compliment. Though too much a wanton to make a wife, she was still considered worthy of being bedded.

Tears pricked at her eyes. "Priceless gemstone" indeed! For a few awestruck, joyous moments, she'd actually been fool enough to dream that this man who challenged and intrigued her was about to make her an honorable proposal.

She wished she'd hit him harder.

Still, there was little point in wasting her emotion raging about the hypocrisy of men. As a helpless captive of a social order constructed and dominated by males, she must now carefully consider what action to take next to protect herself and Parry.

Her most immediate problem was what to do with the

horse and carriage. Any suspicion of theft would be harshly dealt with, and she had difficulties enough.

Simmering anger strengthened her resolve. She'd drive them to Lady Alice's and hand them off to her groom with the explanation that, when his lordship stepped down for a moment, the horses bolted. Given her earlier demonstration of skill, Lord St. Arrogant Abrams would not believe that— indeed, she sincerely hoped he did not—but ton gentlemen in general had such a low opinion of a woman's abilities, the story would be readily accepted. St. Abrams would not dare dispute it, lest he look a fool for having had his equipage stolen out from under him by a mere female.

Considering the enormity of this afternoon's debacle, 'twas a very minor victory, but it gave her some small matter of satisfaction.

After returning the curricle, her next imperative was to determine what to do now about His Leering Lordship.

After soiling his perfectly polished boots with the dust of nearly a mile-long walk, he was apt to be in rather a temper. She grinned at the thought. Doubtless he'd be foaming at the mouth for a chance to get back at her.

He had at his disposal, she knew, a great many more resources to effect his revenge than she possessed to counter him. Her smile faded and her head began to pound.

By now she'd reached the more congested area of the city. For the rest of the transit back to Lady Alice's, the tricky task of guiding the high-spirited carriage horses through the crowded streets kept her fully occupied. By the time she at last reached the safety of the stableyard, her shoulders ached, her fingers were numb, and she was nearly sorry she'd decided to abscond with the beasts.

Jem swallowed her story of runaway horses with a barely lifted eyebrow, but to her relief, did not dispute it. Leaving the matter of returning them in his capable hands, she crept cautiously up to her room, not wishing to encounter her aunt until she'd determined what to do next.

She collapsed on the chair in her sitting room, her fingers gone from numb to shaking and her head throbbing worse than ever. Which, she thought, groaning as she eased the back of her neck into the cushioned chair's embrace, might turn out to be a blessing.

She ought to begin immediately to bathe and dress for dinner and the musicale Lady Alice had intended them to attend this evening. Mr. Masterson had already told her he could not be present, as his grandfather required his attendance at a family dinner. Since it was entirely probable that the viscount would track her down and make his first attempt to administer retribution, she was willing to use her headache as an excuse to avoid the entertainment. Missing Colonel Howard would be unfortunate, but she needed time to plan out her defenses.

The first step of which would be to visit the jeweler in the morning and replenish her reserve of funds. Though it nearly choked her to have to admit it, her safest alternative might once again end up being flight.

The unfairness of it recalled the lingering humiliation of the viscount's ignoble offer, and a swell of anger and resentment rose in her breast. Her lips trembled and her eyes stung, but she battled back the tears.

She needed to be strong, not weak. She would make her plans and gather her funds. This time, she vowed, the Invincible Viscount's schemes would not catch her unawares.

Chapter Twelve

Nearly an hour later, Gilen reached the outskirts of Harrogate. Initially in a blazing fury at being dumped beside the road like so much refuse, after the leisure to consider the matter afforded him by the stroll back to town, he had ended up more amused than incensed.

Under a clear blue sky, the late-afternoon sun's warmth hinted at the spring that was soon to arrive, and the walk in the clear air was quite invigorating. Within a few more moments he would reach the environs of the park where he might come across a hackney to bear him the rest of the way home. He would be quite interested to discover, he thought with a chuckle, what the enterprising Miss Southford had done with his curricle and team.

Obviously, despite the desire between them she hadn't bothered to deny, that saucy minx still believed she had a chance to extract an offer of marriage from Jeffrey. He could understand, given that delusion, why she might so unceremoniously rebuff his less-respectable—but much more appropriate—offer. And he had to admire the spirit-edness of her reaction almost as much as he had her driving skills. She threw a pretty mean roundhouse punch.

He grinned, recalling the passion sparking in those violet

eyes. She certainly played her part well. Did he not know her response stemmed from anger and pique at having her plans foiled, he might almost believe her a gently bred virgin aghast at receiving a disreputable offer from the escort into whose care she'd been entrusted by her guardian.

For an instant, his certitude about her identity wavered. Surely he was not mistaken!

He shook his head, firmly dismissing that uncomfortable shaft of doubt. No, 'twas impossible—mercifully. To have offered so unforgivable an insult to a virgin of his own class would have been even more shameful than betraying Jeffrey for no purer motive than assuaging his own lust.

No, whatever Miss Southford might be maiden debauched by a venal relation, wanton who'd willingly participated in her own ruination—the girl who had danced like Eve herself for him in the gypsy camp was no innocent. He hadn't wanted to sour the delicate negotiation this afternoon by resorting to crude threats, but Miss Southford was too intelligent not to realize that Gilen would do whatever was necessary to stymie her pursuit of Jeffrey, and bring her where she belonged—into Gilen's arms.

He would concede her this round. But he had no doubt that, in the end, he would triumph. And then, ah then, all that fire and spirit would be his, in his life, in his bed.

Would passion spark in her eyes once again as he undressed her? Would those lovely orbs glaze over with desire as he filled his hands with her pale plump breasts, the rosy pink nipples puckering as suckled them? He could almost feel the silk of her bare skin under his fingers as he traced them down the soft round of her belly. Stroking, then parting the wiry dark curls at her slick center to caress and tantalize. Would she moan his name as he tasted her, use the hand that had so indignantly slapped his face to clutch his shoulders when he answered her hoarse cry for fulfillment, opening her smooth white thighs and driving himself home?

Yes, home, he thought, almost shaky with need, in that discreet little house in Mayfair where he soon expected to spend most of his days and all of his nights.

Despite the chill of the approaching evening, sweat dewed his brow and dampened his shirt. He had to have her, and he would. 'Twas only a matter of when.

Anticipation springing his steps, he spied a hackney farther down the street and sprinted toward it. The gauntlet had been well and truly thrown this afternoon by an adversary who was proving herself worthy of his skill. He couldn't wait to take it back up.

As Gilen dressed to go out, he considered how he would approach Miss Southford. Mercifully, while advising Gilen that he was promised to his grandfather this evening, Jeffrey had let slip that Miss Southford was to attend Lady Huntville's musicale. He'd have one more evening to try to coax her submission before the complication of Jeffrey's return to the field.

Watching in the mirror as he set the perfect knot on his Mathematical, he frowned, wondering what the minx would say to Jeffrey if Gilen did not win her over tonight.

Might she tell him of Gilen's offer, trying to drive an irreparable wedge in their friendship?

The threat was sobering, and he considered it carefully. However, at length he decided that she was not likely to do so. As Jeffrey still labored under the illusion that Miss Southford was a lady, he would not, Gilen felt sure, believe his friend capable of such reprehensible behavior as offering carte blanche to the decorous maiden being courted by his best friend. Horrified and disbelieving, Jeff would try to excuse or explain away what that damsel thought she heard, in the process asking a great many questions which Miss Southford would probably prefer not to answer.

No, 'twas safer for the successful outcome of her deception that she keep Jeff in ignorance of any quibbles about her honor until after she'd finagled his betrothal ring onto her finger.

As for his own plans, Gilen meant to use this final opportunity to detach her from her party by whatever means necessary and spirit her away for a private chat. This time, he'd warn her quite bluntly he would never allow her to entrap Jeffrey. Then, while she sputtered in outrage, he'd haul her close and add the persuasion of his lips and tongue and hands to his verbal arguments.

The idea of once again having her in his arms filled him with a fever of anticipation that made him view with impatience the hours that remained until he might present himself at Lady Huntville's.

How would she react when he first approached her?

He hadn't the vaguest notion, though he'd wager a monkey she'd not give up her illusions of marriage without attempting some further mischief. But, he thought, a grin once more springing to his lips, the more difficult the hunt, the more satisfying the capture.

Late that evening Gilen sat before the snug fire in his rooms in a far less sanguine mood. Not only had he been forced to endure the screeching of the coloratura soprano— a pitch of voice he had never enjoyed—borrowed for the evening by Lady Huntville from the local opera house, after several hours of gritting his teeth through that purgatory, Miss Southford had failed to appear.

He'd considered trying to track her down, but not having any idea which of the evening's several society entertainments Lady Alice might have seen fit to grace with her presence, he concluded such a clueless search would likely result in nothing but a waste of his time.

He'd returned to his rooms in considerable dudgeon, dismissing his valet as soon as he'd allowed the man to strip off his coat, and flinging himself into the comfortable armchair in front of the hearth for the consolation offered by a large glass of brandy.

Jeffrey was so assiduous in attending the baggage at every opportunity, 'twas unlikely Gilen would be able to get Miss Southford alone during a social event unless he were willing to purloin her from under the very nose of his friend—an action for which Jeffrey would surely later take him to task. Though Gilen intended to make a full confession after the fact, to have the best shot at detaching the wench and still salvaging their friendship, Gilen needed to spirit her out of Harrogate without Jeffrey's becoming aware of his intentions.

So—when could he corner her again? While he stared glumly at the fire, thumb rubbing the smooth round of the brandy glass, the answer to that dilemma suddenly surfaced out of memory.

Early tomorrow morning, attended only by a groom, Miss Southford planned to ride the mare Colonel Howard had sent over. She'd turned down the gentlemen's offer of escort, saying she wanted but one attendant during her ride.

One attendant she'd get, Gilen decided. But it wouldn't be the groom.

Suspecting that "early" might be early indeed to a country-bred girl, Gilen astonished his valet by shaving and dressing before dawn. He arrived at the mews behind Lady Alice's town house just as the first sunlight of the new day gilded the east facades of Harrogate.

There was no sign yet of Miss Southford. Gilen strolled

into the stable, encountering the groom who had attended his mount on his previous visits.

"Is Miss Southford's horse ready?" Gilen asked, as if his presence in the stable had been prearranged.

The groom gave him a speculative look after politely tugging a forelock. "Aye, my lord, though I don't suspect she'll be a-ridin' until nigh on eight."

Gilen sighed. "Ah, ladies. And here she told me only yesterday I should be here just after seven."

"I doubt the ladies are meetin' company yet, but I imagine Cook could fetch you a tankard of ale if'n you was to step into the parlor, my lord."

"Thank you—Jem, isn't it? A tankard would be welcome, but I'll take it here in the stables. Since I can intervene to assist Miss Southford during her ride, if necessary, you may resume your regular duties."

In the absence of explicit orders to that effect from his mistress, the groom looked rather uncertain. After a moment, however, doubtless recognizing the voice of authority, he nodded. "As you wish, my lord. I'll see about that tankard."

Half an hour later, Gilen was finishing the last of the dark, sharp brew, approving the neatness and order and breathing in the well-loved tang of horses and leather tack, when the door opened.

His senses alerted. Entering the stables, however, was not Miss Southford but her stepbrother Mr. Wakefield.

Gilen stiffened, not sure after that drive yesterday whether the young man would order him out or try to mill him down. But the lad offered a cordial smile and a friendly greeting that held not a bit of reserve.

Cautiously Gilen responded in kind. Apparently Miss Southford had not apprised her stepbrother of what had transpired during their outing.

Relieved he would not have to finesse his way out of a challenge from a pup too old to brush off and too young to fight, Gilen was about to let the boy walk away when a new stratagem suddenly occurred to him. Since Parry Wakefield neither held him accountable for insulting his sister nor remembered encountering him at the gypsy encampment, with a bit of deft questioning, he might discover more about how Miss Southford and her stepbrother came to be traveling by so unusual a means.

"Your Aunt Alice keeps a very fine stables," Gilen began.

"Yes, she does. I like that. A household's animals should be as comfortable as the humans, don't you think?"

"Perhaps more so, since they do much work for their masters. You are particularly fond of horses?"

Parry Wakefield smiled, an unselfconscious gesture totally free of artifice. "Yes, my lord."

"I understand your sister is a bruising rider. Did your father keep many horses at Southford?"

The young man's smile faltered. "Papa is dead, my lord. His horses aren't ours anymore, Gwen told me, though I don't understand why." The boy shrugged, as if used to accepting the inexplicable whimsy of fate.

Gilen examined the boy more narrowly. He appeared to be at that awkward age when a lad has one foot still in childhood and the other in the adult world. Though quite normal in appearance—handsome, even—Mr. Wakefield did not seem to possess the depth of understanding Gilen would have expected in one of his apparent age.

Perhaps he was simple? That would explain why Gilen had never encountered him in Lady Alice's drawing room or at other social affairs in town.

It also rendered Gilen's behavior in questioning him somewhere between ill-judged and reprehensible. However, he reminded himself, to soothe the tweak of conscience, Jeffrey's salvation required strong measures, and he had no intention of abusing the boy.

"Were they fine animals, your father's horses?"

"Papa had splendid horses. Rabbits, too."

Casually Gilen inserted, "I understand the gypsies keep excellent horses."

The boy's face lit with enthusiasm. "Yes, indeed. I helped Remolo birth a fine colt."

Shock, then excitement coursed through him. Dismissing another guilty pang, he asked, his voice deliberately nonchalant, "Did you do that on the journey you made with them?"

The boy's face took on a guarded look. "Journey?"

Careful, Gilen. "A few weeks ago, when you were journeying to visit your aunt."

The boy's face brightened again. "I like Aunt Alice. She never speaks in a loud voice, and she doesn't mind my animals." He frowned. "Not like cousin Nigel."

"Did cousin Nigel send you on the trip?"

A gathering alarm added to the confusion already evident in the young man's face. Had his slow wits finally gathered he was revealing something he should not?

The lad swallowed hard. "I'm sorry, my lord. I—I don't remember." Parry Wakefield gave him a pained, apologetic smile.

"I, too, like horses very much," Gilen said, shifting focus. "In fact, I'm looking to purchase some. A friend told me the gypsies might consider selling some of their stock. Where might I find Remolo, do you think?"

The boy's eyes flickered away from him and he clenched and unclenched his hands. "I—I don't know, sir."

"There's no hurry, Mr. Wakefield. Take a few moments and try to recall."

"I am trying, my lord," he burst out, distress and a panicky desperation in his tone.

His concentration riveted on Mr. Wakefield while he attempted to ascertain how much of the story was truth, how much evasion, Gilen didn't at first notice the cool draft of air that telegraphed the opening of the stable door. Not until the agitated look on Parry Wakefield's face changed to one of relief.

"Gwen!"

Gilen whipped his gaze around—to see Miss Southford halted just inside the door, garbed in a worn charcoal riding habit, whip and gloves in hand. Jaw slightly dropped, she stared at him.

"Lord St. Abrams?" she asked, as if unable to believe the evidence of her eyes.

Her stepbrother rushed up to her. "Gwen, I'm sorry! The gentleman keeps questioning me, and I can't remember. I've been thinking and thinking, but it's all just…blank. I'm sorry, Gwen!" The lad pulled at his hair, anxiety evident in his face and a glaze of tears in his eyes.

"It's all right, Parry," she soothed, stilling her stepbrother's agitated hands. "It's not important."

Perhaps the lad truly was simple rather than merely a poor liar, Gilen thought, feeling guiltier still.

After skewering Gilen with a quick, scathing glance, Miss Southford reached up to cup the boy's chin between her hands. "Look at me, Parry." When the young man's wildly shifting gaze connected with hers, she continued. "You mustn't be upset, my dear. 'Tis a trifling matter, much less important than the animals awaiting your care. I can take care of it while you see to them. We lingered so long over our tea, I expect they'll be nibbling up the bars of their cages if you don't hurry."

"It's truly all right? You're not an-angry with me?" he asked, his voice breaking a little over the word.

"Of course not, dearest."

"I didn't…make a mistake?"

"No, not a bit. But you will be making one directly, if you don't get your menagerie fed soon! Especially that gray tabby, who looks as if she's about to give birth at any moment."

The lad's face began to clear. "Yes. Will they be all gray like her, do you think? I wish we knew who the father of the litter was."

Miss Southford threw Gilen another quick dagger of a glance. "I'm afraid *some* males are utterly irresponsible in their conduct. Off with you, now! I'll come check on them after my ride." Giving her stepbrother an encouraging smile, she patted his cheek and then released him.

Parry Wakefield nodded, apparently reassured. He looked startled and once more uncertain when he turned to find Gilen still standing there. "Oh—L-Lord St. Abrams! I'm sorry I couldn't help you, sir." He sketched Gilen a bow and then strode quickly away.

Miss Southford's smile vanished with the sound of the door banging closed behind her stepbrother. "How *dare* you?" she demanded, her voice pitched low with outrage. "How *dare* you invade my aunt's home and harass my brother!"

Before Gilen could begin to stutter out an explanation, Miss Southford advanced on him, brandishing her riding whip. "Was it not bad enough that you offered me the worst possible insult yesterday? Get out, and don't ever darken our door again!" So suddenly Gilen had no time to anticipate the move, she snapped her arm back and cracked her whip in his direction.

The thin leather thong whined dangerously close to his

cheek. Miss Southford continued to advance, as if she intended to drive him out of the stable by force.

"You miserable arrogant excuse for a gentleman," she all but snarled, punctuating her epithet with another swipe from the whip.

Gilen dodged the whirling thong and backed away, his initial astonishment giving way to incredulous delight. By heaven, she was magnificent! Whatever lingering doubts he might have harbored dissolved as this girl, still garbed like a proper ton maiden, changed before his eyes from demure virgin into the passionate creature who had told his fortune, teased his wits and tantalized him with a dance.

He couldn't help grinning, and had the pleasure of seeing fury spark anew in those wide violet eyes.

"You find this *amusing?*" she choked out. And lashed the whip at him again.

He ducked as the leather tip nearly caught his left ear. "Damn—dash it, Miss Southford, that was too close! Please, ma'am, if you can't control yourself I shall have to grab hold and disarm you."

Ah, that she might compel him to do it! With her body bound closely to his was exactly where this astonishing, intoxicating, intemperate vixen belonged.

He couldn't wait to see how her passionate nature played out in his bed.

Her mouth tightened in a furious line, Miss Southford stalked him, her whip at the ready. "You'd better hope—" a mosquito whine sliced the air beside his right ear "—I never get hold—" he jumped to avoid a lash at his left side "—of you!—" he dodged a swipe to his knee and took the *thwak* of the quirt on his boot.

Still grinning, he retreated, leading her toward the stable wall opposite the door to the tack room. When his back was nearly to the wall—and her back was to the door—he abruptly halted and craned his neck, as if to look at someone behind her.

"Jem, come in quickly!" he called out.

Whip still raised, Miss Southford glanced over her shoulder.

One instant was enough. In a lightning movement Gilen leapt toward her and seized the whip.

She whirled back and grappled with him for control of the weapon, but she was no match for his height and strength. After a few moments, Gilen wrestled her around and pinned her against the stable wall, whip still in her hand but trapped behind her skirts.

Once more he savored the delicious pleasure of Miss Southford's soft warm body pressed against his, her face flushed and her bosom heaving from exertion. Soon realizing she could not break free, Miss Southford ceased struggling and raised indignant violet eyes to his face.

"That, sir, was vilest trickery!"

"Considering you were attempting to flay me alive, I think it forgivable!"

"*Nothing* in your behavior toward me for the whole of our overlong and unfortunate acquaintance has been f-forgivable!" she pronounced, her voice breaking and a suspicious moisture gathering at the corners of her eyes.

Amazingly, a tenderness fully as fierce as his desire invaded his chest at that evidence of her distress. Though he eased the pressure of his grip, he could no more halt the descent of his lips toward her trembling ones than he could have commanded his heart to cease beating. "Nothing at all?" he whispered, angling her chin up.

Her momentary weakness gone, she jerked her chin free and glared at him. "Release me at once, you scoundrel!"

He might have known his gypsy enchantress would fight to the end—and issue orders like a queen.

"I'm no more a scoundrel than you, my sweet vixen. At least I'm not masquerading as something I am not!"

"Indeed you are, sir!" she flashed back. "You *pretend* to be a gentleman."

He chuckled. "Come now, my sweet, 'tis past time to be angry with me for discovering your secret. You must know I could never let a wench from a gypsy wagon marry Jeffrey—or any other gentleman. But promise to come away with me, and I pledge to let you leave Harrogate with your good name intact. Without revealing your duplicity and humiliating your aunt, if Lady Alice is indeed such."

The mutinous silence in which she heard his speech was so enchanting, he had to lean toward her again, and once again she evaded his kiss. "Silly girl," he chided. "Why not admit we belong together? I'm a generous man. You'll never regret coming under my protection."

Miss Southford opened her mouth as if to retort, then hesitated.

At the temptation of those pouting lips so near his own, a wave of desire too powerful to suppress crashed through him, and he simply *had* to kiss her. Leaning her back, he clutched her chin tighter. "Never any regrets," he whispered as he brought his lips to meet hers.

Which at first remained stiffly unyielding. But as he added the coaxing of his tongue, he felt them soften and her body grow pliant in his arms.

Greedy exultation licked through him, sent the blood roaring through his veins. He tugged at the whip she still held and lifted his mouth a fraction to whisper, "Give up your weapon now, and I promise to wield mine for you—long and thoroughly and often." He punctuated the words with a sinuous slide of his straining breeches against her skirts, making the bawdy nature of the offer quite obvious as he once again claimed her lips.

Then yelped, loosening his hold on her when she bit him, hard.

She used his momentary shock to wriggle out of his grip and scuttle away. Once free, she whirled, whip once more at the ready. "You obnoxious, *vulgar*…vulgar…oh, I can't think what to call you!" she cried. "You must be mentally unbalanced! Leave my aunt's property this instant. If you ever return and disturb my family again, I swear I'll call the constable on you for trespassing!"

Barely had she finished those impassioned words when the back stable door slid open and the groom returned, leading a trim chestnut mare with a star on her forehead.

"Your horse be ready, Miss Southford."

Her chin lifted and she swept Gilen a glance of magnificent disdain. "Thank you, Jem. Shall we depart?"

The groom stopped short, looking from Miss Southford to Gilen and back. "You mean me, Miss? But his lordship said—"

"I can imagine," she snapped. "No matter. 'Tis rather late, and I wish to leave immediately. I shan't be able to take the mare to any speed in town. You'll have time to saddle another beast and meet me at the park."

Pointedly ignoring Gilen, she walked over to the mare, and motioned the groom to help her mount.

"Thank you, Jem," she said as she settled onto the side-saddle. "Please tell my brother before you join me that I shall find him as soon as I return."

Without so much as a parting glance, Miss Southford clicked the reins and guided the mare out.

The groom gave him a wondering look, but after Gilen returned one of well-practiced hauteur, the man made a swift bow and took himself off.

Gilen strolled out of the stable to see Miss Southford just about to round the corner, the new mount seeming under her complete control. The ease with which she rode, the way she held the reins, displayed the grace of an accomplished horsewoman.

Not at all cast down by this latest reverse, Gilen watched until she disappeared. What an extraordinary creature! He still couldn't believe she'd had the courage and audacity, first to punch him on the road outside Harrogate, then to try to carve him up with her whip. He grinned and then winced, tasting blood on the corner of his lip where the vixen had bitten him. Unpredictable, volatile, fascinating minx, an innocent maid one moment, a raging virago the next.

Thank heavens her true persona was the latter and not the former! Though Gilen still had no inkling which of his theories accurately explained her fall from grace, given her stepbrother's comments about the new Baron Southford, he was inclined to suspect that perhaps her cousin had been venal enough to have seduced or raped his ward. He simply couldn't imagine any man not wanting to bind such fire and passion to him permanently, once he'd tasted it, unless he were a relation within the prohibited bounds of propinquity—or a married man.

Under normal circumstances Gilen would have wanted to put a bullet through any individual despicable enough to have ruined a passionate young innocent. In this case, however, he could only be thankful that since the foul deed had already been perpetrated, fate had led her to him, a man prepared to overlook her unfortunate past and cherish her strength and uniqueness for the indefinite future.

His pleasure at contemplating that future was tinged by more than a little guilt that he should be so thankful for what had to have been the greatest misfortune of her life. Had her sojourn in a gypsy camp not confirmed beyond doubt that her virtue was already irretrievably lost, regardless of the steadily increasing strength of his feelings for her, honor would compel him to stand aside and let her pursue a proper future with Jeff.

By now, he could not imagine allowing any other man to have her. No, this strong-willed, tempestuous woman belonged with him and no one else.

He glanced down at the probably irreparable gash in the leather calf of one of Hoby's best boots. His valet would have palpitations when he saw it.

Gilen licked his injured lip, grinning wider despite the sting. Though she hadn't yielded—yet—she was weakening. Another rush of heated sensation coursed through him at the memory of her softening in his arms.

He just needed to do a tad more convincing to get the volatile Miss Southford to succumb completely.

Chapter Thirteen

Scarcely able to concentrate on guiding her unfamiliar mount through the busy street, Gwennor proceeded toward the park, her face still crimson with embarrassment.

How dare the unspeakable Lord St. Abrams address her in such wanton terms? And to…stroke her like that! She might be an innocent in the ways of a man with a maid, but being country-bred, she knew quite well what occurred in the mating of male and female.

She should have fainted with mortification. Instead, she recalled with a deepening sense of chagrin, despite her outrage, she'd felt an intense and shocking warmth flowing outward from her center at the friction of his hardness against her skirts. A warmth that intensified in the instant during which she imagined where and how he meant to sheathe his ''weapon,'' before sanity returned and she put a violent stop to both their reactions.

Of course, had she not actually begun to *respond* to the blackguard's kiss, he probably would not have accompanied the repetition of his dishonorable offer with that even more blatant and insulting motion.

Whatever had come over her? she wondered. Cheeks turning cold and then hot again, she pulled up the fortunately docile mare inside the park entrance and jumped down from the saddle. Where was the calm, controlled, rational woman she knew herself to be?

It must be the unsavory influence of Lord St. Abrams, she decided as she walked the mare. Since she'd met him, she had danced like a wanton, responded to a passionate kiss from a near stranger, slapped a viscount, stolen his carriage, and then nearly horsewhipped him. From what deep, repressed place within her had this unprecedented violence proceeded?

She ought to despise him for provoking her to it. But when she examined where there should be a hard lump of dislike, she discovered instead…an exhilarating fascination.

She'd found his quick wit invigorating since their first exchanges over his palm at the gypsy camp. He caught her inferences and comprehended her innuendo without a hesitation. Add that liveliness of mind to the natural charm he could exert when he chose, and 'twas not so surprising that her proper suitors seemed somewhat…dull.

And of course, there was that undeniable if regrettable physical pull between them. Lud, the man had only to approach and her body sang with anticipation, excited alertness speeding through every nerve.

Though she ought to wish him to Jericho and want to avoid him like a virulent contagion, she found herself, despite the danger he posed to her well-being, instead…drawn to him. As if, until she met St. Abrams, she had been sleepwalking, drifting along on some quiescent current, awaiting his vital presence to jolt her into vibrant life where every experience seemed more vivid, sounds purer, colors richer. As her anger over this latest confrontation cooled, she had to acknowledge the frightening truth that he attracted her on levels far beyond the merely physical.

Oh, this was idiocy, she thought with exasperation. What

whimsical fate had conspired to have the one man besides cousin Harry who had ever fired her spirits and filled her with such a zest for living turn out to be the individual who meant to destroy all her plans for a future?

She would *not* allow herself to recall the thrill she'd experienced during their carriage ride when, for a few precious minutes, she'd thought he'd meant to make her an honorable offer.

'Twas so unfair! But life often was, she reminded herself. Did cousin Nigel's inheriting *her* beloved home not confirm that?

In fairness, though, she had to admit that though his lordship's erroneous conclusions about her identity might have initially led him to misinterpret her character, 'twas in large part her own subsequent actions that had sealed that unfavorable opinion.

Given what he believed her to be, the viscount's actions were understandable. Especially after Lady Alice had confided to her the story of Mr. Masterson's broken engagement, she could hardly despise St. Abrams for acting to prevent his friend from being maneuvered into a decision that the viscount believed would blight the rest of his life.

Had she not taken equally audacious steps to protect the brother she loved?

A wry smile came to her lips. Would that she and Parry had so zealous a champion to defend them.

A flicker of hope gleamed through her bleak thoughts. Despite the fact that the viscount was directly opposing her plans, she could still understand—even sympathize with his actions. Were she to confide her true situation to him, would he not understand and sympathize with hers?

With her future and Parry's at stake, perhaps it was time to abandon the pride that prompted her to try to best him and confess the truth, whether or not he deserved to hear it. But…would he believe her?

That she was bold enough to embrace so desperate a means of escape, probably. But would he be able to accept that she was still a virginal maid deserving of a gentleman's protection?

Ah, how comforting 'twould be to lean upon his strength rather than oppose it! But 'twas far too late to undo either that firelit dance—or the kisses they'd shared.

Given those unfortunate events, she simply could not be sure she'd be able to convince him of her innocence.

Not that she still feared he meant to harm her. Indeed, he seemed to appreciate her company as well as her person and sincerely wish to "protect" her, albeit in a manner he considered more suitable than wedlock. But unless he believed in her honor as well as her daring, he would not cease his efforts to thwart her plans.

If she could not gain St. Abrams as an ally, it might be wiser to discourage Mr. Masterson's attentions. Would the viscount then abandon his campaign against her?

She sifted through the shocks and chagrin of their latest exchange, trying to recall his exact words. And with a sinking feeling, heard him assert he would not permit her to entrap Mr. Masterson—or any other gentleman.

If he were to scare off all her suitors, how was she to safeguard Parry?

Her mind leapt to her first evening dealing cards at the gypsy camp, when she'd discovered the leering looks directed by the men at all the gypsy women and realized that, should her presence among them become common knowledge in the fashionable world, her reputation would be ruined. It appeared that fear had been justified.

Perhaps she should acknowledge defeat, leave Aunt Alice and make her way elsewhere.

Or give in to his blandishments, and go to St. Abrams.

A tiny thrill skittered over her nerves in the instant before she contemptuously dismissed that alternative.

St. Abrams's motives in trying to rescue his friend might be pure, but so were hers in trying to rescue Parry. Just because the viscount, with his wealth, his contacts, and his power had many more resources available to exert his will against her didn't render her cause any less just. It was certainly more urgent.

And St. Abrams's methods were less than noble. A man's seduction of a woman he desired and believed a wanton was no great sacrifice.

How, then, to contravene the ongoing threat he posed?

She could, at her next meeting with Mr. Masterson, pour into his astounded ears the whole story of his friend's vile behavior this morning and on the Harrogate road. Such an action would surely damage the viscount's standing with his friend.

It would also almost certainly cause Mr. Masterson deep distress, subjecting him to the pull of conflicting loyalties between his longtime friend and the woman he was courting. And regardless of what happened between herself and her suitor, would probably end by ruining a relationship she knew Mr. Masterson prized.

No, even if it meant losing the chance to win a man who might make her an excellent husband, she could not reward his kindness in such a manner.

Should she set her sights on some other suitor, would St. Abrams carry out his threat of exposing her?

He might—but she didn't think so. Every instinct argued that this struggle had become a contest between herself and St. Abrams alone.

He'd be more apt to try to entice her to a private resolution. His actions in the stable this morning—and hers—recurred vividly, and once again her cheeks heated.

Perhaps she should give up on the idea of marriage completely and seek a position as a housekeeper or companion. But Lady Alice would never understand her dismissing two such excellent prospects as Mr. Masterson and Colonel Howard to become a mere paid companion. No, if the viscount's pursuit forced her to that, Gwen would have to leave Harrogate to find employment.

Leaving did offer the advantage of protecting Lady Alice from potential embarrassment. And Gwennor didn't think the Presumptuous Peer would take the trouble to trail her elsewhere. Would he?

By now, her head was once again aching and she saw the groom approaching in the distance. Botheration, she would dismiss all thoughts of her dilemma and just enjoy the sheer beauty of the fresh new morning and a hard gallop.

With her plans so unsettled, her previous decision to restock her funds by selling a few more pieces of her mother's jewelry seemed more imperative than ever. Stifling her sorrow at the idea of parting with yet another of the few remaining links to her mother, she determined that once she'd returned from her ride, she would force herself to look through the collection and select several suitable pieces. While Aunt Alice was still abed, she would slip out to the jewelers.

Aside from that action, she hadn't yet figured out how she was going to save Parry, sort out her suitors, evade the risk of humiliating Aunt Alice—and defeat My Lord Presumptuous.

She might not be certain what she meant to do, but she was quite certain what she would *not*. After the way he had humiliated, embarrassed and tempted her, she would never give St. Abrams the satisfaction of admitting the truth.

Most of the inn's other fashionable guests had not yet stirred from their chambers when Gilen arrived back at his rooms. After ordering up breakfast, he took his favorite seat by the fire and contemplated what his next move should be in the ongoing battle with Miss Southford.

He was finishing his beefsteak when a knock at the door was followed by the entrance of Jeffrey Masterson.

A wave of guilt flushed his face. Before he could speak, though, Jeff hailed him cheerfully.

"Dreadful dull evening with grandfather." He poured himself some ale from the tankard on the tray beside Gilen. "So, did you head off Colonel Howard and take Miss Southford driving?"

"Y-yes," Gilen replied, wondering how he was going to explain the rest of that excursion.

"And did you not find, upon closer acquaintance, she is as delightful as I said?"

A vision of outraged violet eyes and a powerful left hook recurred, and he smiled. "She does indeed improve upon acquaintance. A most...resourceful young woman."

Jeffrey grinned back. "Did I not tell you? And an excellent driver—you did allow her to handle the ribbons?"

"Oh, yes. Most impressive."

"How she must have enjoyed the drive! I hope she did not find you *too* charming, however."

Recalling how that interlude had ended, Gilen's grin widened. "I think you may safely assume that."

"Which reminds me," Jeff continued, mercifully oblivious. "Knowing how much Miss Southford loves riding, it was particularly aggravating of Howard to steal a march by offering her the use of that mare. 'Try the horse for his sister,' indeed." Jeffrey gave a disbelieving sniff. "I have no doubt he means to make her a present of the beast, if he can finagle her into accepting his suit."

"We certainly can't allow that," Gilen replied, indignation stabbing in his gut at the notion. If he weren't prepared to let her go to a friend, he'd be damned if he'd allow the colonel to claim her.

"Indeed! Thank heavens you were there to forestall him," Jeffrey replied, giving him a hearty clap on the shoulder. While guilt again sank its talons into Gilen, his friend continued, "Impatient to see her, I awakened early today and couldn't get back to sleep. So I took a stroll through town, trying to think of some token *I* could offer her—a book, perhaps, or some sweetmeats. You'll never guess what I discovered!"

"A rare first edition?"

"No, something even more unexpected. As I was walking down High Street at that very early hour, I observed Miss Southford entering the establishment of Smythe and Hawkings, the jewelers. I followed her, of course, and discovered her doing the most amazing thing!"

Given her previous unpredictability, Gilen would not have been surprised to learn she was working in the shop— or robbing it. "I can't imagine."

"She was none too happy to see me at first, though I am still glad I happened along, else I should never have learned the truth. Gilen, she was selling some of her mother's jewelry! I could see she was much chagrined to admit it, poor darling. Imagine her guardian leaving her so badly circumstanced as to have compelled her to part with family heirlooms! The man should be shot."

His eyes narrowing on a vision of Miss Southford and her guardian playing out a very different scene, Gilen replied grimly, "Indeed he should."

"I knew you would agree! Well, I begged her to keep the jewels and allow me to lend her a sum instead, but naturally she refused. So after I escorted her back to Lady Alice's, I returned to the jeweler with the intention of redeeming the gems. As it turns out, the jewelry is more valuable than I anticipated, and I haven't at present the cash to complete the transaction. Would you lend me some of the ready, until I can arrange a draft on my bank? I'd ask grandfather, but he would wish to know all the circumstances, and might…misinterpret the situation."

As the full implications of the little scene in the jeweler's shop struck him, Gilen felt a surge of outrage.

The wily little witch! So much for abandoning her pretensions to Jeffrey! Gilen had barely let her out of his sight when she'd turned around and come up with a new scheme to sink her claws into his friend!

Family heirlooms, indeed! Gilen thought, barely suppressing a snort. The wench was probably fencing gems she stole during her sojourn in the gypsy camp, or won off lads too drunk to read the cards in their hands.

Small wonder Jeffrey was reluctant to relate the tale to his grandfather. Lord Masterson would probably suspect— with good reason—that Miss Southford was a clever harpy out to get her clutches on some of the Masterson fortune.

He surfaced from his angry ruminations to find Jeff staring at him. "I *can* count on you, can't I, Gilen?"

His friend's artless inquiry and the look on his open, trusting face, smote Gilen like a blow. He was almost tempted to confess the real nature of his dealings with Miss Southford. Almost.

"Gilen?" Jeff repeated when he did not immediately reply. "Surely after spending time with her, *you* could not believe her a—a conniving woman."

He swallowed the strong impulse to inform Jeff just what

sort of woman he thought her to be. "I trust I have a pretty accurate assessment of her character," he said instead. One which made it all the more imperative for Gilen to remove her before she could entangle Jeffrey any further in her schemes.

"Of course you have," Jeffrey said, looking relieved. "You always were the most discerning fellow—only see who you chose as your best friend, eh?"

Jeff grinned and clapped him again on the shoulder. "Shall we go there now? The necklace and bracelet were fine indeed. I don't want to risk having someone else come into the shop and snap them up before I return."

Unlikely as that prospect was in Harrogate, Gilen pushed his chair back. "Let me get my coat. I must confess," he added with a dry irony lost on his trusting friend, "I'm eager to see these family heirlooms dear Miss Southford was forced to give up."

A short hackney ride later, they entered the shop. Mr. Smythe greeted them with a deep bow for Gilen and a knowing look on his face. "Welcome, my lord, and welcome back, Mr. Masterson. You were here earlier with the young lady, Miss Southford, were you not?"

"Yes. I should like to have Lord St. Abrams inspect the jewelry you so kindly bought from her."

"Right this way. Lovely pieces, quite valuable. And the negotiations so delicately done by the young lady, though I suspect 'twas on her aunt's behalf that she came."

Gilen looked over in surprise. "Indeed?"

"A most excellent woman, Lady Alice," Mr. Smythe said. "Unfortunately, her late husband left her not terribly well circumstanced. She has over the years occasionally suffered financial...embarrassments."

Jeffrey smiled wryly and turned to Gilen. "She has a weakness for piquet and silver loo, grandfather told me," he said, "though I'd not realized the addiction severe enough for her to become badly dipped."

The jeweler coughed delicately. "On several occasions our firm has been honored to assist her by purchasing items similar to those we obtained today. Ah, here they are."

He extracted a box from a locked case and opened it. Reposing on a satin surface were a filigreed gold necklace set with rubies and diamonds, a matching bracelet and large earbobs. The design was obviously antique and the stones, even to Gilen's untrained eye, of superior quality and cut.

Jeffrey named the sum previously quoted by the jeweler, who confirmed it, and Gilen took out his purse.

So at last, money was changing hands over Miss Southford, he thought. A fitting sortie in a battle in which he was still confident of prevailing.

After the beaming merchant bowed them out of the shop, the jewels polished and tucked into a new box tied up with satin ribbon, Jeffrey turned to Gilen.

"I've another favor to ask. Would you keep the gems for me? Though the jewels by rights belong to her, I cannot offer Miss Southford so valuable a gift until we reach the...proper point. I shouldn't wish grandfather or a cleaning maid to find them prematurely."

Not that Gilen could ever allow it to progress to that. Steeling himself to the wreckage of his friend's hopes with a reminder that Jeffrey would thank him in the end, Gilen replied, "If you wish it."

"You will guard them carefully? They are...*hers*."

The awe with which Jeffrey spoke of the baubles, simply because they had adorned Miss Southford's neck, filled Gilen with an equal mix of exasperation and discomfort. "Of course."

"Again, my thanks for both good turns. I couldn't ask for a better friend."

Knowing the sort of good turn he soon intended to do Jeffrey, Gilen mumbled an inarticulate reply.

"By the way," Jeff added, "when it comes to rings, do you think a lady would prefer something new, chosen just for her, or a family piece?"

In his friend's clear green eyes Gilen could read all his tender hope and intensity of emotion. A wave of anger at the cruel blow Miss Southford's duplicity would soon deal his friend washed through him, and in that moment he could cheerfully have ripped the antique necklace out of its velvet box and garroted the wench with it. "I—I couldn't imagine," he gritted out.

"I've time still to decide, I suppose," Jeffrey said. "But given the threat of Colonel Howard, not too long! I must meet grandfather at the Pump Room now—a fate I won't invite you to share. Until later?"

"Later," Gilen agreed, and watched as his friend, with a jaunty wave, walked down the street, whistling.

If—when—Gilen managed to convince the wench to break off with Jeff, eventually he would have to reveal the truth of his machinations to his friend. Although Miss Southford's acceptance of a carte blanche would be all the proof Gilen would need to demonstrate her unworthiness to become Jeff's wife, the warmth in his friend's voice when he spoke of her and the eager anticipation with which he discussed choosing a betrothal ring filled Gilen with a deep and uncomfortable foreboding.

Even if Jeffrey could not avoid acknowledging her true character, still he might never forgive Gilen for carrying her off from under his nose. It was beginning to look more and more as if Gilen would not be able to rescue Jeffrey without permanently alienating his friend.

He knew how he would feel if he discovered that *Jeff*

had lured the beguiling wench away from *him*. No matter how valid the reason.

The charms of the lady notwithstanding, the looming prospect of forfeiting the friendship of the man who'd been closer to him than a brother for the better part of twenty years was so distressing that Gilen seriously considered abandoning his attempt to seduce her away.

If he could come up with any other means of detaching her that he felt had even a fair chance of success, he'd sacrifice the pleasure he knew she would bring them both and take it.

For a moment, he allowed himself to contemplate such satisfying if improbable scenarios as runaway carriages, paid abduction, hired assassins. And then the idea occurred to him.

Perhaps he could use the jewels he'd just redeemed, added to whatever additional sums he could come up with, to bribe her into relinquishing her hold on Jeffrey and leaving Harrogate.

'Twas most unlikely she'd agree, when she doubtless knew that, with a bit of perseverance on her part, both Jeffrey and the jewels would soon be hers. Still, he could make the attempt.

He looked at the box in his hand and sighed. If that ploy failed, he'd add the jewelry to his own offer, dangling before her a vision of his largesse along with pointed reminder that both were the most a wench from a gypsy wagon could ever hope to obtain.

However he managed to finesse her departure, it must be soon.

The prospect of her coming to him filled him with a contradictory mix of wild anticipation, shame, regret and desire. Damn the consequences, he wanted her, plain and simple, on every level.

As he was betraying his best friend to do it, that probably made him not much better than the seducer who ruined her to have her.

Thank heaven she was so intoxicating a woman, he thought with gallows humor. If she were to be the means of losing him his oldest friend, at least she was going to make him enjoy the dismal prospect.

Chapter Fourteen

Eschewing the idea of dropping by the Masterson town house, Gilen lunched alone before his own hearth, the box containing Miss Southford's jewels on the table beside his favorite chair. How to turn the gems to advantage?

As Jeff had observed, one couldn't just offer them back to her in some crowded drawing room. Once again, he would need sufficient private time—and space, given her skill with a whip—to negotiate effectively.

After this morning, his chances of getting her alone were growing slimmer than a hardened gamester's odds of winning a fortune. Her bold threat to the contrary, he didn't think Miss Southford would go so far as to attempt to have him arrested. Should he pay a call during Lady Alice's afternoon at home, though, he wouldn't put it past the volatile wench to order him out of the drawing room, unmoved by her aunt's protest or the gasps and scandalized speculation of her other guests.

If he weren't ejected forthwith, he could still call on the support of Lady Alice, who doubtless harbored a warm affection for his wealth and title. However, her niece would probably sooner muck out the stables than allow herself to be maneuvered into a private chat with him. His entrance *into* her aunt's drawing room would likely signal Miss Southford's abrupt departure *out* of it, on whatever suddenly "urgent" pretext she could manufacture.

No, trying to arrange a meeting during a normal social call would not suffice.

By the time he'd finished his beef and ale, Gilen had hit upon a new scheme that, he thought with some satisfaction, was nearly foolproof. First, he would devise an opportunity to chat with Lady Alice without her niece's knowledge. Despite Jeffrey's prior claims, Gilen was sure if he dropped enough inferences about his strong feelings for her niece, Lady Alice, like any fond chaperone wishing to snag the most advantageous offer for her protégé, would exhibit few qualms about arranging access to the lady.

The by-now familiar sting of conscience pricked at him. The success of this stratagem required him to knowingly mislead a genteel lady about his intentions toward the supposed innocent in her care.

Add that sin to the evasions—if not outright lies—he'd already told in a campaign whose central strategy involved the betrayal of his best friend, and Gilen had to conclude that Miss Southford was definitely exerting a detrimental influence on his conduct. The sooner he captured her and saved Jeffrey, thereby accomplishing at least one laudable aim, the sooner he could begin to redeem what had previously been a stainless moral character.

Ah, yes, having her would be better—for his character and every other part of him. For a moment, lost in a swell of desire and anticipation, he contemplated the delightful prospect of housing her, clothing her, unclothing her and luxuriating in a continuation of their lively battle of wits. And to think, before leaving London for Harrogate he'd been suffering a touch of ennui!

With the unpredictable and spirited Miss Southford in

residence, he didn't expect to be bored in the foreseeable future. Possibly not until the next millennium.

He couldn't wait to cross swords with her again.

To put his plan into practice, however, he needed some additional reconnaissance. Setting out again after luncheon, he made his way not to the imposing facade of Lady Alice's town house, but to the servants' entrance.

The astonishment of the maid who admitted him soon transformed, with the addition of a few well-placed coins, into voluble appreciation. Armed with the knowledge that Miss Southford spent the post-noon interlude in the library while Lady Alice reposed herself in her room, he exited the kitchen and strolled around to the front entry.

After first admonishing the butler, buttressed by another flow of gold coinage, on no account to allow Miss Southford to learn he was in the house, he bade Mercer summon his mistress. As expected, the news that Viscount St. Abrams desired an urgent audience with Lady Alice on a matter of great delicacy elicited a swift response from that lady, who begged him to make himself comfortable and promised to be down forthwith.

Little more than a quarter hour after Mercer had escorted him into the front parlor, the lady herself hurried in, her face wreathed in smiles and her cap slightly askew.

"Lord St. Abrams!" she exclaimed, offering her hands to be kissed. "Such an unexpected surprise! With what urgent matter can I assist you?"

"As I mentioned," Gilen said, taking the seat she waved him to, "the situation is extremely...delicate. It involves, as I supposed you have guessed, your niece."

"A delightful child!" Lady Alice pronounced. "But may I ask on whose behalf you wish to speak? Mr. Masterson's, or—" she gave him a shrewd, penetrating glance "—your own?"

Gilen felt his face heat. "My own," he replied baldly. "Which is what makes the matter so delicate."

"Oh!" she replied, looking intrigued—and gratified. "Are you saying that...*you* wish to fix my niece's interest?"

"I find her a most...exceptional creature," Gilen said, attempting to choose words that would further his aims without perjuring himself completely. "And I flatter myself that perhaps my strong feelings are...reciprocated."

Lady Alice's eyes widened. Gilen could almost see her calculating the relative worth of his fortune against Jeffrey's. "And...what of Mr. Masterson?"

Gilen sighed, not having to feign how ill at ease the whole business made him. "Of course, given the fact that my friend has also expressed a marked interest in your niece, I find myself in a most uncomfortable position. Indeed, I engaged in quite a struggle, trying to determine whether it would be better to speak out or remain silent. Mr. Masterson is an admirable gentleman in every way, as well as my dearest friend, and under no circumstance would I wish to do him an injury."

He paused, considering how best to proceed.

"And now that you have determined to speak?" Lady Alice prompted.

"After much rumination, I felt I could not ignore the intuition that tells me Miss Southford reciprocates my...interest. Naturally, I have no wish to...step in unless this is in fact the case. If she does, and I were to say nothing, being unaware of my regard, your niece might make a decision that would have lasting, and unhappy, results for us all. If her emotions are not engaged, I will withdraw quietly, with no one but you, she and I the wiser."

"How kind! How...subtle!" Lady Alice exclaimed. Practically beaming at the notion of balancing the competing claims of two highly eligible suitors, Lady Alice asked, "What would you have me do, my lord?"

"Summon your niece to receive a visitor without telling her who awaits, and allow us a private interview. I should be able to swiftly ascertain her feelings."

Lady Alice extracted a lace handkerchief from her reticule and dabbed at her eyes. "So gallant and romantic, my lord! When should you like to see my niece?"

Gilen felt a flush mount his cheeks. He supposed he should be gratified to discover he was not so steeped in prevarication as to be lost to all sense of shame, but by now, there was naught to do but proceed.

"Immediately, if your niece is at home and you can forgive the haste of a man in the throes of…deep emotion."

"My dear Lord St. Abrams!" Lady Alice said, deploying her handkerchief again. "I shall send for her at once."

"You are all compassion, my lady."

After ringing the bell pull and giving Mercer her message for Miss Southford, Lady Alice walked with Gilen to the door. "I do hope all will be resolved as you both deserve," she said as she exited the parlor.

Gilen felt another twinge of conscience. "So too do I, my lady. Whatever the outcome, you have my deepest thanks for your assistance."

His hostess then left him to await the arrival of her niece. Too edgy to sit, Gilen paced about the chamber, rehearsing his speech and dismissing the ridiculous notion that suddenly came to him of going down on one knee.

He was not, after all, about to make her that sort of declaration. And he must remind himself that however innocent she appeared, she was also a cunning jade. Only consider this morning's scheme to wrest away some of Jeff's—now his—money.

And yet… With another uncomfortable pang, he recalled

the tenderness that had engulfed him when, with her held captive in his arms, she chided him for his persecution.

Despite his irritation at her conniving, he could not forget that she had—he was nearly certain—been born a lady of quality, most probably betrayed by a man of her own class. And because of that would be forever denied what should have been her birthright—an ardent young gentleman going down on one knee to tender her an honorable proposal.

Were circumstances different, might that young man have been him?

Though he rapidly dismissed so whimsical a fantasy, he was impartial enough to admit Miss Southford was rather a splendid creature. He could not imagine any other lady of his acquaintance having the fortitude to land on her feet after such a disaster, or the wit and determination to try to avoid the inevitable consequences.

His pulse leapt and his breath quickened as he heard footsteps approaching. A moment later, her familiar voice penetrated through the paneled door into the chamber.

"A mystery caller? Really, Aunt, how very…gothic!" Though she uttered a short laugh, Gilen could hear uncertainty in her tone. "A pleasant surprise, I trust?"

"Oh, I believe you shall thank me for it!"

"'Tis not…cousin Nigel, then."

The note of mingled alarm and distress in her voice strengthened Gilen's conviction that the new baron had indeed played a major role in the events that had led her to the gypsy camp. Anger washed through him, and he had a strong suspicion that someday, once he finally got the truth out of Miss Southford, he would feel compelled to pay a most unpleasant call on the baron.

"Certainly not!" Lady Alice was protesting. "As if I'd allow *him* to see you alone! Go on, now."

Suddenly it struck him to wonder how much Lady Alice

knew about the circumstances of her niece's departure from her home. Was she a party to the deception Miss Southford was trying to perpetrate?

Gilen supposed it wouldn't be the first time a chaperone had tried to pass off a charge who was less than virginal. Not that it mattered, except that if Lady Alice did know of her niece's disgrace, Gilen would feel less guilty about having manipulated her.

A moment later, his nerves jolted to the alert as the door opened to admit Miss Southford.

She took several steps toward the fireplace; finding the sofa before it unoccupied, she halted.

Gilen had been wise enough to take up position just inside the door, for once she turned and spied him, the cordial smile vanished from her lips. Inhaling sharply, her eyes sparking and her expression turning murderous, without a word she stalked back toward the oaken portal.

Gilen jumped forward to block her path.

"Miss Southford, wait! You must hear me out."

She looked down pointedly at the restraining hands Gilen had placed on her arm. Staring through, rather than at him, she said coldly, "I believe I have already said everything I need to say to you. And I am absolutely certain you have said everything—and more—that you ever needed to say to me."

"Not everything! You must at least allow me to apologize for questioning your brother before I realized…his condition. But with you so unforthcoming, how can you fault me for wishing to learn more?"

Miss Southford remained silent, neither pulling away nor acknowledging his presence.

"What…is his condition, if I might ask? He seems so engaging and amiable a lad."

At first Gilen thought she would not reply. But then, as

if the words could not be repressed, she said hotly, "He is the sweetest, most innocent soul in nature, and despite what *some* might think, neither an embarrassment nor a threat to normal folk. And I would murder anyone who tried to injure him!"

"So I observed," Gilen replied with a smile. "But I don't wish to harm him—or you. Quite the opposite."

Miss Southford gave a derisive sniff. "You've delivered your apology, my lord. Now go."

"But since this morning, there have been new developments," Gilen countered. Keeping one hand and an attentive eye on her lest she jerk free and attempt to scoot around him, Gilen extracted a pouch from his pocket.

Miss Southford eyed it with distaste. "My mother's jewels, I suppose. Did you steal them, my lord?"

"Are they truly your mother's jewels?"

Her chin jerked up and he saw a flash of something like—hurt?—in her eyes, as if it pained her that he doubted her veracity. Ignoring the question, she said, "Release me immediately or I shall summon the butler."

"But you have not yet heard my latest proposal."

"Nothing you could propose would be of any interest."

"Even if I promised to return these?"

Her eyes flashed to his, then dropped again to the pouch in his hand. Instead of fierce, her expression now ooomed...longing. "At what price, my lord? You must know, had I sufficient funds, I should not have parted with them in the first place."

"That you were reduced to doing so indicates you are experiencing some severe pecuniary difficulties. Accept my offer, and you'll never suffer such a thing again."

Before he realized her intent, she abruptly jerked free of his hand and stepped toward the door. He grabbed her shoulder, halting her flight.

"I'll give you the gems, plus a sum handsome enough to keep you from want for the foreseeable future, if you will perform one very simple task. Leave Harrogate."

"In your company?" she asked, her voice scornful.

"I can't deny that would be my preference. But…I offer all that merely if you will agree to leave here and have no further contact with Mr. Masterson. Leave alone if you prefer, so long as you go."

Her wary gaze flew back to his, assessing. In her eyes he read confusion—and indecision.

Might she really accept the bribe? Gilen was dismayed at the panic streaking through him—shaken to realize he didn't want her to accept anything that did not include him in her life, even at the risk of losing Jeff's friendship.

By the time he'd sorted through his unexpected and unsettling reaction, Miss Southford's hesitation had vanished. Her eyes shuttered, her voice cool, she said, "I wish to leave now, sir. You will release me."

At least her voice had not broken, Gwen thought—a small miracle, that. After St. Abrams tried to buy her off, like some…mercenary harpy!

Almost as bad was the realization that she'd actually been tempted to take him up on the offer. Ah, to have mama's jewels back again! But she'd swiftly realized he would not have tried to bribe her if he'd thought he could detach her from Jeffrey by other means, nor would he have offered his own money—a proposition that, given his opinion of her, he must have nearly choked at uttering—if he were planning to expose her. However, whatever sum he was prepared to offer, no matter how handsome, could never match the permanent security of marriage.

Besides, accepting his bribe would only prove correct his opinion of her as a dishonorable deceiver. If she were starv-

ing in the streets, she swore she would never give him the
satisfaction of doing that.

"If that doesn't tempt you, my sweet," he murmured,
"my original offer is still very much open. These jewels
could be my welcome gift to you, the first of many."

Keeping a wary eye on her, he let go her shoulder, loosened the strings on the bag and dumped her mother's necklace into his hand. "Magnificent, is it not?" he asked, holding it out. "I can see the rubies glowing against your skin
above a gown of yuletide red."

Before she could arm herself against it, a blow of grief
hammered her. Scarcely knowing what she did, she reached
out to touch the necklace. *I can still see Mama wearing
this at our Christmas ball just before she died.*

She didn't realize she must have spoken the thought
aloud until she looked up to see the viscount's eyes on her.
Surely that wasn't…sympathy in his gaze?

"How old were you?"

"Eight," she whispered, all her will concentrated on
suppressing the tears that threatened.

To her utter astonishment, the viscount touched her
cheek, so gently the burn in her eyes became a tear that
rolled down to wet his fingertip.

Even arrogant, wrong-headed, and masterful, she found
St. Abrams compelling. Compassionate, he was irresistible.

"How did you come to be at the gypsy camp?" he asked
softly. "Fleeing a failed love affair? Or had the new baron,
God rot his black soul, betrayed and seduced you?"

Occupied in fighting the powerful pull of the unwanted
attraction flowing between them, she made no reply.

St. Abrams sighed and shook his head. "I suppose you'll
never tell me. But *I* will tell *you* that for me, it no longer
matters. With your courage, your spirit, your wit and de-

termination, you are an extraordinary woman, Gwennor Southford. I can withstand you no longer.''

Her eyes widened and she looked up at him in shock. He couldn't be saying what she thought she was hearing!

He took her numb hand and kissed it. ''You've already admitted the force of what is between us. All I wish is to keep you safe from want and worry. Only say the word, and make us both happy.''

He found her irresistible—despite the gypsy camp and his initial prejudice? Then—he must truly love her!

He shifted his weight, and seized by dizzy euphoria, she waited for him to drop down on one knee.

''Say yes, my darling,'' he murmured, still standing.

Only then did it strike her that ''will you be my wife'' was the one phrase missing from his touching declaration.

The realization that he'd once more misled her into confusing his dishonorable offer with a proper proposal shocked her out of befuddlement. The knowledge that she would have accepted an honest offer fired shock into anger.

And the shameful awareness that, even knowing all he offered was carte blanche, she was still tempted to accept, made her want to shriek with fury and hit him again, much harder.

But she'd already struck him once. She would remember she *was* a lady, even if *he* did not believe her such.

She jerked her hand free. ''Though I marvel at your effrontery in presenting yourself today, I should have realized by now there are no depths to which you will not sink to achieve your aims. Even shamefully misleading my poor aunt about your intentions, as you must have done to induce her to permit you this private interview.''

He winced and opened his lips, but she cut him off. ''Not another word, or I shall scream the house down! Please understand that no ploys will avail you in future. I shall tell

Lady Alice and all the staff that you are not to be admitted again on any pretext. Good day, my lord.''

Gwennor drew herself up to full height, staring past the viscount as if he'd already departed. Despite the emotional tumult that made her limbs tremble, she would, she vowed, ignore him until he left, if it took all day.

Though he didn't attempt to touch her again, St. Abrams did not budge.

"Come now, my sweet, you must face the unhappy truth," he said, his tone coaxing. "I now believe you to be gently born, even concede that your...ruination might remain hidden. But I remind you that half a dozen friends accompanied me to the gypsy camp. I don't wish to wound you, but what gentleman who values the purity of his family name would knowingly offer marriage to a woman who'd been seen by his peers dealing cards in a gypsy wagon? Not even a gentleman as forgiving as Mr. Masterson! Unless you lead him into that certain disgrace by omission and trickery.''

Tears stung her eyes and for a moment she wavered. Could St. Abrams be right?

Of course, she'd fully intended all along to give to the man who begged her hand in marriage a complete account of her flight from Southford...eventually. But she could now see that withholding that crucial information until *after* a proposal had been tendered might place a true gentleman in a very difficult dilemma.

Being a gentleman, he could not retract the offer. But if learning of the contrivance to which she'd been reduced altered his opinion of her in the way the viscount indicated, her betrothed might also feel that in honoring his proposal, he would be shaming his family.

Would it make any difference to St. Abrams that she had not, as he believed, been ruined before her flight?

She asked herself the question only to realize he'd already answered it. Her supposed fall from virtue might be hidden—but not the disgrace of being recognized as working in a gypsy camp.

Perhaps the viscount was right after all. Perhaps she should abandon marriage as a goal and seek instead a position as a nurse or companion.

As that confusing and distressing jumble of thoughts ricocheted through her head, she suddenly realized St. Abrams still stood beside her. Waiting.

"You are a fighter, Miss Southford, and I admire your spirit. Despite all the evidence to the contrary, I can't believe you would really commit so heinous a deception."

Uncertain now what she should do, she opened her lips, shut them. "I believe I asked you to leave," she said finally in her coldest voice.

"Come to me instead!" He seized her hand, pressed it his lips. "I promise you, there will be no regrets."

His promise—to his doxy! Fury returning, she jerked her hand free and slapped his face with all her strength.

"Mercer!" she cried. "Mercer, come at once!"

The parlor door opened so quickly, she realized the butler must have been hovering in the hall just outside.

"Lord St. Abrams is leaving, if you will escort him, please? And Mercer—he will not be coming back. Ever."

For an instant, the butler's habitually impassive face showed surprise. Recovering rapidly, he said, "As you wish, Miss Southford."

Counter that! she thought, throwing St. Abrams a defiant glance.

She expected to see anger in his eyes. Instead, they looked...reproving. "Don't be so sure," he murmured.

And then he refueled her indignation by bringing the fingers with which she'd just slapped him to his lips and, under the butler's interested gaze, kissing them, all the while caressing the palm beneath with his thumb. By the time he released her hand, her senses were swimming.

He had the colossal nerve to make her a deep, courtly bow. "Your servant, Miss Southford."

Ushered onward by Mercer, he walked out.

Gwennor closed the door behind them with a slam and tottered back to the sofa.

Damn him! The Presumptuous Peer was unfailingly arrogant. Opinionated. Overconfident. Manipulative.

He was also perceptive. Quick-witted. Indefatigable in defending his friends. Unexpectedly compassionate.

Gwennor groaned and buried her face in her hands. And she, surely the most addlepated woman in the whole of England, seemed somehow to have fallen in love with him.

Chapter Fifteen

Rubbing his stinging cheek, Gilen climbed into the waiting hackney. Despite failing to achieve his ultimate goal, he was exultant.

Miss Southford had almost confessed! He had watched her resolve waver as she weighed his arguments.

If only she would tell him the truth. If he couldn't offer her the redemption of marriage, he might at least be able to exact a knockout blow's worth of vengeance from the irresponsible blackguard who had ruined her.

He chuckled to recall with what haughty disdain she'd treated him, as if she were a princess royal. By heaven, had she not suffered so unfortunate a fate, he'd be strongly tempted to make the spirited vixen a proper offer.

After all, whatever else she'd done, it seemed obvious she was gently bred. Unless she were the cleverest actress in the world, the jewels she had sold were in fact her mama's, her regret over parting with them and the memories they represented touching even his skeptical heart.

It also seemed apparent that her fall from grace had not left her with child. Since as far as he could ascertain, he was the only person who knew of her running away and

Her chin lifted. "Still, my lord, there are some that cannot be broken."

"Occasionally," he acknowledged. "But one must have patience."

"Are you having difficulties with your stallion?" Jeffrey asked, his tone perplexed.

"We're speaking in theoretical terms," Miss Southford replied quickly. "Now, you must tell me about the incident yesterday afternoon at the Pump Room. Lady Alice says you very gallantly came to Miss Aylesbury's rescue!"

To Gilen's surprise, Jeffrey blushed. "'Twas nothing, truly."

"A rescue in the Pump Room? Was the young lady about to choke on the waters?" Gilen asked, his eyebrows raised.

"No, of course not, Gilen. It's just…well, you know how…determined Lady Aylesbury can be, and she was pushing poor Mary Anne—Miss Aylesbury, that is—to engage the Duke of Hartford in conversation."

Mary Anne? Gilen thought. When had Jeffrey grown to be on terms of such intimacy with the Aylesbury chit?

"Whereupon you asked the lady to stroll with you, preventing her overbearing mama from forcing her into receiving what at best would have been a snub, at worst a cut direct," Miss Southford said warmly.

"Now you, Miss Southford, would probably have rescued yourself by bluntly refusing, or distracting Lady Aylesbury's attention to a less-desirable but more approachable gentleman," Gilen observed.

"Yes, Miss Southford can be very forthright," Jeffrey replied. "Perhaps Miss Aylesbury does lack…fire, being rather shy and biddable, but I assure you the sweetness and gentility of her nature makes up for any want of dash."

A chit with no backbone, Gilen thought dismissively.

"A very lovely lady as well," Miss Southford said. "And most grateful for the assistance of so valiant a champion. Well done, Mr. Masterson!" She patted his hand.

Instantly resenting the gesture, Gilen focused on them with narrowed eyes.

There was, Gilen noted with relief, no betraying color in her cheeks when she pressed his friend's fingers, no hitch in her breath when Jeff took her elbow to guide her around a puddle. Nor could he perceive between them the hum of attraction such as always vibrated between himself and the lady.

Unquestionably, Miss Southford belonged with him, not with Jeff. Surely she knew that!

Miss Southford did color then—as if conscious of the intensity of Gilen's stare. "My lord, your horse must be growing restless. You should proceed with your gallop."

"He is content to walk, I assure you. A slow pace now makes anticipation of the ride to come all the keener."

In what might have been exasperation, Miss Southford huffed in a breath, but made no further reply. The tolling of a distant church bell broke the silence.

"Is that five of the clock?" Miss Southford exclaimed, halting. "Mr. Masterson, if I might prevail upon you to escort me home? I have just remembered that Lady Alice asked me to wait upon her at five. Her...her, ah, mantua-maker is to bring a gown for her to try."

"Of course, Miss Southford. I shall summon a hackney at once. Gilen, stop by grandfather's this evening, won't you? I have something...of particular import to convey."

"Certainly, Jeff. Miss Southford—until *later*."

Choosing not to strike at his bait this time, she merely inclined her head.

Gilen watched them walk away. Despite his conviction that Miss Southford had not formed a strong attachment to his friend, he remained more disturbed than he wished to admit by the cozy picture they presented, walking arm in arm. He was *not* jealous of her apparent approval of Jeff, he told himself firmly.

He reviewed their conversation and chuckled. Miss Southford had picked up instantly on the innuendo underlying his words. Needle-witted and determined, she gave as good as she got, showing herself a worthy opponent.

Who would make an even better partner. Ah, yes, you belong with *me*, he silently informed her departing back.

And then wondered uneasily what matter ''of particular import'' Jeff wished so urgently to convey to him.

Responding to an invitation sent round to his lodgings, Gilen presented himself at the Masterson town house for dinner. Jeff greeted his entrance into the salon with an air of repressed excitement.

''So glad you could come dine! Grandfather's been wishing for more of your company. Even better that you arrived early, for I have been waiting to tell you the news. Indeed, tomorrow is likely to be the happiest day of my life! I expect—ah, grandfather! Let me help you in.''

Cold dread settled in Gilen's stomach. But whatever event his friend was anticipating, he evidently did not wish to share it with his elderly relation. Once Lord Masterson had been assisted to a seat, Jeffrey allowed his grandfather to direct the conversation toward the usual masculine subjects of horses, hounds and estates.

Though he genuinely enjoyed the company of the feisty, irascible baron, Gilen had a hard time concentrating on the conversation, his mind continually straying to conjectures about the news Jeff was so agog to impart.

Though he tried to reassure himself his friend's excitement could have any number of explanations, the one he most feared kept grating on his mind like a burr beneath a saddle that would not be dislodged, dimming his pleasure in the company and destroying his appetite.

Did Jeffrey intend to make Miss Southford an offer to-morrow?

And if he did—what was Gilen going to do about it?

By the time the old baron excused himself after the brandy, Gilen's patience was stretched thin. Barely had the door closed behind Lord Masterson when he turned to Jeff, trying to school his face into a mask of friendly interest. "Now, what's this grand news?"

"I imagine you've already guessed it. While I waited for Miss Southford to come down this afternoon, Lady Alice informed me that Colonel Howard plans to drive her to the theater tomorrow night, and strongly hinted he intends to deliver a proposal! I pondered and pondered during the whole of our outing, and I'm nearly convinced that I cannot allow him to speak to her first. So, I shall call upon her right after nuncheon tomorrow and try my luck. Wish me well!"

Even though expected, this confirmation of his worst im-aginings struck Gilen like a blow to the chest—until one of Jeff's phrases pierced the thick layer of panic enveloping him.

"'Nearly' convinced?" he repeated. "You are not sure Miss Southford is the lady you wish to make your wife?"

Jeff shifted to avoid Gilen's gaze. "Of course I am, I suppose. It's just—well, having never had any desire to get leg-shackled, you probably can't appreciate this, but when it comes to actually making a declaration, a fellow naturally has some…reservations."

Reservations about claiming Miss Southford for his own? Gilen had none at all. Panic receded and the vague outlines of a plan set his mind racing.

"'As long as you both shall live,' is a rather extensive time, Jeff. If you still have 'reservations,' I counsel you to wait. Besides, how can you know that Lady Alice did not hint of Colonel Howard's intentions merely to get you to the sticking point? Don't settle your future in haste simply to avoid being beaten out by a rival."

"Perhaps you are right." Jeff sighed and sipped his brandy. "'Tis unusually difficult to decide how to proceed, for I shall shortly be obligated to…go out of town for a few days. Even if you are correct and Colonel Howard does not declare himself tomorrow, what is to say he will not do so before my return? I'm not sure I want to risk that. Unless—" Jeff slammed down his glass and turned to Gilen, eagerness chasing the frown from his face. "Unless I could prevail upon you to squire the lady about and make sure Howard has no opportunity to declare himself before I return! But I couldn't ask that—"

"Of course you could!" Gilen interrupted. "What are friends for, after all? I can willingly pledge to insure she does not accept an offer from Howard in your absence."

"You would do that for me, best of my friends?"

Gilen nodded. *You planned to do this anyway, so renounce useless guilt,* he told his protesting conscience.

Jeffrey stuck out a hand and shook Gilen's fervently. "A bargain, then! How can I thank you enough? I suppose I should also tell you—but, no, it can wait upon my return."

"Where is it that you must go in such haste?"

"Oh, a…a trifling matter for grandfather. It…came up rather recently, and shouldn't take above a few days."

Exultant at the opportunity just afforded him, Gilen listened with only half an ear to Jeff's answer.

Several days. He would have several days to work on Miss Southford, free of the constraint of Jeff's presence.

Surely in that time he could figure something out. Colonel Howard's competition he dismissed out of hand.

"By the way," Jeffrey broke in on his reverie. "Apparently Lady Alice is not in good pin financially. Grandfather told me the bank is carrying a note on both the house and her cattle. Assuming Miss Southford accepts me, I may need another small loan to redeem them until I can make arrangements with my bank. Can't have the aunt of one's betrothed under the threat of debtor's prison! Now, one final round, and then good night. With you watching over Miss Southford, I can leave early in the morning."

A short time later, Gilen departed, finally able to occupy himself considering new ploys to capture the elusive Miss Southford. As he sat in the hackney bearing him back to his rooms, an idea occurred so truly despicable that he was initially ashamed even to have conceived of it.

There could be no more telling indication of how depraved his character had become since he'd fallen under the spell of Miss Southford than the fact that he could imagine—much less, as he was now doing, seriously envision—buying up Lady Alice's debts to use as a bargaining tool against her niece.

The fires of hell were surely being stoked to receive his black deceiving heart.

Not that he would actually turn them over to the magistrates, of course. But given Miss Southford's low opinion of his character, she would probably have no trouble believing he intended to do so. And might be concerned enough about the threat to her aunt to finally give up her pretensions to Jeffrey—and yield to him.

How he was going to turn up sweet a woman who, having had played against her such a low disgusting trick would likely despise him, he would worry about *after* he'd routed the lady.

* * *

Gilen de Mowbry, how low you have fallen. Having just come from the bank, Lady Alice's redeemed mortgages in his vest pocket, Gilen stood across the mews from the servants' entrance, watching for the maid whose assistance he'd purchased yesterday. He hoped that the shiny coins he'd dropped in her eager fists had left her with a more favorable opinion of him than the one that would be held by the butler and the residents above stairs.

He'd have to somehow cozen the girl into admitting him, since there was no chance that the glibbest of excuses would gain him admittance from either Mercer or Lady Alice.

Despite the infamous stratagem to which he'd been reduced, Gilen's senses sang and his mind raced in anticipation of encountering Miss Southford again. This battle, this time, he knew he was going to win.

At last the sandy-haired lass appeared, broom in hand as she began sweeping the steps. He sprinted over to her.

"My lord!" she gasped, belatedly dropping a curtsey.

"Hello, Mitsy." He offered a coin, which she quickly slipped into her apron pocket. "Are your ladies about yet?" He held up another coin.

She snatched it from his fingers. "Lady Alice don't never leave her chamber 'til after ten, but Miss Southford's out ridin' with her brother. Then she'n Lady Alice are to go directly to the mantua-makers. Expect to be gone all afternoon, Tilly said."

Gilen frowned. He'd hoped to catch the wench this morning before her chaperone was about. And he certainly needed to settle matters before she could set her claws into the innocent Colonel Howard tonight.

"Is there no time before this evening that I might catch Miss Southford alone?"

He thumbed out another coin, offering it just out of reach.

The maid moistened her lips, eyeing the coin covetously. "I…I dunno, sir. Now's I recall it, I think I heard Mercer say he had orders you wasn't to be received."

Gilen shrugged, not having to feign the heat that flushed his face. "Miss Southford is…angry with me. As I'm sure you know, she has several suitors, and I fear I let my…jealousy betray me into saying something rather unwise. Now, to punish me I expect, she's to go off with Colonel Howard tonight, and—"

"Yes!" the maid interrupted, her face aglow. "Tilly told us as how the Colonel meant to make Miss an offer this very—" She halted and clapped a hand over her mouth.

Nor did Gilen have to force the grim set his mouth took on at that confirmation of the unwelcome news Jeffrey had imparted. "So have I heard. Then you understand the urgency of my mission! Mitsy, can you not have pity on a man in love—and let me state my case to your mistress before it's too late?"

The maid's enthusiasm dimmed. "M-my lord, if'n Mercer was to learn of it, he might have me turned off."

"Mitsy, my whole life's happiness is now in your hands! Besides," he dug a fistful of coins out of his waistcoat pocket, "my household on Curzon Street in London could always use an intelligent, dependable maid. If it should come to that, you need not worry about employment."

Her eyes widened still further. "L-London!" she gasped. Quickly she raked the coins from his fingers into her apron pocket. "If'n you was to return about six, my lord, you might catch her. Lady Alice always lays down on her bed afore dressin' for the evening, and Miss works in the bookroom."

Gilen gave her his most beguiling smile and bowed with

a flourish. "You are a veritable angel of mercy! I shall come to the kitchen entrance at six, then."

"Oh, la, sir!" the maid exclaimed, blushing. "But you mustn't come by the kitchen. There'll be too many folk about, what with dinner cooking 'n all. Best come to the side door by the stillroom. I'll fetch you there."

"I shall be there. Thank you, Mitsy."

He would have to make the best of that opportunity, Gilen told himself with resignation as he stealthily slipped back out. And then had to grin.

If his noble sire could have seen his son reduced to bribing favors from an under housemaid, Gilen thought wryly, were the man not already dead, he would doubtless have expired from apoplexy on the spot.

Impatient for evening, Gilen filled the intervening hours with a long ride, a lingering lunch, and a protracted period sitting over the London newspapers, where instead of reading, he made mental notes of the details of the house and furnishings he would soon be setting up for Miss Southford. Having concluded that happy exercise, he was at last able to sneak back to the side door of the town house.

Mercifully, he had but a few moments to wait before Mitsy appeared. "Miss Southford be in the bookroom now, just like I said," she informed him as she beckoned him inside. "This way, my lord."

Silently he followed her through the deserted stillroom, up a back stair, and into a narrow hallway. Halting, she gestured to a closed door.

He nodded and made her an elaborate bow. She bobbed a curtsey, fingers over her lips to stifle a giggle, and fled back to the stairs.

His heart thumping hard in his chest, Gilen slipped noiselessly into the room.

Chapter Sixteen

Miss Southford sat at a small desk across from the door, her face in profile as she bent over a ledger, frowning. So absorbed was she in her work, she did not notice his stealthy entrance. Given the quantity of Lady Alice's debt, he was not surprised at her concern.

For a moment he allowed himself to admire the lustrous dark hair pinned in a thick coil atop her head, the fine straight nose, the plump lips pursed in concentration, the luscious outline of her chest in the becoming dove-gray evening gown. Soon, it would his happy task to smooth the frown from her face, lift the burden of worry from those slender shoulders and shelter her close.

Remembering his mission, a bit of his enthusiasm dimmed. She'd likely not come to him unless he invoked the power of the debt instruments burning like a reproach in his waistcoat pocket. If it came to that, could he actually bring himself to threaten her with them?

Before he could arrive at an answer, her fingers tensed on the ledger, as if even in the absence of sound or sight, the flash of energy that always pulsed between them alerted her to his presence. She looked up.

Gilen leapt over to press a hand over her mouth. "Please,

Miss Southford! I must speak to you on a matter of urgent concern to your aunt!''

He gritted his teeth as she attempted to bite him, her eyes glaring at him over his palm.

"If you give me your word not to call out, I will release you. Do you give it?''

After a moment she nodded. Gingerly he let her go.

"You ask my word as a lady? For I'm sure I cannot trust yours as a *gentleman*."

Ignoring that jab, he soldiered on. "You've had ample time to reflect. Have you reconsidered my offer?''

After a scathing glance, she returned her attention to the ledger. "If you've merely come to insult me again," she said, taking up the pen, "you waste my time. Kindly sneak out by whatever means you slithered in."

"That you're tempted to accept you cannot deny. The way you respond in my arms proves that beyond doubt."

Miss Southford not deigning to reply, the scratching of her pen on the ledger was the only sound in the room.

It would have to be the debts, then. Taking a deep breath, Gilen pulled the papers from his pocket.

"Since you appear to be concerned with matters of household finance, you might wish to look at these." He held out the documents.

Miss Southford did not so much as glance at them. "I have absolutely no interest anything you could show—''

Gilen pushed the mortgage under her nose and pointed out her aunt's name. "Are you sure?''

She threw him a suspicious glance, then pulled the parchment from his hand and scanned it rapidly. He heard her shocked intake of breath before she whirled to face him. "How did you get this?''

He shrugged. "Does it matter? The fact is, I have it— and these." He displayed the other documents.

She stared at them a long moment. Her hands gripped the pen tightly, the knuckles whitening.

"And what," she asked, her voice carefully even, "do you intend to do about them?"

"That depends on you. If you leave Harrogate, as we discussed, I will tear them up."

"And if I don't…" Her eyes widening in full comprehension, she sprang to her feet. "No! Not even *you* could be that despicable!"

Her accusation echoed the one being hurled by his own indignant conscience. He forced himself to continue. "I advise you not to remain and find out, unless you wish to see your dear aunt removed to a debtor's prison."

"But that is m-monstrous, sir!" she cried, her voice breaking with anger. And fear—he could see it lurking in her eyes, in the tense set of her shoulders. Another arrow of remorse stabbed him in the chest.

"Please, my lord, whatever you think of me, whatever our quarrel, let it remain between us! Do not allow my innocent aunt to suffer for wrongs you lay at my door!"

Her fierceness and courage, her impassioned voice, were irresistible. Gilen seized her hands and kissed them.

"You know I wish Lady Alice no harm, you stubborn creature! But I cannot allow you to go to Jeff—or any other man. I don't want to injure you, but to cherish you, here with me where you belong. Surely you believe that?"

They stood motionless, gazes locked, her hands still imprisoned by his. To his surprise, after a moment she gave him a reluctant smile.

"I suppose, in your own misguided way, *you* believe it," she said softly, tugging her hands free. "And despite your relentless, single-minded persecution of me since nearly the moment we met, *I* cannot believe you would really do this.

To my aunt—or me. You will return those, please.'' She held out her hands for the documents.

The debts—his last bargaining chip.

And yet, she was right. He could malign his honor and sense of decency no further. If he really could not bear to see her wed another, he might simply have to ignore the shame of her past, the outrage of his ancestors, and marry her himself. Dare he act so irresponsibly?

With a sigh he tossed the papers on her desk. "You are correct. I cannot harm your aunt—any more than I can resist you, my impossibly bewitching Miss Southford."

Slowly he reached over to touch her face, his heart exulting when she did not pull away. He traced her chin, her lips, her brows, before bringing his hands back to cup her face. "Will you not let me cherish you?" he whispered.

"I ought to send you packing," she said softly.

"Have mercy on me, I beg you."

"You are a despicable, conniving knave—"

"Undoubtedly correct." He drew her into his arms, using the barest bit of pressure so she might easily break free. To his infinite delight, she did not.

"—Who has behaved much more badly than anything he could accuse me of."

"True enough, my darling."

"I should probably resort to my whip again," she breathed while he tilted up her chin.

"Later," he murmured, his lips descending.

Over the starburst of pleasure that exploded in him when their mouths connected, he heard a moan—his or hers, he wasn't sure. He held himself to gentle, nuzzling touches, letting her set the pace. And uttered a muffled groan of bliss when, with a timid flick of her tongue, she probed at his lips.

Mesmerized by her cautious exploration, at once seductive and innocent, he let her taste him, wondering that his bones did not melt and fuse on the spot. He would not have believed he could derive such sheer erotic pleasure from an act performed while still fully clothed.

Despite his intention to let her lead him, he could not help tightening his grip. His heart raced as, twining her fingers in his hair, she moved closer, her body arching as she fitted herself against him.

And fit she did, so well he wanted to lift her, grind his hardness against the soft cleft at the junction of her thighs. His hands clenched on her arms to do just that when a loud noise penetrated his sensual spell.

Still, it took another moment for his addled wits to identify the unpleasant sound as a feminine shriek, still another before his sensation-drugged fingers could release Miss Southford. Groggily, he sought the sound's source.

And saw Lady Alice, hand to her bosom, half fainting as she gripped the doorframe to the bookroom.

"Gwennor! And L-Lord St. Abrams!" she gasped.

Miss Southford jerked away from him, stumbling in her haste. He put an arm around her to steady her.

Gradually a smile formed to replace the shock on the widow's face. "Why, what a sly dog you are indeed, my lord! So you stole a march on Mr. Masterson after all. I must admit, I did feel from the beginning that there was something between you and my niece. Let me be the first to offer congratulations!"

Belatedly Gilen realized his arm was still wrapped around Miss Southford's shoulders. Hastily he removed it—but 'twas already too late.

Lady Alice rushed over to give her niece a kiss. "Oh, I cannot wait to see the announcement in the gazette! Your wedding shall be the event of the season!"

Your. Wedding. Lady Alice's beaming face uttering those

shocking words finally evaporated the last remaining bit of sensual fog.

He looked to Miss Southford to correct her aunt's error, but she stood mute as if cast in stone. He opened his own mouth to dispute Lady Alice—and then shut it.

Having been found in passionate embrace with Miss Southford, what could he say? There was only one honorable exit from this room—the one Lady Southford had detailed.

For a moment he was numb with shock. Then a blistering rage at his folly—and Miss Southford—nearly choked him.

He could refute Lady Alice's conclusion, coolly indicate that he had no intention of offering marriage to her niece. And within a day, the report would fly about Harrogate— and from thence, through the links of kinship that tied the local aristocracy to families all over England—that Lord St. Abrams had compromised a maiden under her own aunt's roof and then refused to marry her.

Miss Southford's reputation would be ruined, of course. But so would his.

The devious, managing baggage! Had she permitted him that kiss, knowing that having given standing instructions that he be denied the house, sooner or later someone would come in to eject him? And that finding them embracing, he would be forced to offer marriage to a jade without honor, lest he forfeit what remained of his own?

With the prize an elevated title and a wealth even larger than Jeffrey's, small wonder that she'd been so receptive to his advances!

For a moment he was too incensed to move or speak. A fine champion, he! So intent on saving Jeff from the wench's machinations that he had fallen victim to them himself. Not that he hadn't, chucklehead that he was, provided her both the opportunity and the manacles with which to leg-shackle him.

Lady Alice was still looking at him expectantly.

"Your niece has just made me the happiest of men," he said, nearly gagging on the words, his furious tone in stark contrast to the sentiments expressed.

Lady Alice clasped her hands to her bosom. "I couldn't be more thrilled if she were indeed my own daughter. Now, sir," she wagged a finger at him, "given your new status as my niece's intended, I will allow you a few more moments of privacy, but no more!"

With a wink to Gilen and a kiss blown to her niece, Lady Alice exited the chamber.

Silence echoed after the door clicked shut. Fists clenching, Gilen wondered how he was going to make it out of the house without seizing Miss Southford and strangling the life from her right here in her aunt's own bookroom.

But when he at last steeled himself to gaze back down at her, instead of the self-satisfied triumph he expected, her face looked—troubled.

"My lord," she began hesitantly, "perhaps I can fix—"

"Haven't you 'fixed' enough?" he interrupted, not bothering to mask his rage. "You ought to be quite satisfied. Rolled me up nicely, didn't you, fool that I am? After all, what is Jeff's name and fortune to that of Viscount St. Abrams? By heaven, to be compelled to offer marriage to a…a *lightskirt* who dealt cards in a gypsy camp! I shouldn't be surprised if my father did not come back from the dead to haunt me for the shame of it!"

She drew herself up stiffly, anger flashing in her eyes. "Yes, I'm the unprincipled jade who lured you into this chamber, barred the door to prevent your exit, and addled your wits making love to you long enough to allow us to be detected."

Her tart—and accurate—reminder of how he had stupidly maneuvered his own destruction set the final seal on his fury. If he were to be compelled to pay the ultimate price for his fascination with this bewitching baggage, by heaven, he'd have his satisfaction! And this very night—not after weeks of waiting for the sham of a wedding.

He seized Miss Southford's wrist. "Come along."

"Wh-what are you doing? Release me at once!"

Paying her no heed, he half dragged, half walked her to the door. Linking his arm in hers, in awful parody of betrothed bliss, he pulled her out the door.

As he suspected, Lady Alice hadn't lost a minute in spreading the joyful news throughout the household. Mercer and several other servants stood beaming in the hallway.

The butler made them a deep bow. "If I may be permitted, on behalf of all the staff, our best wishes, my lord, Miss Southford, for a lifetime of happiness."

"I expect we shall have exactly as much happiness as we deserve," Gilen retorted with a clenched-teeth smile. "If you would fetch Miss Southford's cloak, I am escorting her to a select gathering where we might celebrate our approaching nuptials. And Mercer—"

"My lord?"

"Let Lady Alice know that Miss Southford will likely be very late returning. However, as she shall be in my *tender* care," he gritted out the word, "the staff need not wait up for her."

"Of course, my lord."

Gilen looked down at Miss Southford, bound so tightly to his side her arm must be growing numb, daring her to dispute his words.

She opened her lips, then shut them, as unable to object

to his spurious outing as he had been unable to refute her aunt's drastically mistaken assumption.

Mercer walked off to fetch Miss Southford's cloak. After assorted bows and curtseys, the other servants went back to their duties.

As the hallway emptied of people, Miss Southford's wary eyes examined Gilen's face. Then, squaring her shoulders and lifting her chin, she straightened.

"You may release me, my lord. I won't bolt."

"Having accomplished more than you could ever have hoped, why should you?"

She gave him an odd, challenging look. "You know nothing whatsoever about what I wished to accomplish."

He let that patent absurdity pass without comment.

After a moment of tense silence, she said, "May I ask where you are taking me?"

"Where I should have taken you that very first night— to receive the only honest thing we have ever shared. I may be forced to offer you my name, but tonight you'll get all I'll ever give you willingly." After a quick glance to insure no servants were still in sight, he leaned down to brand her mouth with a brutal kiss. "In my bed."

Fighting a strong desire to burst into tears, Gwennor let Lord St. Abrams lead her down the stairs. Why should it distress her so that he believed her capable of blatant entrapment? Given his oft-expressed low opinion of her character and the predicament they'd been placed in when her aunt stumbled in upon them, 'twas a logical assumption. And his fury at being coerced was also understandable.

Surely by now she should have mastered the ridiculous hope that he might come to recognize her true nature and revise his initial, degrading estimate of her. And 'twas past time to eradicate the ludicrous wish that he might learn to value—mayhap even to love—her.

He might have acted foolishly in maneuvering himself into that scene with Lady Alice, but he was not simpleton enough to fall in love with woman he thought to be a jade. Unlike Gwennor, who'd stupidly lost her heart to a man who would never respect her, and after this latest imbroglio, no longer even like her.

His angry words made it clear that in future, she would be no more to him than an object of temporary lust.

She could, of course, take advantage of his mistake and compel him to marry her. Given the fact that he hadn't immediately tried to charm Lady Alice into overlooking the compromising situation in which she'd discovered them, Gwennor didn't think he would later attempt to wriggle out of the agreement.

For a moment she entertained the idea. Gilen de Mowbry at her side for the rest of her days, bedeviling her wits, tantalizing her body, enrapturing her nights.

Coerced into wedlock and furious over it, Gilen de Mowbry, exiling her from his presence except for occasional interludes during which he tried to get her with his heir.

Arrogant and stubborn as he could be, he would likely never sway in his belief that she'd deliberately entrapped him, no matter how logical her explanations, no matter how stainless her character or single-minded her devotion after they were wed. Strong-willed and stubborn as he was, he could probably remain angry for a very long time.

No, she couldn't bear it. Though such a marriage would provide the material security she and Parry needed—and had the potential to fulfill her fondest fantasies—forcing the viscount to marry her would likely condemn her to living with his enmity for the rest of her life.

Better to hire herself out as a housekeeper or companion.

They reached the street, and with an elaborate show of courtesy—no doubt to impress Mercer and the footman—he handed her into the waiting hackney. Rather than argue in front of the servants with him in such a towering rage, it had seemed better to go along with his spurious plans. But now that she was seated in the hackney, before they reached his rooms, 'twas time to apply the soothing balm of reason before she found herself ruined in truth.

The viscount seated himself beside her. As she opened her lips to speak, he pulled her roughly into his arms and kissed her.

Like his quick kiss in the entryway, there was nothing of tenderness in it. His arms binding her close, his tongue invaded her mouth, plumbing its depths with all the subtlety he might have accorded a street-corner strumpet.

Which, of course, was how he saw her. Lord St. Abrams's whore, purchased at far too high a price. The tears she'd been trying to suppress welled at the corners of her eyes, and her trembling mouth offered no resistance to the force assaulting it.

But after a moment, his kiss gentled, the pressure of his mouth on hers softening, the touch of his tongue turning featherlight. He lifted a hand to her face, his fingers caressing her chin, her cheeks, her eyes. Where they encountered the hot drip of her tears, and halted.

With a shuddering breath, he broke off the kiss and eased his grip on her. "Gwennor, Gwennor," he sighed. "I've never known a woman who could inspire me with such rage one moment—" with a finger he carefully wiped her tears from the corners of each eye "—and such tenderness the next. What am I to do with you, wench?"

Take me back home, she almost said. 'Twas the logical thing to do, the only way to avoid disaster until she found a way out of this tangle. Somehow she knew, despite the ferocity of the anger he'd expressed just moments ago, if she asked that of St. Abrams, take her home he would.

Is that what she wanted?

She couldn't marry him. But if she remained in Harrogate, trapped between her aunt's expectations and St. Abram's fierce sense of honor, she'd be forced to.

No, that could only lead to misery for them both.

She would have to leave the city. Whether or not she was still worthy to be some man's wife no longer mattered. Knowing she loved the viscount, she could no more imagine giving herself in marriage to another man solely to secure a future than she would have contemplated going to Nigel's friend and leaving Parry behind.

She would never have the viscount's love or respect. But if she went to his rooms now, she could claim the one thing he willingly offered—his passion. She might have it only for one night. But it would be a soul-stirring, mind-bewitching, body-bedazzling night such as she was unlikely ever to taste again, unlikely to experience even once if she did not seize the chance to sample it now.

Was she brazen enough to do it?

Gwennor Southford, sensible, capable manager of her father's home, diligent chatelaine of Southford land, industrious member of the parish Benevolent Aid Committee, would never do anything so shocking and sinful.

Gwennor Southford who traveled with a gypsy troupe, danced to the wild music of violins, kissed and slapped, and kissed again this aggravating, infuriating, impossibly attractive man, would not settle for less.

He already thought her a wanton, else he'd never have given her this opportunity. For once, his degrading opinion worked to her advantage.

Abandoning any last doubt—and all her remaining scruples—she raised her face. "Kiss me," she said.

With a sound that was half chuckle, half groan, he grasped her by the shoulders and complied.

Chapter Seventeen

She opened her mouth to him eagerly this time, sought out his tongue, followed it in a teasing, gliding dance that ignited a molten pleasure deep within her with each languid stroke. He groaned, slid one hand beneath her cloak and cupped her breast, then stroked his thumb across the tender nipple, unleashing a rush of such exquisite sensation she gasped.

"Ah yes, sweeting," he murmured, and pushed her back against the squabs. Bringing both hands down to cup and caress her breasts, he kissed her again, his tongue laving hers in time to the seductive rhythm of his thumbs.

By the time the hackney halted a quarter of an hour later, her breath was reduced to uneven gasps, her chemise clung to her moist skin—and she craved with greedy desperation to have him bare and caress naked the skin his skillful fingers had tantalized through the too-thick cloth of her gown.

St. Abrams's breathing was no steadier, she noted when he pushed himself away. And he let his hands linger on her breasts until the hackney driver knocked on the door. "We's 'ere, govnor," the man said as he opened it.

The viscount handed the journeyman some coins, then

turned back to wrap her cloak around her and pull up the hood. "Keep your head down," he murmured as he handed her out.

The hackney had halted in the alleyway behind the viscount's chambers. Tugging the hood further down over her face, he hastened her up the dimly lit back stairs.

"Can't have all of Harrogate knowing my supposedly virginal bride seduced me in my chambers before the wedding," he whispered as he unlocked the door.

As soon as he'd closed it behind them, he pulled her to him for another long, tongue-melding kiss that immediately refired all the molten desire surging in her veins. Still kissing her, he picked her up and carried her through the sitting room and deposited her on the large canopied bed in the room beyond.

"Give me a few moments, my sweet, to seek out my valet and dismiss him for the night. There's wine in the decanter beside the bed. Pour us a glass." After another lingering kiss, he walked out, closing the chamber door.

A single candle glowed on a stand beside a large wing chair, casting wavering gold light on the bed already dappled with moonlight.

'Twas said moonlight could cause madness. Was that the reason for the urgency that gripped her?

She'd best make sure what she truly wanted. When St. Abrams came back she would have one last chance to return to sanity before setting in motion a spiral of events that would end with her well and truly ruined.

Reason clamored to repossess her fevered brain, arguing the danger of discovery, of getting with child, of recklessly throwing away any chance of achieving the permanent security of marriage.

Ignoring that rational voice, she raised her hands to the

breasts he'd tantalized and caressed with her own thumbs the still-throbbing nipples.

No, *this* was what she wanted. Ultimate pleasure, the infinite variety of sensation he'd promised her in his arms. She had the rest of her life to be sober, serious and sensible.

St. Abrams thought her a gypsy wanton, and tonight, she would be one.

She threw off her cloak, poured a glass of wine, and, blood thrumming in her veins, sat on the bed to wait.

A few minutes later, St. Abrams returned. His teeth gleamed white in the dimness as he saw her still on his bed, wineglass in hand.

"No second thoughts?"

Rather than reply, she offered him the glass. He downed a long sip, but instead of swallowing, he cradled her head in his hands and bent to lick at her lips. When she opened to him, he transferred some of the tart liquid into her mouth.

She drank it down, the warmed wine making her head giddy. Or perhaps it was the taste of him lingering on her tongue.

"Sweet Gwennor," he murmured, sitting beside her and bringing her hands up to kiss. "What a fascinating mix you are, at once lady and wanton, siren and innocent. Are you ever going to tell me the truth?"

"The...truth?"

"The truth about how—why—you ended up with the gypsies."

Though she wasn't about to reveal the whole, 'twas better not to lie. "I'd...rather not talk about it. Besides, what difference could it possibly make now? You formed your opinion of me long ago."

He put his hands on her shoulders and massaged them gently. "Perhaps, but I'd like to know which of my theories is correct. Though I can't imagine how your ravisher let you slip away, I can only be grateful he did. Should I shoot the careless bastard for you?''

She leaned into his caressing fingers and smiled slightly. ''That would be suicide.''

''You think me so poor a champion?'' he retorted, obviously stung. ''I'll have you know I'm accounted a superior shot.''

She shook her head. ''It no longer matters. I've given up on girlish dreams of a knight galloping up on a white destrier to carry me away.''

He drew her back against his chest and wrapped his arms around her. ''I shall carry you off and be your champion. And as I promised, you will have no regrets.''

No regrets? That was impossible, but she would not spoil tonight with thinking of them.

''So tell me, my sweet,'' he whispered, sliding his hands slowly down her sides and back up, almost but not quite grazing the edges of her breasts, ''what do you want?''

Your respect…your trust…your whole heart. But he wasn't interested in a love beyond the carnal, so with a sigh she replied, ''Despite what you think me, I'm not very…experienced.''

His caressing fingers stilled. ''Did that seducing scoundrel not even teach you pleasure? May he be doubly damned!''

She moved his hands to once more cup her breasts. ''You teach me.''

He bent to kiss her neck. ''Willingly, my sweet.''

He must be mad, Gilen thought while his hands expertly freed the tiny buttons at the back of Gwennor Southford's gown. In the heat of anger, there might have been some excuse for his behavior. But anger had long since fled, replaced by an all-consuming fire of another sort.

Still, though Gwennor—he could no longer, while he

nuzzled the skin he bared with each succeeding button, think of her as Miss Southford—might not be a virgin, she was still gentry-born. He shouldn't have brought her up to his rooms like a common courtesan.

But with desire raging in his blood and her willing acquiescence, he knew he could not make himself take her home—not yet.

Oh, he'd been furious, and with good reason. But perhaps this forced marriage wouldn't be such a disaster after all. Despite the argument he'd flung at her, he knew that he alone of his party would recognize her as the wench from the gypsy encampment, and he certainly wouldn't spread such tales about his own wife. If she came to his bed not still a virgin, who but he would ever know?

Since the maddening minx had done such a thorough job of infiltrating his senses and captivating his mind, there would be definite advantage in binding her to him in marriage. He'd have her at his side forever, challenging his opinions and provoking his intellect as handily as she fired his blood and warmed his bed. He'd not have to worry about her being lured away by someone with a glibber tongue or a fatter purse.

Unlikely as that would be. He knew himself to be tolerably glib, and few men possessed a plumper purse or a more impressive pedigree. But she'd already shown herself alarmingly independent and virtually unpredictable. If she took it into that stubborn head of hers to leave him, she'd be damnably difficult to dissuade.

He finished the last button and urged her to her feet, then freed her from the gown and turned her to face him, clad now only in her chemise and stockings.

Her dark-violet eyes, glazed with desire and yet uncertain, regarded him. "W-what now, my lord?"

"Gilen," he said huskily, drinking in the sight of her—

the pert breasts, nipples peaked and rosy beneath the thin linen chemise, the dark triangle of curls at the junction of her thighs.

He patted his knees. "Sit, and take down your hair."

She sat. He eased her rounded bottom against his hardness, the exquisite pressure waxing and waning as she reached up to extract the pins from her hair.

He sighed with delight when the whole heavy mass tumbled down. Leaning her once more back against his chest, he contented himself for some minutes with combing through the thick locks, letting his fingers as they pulled free continue downward to touch her arms, sides, belly. "Ah, what glorious hair you have, my sweet."

"What now, my l...Gilen?" she whispered.

He settled her more snugly against his erection and reached around her to unlace the top of her chemise. Taking two handfuls of hair, he brushed the silky strands over her nearly bare breasts, delighting in her gasping intake of breath when he tantalized her nipples.

"Do you want this, my siren?"

"Y-yes."

Already he was aching for release. But he wanted this slow seduction to last and last, so he urged her to her feet and led her to the center of the room, then pulled over a stool and sat before her.

"A thousand times I've envisioned what would have followed, had we not been forced to stop that first night," he said, stroking her arms, the curve of her hips. "This time, there will be no interruptions. So, my gypsy enchantress, I hear the sound of violins, the jangle of bracelets, the clapping of hands. Dance for me."

At first he thought she would not comply. But then, a half smile on her lips, she closed her eyes and began to sway her hips, move her arms and shoulders in the rhythm of some silent music.

In his head he could hear it too, the plaintive, mournful violins, the staccato clatter of bracelets, the shouts of encouragement from the onlookers. After a few moments of sinuous motion, the loosely laced bodice slipped lower, unveiling her breasts completely.

"Perfect," he breathed, rubbing his fingertip over one taut rosy tip.

Ah, this was a thousand times better than his best erotic memories. Instead of a bonfire's blaze behind them, they had the glow of a small fire in the grate and a golden dazzle of candlelight. The low-cut gypsy blouse had revealed the top swell of her breasts, her full gypsy skirt her narrow waist, but the unlaced chemise displayed those breasts in their full glory while through its thin material gleamed the opaque outline of her limbs and the shadowed curls he thirsted to taste.

Best of all, instead of a camp thronged with witnesses and a hard wagon bed, when this dance was done they had the privacy of his room and a wide, soft four-poster.

She opened her eyes and saw him staring. Her smile widening, she swayed closer, dipping her naked breasts near his lips.

He swiped his tongue across one pebbled nipple, but before he could seize it in his teeth, she laughed and danced away. Skipping behind him, she wrapped her arms around his shoulders and leaned close as she moved, rubbing her hardened nipples and the wiry curls at her thighs against his linen shirt.

'Twas almost enough to make him lose control. Groaning, he reached behind him to cup her bottom and pull her closer. She nipped his neck and reached down to rub his rigid length through the chamois of his breeches.

A wave of pleasure shuddered through him, numbing his fingers, stealing his breath. As his hold on her dissolved, she stepped back and danced away. When his eyes could focus again, she was once more in front of him, her hands stroking his chest, his face as she moved.

He jerked up her chemise, stripping down her stockings until they pooled at her feet. Laughing low in her throat, she kicked them off. Her hands went to his cravat, dissolved the knot and pulled the fabric free.

Before she could drop it, he took it from her.

"Bind up your skirt with this," he whispered.

Slowing her undulating motion, she raised the linen fabric and wrapped his cravat low about her hips, fixing the chemise in place. Then she raised her arms and twirled before him, the shortened skirt swirling about her thighs.

His pulses drumming in his head to the accelerating beat of his heart, he ran his hands along her bared calves, across her knees, up to the silk of her inner thighs. She moved her hands to mimic his movements, sliding them down the length of his arms, his chest, prying free the buttons of his shirt and waistcoat, running the pads of her fingers on the skin beneath. Feverish with the need for her touch, he stripped the garments off.

He held his hands lightly against her gyrating body, letting her sinuous movements guide the skim of his fingers over her buttocks, her hips, his playful tug of the tight curls above her mound.

Perspiration dewed her forehead as his fingers dipped beneath the chemise and crept up her thighs. He urged them apart and she widened her stance, moving into his caressing touch. When he at last flicked a fingertip over the sensitive nub, she stiffened, her sure steps faltered. She grabbed his shoulders, her nails biting into his neck, and arched her head back, uttering a hoarse growl.

"Yes, my beauty," he murmured. "Dance for me."

Fiercely gratified to find her wet and ready, he worked his fingers over her dewy pearl and into the slick canal beyond. "Do you want this, Gwennor?"

"Yes," she gasped. "Oh, yes." Haltingly she picked up the rhythm again, this time swaying her hips into the touch of his stroking fingers. He continued until she was unsteady and gasping, until the tightness of his breeches neared pain.

He moved one hand to tug at the fasteners of his trouser flap, his other still caressing her. Sensing the change of position, she opened heavy-lidded eyes, smiling when she comprehended his intent.

"Unsheathing your weapon?"

The thought of her watching him bare himself sent a bolt of sensation flooding through him, further complicating the business of freeing the straining buttons.

She reached down and tugged them free. "Shall I?" she murmured.

He managed an inarticulate mutter that she took for assent. And then he ceased to breathe at all as she drew his hard velvet length out of the encumbering breeches. "Do you want this, Gilen?" she asked, and slowly stroked down his whole length.

"Yes," he groaned, nearly paralyzed by the intensity of the sensation. The blood in his body seemed to pool beneath her caressing fingers and he lost all feeling in his extremities. His now-nerveless hands fell back to his sides.

She uttered a protest at the cessation of his touch, then followed his lead bonelessly as he parted her knees and pulled her onto his lap, nudging his throbbing length into the soft heat of her thighs. Easing her legs wider, he guided himself within.

And then held himself motionless, barely penetrating, letting her adjust to his fullness. She clutched at his shoulders, her peaked nipples grazing his bare chest, her breathing ragged. "Now," he said unsteadily, his skin sheened with sweat as he tried to hang on to the last shreds of his control, "let us finish the dance."

He took one nipple into his mouth, sucking greedily as he slowly rocked his hips. She shuddered and caught his rhythm, moving in time to that ancient, primal melody.

As she rocked him deeper, control began to ravel. He clutched at her bared bottom, urged her to clasp her legs behind his back, accelerated the pace.

Until she tensed, gasping. He thought at first she'd reached completion, but she braced herself away from him.

Her seducer must have finished quickly, he realized, or perhaps the bastard had been less manfully endowed.

"Hush, my lovely," he whispered, stilling. He moved a hand to stroke her where their bodies joined and resumed the ministrations of his lips.

Not until she relaxed, once again sinking into him, burying him deeper, did he begin moving again. Wrapping his fists in her thick dark hair, he drew her face down for a long sweet kiss.

He released her lips and framed her face with his hands. "Now dance with me, my darling." He pulled her close, crushing the heavy softness of her breasts against his chest, and captured her mouth, stroking with his tongue in time to the rhythm of their joining.

When he thought he could stave off satisfaction no longer, she cried out and writhed against him. In triumphant jubilation, he joined her through the last exquisite measures.

Bodies sated, muscles rubbery, they sagged against one another while the beat of their pulses slowed and the hissing of breath quieted to a murmur. When at last strength and feeling returned to his limbs, Gilen lifted her, still joined to him, carried her to the bed and eased back against the pillows, pulling her against his chest while she cradled him within her depths.

Ah yes, he could dance with her like this all day and all night, forever.

So many other pleasures he would teach her. But all he wished at this moment was to remain quiescent in this bed, her body still possessing his in intimate embrace.

They must both have dozed, for her bare back was chilled when he returned to himself. She murmured and stirred, then startled awake.

"Hush, my sweet, we've time yet."

She opened dazed eyes. "Time...for another dance?" she asked, shifting her position.

The subtle change in pressure sent an aftershock of pleasure through his captive member. She must have felt him surge within her, for she shuddered and thrust instinctively against him.

Though it should be far too soon for him to respond, nonetheless he felt that exquisite tightening, the slowly building pressure as he hardened within her depths.

Cupping her bottom, he pulled her close. "Yes, my love, let us dance again," he replied, and claimed her mouth.

When he woke again after that joining, Gilen knew he must take her home. But filled with a euphoric lassitude, he couldn't make himself move quite yet.

Her body still pliant in sleep, Gwennor dozed on his chest, her tangled curls blanketing her back and shoulders. Moonlight played over the planes of her face, cast silvery shadows on her inky eyebrows and thick velvet lashes.

Gwennor, who was soon to be his wife. Somehow the notion didn't sting nearly as much as it had earlier in the evening, as in loving detail he relived the events of their night together.

Sometime before they were wed, he would extract the truth of her past. Though he wouldn't want to engender the speculation about her honor inherent in a duel, he was fairly certain that some venal blackguard inhabiting the Welsh countryside was going to feel the fury of his fists.

Though he shouldn't punish the man too much, he supposed. For if Gwennor Southford had not been forced from her home, he would never have met his gypsy enchantress—or experienced this wondrous night.

To his regret, she stirred awake. Looking at him at first dazedly, she gasped and pushed against his chest, her eyes widening as if not sure how she came to be naked in his arms, in his bed.

"Hush, sweeting, you're safe with me."

She stilled, still staring. "Gilen?" Comprehension returned, but though her rigid grip eased, she once more pushed away.

He let her go, feeling a curiously intense sense of loss. Ah, well, they would have months, years, decades of nights like this.

Avoiding his eyes, she faced away, apparently embarrassed by her nakedness, now that the fire of passion had banked. Touched by her modesty, he dragged his dressing gown off the chair beside the bed and offered it.

"Thank you." She took the robe and belted it about her with an expression of relief. "I must get home now."

"Must you?" Again he felt the oddest compulsion to hold her, keep her here, never let her go.

"Yes. We can't have all of Harrogate knowing your supposedly virginal bride seduced you in your rooms."

He smiled at her parroting back of his words. She did not, and a flicker of alarm licked through him.

"'Tis a bit late for second thoughts now, my sweet," he murmured, watching her closely.

"No second thoughts," she replied, to his unaccountably sharp relief. "But every…happening has its moment. This has now ended and I must go."

She had slipped back into her ton maiden pose so completely it was as if another woman now inhabited his rooms. Though he regretted the departure of the gypsy siren, the mere fact that she could present in one body two so wholly different facades amazed and fascinated him.

She was pacing about the room, hunting her scattered garments. He rose from the bed.

"Can I help?"

She turned. For a long, luscious moment, the proper virgin disappeared and she was once again his gypsy dancer, her eyes slowly caressing his bare body from head to toe with such heated intensity that he felt his loins tighten once again. Then the hot light faded and she looked away.

"I shall require your assistance doing up the buttons, if you please." She offered him her back.

He stepped behind her, but instead of beginning on the fastenings, he pulled her against his naked length.

She stiffened in his arms, setting off another alarm in his chest. Did she truly have no regrets?

When he considered what he had just induced her to do, he could well understand her unease. Should anyone learn that a supposed lady of quality had come unchaperoned at night to the rooms of a single gentleman—and shared a rapturous and thoroughly illicit interlude with him—the scandal would ricochet all the way to London.

"Don't worry, we shan't be discovered," he reassured her. "Besides, I'm soon to make an honest woman of you."

"Are you?" She raised an eyebrow. "Can even the mighty Viscount St. Abrams change who I am?"

Her odd tone alarmed him further, and he clasped her

closer, as if to reaffirm his hold over her. At last, with a shudder, she relaxed against him.

When he released her, to his immense satisfaction, she turned and slowly stroked his jaw. "Ah, Gilen," she whispered. His chest tightened at the tenderness in her tone. "The buttons now, if you please."

He did them up unwillingly, then poured her a glass of wine to sip while he dressed himself and came to stand by her, watching as she rebraided her thick curly hair.

After previous trysts, he had always been the impatient one, ready to leave once the intimacy was finished. He found it unsettling that, though the sensual spell simmered in his veins, his proper Miss Southford seemed to have put it all behind her.

Hair repinned, pelisse buttoned, she turned to him, quiet and composed as a nun. "I'm ready, my lord."

"Gilen," he corrected. With unaccountably reluctance, he rose to his feet. "Wait here, my sweet. I'll summon a hackney and come back to fetch you."

He started toward the door, but then, compelled by something he couldn't name, walked back to her, cupped her chin and raised her face to his.

"No regrets?" he asked, hardly breathing.

She gave him a slight smile, such an edge of sadness in it that he could almost believe her a proper maid who'd just lost her virtue. "No regrets," she replied softly. "Thank you, Gilen."

He grinned, immensely relieved. "You are welcome."

"And—I'm...sorry about the scene with Aunt Alice."

He shrugged a shoulder. "We shall deal with that later. Even should there be...consequences to this night."

"There shouldn't be. I...I am near my woman's time, and 'tis unlikely then, I'm told."

"As we're soon to be wed, 'twill not matter. I shall be back shortly."

A half hour later, he guided her down the darkened stairs into another hackney. She sat quietly during the drive back to her aunt's, responding so briefly to his attempts at conversation that he soon fell silent as well.

They arrived without incident, roused the night porter to admit them and entered the shadowed hallway. Glad the porter's presence gave him the excuse to play the proper fiancé, he bent to kiss her.

She accepted the salute chastely, like a virtuous maiden. He found himself wishing for a return of the gypsy siren. Would she befuddle and bewitch him all their life together with her vacillation from one to the other?

He couldn't let her go without a taste of his gypsy. Before lifting his mouth from hers, he slid his tongue over her lips, seeking entry.

In a sense-quickening reverse that once more caught him off guard, she not only opened to him, but became the aggressor, pursuing his tongue, alternating light touches with bold lingering stokes until his whole body tingled and he cursed the fact that they stood in her aunt's hallway instead of in the corridor outside his rooms.

"Miss Southford," he said unsteadily when at last she broke the kiss, "you are an amazement."

She gave him an enigmatic smile. "You have no idea. Good night, Lord St. Abrams."

He grinned. "My very dear Miss Southford."

He watched her until she disappeared up the stairs. Walking out into the night that was already lightening with approaching dawn, his grin widened.

Yes, he supposed he could accustom himself to a lifetime of nights like this. Even if it meant battling papa's shade for having had the temerity to bring into the august St. Abrams family probably the first unchaste bride.

He should be angry. His original plans for Miss South-ford were much more suitable. Without doubt, she belonged in his bedchamber, but she simply wasn't worthy of stand-ing in the drawing room of Abrams Castle receiving guests as viscountess. He'd been tricked, maneuvered and be-trayed by a cunning jade.

He ought to leave town for a few days, let her worry and wonder whether he was truly going to honor his obligation. Not give the brazen baggage the satisfaction—yet—of pa-rading him about Harrogate on her arm, gloating over her triumph.

Or of realizing how quickly her chin trembling with ag-itation, her eyes welling with tears she would not allow to fall, could touch his heart and bend him to her will.

Yes, he'd go away. And prove to himself that he could control this disturbingly intense desire to be with her again.

Chapter Eighteen

Less than a week later, Gilen rode back into Harrogate. Considering that he would shortly have to reveal his crass betrayal to his best friend and send an announcement of his coerced engagement to the journals, he ought to be in a smoldering rage. Instead, a totally illogical sense of anticipation lightened his heart.

Not that he was looking forward to the interview with Jeffrey. Reasoning 'twas best to get over rough ground quickly, however, on his way into town Gilen stopped at Lord Masterson's stables, where he ascertained from a groom that the master's grandson had just returned from his trip. Gilen then proceeded to his rooms to tidy up and marshal his arguments.

But the thoughts that rattled around his brain as he soaked in the hip bath made no more sense of his actions than those that had circled endlessly through his head during the interminable four days that had been the longest he'd been able to absent himself from Harrogate.

After escorting Miss Southford home, he'd returned to his rooms only long enough to throw together a traveling kit before riding off to Lacey's Retreat. Though his brother and companions had already left for university, the viscount had extended a cordial welcome to the elder brother of his son's friend. But whether hunting in the home woods or fishing the swift-flowing river, he found himself drawn again and again, like a lodestone to the north, to the clearing west of DeLacey land. Where, one star-spangled night, the logical, responsible course of his life had been diverted from its channel with flash-flood force by an enchanting gypsy dancer.

During his solitary rides he also found himself holding silent conversations with the late Lord St. Abrams, trying to explain to his dead father—and himself—the circumstances that had led him into behavior his illustrious forefathers would doubtless deplore.

I know 'tis a rare coil, Papa, but I shall sort it out, he'd assured his dead sire. The snap of a fallen branch beneath his horse's hooves a moment later had sounded suspiciously like a derisive sniff.

Being no closer at the end of four days to reconciling his actions, and giving up the losing battle to resist the sharp need to see again the bewitching minx who'd driven him to them, he abruptly bid farewell to his puzzled host and galloped back to the city.

And so, two hours after his arrival, he stood in Lord Masterson's parlor, hands damp within his chamois gloves, girding himself to attempt to explain what his oldest friend might well find neither explicable nor forgivable. At least, he comforted himself, the chances of their long friendship enduring his theft of Jeffrey's lady were better with him about to make that lady his wife than they would be had he succeeded in his original intention to turn her into his mistress.

Much as he told himself he was prepared, still his stomach tensed when the door opened and Jeffrey walked in. It twisted even tighter when his friend stopped short, neither responding to Gilen's tentative smile nor meeting his gaze.

Gilen opened his lips in greeting, but no sound emerged. All the sentences in his head scattered like leaves in a high wind, leaving only the heart-wrenching fear that their long friendship might truly be over.

Jeffrey motioned him to a chair. Not until he'd seated himself did his friend finally look at him, an awkward, strained expression his face.

Gathering his courage, Gilen began, "I don't quite know how to say this, but—"

"No, let me speak first," Jeff broke in. "Though it may be hard to explain—'tis hard enough to explain to myself! I am sorry, Gilen. But we've been boon companions for so many years, surely that friendship is as dear to you as it is to me. Dear enough, I earnestly hope, that you'll be able to forgive me." His face grew suddenly fierce. "Whether you can or not, however, I am still going to ask you to wish me happy."

Gilen focused on the changing expressions of Jeffrey's face, trying to make sense of his words. Alarm began skittering across his nerves, like the flash of distant lightning as a storm approaches. "F-forgive you?"

"I certainly never intended affairs to turn out like this. And after what I coerced you into doing for me—well, I only hope you don't feel I've betrayed our friendship."

Gilen shook his head slightly, trying to put Jeff's words together into some pattern that made sense. After a moment's cogitation, two phrases flashed back into mind. *Wish me happy…betrayed our friendship.*

A possible solution clicked into place and his bewilderment exploded into shock—and rage.

No, it couldn't be! Hadn't he been through enough to

capture the wily wench? Jeffrey simply could not have countermanded his offer to Miss Southford!

"Y-you o-offered for her?" he stuttered, unable to credit such effrontery.

"Well…yes." Jeff's face heated and his look turned sheepish. "As I understand it, 'twas the very morning you left Harrogate."

"A-and she *accepted* you?" he asked, his voice rising with incredulity. The brazen baggage! How could she have shared a night like that with him—and abandoned him for another man the very next morning?

"Well, see here!" Jeff objected, his tone a little affronted. "I may not be as prime a catch as the mighty Viscount St. Abrams, but I'm still accounted by most of Society as a fairly eligible parti."

Unable to remain still, Gilen sprang up from his chair and began pacing the room, teeth clenched and hands balled into fists. He was going to murder her. He whirled to face his erstwhile friend. No, he was going to murder *him*.

Uneasiness flickered across Jeffrey's face at what he must have read in Gilen's eyes. "Now, I expected you to be somewhat upset, but there's no need to go round the bend. I know you despise the family, but despite Mary Anne's unfortunate connection to Lady Aylesbury, most members of the ton concede the lady herself is as genteel and pretty-behaved as a man could wish in his wife. Though I do readily admit my behavior has been less than honorable toward Miss Southford, a fact which I heartily…"

As his brain sifted through Jeffrey's tangled discourse, Gilen stopped in midstride. A bolt of relief, so powerful his head went dizzy and all his limbs tingled, blotted out the rest of his friend's sentence.

He pivoted to face Jeffrey. "Are you telling me you offered for Miss *Aylesbury?*"

Jeffrey wrinkled his brow. "Of course. What did you think I've been trying to tell you?"

On knees gone suddenly rubbery, Gilen stumbled back to his chair. "I—I'm shocked, that's all. But...I had no notion you were enamored of the lady! How did this all come about?"

Jeffrey's look again turned sheepish. "You'll remember, the day before I left town, I mentioned there was something I wished to tell you?" After Gilen nodded, he continued, "I had encountered Miss Aylesbury in the Pump Room nearly every day since I arrived in Harrogate. Initially I felt just a strong sympathy for her, living under the thumb of so vulgar and domineering a mother. But as time went on, I became more and more aware not just of her beauty but also of the goodness and sweetness of her nature. However, I'd sung the praises of Miss Southford to you on so many occasions, I concealed my steadily increasing regard for Mary Anne, fearing you would both take me to task for fickleness and lodge strong objections about the lady's family. So, not being sure what I wished to do, I...dissuaded you from accompanying me to the Pump Room with grandfather and continued to pay court to Miss Southford."

"Paying court at once to two females? What a rascal you've become, Jeffrey Masterson!"

Jeffrey flushed. "I didn't intend to mislead Miss Southford—or you. At the time I was still seriously considering marrying her."

"Seriously enough that you asked me to fend off Colonel Howard," Gilen observed drily.

Jeffrey's blush deepened. "I do feel badly about that, but truly the matter wasn't decided until the house party."

"A house party? Was that the urgent 'errand' on which you had to go for your grandfather?"

"Yes. Lady Aylesbury insisted on dragging Mary Anne to the annual gathering old Lord Rumpsfeld has at his estate. I only went because Miss Aylesbury begged me most piteously to come and protect her from the attentions of that old reprobate. Her mama was impatient with her for not yet bringing any acceptable suitors up to scratch, and Mary Anne very much feared during the course of the party Lady Aylesbury would maneuver her into a compromising situation with Rumpsfeld, and then force them to marry. As if one could abide the notion of her being pawed by that randy old goat!" Jeffrey said hotly.

"So you promised to come along and—protect the lady?" Gilen prompted.

"Yes. That first morning, to forestall an approach by Rumpsfeld, I agreed to take her walking in the garden. She was still frightened, and looked so worried and irresistible, I…well, I just had to embrace her! And who should have been lying in wait in the shrubbery but Lady Aylesbury, thinking to catch her out with Lord Rumpsfeld!"

Gilen stifled his first, cynical reply. Not a believer in coincidence, he had little doubt Jeff's inclusion in the house party had been a clever ploy on the part of Lady Aylesbury, with or without her daughter's collusion, to bring up to snuff not the aging roué, but Gilen's susceptible and innocent friend.

"Naturally," Jeffrey was continuing, "I chose to do the honorable thing and make her an offer."

"I don't know, Jeff. It sounds like entrapment to me. Are you sure you wish to do this?"

"I am, actually. Now I know you'll protest that in the past, I've been rather…fickle. And I readily admit, in the last two weeks I've behaved very badly in leading on Miss

Southford, who is truly a lovely and admirable lady. But she is rather…forceful and independent. Whereas Mary Anne is so gentle, so grateful for every little courtesy. She actually thinks me something of a hero, which is ridiculous, I know, but gratifying nonetheless. She…needs me, Gilen. And I think we shall deal very well together. Especially after I send her mama to the rightabout, which I intend to do as soon as we're wed! Well, suffice it to say, I'm quite content. And I do thank you for your help with Miss Southford.''

Gilen grinned, the euphoria left in relief's wake making him feel expansive. Everything would be all right after all. He would get his gypsy enchantress—and keep his best friend. "I'm pleased to have been of service.''

"Thank you, Gilen!'' Jeff walked over to clap him on the shoulder. "I'm so glad you feel that way.''

Perhaps now he should reassure Jeffrey that his friend needn't worry about Miss Southford, for Gilen intended soon to make her his bride. But no, admitting that at the very moment Jeff confided that he'd given up his own claims to the lady was bound to reveal to his friend that Gilen had been courting the lady behind his back. Better to wait a decent interval before confessing his intentions.

A huge burden of worry now lifted from his shoulders, Gilen's immediate desire was take himself off to visit his vixen and discover what sort of mischief she'd been up to since his departure. And see if she had missed him as keenly as he had missed her.

"I must go now,'' he told his friend as he rose from his chair, "but I shall return later. We should share a bottle of champagne to celebrate!''

Jeff escorted him out. "Indeed we must, old friend.''

Already consumed with a fierce desire to gaze on the lovely face and bandy words with the tart-tongued wit of his lady, Gilen had difficulty restraining himself to a decorous walk. Full of the sheer joy of living, he wanted to leap into the air shouting hurrahs and race at full speed straight to Lady Alice's town house. If, as he hoped, her aunt would allow the betrothed couple a few moments of privacy, he knew exactly how he intended to use them.

His boisterous spirits received a check when Mercer ushered him in—and disclosed, after giving him an odd look, that Miss Southford was not at home.

Disappointed more than he wanted to admit, he nonetheless settled himself to impatiently await Lady Alice. After paying his compliments to her chaperone, he could discover where his lady had gone and track her down.

Would her expressive eyes widen with surprise—and then delight—when she saw him? Her heart leap in joyous anticipation as he approached?

Lost in pleasant imaginings of how that joy might best be expressed before—and after—their nuptials, Gilen did not at first hear Lady Alice enter.

"My dear Lord St. Abrams!" she exclaimed, sweeping in to offer him her hands. "An unexpected surprise! And how kind of you to stop by and pay your regards."

"How could I not fail to call immediately upon my return on a lady who is not only one of Harrogate's most charming residents, but also one to whom I owe so much?"

Lady Alice blushed. "What pretty compliments you pay, to be sure! Though I suppose 'tis I who should thank you, not to have mentioned to anyone how very foolishly I reacted the other morning, for no one has yet taken me to task for it, and I should certainly have heard of it by now. Though I do not doubt, as Gwen told me, that the two of you shared a great laugh over it!"

Once again Gilen felt he'd been dropped into the middle

of a conversation with no inkling of the salient facts that had preceded it. "A...good laugh, my lady?" he repeated, totally at sea.

Lady Alice chuckled. "I still think it a very naughty play you two were rehearsing that morning in the bookroom, most assuredly not something that would have been acted out in my day! Which made my...premature conclusion about your conduct and intentions only natural and forgivable, as Gwen assured me after she'd explained the matter." Lady Alice shook her head. "*School for Scandal,* she said the play is called, and a very apt title in my opinion! Still, I am most thankful she sought me out the very next morning, before I embarrassed all of us by announcing my erroneous assumptions to the whole of Harrogate!"

His mind once again trying to make sense of unexpected developments, Gilen scarcely heard her. Miss Southford had told her aunt they'd been...rehearsing a *play?* What sort of rig was the minx running now? A knot of dread formed in his stomach.

"Y-yes, I shall doubtless share another chuckle with Miss Southford over it. Where would she happen to be now?"

Lady Alice looked at him in surprise. "Why, she's still at that house party. The one her cousins invited you to, where you were to perform the play together. Indeed, I thought you would still be there as well. Has it broken up early?"

Gilen felt as if a hole had opened up under him into which, ripped from his moorings, he was falling at dizzying speed. He needed to escape the room and regain his footing, sort out the startling information Lady Alice had just imparted.

"I, um, received a summons and was forced to depart," he fumbled. "And so must now leave you as well to, ah, complete that urgent errand.'' He popped to his feet. ''Your servant, Lady Alice.''

Looking bewildered, his hostess rose as well. ''Good day, my lord. Whether my niece has returned yet or not, please feel free to call whenever you like.''

Gilen paused in his march to the door and glanced back. ''When do you expect her?''

''Oh, not for a week or so. She was rather vague about when the party would finish up.''

With another bow, Gilen stumbled out.

He rode back to his rooms in a fog of speculation.

The first and most important fact seemed to be that, by clever manipulation of the facts her aunt had observed, Miss Southford had managed to convince the lady that their passionate interlude had been a rehearsal for some sort of amateur theatrical. He had not compromised her niece.

There was no engagement.

He ought to be ecstatic. His honor would remain unblemished without his being forced to wed a woman who could not come to her marriage bed a virgin. Doubtless the assorted generations of St. Abramses were applauding in their tombs. He'd even salvaged his friendship with Jeff.

Why, then, did he feel so...bereft?

Back at his rooms, sitting before his own hearth while he ate a nuncheon of which he tasted not a morsel, Gilen tried to make sense of Lady Alice's story. He could not seem to get the separate facts to combine into any coherent or logical whole.

Why, after managing to snare an even richer matrimonial prize than Jeff, would Miss Southford have let him go? Having been accustomed since the day he left Eton to being accounted one of the primest catches on the Marriage Mart, it seemed inconceivable that a maiden with a particle of practicality and any knowledge whatsoever of the workings of Society would have whistled down the wind a chance to end up Viscountess St. Abrams.

Underlying that was a more personal sense of injury. Miss Southford had apparently abrogated her claims not just to Viscount St. Abrams, but also to Gilen de Mowbry.

She hadn't wanted…him.

A surge of indignation brought him to his feet, sloshing the wine from his glass down the front of his pristine waist-coat. The chit had bloody well wanted Gilen de Mowbry that night in his rooms! How dare the wench tease him, beguile him, befuddle his mind and bewitch his senses and then just—depart, giving him no hint of her whereabouts?

Which was exactly what he had done to her, his precise conscience had the temerity to remind him.

He swabbed at the stain on his vest and dropped back into his chair, still furious and disgruntled. It simply didn't make sense.

Other, less comforting memories drifted back from the magical night. The odd feeling, as she dressed to return to her aunt's, that Miss Southford had already left him and retreated into some private place within herself, well beyond his reach.

Her strange remark in her aunt's entry hall before he dragged her to his rooms— "You know nothing whatsoever about what I was trying to accomplish."

Well, of course he did! She wanted what every maiden wanted—and what, in her case, was even more imperative: to cover up her disreputable past by snagging as socially elevated a suitor as possible into marriage.

Didn't she?

Gilen shoved that dismaying doubt aside. Though it seemed clear no public notice had been given, after that night in his rooms he wasn't sure that honor did not still demand he marry the chit, however coerced his proposal.

After all, she might have been a gypsy dancer—but she was also a lady bred. He would never have taken such liberties had he not fully intended to make her his wife.

He did know with absolute surety that he must track her down and find out what the devil she was trying to do to him.

And when he did find her, he wasn't sure whether he ought to kiss her breathless—or strangle her.

Since he could hardly inquire Miss Southford's current whereabouts of Lady Alice, Gilen was mulling over how best to ascertain where she had disappeared when he reached the stables to collect his stallion. Perhaps he could seek out her brother, he thought suddenly.

Not to interrogate the lad at length, of course, he thought with a pang at his previous encounter with young Mr. Wakefield. But Miss Southford was so protective of the boy, she was sure to have explained her absence to him and perhaps have repeated the name of her destination often enough that he might recall it. He'd ask the lad one brief question and not pursue the matter if the boy couldn't answer it.

So as Jem led Raven out, Gilen asked casually, "Is Mr. Wakefield about?"

"No, my lord. He done left with his sister a few days back." The groom grinned. "Some right fine rabbit stew we been having since his departure too!"

"Best not let the lad know that!" Gilen replied, returning a smile.

A smile which faded as he rode off. It seemed strange that Miss Southford would have taken the boy with her. Here in Harrogate, he might remain cloistered at her aunt's house without being presented to Society, but at a house party his presence—and his condition—would be much more difficult to conceal.

He pulled up his mount a few streets away, unsure which way to ride. Since Jeffrey had just arrived back in town, he obviously did not know where the wench had gone.

But her other devoted suitor, Colonel Howard, probably would. And if he were not a guest at the party himself, he would most likely be congregating with his friend Colonel Haversham and the rest of Harrogate society at the Pump Room. Gilen urged his horse in that direction.

Gilen circulated through the crowd in the Pump Room, pausing to chat briefly with various acquaintances while keeping an eye out for his quarry. He had the pleasure of delivering his congratulations to Jeffrey's blushing betrothed while still managing to evade the attempts of her overbearing mother to cement his socially prominent presence at her side. Finally, his persistence was rewarded by the entrance of the two colonels, Lady Alice on the arm of Colonel Haversham.

After an exchange of compliments, Gilen deftly cut Colonel Howard from the group.

"Colonel, I'm somewhat surprised to see you here," he said once they were out of Lady Alice's earshot. "I had thought certain you would have attended the house party to which Miss Southford has gone."

A look of pique crossed the colonel's face. "I'm afraid I was not invited. Miss Southford had the courtesy to send me a note announcing her departure, otherwise I would not have been aware of the event."

"The hosts were not friends of yours, then?"

"To be frank, I do not know who the hosts are. When I inquired of Lady Alice, her response was so...garbled that I could not be quite certain of their identity."

"And she told you…"

"That Miss Southford had received a note from the friends of her cousin, whose name Lady Alice could not perfectly remember. I must admit I'm somewhat surprised by your inquiry, my lord. Lady Alice seemed to think that you, if not escorting her niece there, were to form one of the party. However, had the proprietor of your hotel not indicated to me that you had departed for Lacey's Retreat, and Lord Masterson assured me that his grandson was attending Lady Aylesbury's entertainment, I would have made…more particular inquiries about Miss Southford's destination."

From that speech, Gilen extracted the unspoken message that the colonel, after determining that neither of his rivals would be present to attempt to bedazzle Miss Southford at the country house party to which he had not been bid, had resigned himself to her absence.

"Did Miss Southford happen to mention in her note when she expected to return to Harrogate?" Gilen asked, risking arousing the colonel's suspicions with one last question.

Colonel Howard gave him a hard look. "No, she did not. May I ask, my lord, why you feel it necessary to interrogate me about Miss Southford's whereabouts?"

"No particular reason, other than that I had…anticipated seeing her upon my return, and was disappointed to find her not in Harrogate."

"There is nothing amiss, then?"

"To my knowledge, nothing beyond the fact that those of us remaining must regret the loss of her charming company."

The colonel raised an eyebrow, as if skeptical of Gilen's explanation. "To that sentiment, I can certainly agree. If you require nothing further of me, my lord?"

Gilen bowed. "My thanks for your information."

Pensive now, Gilen spent another hour mingling with the crowd, but could find no one who had seen Miss Southford recently, nor anyone with any knowledge of the house party to which she had supposedly traveled.

Why would Miss Southford have deliberately undone the illusion of their engagement and then run off to visit friends of whose existence neither he nor any of her other acquaintances in Harrogate had previously been aware? Traveling apparently without escort to an equally unknown destination?

Abandoning him without a word of her intentions, after the intimacies they'd shared?

Mystified, and a good deal more worried than when he'd arrived, he was about to depart when Lady Alice, now chatting with a dowager in a tall plumed headdress, beckoned to him.

As he approached, she pressed the arm of her companion and walked to meet him.

"My lord, I must apologize! I was so surprised to see you today that I quite forgot, but," she glanced around and lowered her voice, "Tilly later reminded me that my niece apparently sent you a note before she departed. As you were not in your rooms when the footman attempted to deliver it, he brought it back. Something about the play, I suspect, so I suppose you no longer need it. But since it *was* addressed to you, I thought you should have it. I had him take it by again this afternoon."

Relief flooded through Gilen. Surely the misdirected note would explain her absence. Though he still had half a mind to throttle the wench when next he saw her for worrying him!

Consumed with eagerness to read the missive, he thanked

Lady Alice and nearly bolted from the room, then spurred his mount at a reckless pace back to his lodgings.

He took the stairs to his chamber two at a time. To his great relief he found there, resting on his mantel, a note addressed to him in a neat feminine hand.

He ripped open the seal and began to read.

"Lord St. Abrams, I realize the declaration you made before my aunt was obtained from you under duress. Since you have made it perfectly clear that you could never entertain toward me those tender sentiments a man should hold for the lady he makes his *wife*—" the word was underlined thrice "—despite the great honor of your proposal, I must regretfully decline your offer of marriage."

Sincerely,
Gwennor Southford

With shaking fingers, Gilen turned the sheet over, but there was nothing more. Still incredulous, he searched for a nonexistent second page and then reread the whole again.

Spilling a little in his agitation, he poured himself a glass of wine and dropped into his chair.

A brief puff of anger blew through him. Her note told him nothing new. Unless she had fled Harrogate to avoid refusing him in person—the little coward!

True, he had not—at least in speech—vouchsafed to her any tender emotion, either before or after taking her off to his rooms. Indeed, remembering his words with a sting of shame, he had called her a jade and condemned her of engineering the entrapment without allowing her to utter a word in her own defense.

And though realizing, after his anger cooled, that she was

most probably as much a victim of his bungling as he was himself, he had not acknowledged that fact to her.

No, he had just assumed that becoming his bride would be the ultimate fulfillment of all her maidenly desires. That there was no need for him to—how had she put it—express any "tender sentiments" to seal the bargain.

Well, what could she have expected him to say about a woman he'd met dealing cards in a gypsy camp? That he was honored to ally his proud and ancient name to hers?

That long before the scene in the bookroom he'd been secretly pondering how he might manage to wed her without dishonoring his family completely? That he'd come to find it impossible to imagine a future that did not include one infuriating, energizing, impossibly seductive gypsy maid?

Then anger surged back. Well, if he had been unforthcoming, so had she! At least *he* had been prepared to honor the vow their bodies, if not their words, had sworn in those enchanted hours under the moonlight. How could she think he could touch her, love her, as he had, and walk away? Although *she* had had no such qualms!

Only then did the obvious conclusion strike him.

Had she not left Harrogate, custom, his declaration, and her aunt would have forced her to wed a man who had, as she justly put it, not avowed a single emotion that a man should feel for the woman he made his wife.

For some reason he could not fathom, this seemed to weigh more with Miss Southford than all the worldly advantages that would be hers as Viscountess St. Abrams.

Regardless of what Miss Southford had told Colonel Howard and her aunt before leaving town, whether she had in fact gone to a cousin or simply departed into the unknown, from somewhere deep within him surged up the powerful conviction that she would not be coming back.

But that was ridiculous, reason refuted intuition. No

gently bred lady would rattle about England, low on funds and with only her fey brother to protect her.

The uncomfortable recollection surfaced that never yet had Miss Southford acted in a normal or predictable fashion. She might even have returned to the gypsies.

Well, that was her choice, after all, he told himself. By dismissing him so summarily without conveying a syllable of her future intentions, despite the magnitude of what they'd shared, she had relieved Gilen of any further obligation toward her and absolved him of the necessity to worry about her whereabouts.

He poured the last of the wine into his glass. Apparently she'd been right after all. He *didn't* have any idea whatsoever what she'd wished to accomplish.

With Jeffrey's future now settled for better or worse, Gilen might as well return to London. Indeed, he thought, indignation swelling, he ought to be counting his blessings that he'd escaped the clutches of a woman so licentious that she could have done what Miss Southford had done to and with him in his rooms that night and walked away without a word. A proper maiden, especially a fallen one anxious to redeem her reputation, should have been chastened by her mistakes. And become doubly anxious to get a wedding ring on her finger.

Ah yes, he was ecstatic to be spared a lifetime of agitation at her irrational behavior, her needle-sharp wit…her magical touch and passionate body.

Heat coiled within him. And a stubborn, persistent anxiety that refused to be dislodged.

Damn the wench! he swore, slamming his fist down hard enough to make his glass jump and spatter wine on the table—and on her note, where it pooled like a single drop of blood on pale skin. She was neither his responsibility nor his concern.

That fact established, he jumped up and retrieved the as-yet-unpacked traveling kit, then pulled on his riding boots and called for his horse. He'd make the rounds of the posting inns to see if a woman of her description, journeying with a dark-haired stripling, had hired a carriage or booked seats on any of the mail coaches leaving Harrogate. If he were lucky, although four days had already elapsed, her trail would not yet have grown cold.

Chapter Nineteen

Gwennor sat at a table in the narrow room she'd taken with Parry in the boarding house at Hunspeth Wells, a smaller, shabbier watering spa for the elderly she'd chosen as her destination upon quitting Harrogate. The employment agent she'd consulted this morning had listened to her qualifications for the post she sought, as a housekeeper or a companion to an elderly invalid, and invited her to return tomorrow after she completed an application and unpacked her letter of reference.

A letter that she, after a stop at the bookshop for ink and velum of suitable quality, had just finished composing in the guise of Harry's mother, her aunt Frances.

Gwennor Southford, how low you have fallen, she thought, re-reading the compendium of fiction and carefully altered fact she had written to confirm the story she'd related to Mr. Hardwicke this morning. With murmurs of sympathy at the appropriate intervals, he'd listened to the tale of her father's death and the sad lack of dowry that rendered a marriage impossible. Lifted an eyebrow at her flat statement that a disagreement with her cousin—without a qualm she'd strongly hinted of an immoral proposal— made remaining in the home of her birth unendurable. And nodded sagely, with expressions of regret that such situations occurred all too frequently, at her contention that, possessing neither the training nor the temperament to hire out as a governess, her best skills lay in managing a household and caring for an invalid. Skills, she'd assured Mr. Hardwicke, that her aunt, though having no use for such, had been pleased to vouch for in order that Gwennor might find genteel employment.

Forgive me, Aunt Frances, she thought as she affixed that lady's signature to the bottom of the letter.

Perhaps, while she was spinning untruths, she should pen a note to Aunt Alice and inform her the house party had been extended. That would allow her time to find a situation, after which, she thought wryly, she would compose a final bit of fallacious nonsense about her cousin possessing a dear old relative in need of a companion and Gwennor not having the heart to refuse tending the invalid for the few short weeks or months until her demise.

Who could have thought that she would find within what she'd previously believed to be her rather plain, practical, prosaic self such a propensity to vice? To her previous sins of wantonness and immoderation, she'd now added deliberately deceiving the aunt who had sheltered her, impersonation of the other aunt who had always been kind to her, making false statements on her application for employment and forging documents.

In addition to which, she had also jilted a viscount. Although could it be considered jilting when the betrothal to which one was calling a halt had been entered into under duress?

An uncomfortable tightness compressed her chest when she thought of St. Abrams, as she did all too frequently. Was he still celebrating his deliverance, or, knowing his friend to be now safe from her machinations, had he returned to the greater diversions of London?

And did he depart still believing her an unprincipled jade? Or had "relinquishing her pretensions" to both himself and Mr. Masterson finally shown him she possessed an honor as fierce and uncompromising as his own?

Too much honor to accept the proposal of a man who wanted her as his wanton but not as his wife.

And even had he loved her, too much honor to allow the ancient and unblemished name he bore to be besmirched by the scandalous actions desperation had forced her to take.

He would not miss the dishonorable wench he believed had tried to entrap his friend. Would he miss the wanton who had danced for him and made love to him and gifted him with her maidenhead?

For the first few days after her departure, she'd wondered if he might come after her. Though she'd been discreet, now that she'd ceased to worry that cousin Nigel might be hot on her trail, she had not attempted to leave Harrogate in complete secrecy. With a bit of persistence, anyone who truly wished to could have discovered from the agent at the posting inn that she and Parry had left on the mail coach north.

But for a man as handsome and wealthy as St. Abrams, wantons—and fiancées—were as easily replaced as obtained. He'd not miss a love he couldn't possibly want and a gift he would never know he'd been given. Her cleverness in warning him in advance that she was near her woman's time would have explained away any questions he might have had about the bloodstains on the sheets.

But she would have the memory of their night together burning bright through the coldness of all the cold winters to come.

For a moment, a glimpse into the bleakness of the future staggered her. Angrily she dashed away a tear. *I will never regret that night.* And if she did regret the bitter fact that she could never share a life with him, as she'd told him, her expectations no longer included a peerless knight on a white destrier galloping to her rescue.

She should feel a sense of freedom, actually. Her whole life had been circumscribed by the men in it, defined first by her duties to her father, then her need to seek a husband to protect herself and her brother. Now that she had thrown away all chance of the latter, her future—and his—depended on her skills and efforts alone, not on the whims of a cousin or the opinions of a viscount.

Gwennor Southford, architect of her own fate.

And what a glorious fate it would be, she thought with a self-mocking grin. As a genteel housekeeper, lower than the governess yet forever apart from the staff, or a companion to some individual so contentious even the most indigent of relatives had been unwilling to tend them.

But as long as she could settle with Parry someplace in the country, where he might train horses and watch over his beloved animals, she would be satisfied. With good honest labor to perform and Parry's affection, she could be content.

Apparently not so perfected in vice as to be able to convince herself of a falsehood, at that pleasant prospect, she put her face in her hands and wept.

Enough mawkishness, Gwennor Southford, she commanded herself a few moments later. *You've chosen your bed; now finish Mr. Hardwicke's papers so you may begin arranging the linens.*

A knock sounded at the door. Anticipation jolting through her body, she dropped the pen, making a blot on Aunt Frances's spurious letter of recommendation.

It will not be St. Abrams, she admonished silently. Cursing herself for the ridiculous hope that, despite her best efforts to squelch it, still seemed to burn deep within her, she mopped up the ink.

'Twas only Parry, returning from visiting the horses in the stables, or the landlady on an errand. Sternly willing her heartbeat to slow, she bade the caller enter.

And then leapt to her feet, shock and gladness coursing through her as she threw herself into the tall young man's eager embrace. "Harry!" she cried.

In the afternoon three days later, mud-spattered and weary, Gilen rode toward the small town of Hunspeth Wells. It had taken him the better part of the first morning to canvass the coaching inns within and adjacent to Harrogate before he discovered, after hard questioning and a flow of gold coins, that a couple matching the description of Miss Southford and her stepbrother had departed on a mail coach bound for the Great North Road. Stopping by his rooms briefly, he had his startled valet pack another saddlebag while he stuffed his purse with as much cash as it would hold. Then, despite the man's sensible recommendation that he not depart until the morrow, he'd collected his mount and in the waning afternoon daylight, galloped out of Harrogate.

But as the clerk at the posting inn, even after a second trickle of coinage, had not been able to recall to which destination the travelers were bound, he'd been forced to halt and make inquiries at each town the coach stopped at to ascertain whether or not the two passengers had broken their journey. Chilled to the bone and weary after nearly eighteen hours in the saddle on a variety of job horses, none of them smooth of pace or light of mouth, he'd finally decided to rest last night at an inn.

But despite his fatigue, his sleep was troubled by fleeting images of Miss Southford, out of funds and on foot, trudging along the post road. Miss Southford accosted by a smooth-talking rogue who offered her a carriage ride into the next town, promising to return later for her brother. Miss Southford, having to hire herself out as a cook or dishwasher—or something worse—to provide them with food and shelter.

Miss Southford, ill, frozen and exhausted, collapsing in a hedgerow beside the Great North Road.

To the pounding of the horse's hooves as he rode out today, he heard the reproving voice of his dead father wondering how on earth his son had allowed matters to proceed to such a stand.

All I wanted was to protect Jeffrey, Papa, he tried to explain. *Well, yes, I wanted the wench, too. Ah, Papa, if you could have seen her dance!* Suddenly recalling with whom he was conversing, he continued hurriedly, *I never wanted to cause her injury—quite the contrary! Well, I know I offered her carte blanche, but you could hardly have wished me to tender marriage to a gypsy cardsharp, even after I determined she was also a lady of quality. Though in the eyes of the family, she could not truly be the latter if she were also the former, could she? Even so—sorry, Papa, for disappointing you—I'm now convinced I must marry her. Now, I know in trying to safeguard Jeff I was also planning to betray him, and to win Miss Southford I was willing to trick her aunt and bribe her maid and blackmail her with her aunt's debts and then, ah, kidnap her to my rooms—*

—*And hound her clear out of Harrogate,* his father reminded him.

Right. Dash it, Papa, I can't really explain why, in trying to accomplish so noble a purpose, I've committed such rep-

rehensible and irrational deeds, like a veritable simpleton or…or…

A man in love, the shade of his sire pronounced with exasperation.

No, surely not that! he argued back. *Though I know nothing about the estate, having never been in love, I'm not sighing over her eyebrows or writing wretched verse in her honor or praising her to the utter boredom of all my acquaintance. Indeed, we can scarcely be together a quarter hour without clashing. She often irritates me exceedingly, although she can also be fierce and brave and determined and brilliant and—no, we shall not discuss the bedchamber. And so reckless and independent she needs a keeper.*

Only a man crazy in love would connive, lie, betray and abduct to be with the gel. Or dash off without a word to anyone to fetch her back, his father replied.

That's not love, that's insanity, Gilen objected.

Same thing, his father replied testily. *Son, just find the wench, marry her, get on with generating the next generation and let me and your poor ancestors return to snoozing peacefully in our tombs.*

In love. He was in love with Gwennor Southford? But who was he to argue with the shade of his esteemed father?

Gilen pulled up his mount and took a moment from jolting on the back of the particularly sorry-gaited job horse to consider the singular notion.

The idea was strange and yet not nearly as terrifying as he'd always imagined it would be when he finally encountered the woman who convinced him to become a tenant for life. It felt—comforting, actually, as if after riding a hard and difficult road, he'd made it home to a warm fire, a hot meal and a snug bed.

Ah, yes, bed. He grinned, reliving the astounding moments he'd spent arriving in it with his vixen.

Did she love him in return? His smug certainty faltered a bit. Surely she would not have come with him as she had if she did not feel some answering emotion. And the virtual sparks that struck between them whenever they were together were certainly mutual.

She already responded to his touch, and, note be damned, must still hope to find the settled security of marriage. Besides, according to that note, all that had prevented her accepting his somewhat irregular suit the first time had been a want of "tender sentiments."

Supplying them must be the key to convincing Miss Southford to accept him for good.

Od's blood, he decided, spurring the horse, between now and the moment he discovered her, he'd compose enough scintillating phrases to dazzle her right to the altar.

But when the hours continued to pass and still he did not catch up with her, his initial confidence dissipated and the underlying anxiety that had destroyed his sleep returned to plague him. When he at last pulled up his exhausted mount at the posting inn at Hunspeth Wells, he'd decided to stop only long enough to rest a bit and eat before setting out again, haunted by that recurring image of her lying lifeless beside the highway.

So accustomed was he by now to receiving negative responses to his inquiries about Miss Southford, after he'd delivered his request for a hot meal and a warm bath along with the description of the travelers he sought, Gilen almost didn't attend to the clerk's response. The man reanimated his weary body and sagging spirits by informing him that two such passengers had indeed disembarked from the mail coach several days previous. The man was even able to hazard a guess as to where the travelers had gone, passing on the information that he'd overheard the young lady ask the innkeeper where she might find genteel accommodations.

Pressing a fistful of coins into the hands of the astounded and grateful clerk, he asked the man to send up the direction of the rooming house along with hot food and water. He'd bolt down a meal, don some clean garments, and go to her.

His spirits—and other things—rose at the heady thought of soon confronting her again. Would she be astonished to see him? Or would the minx throw him a saucy look and wonder what had taken him so long to find her?

A bare half hour later, Gilen stood before the small pier glass, tying a fresh cravat and rehearsing his speech.

Miss Southford, you must have been aware for some time of the steadily increasing strength of my emotions. Nice enough beginning, he thought, settling his chin and creasing the intricate linen folds into a perfect Mathematical.

I suppose, given my less-than-honorable behavior— might as well admit fault where fault was—*you might have considered I regarded you with enmity, but I assure you, from the very first I've found you irresistible. I know my initial offer cannot have been pleasing—*he grinned at the memory of her sharp right hook—*but even that was merely testament to the intensity of the sentiments you evoke in me. My lovely, intelligent, bewitching and altogether enchanting Miss Southford, I cannot conceive of living without you.*

In short, he shrugged into his coat and began walking down the stairs, *I love you, Gwennor.*

He had to practice several times as he walked to her rooming house before managing to get his lips around that still-daunting phrase, but it was growing easier with each attempt. When he at last confronted her, he hoped it would slip facilely off his tongue, as well as the requisite follow-on: *Miss Southford, will you do me the honor of granting me your hand in marriage?*

Whereupon—he envisioned this scene with relish—she would confess her own love, fall into his arms, and bewitch him with her kiss.

Wouldn't she?

He glanced at the scrap of paper that denoted the location of the rooming house. The two-story dwelling before him must be it. Squelching his doubts, he hurried up the front stairs.

The landlady, a Mrs. Ames, answered his knock and ushered him in.

"I'm Mr. de Mowbry, ma'am, come seeking my cousins, Miss Southford and her stepbrother Mr. Wakefield," he began. *Just this one last falsehood, Papa.* "Shortly after they set off on their journey, our dear uncle died. The will is to be read soon, and the attorney felt it essential that they both be present."

Mrs. Ames's eyes brightened. "A bequest, is it?"

"I'm not certain, ma'am. 'Tis highly likely, which is why it's imperative that I return with them at once. The innkeeper of the Rose and Crown believed that they had taken rooms here."

"And so they had. A fine, genteel young lady she was, and her brother such a quiet, polite lad."

"Indeed. If you would show me up, ma'am?" He discreetly slipped a coin into her hand.

Mrs. Ames shook her head and handed it back. "Now, if'n you'd have asked me that two days ago, I'da been happy to take your money, sir, but 'tis too late."

"They—have left?" Damn and blast! Consternation warred with frustration in his breast.

"Aye, sir. Though I think that lawyer musta told her sweetheart as well, for he was here before you."

The excitement that had filled him soured in his gut. "S-sweetheart?" Gilen repeated.

"So handsome he was in his regimentals, and as honey-lipped as they come! I do swear, by the time he gathered their belongings and led them away—paid me for a whole month's rent, too, though they'd been here less than a week—I was half in love with the charming devil myself. Off they went, all arm-in-arm. 'Twas so romantical, I thought I'd weep."

"M-Miss Southford went off arm-in-arm with…a soldier?" Gilen repeated, shaking his head to make sure he was hearing the woman aright.

"Aye, sir. She and her brother, this two days past."

There must be some mistake. Miss Southford couldn't have left with a soldier. Arm-in-arm or any way! Gilen loved her—and she'd loved him in return!

But standing before him was not Gwennor Southford, radiant with happiness that he'd come for her, but the little landlady who'd just related a tale he had no reason not to believe, and who continued to eye him curiously, sharp gaze focused and chin angled up.

Anger rose in him like fog over cold ground, fueled by fatigue, disappointment—and hurt. It still seemed incredible she could have so deceived him, yet with her departure from here all the puzzling facts fell so neatly in place.

Why she'd had to leave her home and travel with gypsies. Why she'd tarried in Harrogate apparently looking for a husband.

Why she'd refused Gilen de Mowbry's heart and hand.

"Be the soldier a friend of yourn, sir?" the landlady asked, interrupting his black thoughts.

"N-no, ma'am." *He's a filthy deceiving blackguard—whoever he is,* Gilen fumed silently.

Or was it that deceitful jade he ought to be cursing?

Numbly he fished two more coins from his pocket and pressed them into the landlady's hand along with the first one she'd spurned.

"For your trouble, ma'am. A good day to you."

"You too, sir." Mrs. Ames dropped him a curtsey. "I hope you catch up with your cousins."

If I do, she's a dead woman, he thought, and stomped out.

Damn her, damn her, damn her! he cursed as he walked back to the inn. He'd spent the better part of a week worrying over her, arguing with his father over claiming her, missing her, aching for her touch and the sound of her voice.

While she was happily journeying to meet her lover.

A house party indeed! No wonder the jade had left without telling her aunt or anyone else in decent society where she was actually going. Had she ever been truly interested in garnering an offer of marriage while in Harrogate? Or had she merely been trifling with her assorted suitors whilst awaiting the return of her soldier boy?

Immediately after leaving *his* bed and *his* arms.

What the name of her mysterious soldier-lover might be, Gilen had no idea, though it seemed obvious this must be the man who'd seduced her back in Wales. Gilen sent a silent apology to the new Baron Southford. In any event, it made no difference now.

Miss Southford had made her choice.

With this business concluded and Jeffrey engaged, Gilen might as well get some sleep and then return directly to London.

But after he'd ascended to his room and settled into bed, despite his fatigue, sleep would not come.

Images of Miss Southford teased his mind. Her indignant violet eyes over the saffron veil when he'd bandied words with her in the gypsy camp. The fire in her expression—and the power of her fist—when she'd hit him after he first offered her carte blanche. Her ferocity as she brandished her whip, protecting her brother. Her tenderness as she stroked his face. Her heated touch as she claimed his mouth and welcomed him into her body.

Damnation! he swore again, punching his pillow and then burying his face in it to shut out the memories. He would think on her no more.

But a pain keen as a toothache seemed to have settled in his chest and refused to be dislodged, no matter what position he assumed on the bed.

After fifteen minutes of thrashing about, he sat up, rang for the innkeeper, and sent for a bottle of brandy.

If he couldn't order himself to sleep, he'd drink himself asleep.

First thing in the morning he'd resume his journey—back to the delights of London. For if this misery was what being in love entailed, he wanted nothing further to do with the sorry business.

Chapter Twenty

In the late afternoon three weeks later, Gilen wandered through the library of his London town house, restless and out of sorts. A silver tray left by the butler on his desk contained a stack of invitation cards, none of which he'd bothered to open.

He'd already attended too many of the same dull entertainments, full of chattering matrons, insipid virgins vying for his notice, and drunken dandies peacocking about in their overbright plumage.

Perhaps he'd go spend the evening at his club. There might be some intelligent conversation to be had. Or if not, the card play was diverting, the dinners excellent and the wine even more exceptional.

Calling for a footman to summon him a hackney, he went to gather his coat and cane.

It being not yet evening, White's was rather thin of company when he entered. Ordering a bottle of claret, he settled into the reading room to peruse the latest papers.

He skimmed the top page idly, until a notice about the Prince of Wales caught his eye, and his chest tightened.

Had she truly been Miss Gwennor Southford, daughter of the late Baron Southford of Southford Manor, Wales?

He'd never even learned that for certain. Perhaps she really was naught but a gypsy princess who'd bewitched him on that never-to-be-sufficiently-regretted night.

Or was it their last few hours together—an experience that still haunted his dreams and made him wake yearning for the scent of her, the taste of her skin—the occasion he should most regret?

Damn, he would not let the wretched jade invade his thoughts again. He'd already spent far too many hours of the last three weeks alternately furious, wistful and wondering.

Had there been something else he could have done or not done? Something that would have made the magic linger—for he could not believe she had not been bewitched as well by the spell that had held him captive through that magical night—long enough for him to return to Harrogate and stop her from leaving.

No, he would not wonder again if she were still with her soldier, perhaps traveling with him on a packet bound for the Peninsula.

Bold, adventurous and independent, she'd make a splendid soldier's wife, he had to admit. And any man would count his blessings to know her ardent spirit and clever hands awaited him in his tent at the end of the day's march.

With a growl, he slammed the paper down on the table.

"Is the news that bad?"

Startled, Gilen looked up—into the face of one of his former Oxford mates. "Beau Bradsleigh! I didn't know you were in town!"

"Just arrived. I understand you're recently returned after visiting old Lord Masterson in Harrogate. Doing well, is he?"

"Still holding his own."

"And Jeff? Has he recovered yet from that fiasco with the Battersley chit?"

Gilen smiled wryly. "I suppose. He's just gotten himself engaged."

Beau laughed. "Again? Should I drink to his happiness, or wait to see how long this one lasts?"

"No, I believe this time the betrothal will stick. Mary Anne Aylesbury's the girl. Dreadful mother, but well-bred on her father's side."

Beau nodded. "Not a brilliant match, but he's got money enough of his own and no need for social connections. We must drink to their health! Order us a bottle, will you, while I go arrange for dinner."

"Did your wife not accompany you?"

"No, I shan't be long in the city, and though feeling quite well, she's not yet fully recovered from young Hugh's birth. I didn't wish her to tire herself with the journey when my stay will be so short."

"My belated congratulations on the safe arrival of your heir."

His friend grinned. "Thank you. Yet another reason to raise a glass. Although you're looking rather down pin. Why not break your evening engagements and dine with me? I promise to cheer you up."

"I've no engagements to break, and will be delighted to have your company."

Beau raised an eyebrow. "The eminently eligible Viscount St. Abrams has no evening engagements? Has London been evacuated? Or did a plague carry off every hostess in the ton?" he asked with a grin.

Gilen merely shrugged.

His friend's smile faded, to be replaced by a penetrating look that belatedly reminded Gilen no one had ever been able to keep secrets from Beau "The Puzzlebreaker" Bradsleigh. Perhaps dining with him wasn't so wise after all.

Or maybe it was. A spark of excitement glowed in his chest. Beau had connections through the whole of England. If Gilen directed the conversation aright, he might at last be able to discover the truth about Miss Southford. And once he knew it, perhaps then he'd finally be able to banish her bewitching memory from his heart and mind.

"Do pour us a glass," his friend was saying. "I'll be back directly."

By the time Beau returned, Gilen had decided he might as well make his inquiry openly, without trying to finesse the matter, and spare himself the embarrassment of Beau puzzling out the sorry facts bit by bit. So, after the wine had been poured, and the usual inquiries made about relatives and acquaintances, he said without further preamble, "Do you have family or friends in Wales?"

Beau slid him a quizzical look. "No. Why do you ask?"

Conscious of an irrational disappointment, Gilen said, "No matter. In Harrogate I encountered some members from a Welsh family—at least, I believe they were Welsh— and was curious about their background."

"I see." For a long moment, his friend studied him. Gilen felt his face heat. "Is it important to you?" Beau asked at last.

"No," Gilen answered quickly. "Well, perhaps." He took a sip from his glass and tapped his fingers on the fragile stem. "Yes, I suppose it is."

"Then I should take you with me to see Lord Riverton. I was planning on stopping by before dinner anyway, and he has quite extensive Welsh connections."

"Riverton? I doubt he'd even remember me, and I don't wish to intrude."

"Nonsense. Once a Balliol man, always a Balliol man.

I'm sure he'll be delighted to receive you. And if anyone in England can answer an inquiry about family connections, 'twill be him.''

Gilen ought to refuse. It really wasn't important any longer. He'd already lost the wench. But a deep need to know the truth, even though it was now too late to do anything about it, kept him silent.

While Gilen struggled to resist the temptation to agree, Beau snagged a passing footman. ''Lord St. Abrams and I are leaving. Bring our coats, please.''

When Gilen started to protest, Beau waved him to silence. ''Come along. Perhaps after Riverton answers your questions, you'll be better company.''

And so, less than an hour later, Gilen followed Beau up the front steps of Lord Riverton's town house on North Audley Street. Gilen was only slightly acquainted with the viscount, an older and very distinguished Oxford college mate who held a cabinet portfolio in the Tory government. But apparently Beau was on more intimate terms with the great man than Gilen had realized, for after greeting the butler affably and ascertaining from him the viscount's whereabouts, his friend waved the servant away and bade Gilen follow him to the library.

After a brief knock, they entered to find Riverton seated at his desk, gazing pensively at a small object which he put aside as they approached. It was, Gilen noted with some curiosity when they reached him, a miniature of a beautiful blond lady with striking blue eyes.

After an exchange of greetings, Beau said, ''St. Abrams needed some information about a Welsh family, my lord, and I took the liberty of advising him you were the best person from whom to seek it. With your permission, I'll leave you to the discussion and go study the excellent collection in your document room.''

"As you wish, Beau," Riverton replied.

"Until later, then." Beau gave Riverton a bow.

As Beau walked out, their host turned to him. "So, St. Abrams, what did you wish to know?"

Pulled from speculating over his friend's relationship with the cabinet minister, Gilen redirected his attention to the gnawing uncertainty he wished to alleviate.

"While in Harrogate, I became acquainted with a friend of Lord Masterson's, Lady Alice Winnerly, and some of her family who were visiting from Wales."

"Ah, yes, the Southfords. Rather a scandal there, though the family attempted to hush it up."

A bolt of excitement jolted through Gilen. So Riverton knew them after all!

"S-so I understood," he stammered.

"How did you learn of it?"

"I became acquainted with the young lady—Miss Southford, whom I'd initially met under somewhat…unusual circumstances."

Riverton's unexpected crack of laughter made Gilen jump. "So it *is* true! I must admit, the man who told me of it often has so much of Irish blarney in his tongue, I'm not always sure I can believe everything he says. What a magnificent, enterprising young woman! She told you the whole story, then?"

Riverton thought her…magnificent? Not sure what to make of that, Gilen replied cautiously, "Only some of it."

Riverton sighed. "I'm afraid Nigel Hartwell is not one of our more illustrious examples of British nobility. Did she describe his scheme to you?"

All Gilen's forebodings returned. So the baron had played a role in her ruination after all! Damn the black-hearted bastard for forcing his kinswoman into the arms of that soldier! "No," he gritted out. "Would you explain?"

"As you seem to have developed some intimacy with the family, I suppose doing so will break no confidences." Riverton tapped his fingers on the desk. "Coming into the title already deeply under the hatches, Hartwell hit upon a ploy to dispose of the former baron's daughter whilst using her dowry to pay off some of his own debts, an arrangement that might, unfortunately, have worked, had he not also planned to sacrifice the lady's stepbrother in the process. You met Mr. Wakefield, I presume?"

"Yes. He seemed a pleasant and harmless young man."

"So you must have observed how zealously Miss Southford looks out for the boy's well-being."

Gilen heard again the whine of a horsewhip, and smiled. "I did indeed."

"Hartwell planned to marry the girl off to a crony to whom he owed money, but knowing the intended bridegroom would not agree to housing the stepbrother, decided to keep the boy at Southford—locked up in the attics. And was ill-advised enough to threaten Miss Southford with the same if she resisted his plans."

"The blackguard!" Gilen cried. Why had Miss Southford never confided this to him? His gaze whipped back to the earl.

"May I ask how you learned of this, my lord?"

The viscount shrugged. "I'm possessed of numerous relations scattered across England—all of whom thrive upon gossip."

Riverton chuckled again. "Hartwell did not reckon on the tenacity and boldness of Miss Southford. As I expect you know, within the space of a few hours she executed a brilliant maneuver that spirited the two of them away from Southford in such a manner that her cousin was never able to trace them. Traveling with gypsies, of all things! You can imagine the dust-up when the happy bridegroom arrived a day later to find his bride—and her dowry—missing. By heaven, I wish I knew more individuals with her ingenuity and daring! Were she a man, I swear I'd offer her a position on my staff.''

She'd run away—to save her brother? Knowing her, Gilen had to admit that made perfect sense. ''Yes, she's very...unusual.''

''I'd heard she ended up at Harrogate under the protection of her aunt, who was attempting to arrange a more suitable marriage for her. Indeed, was she not almost on the point of receiving an offer from your friend Mr. Masterson?''

''Yes, I—I believe she was.'' Gilen's hands began to sweat. Riverton seemed uncomfortably well-informed. Just how much more did he know?

''And then she suddenly quit the city with very little explanation, traveling alone but for her brother. A foolish and rather dangerous thing to have done, wouldn't you agree? Thank heaven for the intervention of her *other* cousin—Major 'Heedless Harry' Hartwell, one of Wellington's staff and an Oxford man. Rather younger than you and Beau, so I doubt you met him there. At any rate, knowing the character of their cousin Nigel, once Harry heard of the former baron's death he took leave and set sail for England to insure that Miss Southford's interests were protected. Fortunately he managed to trace her after she'd fled Harrogate before anything untoward occurred. And before she hired herself out as some sort of housekeeper, which had apparently been her intent.''

So handsome he was in his regimentals...gathered their belongings... Off they went, all arm-in-arm...

All *three* of them. The soldier was her cousin—not her lover. For a moment Gilen thought he would be sick.

He looked back up to see Riverton regarding him with

an air of concern. "Have I said something distressing, St. Abrams?"

"N-no, on the contrary, I'm...reassured. I had known the young lady left Harrogate suddenly and was... concerned for her." Gilen's words trailed off and he stared sightlessly at the bookshelves, trying to grasp the enormity of his misconceptions.

"Was she perchance angry with you when she left?"

He whipped his gaze back to Riverton. "She m-might have been."

As if involuntarily, Riverton's eyes flickered to the miniature on the corner of his desk. "Women," he sighed.

Too numb to speak, Gilen merely nodded.

"At least, being acquainted with the lady, I trust you were able to avoid falling into the erroneous but common generalization our class is apt to make about gypsies."

Another flicker of alarm shook Gilen. "Generalization?"

"Yes, the one that claims all their women to be wanton." Riverton chuckled again. "My good friend Teagan Fitzwilliams, who, like most Irish rogues, has an alarming penchant for low company, traveled with them once and nearly got his liver cut out when he attempted to become overly familiar with the lass who was telling his fortune. Despite the freedom their culture allows them in dress and manner, the wenches are, Teagan reports, chaste as nuns. But then, you already knew that."

Gilen smiled weakly. "Of course."

"Naturally, given the unfortunate prejudice so widely prevailing in our Society, you intend to keep your knowledge of Miss Southford's presence among the gypsies a secret. The, ah, relation who passed the story along to me was quite insistent on its remaining absolutely in confidence. 'Twould cause quite a scandal should the tale emerge, and I should hate to see so excellent and resourceful a young lady suffer for precisely the qualities that make her unique.''

"Naturally." Memories of a star-splendid night overcame him, the sibilant swish of long skirts and jangle of bracelets under a wail of violins. The wine-heady taste of her lips—and the vicious curve of the blades pointed at him by the gypsy men as their leader pulled him away.

He jerked back to the present to find Lord Riverton watching him.

"In case you should wish to inform the young lady of your relief at her safe homecoming, I understand Major Hartwell escorted his cousins back to his estate in Llanarth. About a day's ride out of Abergarenny, I believe."

"Th-thank you, my lord. Perhaps I shall send her a note."

Riverton smiled. "A lady as stalwart and resourceful as Miss Southford is likely to require a bit more persuasion than could be conveyed in a letter. May I wish you a safe journey to Wales, and good luck. I rather expect you'll need it."

The magnitude of his erroneous assumptions still taking shape in his disbelieving brain, Gilen had difficulty managing an answer. "Thank you again, my lord, for your very…interesting information."

Still dazed, he stumbled toward the door. As he paused on the threshold to make his final bow, he was suddenly swept with a strong, inexplicable conviction that Lord Riverton had known the whole of his story before ever Gilen had spoken a word. That the viscount had spun out the tale merely for his own amusement.

The viscount must possess a damnably knowledgeable family!

He opened his mouth to demand if that were true, then closed it. No point looking any more the fool.

The viscount flashed him an enigmatic smile.

Gilen returned a slight nod, made his bow and fled.

As he walked out, his rattled brain kept tossing up bits from Riverton's conversation. Rather than thinking her ruined by having traveled with the gypsies, the viscount—a most influential member of the ton—had pronounced Miss Southford "enterprising," "ingenious" and "daring" to have defied her cousin and averted his plans, saving her half brother from an ignoble fate.

And so she was—all those things. Not until he'd exited the town house, however, did the most awful of realizations hit him.

If the company in which she'd traveled hadn't been wanton, and if Miss Southford had left her ancestral home still a maid—then the man who had debauched her wasn't her loathsome cousin Nigel or the handsome soldier who'd carried her off from the boarding house.

No, the seducer who had claimed her maidenhead was the wrong-headed, dictatorial Viscount St. Abrams.

In precise detail, the memory returned of the moment he'd claimed her—her sharp intake of breath, her arms braced against his entry. Her now all-too-understandable hesitation. Another wave of consternation swept him.

As if everything he knew of her life were shapes in a kaleidoscope that had just been shaken anew, the pieces he'd thought to have fitted together so neatly now fell into a radically different, but no less coherent, pattern.

Her reluctance to dance for him. Her outrage at his immoral proposal and her hurt at his assumption of her dishonesty. Her fury at being called a jade, and the quiet withdrawal that night in his rooms, as she must have realized the enormity of what he'd done to her—what she'd allowed him to do.

Why *had* she allowed it?

The villainy he'd perpetrated against her staggered him. Offering carte blanche to a virginal lady of quality, persecuting her to accept it, insulting her virtue and finally seducing her out of her it.

And yet…she must have known, even after he'd forced her into that hackney to take her to his rooms, that had she asked him to, he would have returned her to her aunt's house untouched. Regardless of his misconceptions of her character and her background, he never would have forced himself on her.

Instead of pleading with him to reconsider, she had requested his kiss. Without a word of protest, she'd begun the dance he begged for. And when that was done, 'twas she who had invited him to dance again.

Given what he now knew of her purity, surely she would not have done any of those things if her heart, as well as her senses, were not fully engaged. She must truly love Gilen de Mowbry—not the soldier over whom he'd been suffering torments of jealousy since the moment he'd quit her boarding house in Hunspeth Wells.

Love him, he realized suddenly, too much to entrap him into marriage. Too much to tolerate a lifetime with a man who'd railed at her for being something she was not, calling her a wanton, a deceiver, a jade.

Since you have made it perfectly clear that you could never entertain toward me those tender sentiments a man should hold for the lady he makes his wife…

He'd been an arrogant, ignorant, presumptuous fool, full of errant assumptions as he pursued his skewed but noble goal of rescuing Jeffrey. But surely she realized that, too, or she would have despised, rather than responded to him.

The fact that she had responded, in spite of all the wrongs he'd done her, must mean she cared deeply. And so there must still be some chance for him to undo all the damage he'd inflicted and win her back.

It seemed, as Lord Riverton had predicted, he was about to journey to Wales. And he did not intend to return until he had somehow managed, with tender sentiments as eloquent and devoted deeds as noble as he could devise, to convince the amazing, unforgettable Gwennor Southford that she held his heart and must now accept his hand.

Ten days later, Gilen stood in the parlor at Hartwell Hall to await the arrival of the master of the house, Major Hartwell. The man he'd thought to be Gwennor's lover. A mixture of embarrassment and jealousy still heated his face at the thought.

And then the major himself walked in. "Lord St. Abrams?" The officer leveled an assessing look at him. "With what can I assist you, sir?"

As the landlady had reported, the major was handsome, and carried himself with that air of assurance forged in men required to make swift and deadly decisions in the turmoil of combat. Now that he knew the fellow to be Miss Southford's *cousin*, Gilen decided he liked him. After all, the major had returned from the Peninsula to look after her interests. Gilen could not help but applaud that.

Especially since he had done such a bad job of it himself.

"I am an…acquaintance of Miss Southford, from Harrogate, and wished to call on her, if you would be so kind as to furnish me her direction."

For another long moment the major subjected Gilen to that same penetrating stare. Finally he nodded. "You must be the missing link, then."

Gilen frowned. "I beg your pardon?"

The major crossed his arms and regarded Gilen frostily. "I could readily believe that cousin Gwen, whom I've known since she was a babe, would have the perspicacity to organize an escape and the temerity to embrace a means no ordinary maiden would dream of employing. But she's also practical and prone to facing facts, however unpleasant. One of which, in our society, dictates that the only means for a young woman to establish herself is through marriage.

"So I found it most odd that, despite being assured I'd frank a Season and insure she has dowry enough to please any man of her choice, she adamantly refused to go to London. Or Bath or Gloucester or even back to Aunt Alice in Harrogate. In fact, she insisted on using her inheritance to purchase a horse farm where she could settle with Parry and live quietly out of Society."

"A horse farm? Where, may I ask?"

In lieu of answering, the major startled Gilen by beginning to unbuckle his sword belt. "Until I figured out the riddle, I thought it best to acquiesce. But since I know quite well she doesn't abhor men in general, I suspected the explanation must lie in her relationship with one particular man."

The major laid his weapon on the sofa and under Gilen's astounded gaze, began to unfasten his collar lacings. "A man who, when I found him, I knew I should have to offer, if not the pistol ball or the edge of cold steel I'd prefer, at least the worst punishment my fists could deliver."

He tossed his shoulder belt after the sword and turned to Gilen. "I expect you're that man. Before I administer the thrashing you so rightly deserve, have you anything to say for yourself?"

Finally comprehending, Gilen started on the knot of his own cravat. "I love your cousin. And I intend to marry her."

"That's good for a start," the major replied, tugging at the buttons on his scarlet regimentals. "Anything else?"

"Were I in your shoes," Gilen said, pulling off the cravat and preparing to struggle out of his jacket, "I'm sure I should feel the same. In fact, I doubt fists would be sufficient. I'd probably insist on swords or pistols."

"Ah, but a duel would engender doubt about my cousin's honor. If we wish to pry her away from the absurd notion of wasting herself running a farm, we must avoid that."

Finally succeeding in freeing himself from the clinging coat, Gilen heaved it on top of the major's shoulder belt and sword. "Such affairs can be hushed up."

The major raised his eyebrows. "Is that a challenge?"

"'Tis what I deserve," Gilen retorted, casting aside his waistcoat and rolling up his sleeves. "But no, that's not correct. I expect only the fiery pits of hell could deliver what I truly deserve."

The major nodded, as if pleased with that answer. "Once I've beaten you to a bloody pulp, what do you intend to do?"

"Pummel you until you tell me where Gwennor is."

The major dragged a side table away and motioned at Gilen to roll up the carpet. "And why would I do that?"

"I told you—I intend to make her my wife."

"I can understand you feel a need to redeem your honor by marrying her, but Gwennor wouldn't have left Harrogate if that had been reason enough for her."

Gilen uttered a deep sigh. "If you must know, duty and honor have virtually nothing to do with it. I…I have to marry her! I tried, before I learned what a grave injustice I'd done her, to forget about her. I went back to London, immersed myself in activity, even tried to interest myself in other women—both honest and the more obliging sorts.

But 'twas no use. The witch has rather ruined *my* life! Entertainments bore me, other company annoys me—the memory of her bedevils me even in sleep. I must have her, wed her, or go I'll go mad.''

The major smiled. "Excellent," he said, and slammed his fist into Gilen's nose.

The major possessed a punishing left hook, but as a skilled veteran of the sparring at Gentleman Jackson's, Gilen was able—usually—to successfully parry it and send home a right uppercut. The match continued roughly even, until with a particularly lusty blow, Gilen managed to knock the major off balance. Blinded on his left side by a cut trickling blood into his eye, Hartwell careened into a side table and went down.

But, with his ears still ringing, and nauseous after his opponent's last superbly successful left hook, the momentum of his swing carried Gilen off balance as well. He tripped over the major's boots and landed on the floor beside him.

For a few moments there was no sound in the salon but their panting gasps and the crash of splintering crockery as the assortment of Chinese vases on the damaged side table slid one by one to the floor.

Finally, with a groan, Major Hartwell hauled himself upright. Grabbing Gilen's wrinkled cravat from the sofa, he mopped the blood out of his eyes and offered Gilen a hand up.

"I might just have to grant your request, St. Abrams," he said, still panting. "A man who throws such an impressive uppercut might be worthy of my cousin after all." He walked over to yank on the bell pull.

After the tight-lipped butler summoned a round-eyed maid to clear away the wreckage, the major offered Gilen wine. "Any bloke who can admit his fault and stand up to me in the ring—or the salon, as it happens—should be offered a second chance. I'll cry pax with you, St. Abrams. I'll even give you Gwen's direction. The farm is but a day's ride from here. Dine with me tonight and you may set out in the morning.''

He was only a day's ride from her? In an instant Gilen forgot his aching jaw and raw fists. "It bids to be a moonlit night. Tell me now, and I'll set out immediately.''

Despite the split on his lip, the major grinned. "I begin to believe you really do love my cousin. If so, accept my heartiest congratulations and this advice, based on years of experience dealing with that strong-willed wench. Given what I suspect has passed between you, I strongly recommend you wait until daylight. You'll need to reconnoiter the ground and mount a surprise attack. Unlike me, Gwen will have no compunction about resorting to pistols.''

Gilen could well believe that of his vixen. "She's a crack shot, I wager.''

Major nodded. "Of course. I taught her.''

Gilen reached over to shake the hand the major offered. "In that case, you owe it to me to share all the intelligence you possess about the grounds and staff. For this coming battle is one engagement I absolutely must win.''

Chapter Twenty-One

As the sun began to set the next day, Gwennor returned to the house. She'd left Parry at the barn, settling in another delivery of prime breeding stock from Ireland. The horses were as excellent as the household and stable staff her cousin had installed here. She felt another wave of gratitude to Harry for so swiftly agreeing to her conditions and expending so much effort to carry them out.

The two weeks since she and Parry had settled at the farm had been busy, full of hard but satisfying work as she acquainted herself with the household and learned the record keeping procedures of the small horse farm Harry had purchased for them. Parry was delighted, his face glowing in a perpetual smile as he worked the horses or roamed the pastures and the woods that bounded their property. Gwennor felt a deep joy in knowing they had found a home where her brother could be safe and happy.

'Twas the nights she dreaded. The fire in the hearth inevitably called to mind the play of golden light over the Turkey carpet in a room now far away, the illumination of the wax tapers, the rugged contours of a beloved face seen under a flicker of candlelight. A flush of shame and longing would rise in her breast as she lay sleepless, recalling every shocking, splendid detail of that forbidden night.

Not that she regretted it. As she'd told herself fiercely from the very first, she would never regret it.

'Twas only that she wished unforgiving reality had not limited their time together to just that single night. If only she could have had one or two more such splendid memories to wrap around her to muffle the bitter blast of loneliness she expected would chill her for the rest of her days....

But she mustn't repine, she told herself as she walked up the entry stairs. Events had turned out better than she'd had any right to expect. Her splendid cousin Harry had come back to England to champion them, brought them back to Southford and coerced Nigel—at the point of his sword, she suspected—into honoring the terms of her father's will and relinquishing the funds meant to be her dowry. He'd then arranged for them to purchase this smallholding that was already being worked as a horse-breeding operation.

And, without badgering her for a better explanation than that it was what she preferred, eventually he'd accepted the fact that still reduced Aunt Frances to tears whenever she thought of it—Gwennor's refusal even to consider accepting a Season at any of the marriage marts from the local county assembly to London itself.

She'd decided to devote her life to raising horses and caring for Parry, she'd told them. Her aunt had bemoaned the decision at tiresome length. Though she suspected Harry didn't believe her, neither had he pressed her further.

She stood before the front door for a few moments before letting herself in, wondering what could have happened to the butler. Once inside the portal, she noticed a tall shadow emanating from within the small front parlor.

Had Harry come to visit? Delighted at the prospect, she quickened her stride. And then halted on the threshold.

Outlined by the fading light from the windows, the tall, broad-shouldered silhouette of her visitor looked so achingly familiar, her breath caught in her chest.

"My darling vixen, I thought you would never get back."

Her heart contracted painfully. She shook her head to clear it, but, reinforced by the timbre of his voice, the illusion still danced before her eyes. "G-Gilen?"

It must be merely a mirage born of heartsick imagining. But so blessed and welcome was it, without another thought, she ran toward him.

Not until she was a step away and realized, in defiance of all probability and logic, 'twas truly St. Abrams who stood there in her parlor, did she remember she must have nothing to do with him.

She skidded to a halt. "Lord St. Abrams! Wh-what are you doing here?"

"Finding you, my angel. Come now, after leading me the devil's own chase, you owe me at least a kiss for my persistence, don't you think?"

He stepped toward her. Hastily she backed away.

He followed, stopped her with a hand to her arm. "Ah, Gwennor, Gwennor my love, I've missed you so."

His words echoed her own feelings so exactly, she couldn't seem to latch on to the phrases she needed. Like "Leave here immediately," and "Don't come again."

Gently he took her shoulders. Before she could instruct her hands to push him away and summon the required phrases to her mouth, he'd lowered his to hers and kissed her.

For several long, immensely satisfying moments she returned the sweet pressure of his lips before her brain succeeded in informing her reluctant body that she really ought not to be kissing Lord St. Abrams.

She pulled away. "Sir, you must depart this instant!"

With a tenderness in his eyes that caused her foolish heart to lurch in her chest, he cupped her chin and angled her face up to his. "Why?"

"Why?" she squeaked. "B-because…" *Because I want too desperately for you to stay. Because if you don't leave right now, whatever it is you came to offer, I'll accept.*

She couldn't say any of that, of course. While she dithered over what she *should* say, St. Abrams let go her chin—and picked her up.

"Put me down!" she cried, finally finding her voice.

Ignoring her command, he carried her into the hallway.

"St. Abrams, stop this at once! Let me go before someone sees us!"

As if he were strolling with her arm-in-arm through Hyde Park rather than squashing her against his chest with her feet dangling off the floor, he continued forward, now headed toward the stairs.

"My lord, this is ridiculous!" When he still made no reply, she wiggled an arm free and punched him in the side.

He yelped and quickly recaptured her hand. "Careful, darling. My ribs are still sore from the pounding Harry gave me."

"H-Harry fought with you?"

"'Twas no less than I deserved for my shameful treatment of you."

The cautious euphoria budding within her died. So that's why he'd come. Somehow he'd discovered the wanton he thought he'd bedded had in truth been a virgin of good birth, a girl his honor would not permit him to seduce and abandon, regardless of her eagerness in allowing that seduction.

"Then, too," the viscount was continuing, "Harry wished to discover if I were truly worthy of you."

"W-worthy?" she echoed. Until he distracted her by starting up the stairs. "Enough of this nonsense, my lord. Release me immediately."

He continued on without pause. "Which bedchamber is yours, my love?"

"B-bedch— No! Put me down, or I warn you, I shall scream!"

St. Abrams reached the landing, paced with her to the nearest door and shouldered it open. "This one, perhaps? Though I don't suppose it matters."

Gwennor gathered as much breath as his arms imprisoning her chest allowed and uttered the loudest shriek she could muster.

In a single motion he kicked the door shut, swung her to her feet and clapped a hand over her mouth. "By the saints, you've made my ears ring! And to no purpose. I gave your staff the evening off, plus a bonus to stay away until noon tomorrow. And the butler's taking Parry off for dinner at the Gilded Hare." Once he was sure she'd stopped screaming, he removed his hand.

At his blatant presumption, she barely refrained from striking him. "How dare you order *my* staff—"

"Sweeting, have you not yet realized I would dare anything for you? Indeed, given the sorry state to which I reduced myself, all that's left is for me to do the most outrageous thing I could conceive. Besides, that's what Harry advised."

"Harry advised?"

"Darling, for a clever girl, you're being beastly dull, repeating everything I say. Yes, Harry advised that a desperate man who had tossed away any advantage he might once have possessed had better do the most daring thing he could imagine in order to seize a second chance. Though nothing could equal the daring of a dauntless girl who defied the head of her family, concocted a brilliant escape, dressed—and performed—as a gypsy, and outwitted an arrogant, opinionated, ignorant ass of an viscount too blind to see the treasure beneath his eyes. Who comes here now prepared to humble himself at your feet—''

''You call this blatant—abduction—'humbling yourself'?''

''But I needed to get you away from your brother and the servants and your duties. And whips and guns—I may be contrite but I'm not stupid. Get you closeted where you cannot escape, long enough for me to vow, Gwennor Southford, that I love you with every atom of my miserable, unworthy being, and that my life will be blighted beyond bearing if you cannot find it in that magnificent, amazing, unpredictable heart of yours to forgive me.'' His voice dropped to a whisper. ''And have the compassion to grant my most fervent request that you become my wife.''

''Not your wanton?''

''Well, that too. But given your talent for slipping off unexpectedly, I thought it best to tie you to me with wedding lines.''

The words were pretty enough, this time. But since he'd somehow discovered the truth she'd refused for so long to tell him, how could she be sure that, knowing he'd blighted his honor by seducing a virgin, he was not simply mouthing the sentiments most likely to induce her to redeem it by marrying him?

''You don't have to wed me, my lord. No one knows of our…prior relationship, except now, I suppose, my cousin Harry. But if you've already fought with him, you've no need to do this. Your reputation—and mine—remain intact.''

"Yes, I know. That's why I intend to lock you in here with me."

"Lock me—" she began, then stopped short as St. Abrams shucked his jacket and began to pull at the knot of his cravat. "Gilen, what in the world are you doing now?"

"Compromising you. Again. And I plan to remain with you in your bedchamber—or whoever's chamber this is— until first your servants, and then the shire, and then the countryside from Wales to London itself, if it takes that, knows we've been together and insists you marry me." He pulled his cravat loose and began on his waistcoat buttons. "Just imagine, my heart, how many fascinating ways we shall think of to pass the time."

"You're insane," she said flatly.

He nodded, as if pleased with her observation. "Indeed. And so I told my father." He reached around her to pluck open the top button on her gown.

Gwen grabbed his hand with a shriek. Giving his head a reproving shake, he bent forward and stopped the sound with his lips. Then he gathered her to him, his hands dislodging the pins from her hair while his mouth worked its magic, gentling her protests, until her flailing hands settled back to his shoulders and pulled him closer.

Finally she forced herself once again to push against his chest, nearly weeping at the effort required.

Immediately he released her. "My dearest darling, what do *you* want?"

If he'd expended so much effort and come so far to find her, perhaps he did love her as he claimed. Still, her cautious self warned that his offer now might be no less coerced by his rigid sense of honor than the one he'd made her in front of Aunt Alice back in Harrogate.

There was no question he held her whole heart. A heart

that would be doomed to permanent misery, should she marry him and discover too late he'd not really loved her.

How could she be sure?

He must have read the uncertainty in her eyes. "Gwennor," he said softly, "do you believe, despite my prior actions, that I have too much honor to lie to you?"

Whatever else he'd done, he'd always been honest. "Yes."

"Then I swear, this time I don't extend to you my hand or my heart—which you've held since that night at the gypsy camp, though I was too stupid for far too long to realize it—in order to conform to some rigid and sterile code of conduct. I offer them solely to honor the unique, enchanting woman you are, Gwennor Southford. The woman I want for my wife—and my wanton—the rest of my life."

He would not lie—of that she *was* sure. So...it must be true. Incredulous joy swelled in her chest.

And as swiftly stilled. "But...what of your DeLacey friends? The embarrassment to your family when it becomes known you wed a woman you met in a gypsy encampment? I would not bring disgrace to your name."

He sighed. "I instilled that notion in your head, didn't I?"

When she nodded, he continued, "Which just proves how much more depraved my character is than yours, my sweet, for 'tis a complete falsehood. No one else in my party at the encampment that night could identify you. Only I had the good fortune to be close to you, and even after kissing you, I still had the devil's own time later trying to decide if the proper lady I met in the Harrogate Assembly Rooms and the entrancing maid who danced under the moonlight were in fact the same woman."

"But what if someone should later discover it? London Society might make you a laughingstock!"

He shrugged. "Bunch of sanctimonious bores, mostly. Having you in my life would more than make up the loss. Though I doubt it will come to that. After all, I am the sole witness to your participation in the gypsy camp. And since I shall insist that any repetition of your delightful performances take place only within the privacy of our bedchamber, no one else will ever know."

She stood very still while the full import of his words filtered through the whirlwind of doubt, longing, uncertainty and hope to lodge in her heart.

He believed in her honor. She would not disgrace his family. They could marry. She need no longer resist her passionate desire to be with him.

"You are sure?" she whispered, hardly daring to believe in such happiness.

"Absolutely. So, my darling, will you marry me?"

A smile began to curl her lips. "Only in *our* bedchamber, you said?"

Quick-witted as always, he caught her meaning, and an answering grin leapt to his face. "I suppose any chamber with a door that locks will do." His sweeping gesture encompassed the room. "This one, for instance."

"Then yes, my love, I will marry you."

His expression turned wicked and a flame lit his dark blue eyes. "Excellent. Let the dance begin."

*   *   *   *   *

*Please turn the page for an
exciting preview of Julia's next book,*

THE SEDUCTIVE STRANGER,

*available in June 2003 as a 2-in-1
with* New York Times
bestselling author Heather Graham's

FORBIDDEN FIRE.

Chapter One

East Anglia, Spring, 1809

Apollo was riding down her drive.

Or so it seemed to Caragh Sudley, hand over her eyes and breath seizing in her chest as she squinted into the morning sun at the solitary horseman trotting down the graveled carriageway toward Sudley Court.

She was returning to the manor after her early-morning ride when the sound of hoofbeats carrying on the still morning air drew her toward the front entrance. At first merely curious about the identity of the unexpected visitor, as the man grew closer she was stunned motionless by the sheer beauty of horse and rider.

The pale sunshine threw a golden nimbus about the gentleman's hatless head, making his blond hair gleam as if the sun king himself were arriving in regal pomp, his chariot exchanged for the gilded beauty of a palomino. The brightness behind them cast the rider's face in shadow and silhouetted in sharp relief the broad line of shoulders and arms now pulling the stallion to a halt.

She shook her head, but that dazzling first impression

refused to subside into normalcy. The tall, powerfully built beast tossing his head in spirited response to his rider's command, creamy coat rippling, was magnificent, the man now swinging down from the saddle no less so.

A dark-green riding jacket stretched across his shoulders and fawn breeches molded over saddle-muscled thighs, while closer she could see his blond locks had tints of strawberry mingled with the gold. His eyes, no longer in shadow once he'd dismounted in her direction, were a shade of turquoise blue so arresting and unusual she once again caught her breath.

The chiseled features of his face—purposeful chin, high cheekbones, firm lips, sculpted nose whose slight crookedness added an intriguing hint of character to a countenance that might otherwise have seemed merely chill perfection—only confirmed her initial perception.

'Twas Apollo, Roman robes cast aside to assume the guise of an English country gentleman.

Should she behold him, her sister Ailis would surely be calling for her palette and paints.

Caragh smiled slightly at the thought of her imperious sister ordering the man this way and that until she'd posed him to her satisfaction. And then she realized this paragon of Olympian perfection was approaching *her*—plain Caragh Sudley who stood, jaw still dropped in awe, her face framed by limp wisps of hair blown out of the chignon into which she'd carelessly twisted it, the skirts of her old, shabby riding habit liberally mud-spattered.

She snapped her mouth shut, feeling the hot color rising in her cheeks, but as the visitor had already seen her, she would only make herself look more ridiculous by fleeing. How unfortunate, the whimsical thought occurred as she tried to surreptitiously brush off the largest clumps of mud and summon a welcoming smile, that unlike Daphne, she could not conveniently turn herself into a tree.

"Good morning, Miss," the visitor said, bowing.

"Good morning to you, too, sir," she replied, amazed to find her voice still functioned.

"Would you have the goodness to confirm that I have reached Sudley Court? I need to call upon the baron."

"That would be my father, sir. You will find him in the library. Pringle, our butler, will show you in."

He smiled, displaying just a hint of dimples. "Thank you for your kindness, Miss Sudley. I hope to have—"

Before he could complete his sentence, her sister emerged from the shrubbery of the garden behind them, a lad laden with an easel and paintbox trailing in her wake. "Caragh! Did that package from London arrive for me yet?"

Caragh waited a moment, but her sister paid no attention to the newcomer. "Well, has it?"

Caragh's delight faded in a spurt of resentment she struggled, and failed, to suppress. With the arrival of Ailis, her all-too-short exchange with the Olympian would surely come to a premature halt.

Wishing her sister could have intruded a moment earlier, or five minutes later, she replied, "If it has, Thomas will bring it when he returns from the village." She steeled herself to glance at the stranger.

Who was not, as she had expected, staring in open-mouthed amazement at her stunningly beautiful sister, but rather, observing them both, his expression polite. For a moment Caragh wondered about the acuity of his eyesight.

"Blast!" her sister replied, still ignoring the newcomer. "I only hope I have enough of the cerulean blue to last out the morning."

Blushing a little for her sister's lack of manners, Caragh

motioned her head toward the visitor. "Ailis!" she said in an urgent undertone.

Her sister cast her an impatient glance. "You show him in, Caragh, whoever he is. I cannot miss the light. Come along, Jack." She motioned to the young lad carrying her supplies and walked off without even a goodbye.

Caragh's blush deepened. "M-my younger sister, sir. As you may have guessed, she's an artist—quite a good one! But very...preoccupied with her work. She's presently engaged upon an outdoor study requiring morning light."

"Who are we mere mortals to interrupt the inspiration of the muse?" he asked, his comment reassuring her that he'd not been offended by her sister's scapegrace behavior. "But I mustn't intrude upon your time any longer. Thank you very much, Miss Sudley. I trust we shall meet again."

Before she could guess his intent, the visitor took her hand and brought it to his lips. After that salute he bowed, then led the stallion off toward the entry.

For a moment Caragh stood motionless, gazing with wonder at the hand he'd kissed. Her fingers still tingled from the slight, glancing pressure of his mouth.

When she jerked her gaze back up, she noted the visitor had nearly reached the entry steps, down which one of the footmen was hastening to relieve him of his horse. Quickly she pivoted and paced off toward the kitchen wing. She'd not want the stranger to glance back and find her still staring at him.

Once out of sight, her footsteps slowed. The handsome visitor had bowed, kissed her hand and treated her as if she were a grand lady instead of a gawky girl still a year from her come-out.

Best of all, he had not been struck dumb when Ailis appeared. He had actually managed to continue conversing intelligently after her sister left them. Nor had his gaze followed Ailis as she walked away; it had reverted back to Caragh's much plainer face.

The few remaining pieces of her susceptible heart that had not already surrendered to the warmth of the stranger's smile and the bedazzlement of his blue-eyed gaze, succumbed.

But of course, in the London from which he must have come, he probably met beautiful ladies every day, all of them elegantly dressed in the latest fashion, and so had schooled himself to maintain a polite conversation, no matter how distracting the circumstances.

Briskly she dismissed that lowering reflection. The thoroughness of his training did not diminish the excellence of his behavior. Indeed, he was a *Vrai* and *Gentil* Chevalier, *beau et courtois,* straight from the pages of an Arthurian legend, she concluded, freely mixing her literary metaphors.

But who was he? Suddenly compelled to find out, she headed into the house.

Creeping past the library, where a murmur of voices informed her the visitor must still be closeted with Papa, she slipped into the deserted front parlor, hoping to catch one more glimpse of the stranger before he departed.

Perhaps when I make my come-out in London next year, I shall meet you again. Only then, I shall be gowned in the most elegant design out of the pages of La Belle Assemblée, *my hair a coronet of curls, my conversation dazzling, and you will be as swept away by me as I was by you today....*

She was chuckling a bit at that absurd if harmless fantasy when the closing of the library door alerted her. She flattened herself against the wall until footsteps passed her hiding place, then peeped into the hall.

Once again, sunlight cast a halo around the stranger's

golden head as he stood pulling on the riding gloves the butler had just returned to him. Caragh sighed, her eyes slowly tracing the handsome contours of the visitor's face as she committed every splendid feature to memory.

After retrieving his riding crop, he nodded to acknowledge the butler's bow and walked out.

Resisting a strong desire to scurry after him and take one last peek through the fan-glass windows flanking the entry, Caragh made herself wait until the tramp of his boots descending the flagstone steps faded. Then she ran to the library, knocked once, and hurried in.

"Papa," she called to the thin, balding man who sat behind the massive desk, scribbling in one of the large volumes strewn haphazardly about his desk.

Making a small moue of annoyance at the interruption, her father looked up. "Caragh? What is it, child? I must get back to this translation of Homer before the rhythm of the English cadences escapes me."

"Yes, Papa. Please, sir, who was your visitor?"

"Visitor?" her father echoed, seeming to have difficulty remembering the individual who had quit the room barely five minutes previous. "Ah, that tall young man. Just bought the neighboring property, he told me. Wanted to pay his respects and inquire about some matter of pasturage. I suppose you shall have to consult with Withers about it before he returns. I simply can't spare the time now to bother with agricultural matters, not with this translation going so slowly."

Apollo would be calling again. Delight and anticipation buoyed Caragh's spirits.

"Very well, Papa. If I will be meeting with him, however, perhaps you had better tell me his name."

"His name? Dash it, of what importance is that? I expect he'll announce it again when he returns. Now, be a good girl and take this breakfast tray back to the kitchen. It's blocking my dictionary.''

Inured to her father's total disinterest in anything not connected to his translation projects, Caragh suppressed a sigh. ''Of course, Papa.'' Disappointed, she gathered up the tray and prepared to leave.

''Goodbye,'' she called from the threshold. Already immersed in his work, her father did not even glance up.

Then a better idea occurred, and her mood brightened. Depositing the tray on a hall table to be dealt with later, she hurried in search of the butler, finally running him to ground in the dining room where he was directing a footman in polishing the silver epergne.

''Pringle! Do you recall the name of the gentleman who just called? He is to be our new neighbor, I understand.''

''Lord Branson, he said, Miss Caragh,'' the butler replied.

''And his family name?''

''Don't believe he mentioned it. But he left a card.''

''Thank you, Pringle!'' Caragh hurried back into the hallway. There, sitting in pristine whiteness against the polished silver tray, was a bit of pasteboard bearing the engraving Quentin Burke, Lord Branson.

Smiling, Caragh slipped the card into her pocket. Her own Olympic hero come to earth now had a name. *Quentin.*

Embark on the adventure of a lifetime with these timeless tales from Harlequin Historicals

On Sale January 2003

LADY LYTE'S LITTLE SECRET
by Deborah Hale
(Regency England)

*Will a wealthy widow rediscover true love
with the father of her unborn child?*

DRAGON'S DAUGHTER
by Catherine Archer
(England & Scotland, 1200)
**Book #3 of *The Brotherhood
of the Dragon* series**

*Passion blazes when a brave warrior goes
in search of his mentor's secret daughter!*

On Sale February 2003

THE SCOT by Lyn Stone
(Edinburgh & London, 1870)

*Watch the sparks fly between a feisty lass and
a proud Scottish baron when they enter into
a marriage of convenience!*

BRIDE OF THE TOWER
by Sharon Schulze
(England, 1217)

*Will a fallen knight become bewitched with
the mysterious noblewoman who nurses him
back to health?*

HHH Harlequin Historicals®
Historical Romantic Adventure!

On the lookout for captivating courtships
set on the American frontier?
Then behold these rollicking romances
from Harlequin Historicals.

On sale January 2003

THE FORBIDDEN BRIDE
by Cheryl Reavis
*Will a well-to-do young woman defy
her father and give her heart to
a wild and daring gold miner?*

HALLIE'S HERO
by Nicole Foster
*A beautiful rancher joins forces
with a gun-toting gambler to save her spread!*

On sale February 2003

THE MIDWIFE'S SECRET
by Kate Bridges
*Can a wary midwife finally find love and acceptance
in the arms of a ruggedly handsome sawmill owner?*

THE LAW AND KATE MALONE
by Charlene Sands
*A stubborn sheriff and a spirited saloon owner
share a stormy reunion!*

Harlequin Historicals®
Historical Romantic Adventure!

COMING NEXT MONTH FROM

HARLEQUIN HISTORICALS®

- **GIFTS OF THE SEASON**
  Mainstream historical author **Miranda Jarrett** joins
  Harlequin Historicals and Silhouette Intimate Moments author
  Lyn Stone and RITA® Award winner **Anne Gracie** for this
  Christmas anthology of three stories set in Regency England.
  HH #631 ISBN# 29231-7 $5.25 U.S./$6.25 CAN.

- **RAFFERTY'S BRIDE**
  by **Mary Burton,** author of THE PERFECT WIFE
  Ravaged by the Civil War, a military man bent on revenge goes
  in search of the bewitching nurse who betrayed him and his men.
  But he never bargained on the explosive desire that would ignite
  between them!
  HH #632 ISBN# 29232-5 $5.25 U.S./$6.25 CAN.

- **BECKETT'S BIRTHRIGHT**
  by **Bronwyn Williams,** second book in the *Beckett's Fortune* series
  Having lost the trail of a man who wronged him, a down-on-his-
  luck rancher takes a job in North Carolina. Sparks fly when he
  meets his boss's daughter, a fiery bluestocking, but will his need
  for vengeance destroy their budding love?
  HH #633 ISBN# 29233-3 $5.25 U.S./$6.25 CAN.

- **THE DUMONT BRIDE**
  by **Terri Brisbin,** Harlequin Historicals debut
  A wrongly imprisoned French count is forced into a marriage of
  convenience to an English heiress with a secret to hide. When he
  discovers his wife is pregnant with another man's child, he must
  choose between honor and a love finally found….
  HH #634 ISBN# 29234-1 $5.25 U.S./$6.25 CAN.

KEEP AN EYE OUT FOR ALL FOUR
OF THESE TERRIFIC NEW TITLES

FRESH FAITH

Resources by Jim Cymbala

Fresh Wind, Fresh Fire
(book and audio)
Fresh Faith
(book and audio)
Fresh Power
(book and audio)
The Life God Blesses
(book and audio)
God's Grace from Ground Zero
(book and audio)
The Church God Blesses
(book and audio)

FRESH FAITH

WHAT HAPPENS WHEN REAL FAITH IGNITES GOD'S PEOPLE

JIM CYMBALA

PASTOR OF THE BROOKLYN TABERNACLE

WITH DEAN MERRILL

GRAND RAPIDS, MICHIGAN 49530 USA

ZONDERVAN™

Fresh Faith
Copyright © 1999 by Jim Cymbala
Study Guide Copyright © 2003 by Jim Cymbala

This title is available as a Zondervan audio product. Visit
www.zondervan.com/audiopages for more information.

Requests for information should be addressed to:

Zondervan, *Grand Rapids, Michigan 49530*

Library of Congress Cataloging-in-Publication Data

Cymbala, Jim, 1943-
    Fresh faith: what happens when real faith ignites God's people/ Jim Cymbala with Dean Merrill.
        p. cm.
Includes bibliographical references.
        ISBN 0-310-25155-9 (softcover)
        1. Fresh.   I. Merrill, Dean.   II. Title.
BV4637.C96 1999
243 — dc21   99-35508
                                                                                CIP

Interior design by Sherri L. Hoffman

Printed in the United States of America

05 06 07 08 09 /❖ DC/ 10 9 8 7 6

Contents

PART 1

~

Something Is Missing

ONE

∽

Stolen Property

I LIVE IN A CITY where things get stolen all the time. Along Flatbush Avenue, where our church is, car thefts are an everyday occurrence. So are muggings, purse snatchings, and apartment break-ins.

Once in a Sunday night sermon I made the mistake of asking our congregation to raise their hands if they had personally experienced some kind of rip-off. The place broke into laughter as 98 percent of the hands went up. What a silly question to pose to a crowd of New Yorkers!

My wife, Carol, and I live in the borough of Queens, east of LaGuardia Airport and Shea Stadium, where the Mets play. I came out to my car parked in front of our house one morning a few years ago and noticed it had been vandalized. As soon as I opened the door and got inside, I saw a huge, gaping hole in the center of the steering wheel where the air bag had been.

Crack cocaine addicts love air bags because they are a quick-sale item. Within minutes they can walk into a "chop shop"—an illicit garage that deals in used auto parts—and trade an air bag for up to $200 cash. It is just one of the ways that crack has devastated New York and other major cities in America. Heroin was one thing, snorting cocaine another— but crack has brought massive destruction.

I moaned to myself about the loss. When I called my insurance agent, he took it in stride. "Well, that's the Big Apple for you," he said. "Happens all the time." We filled out the claims paperwork and ordered the part from the dealer. I didn't ask what this would do to my rates next time around; I didn't really want to know.

A few months passed before I finally got around to taking the car in for the replacement. At last the damage was repaired.

And wouldn't you know—within three weeks I got ripped off again! Same parking place in front of my house, same window forced open. I'm almost sure it was the same thief.

This time I didn't even bother to file an insurance claim. I just paid the $800 for replacement out of my pocket rather than risk my rates going through the roof.

I even found a way to joke about it with someone: "You know, maybe I should leave coffee and cake for this guy on the front seat ... with a note that says, 'Hey, let's be friends! If I'd just supply you with other stuff to sell, at least you wouldn't have to break into my car every few months.'"

MORE THAN MERCHANDISE

FORTUNATELY, AIR BAGS CAN be replaced. As much as you hate the loss and inconvenience, you gradually go on with your life. A year later, you won't even remember that it happened.

But in the spiritual realm, a kind of stealing is going on in many lives that is much more serious. Satan is in the business of ripping off things far more important than an air bag. That is his nature. As Jesus said in John 10:10, "The thief comes only to *steal* and kill and destroy."

Satan obviously doesn't want car parts. Nor does he want your house; he doesn't live in a house. He doesn't need your vehicle, for he has other modes of transportation. He has no interest in your clothes; he's a spirit being. He doesn't care about your investments; what would money mean to him?

In the spiritual realm, a kind of stealing is going on in many lives. Satan is in the business of ripping us off. ~

But he is very interested in stealing *spiritual treasures*—things that have value with God and are of eternal significance. Take, for example, our very purpose for living. Satan loves snatching men and women on the streets of my city and your city—people who have potential—and turning them into glassy-eyed wanderers through life, with no goal from day to day. They lie in bed at night staring at the ceiling, saying, "What's the point? Just to make money? Just to have kids? Why?"

People turn to drugs and alcohol because they don't have a clue as to why they're alive. Others turn to career achievement, or pleasure, or materialism ... something, anything to fill the void. But it doesn't work. God created them to worship and enjoy him forever, but this awareness has been stolen from their consciousness.

Notice the progression in John 10:10. Satan's first move is just petty larceny. Once he manages that, he can move on to actual killing, and from there to mass destruction. "Steal ... kill ... destroy." But it all starts with stealing.

WHAT HAPPENED TO "FIRST LOVE"?

EVEN AMONG THOSE WHO are Christians, the devil has a strategy of theft. For example, as a pastor I have seen over and over the tragic loss of our *"first love"* for Jesus. There was a time in our lives when we loved Jesus so much more than we do today. Our appetite for God's Word was voracious. Our love for God's house was enthusiastic. Our eagerness for spreading the gospel was so strong. . . . Now, how is it? Yes, we still love the Lord. We still come to church. But what happened to all that energy and passion?

That is the problem Jesus addressed with the Ephesian church in Revelation 2:2–5: "I know your deeds, your hard work and your perseverance. . . . Yet I hold this against you: You have forsaken your first love. Remember the height from which you have fallen! Repent and do the things you did at first. If you do not repent, I will come to you and remove your lampstand from its place."

Where does "first love" go? Our zeal and our intensity don't evaporate. Satan steals the hot embers of devotion and consecration. We get ripped off.

> **The Bible has no retirement plan. God can keep his people on fire for him, keep them sharp and intense.** ～

Someone might say, "Well, you have to understand that back when I met Christ, I was an energetic teenager. A lot has happened since then. You know, we all mellow out with time." Does anyone really believe that? The Bible says God's plan for us is that we be "transformed into his likeness with *ever-increasing* glory, which comes from the Lord, who is the Spirit" (2 Corinthians 3:18). There is no end to the power he wants to exhibit in our lives. The Bible has no retirement plan. God can keep his people on fire for him, can keep them sharp and intense. We need to be honest and admit what has really happened. There is no point in conning ourselves. We've been ripped off by the master thief.

FADED CALLING

OR HOW ABOUT THAT unique *calling* that rests on every Christian's life—the gifting to serve others in the name of the Lord? Ten years ago there was a stirring inside of you; he gave you a dream about what he wanted to do in your life. Maybe he wanted you to teach children. Maybe he wanted you to sing. Maybe he wanted you to be a prayer warrior, standing in the gap for other people in need. Maybe there was even a pull toward the mission field that was birthed by the Holy Spirit himself.

But then . . . you got discouraged. Somebody let you down. Something went sour at your church. You tried once or twice, but somebody criticized you. Soon the dream was gone, and the calling wasn't so real. All the inspiration you had felt was missing.

Sometimes I meet pastors in this condition—a hollow shell of their former selves. All the energy is gone; they're just going through the ministerial motions now.

You would tend to imagine this happening mainly through the many discouragements that ministers face and their over-burdened schedules leading to burnout. Actually, those are only two of Satan's strategies for going after the shepherds who work among God's flock. He has many others as well.

Years ago I met a man who really seemed sincere as he labored tirelessly to build up a congregation of believers in a major city. God's blessing upon his preaching was evident. The church began to flourish.

A few years later, I happened to visit one of his services. Something had obviously changed. The pastor had somehow come to believe that *he* was special. The spotlight was now more on him than on Jesus Christ. The messenger had tragically become bigger than the message.

We chatted afterward, and he pointedly asked me what I sensed about the direction of his church. I encouraged him as best I could, but then added, "Remember, my friend—don't take yourself too seriously. This is about God's Spirit working in the lives of people to draw them nearer to Jesus. We're just called to serve them. Preach the Word faithfully, and then disappear into the background so God will get all the praise."

He didn't seem very excited about my last remarks.

His limited fame seemed to go quickly to his head, and soon the simple sincerity and childlike faith that had characterized his earlier efforts for God were replaced by a slick, affected flamboyance, which is very destructive to the cause of Christ. The man's effective preaching and spiritual fruit quickly disappeared.

Where do you think they all went? Something very precious was stolen along the way.

The devil is always trying to rob us of something God blessed us with. When he succeeds, the spiritual gifts seem to fade, and the material things occupy our attention twenty-four hours a day.

HOME BURGLARIES

CONSIDER THE SUBJECT of marriage. The latest surveys by researcher George Barna show that the divorce rate among churchgoers is just about equal with the population at large. If I were an atheist or an agnostic, I'd say, "Look—how come Jesus can't keep you two together? I thought you said he was so wonderful. . . ."

Why are Christian couples breaking up? Is it because they shouldn't have gotten married in the first place? Or because they came from dysfunctional homes and had bad role models? There is more to it than that. *The thief comes to steal....*

> **The divorce rate among churchgoers is just about equal with the population at large. If I were an atheist, I'd say, "How come Jesus can't keep you two together?"** ～

In fact, Satan fully intends to destroy my marriage to Carol, even though we have served side by side in the ministry for more than twenty-five years. These are the realities of spiritual warfare. Only the power of Christ can keep the two of us together as God has planned and can give us victory over Satan's destructive power. No honest minister of the gospel will deny the fact that the devil has made major assaults on his or her marriage. It's usually not talked about in public, but many tears are shed and prayers offered up to God as sincere servants of the Lord do battle against the demonic forces set on stealing their marriages, credibility, and effectiveness.

What about *our children* and *our grandchildren?* They were dedicated to God at an altar once upon a time. We stood before a minister and said with all sincerity, "O God, this baby belongs to you." But something has happened in the years since then. Now the young man or young woman is not living for God—there's no use pretending that they are.

Let's not close our eyes and make-believe otherwise. Before we can see God do what only he can do, we must spiritually diagnose exactly what is going on around us. Denying reality is not part of true Christian living.

MOST OF ALL: WHERE DID THE FAITH GO?

AT THE CORE OF ALL these losses I have mentioned is the silent theft of the most crucial element in our spiritual walk: our *faith*. What is faith? It is total dependence upon God that becomes supernatural in its working. People with faith develop a second kind of sight. They see more than just the circumstances; they see God, right beside them. Can they prove it? No. But by faith they know he's there nonetheless.

Without faith, says Hebrews 11:6, it is *impossible* to please God. Nothing else counts if faith is missing. There is no other foundation for Christian living, no matter the amount of self-effort or energy spent. Nothing else touches the Father's heart as much as when his children simply trust him wholeheartedly.

I meet people who at one time would pray over anything and everything! Even if they lost their glasses, they would pray to find them—and amazingly, the glasses would show up. Now the same people seem not to believe that God can do much of anything.

Oh, they will still give you the standard confession of faith: "Yes, I have faith in the God who answers prayer." But that vibrant trust and expectation are no more. They aren't saying, "Come on—let's go after this problem in the name of the Lord." They've been robbed.

There is an obscure story at the end of 1 Samuel that speaks to this matter in vivid detail. It is one of the low points on the roller coaster of David's life. The young conqueror of the giant Goliath is now on the run from King Saul. So many threats, so many close calls . . . he actually goes to live among the Philistines for a year, for he has run out of places to hide in Israel.

David has his own little militia of six hundred men, plus wives and children. They set up at a place called Ziklag.

When the Philistines decide to go to war against Israel, it puts David in a real crunch. He's a fighter, of course, a warrior, so he lines up with King Achish. But the Philistine generals spot him and say to their king, "What does David think he's doing?"

"Why? What do you mean?"

"The famous son-in-law of King Saul, right? No way is he going on this campaign with us!"

Achish tries to defend David's loyalty but gets nowhere. The generals say, "Look, don't you know that song they sang all over Israel? 'Saul has slain his thousands, and David his tens of thousands'—and some of those tens of thousands were us! He is definitely not going into battle with us."

So David and his militia get sent back home.

When they come close to Ziklag, they start to see smoke on the horizon. They begin a fast trot—and soon discover something dreadful: Every wife, every son, every daughter, every cow and lamb is gone. Someone has made a secret raid, burning down the city and stealing everything.

These husbands and fathers are stunned by the desolation. They are heartbroken . . . imagine them thinking of their wives and daughters being captured by some roving band of marauders. *My lovely wife is missing! What is happening to my fourteen-year-old daughter right now?* They can only imagine the unrestrained brutality and heartlessness that have surely occurred. They begin to cry so hard that they run out of tears. They are devastated.

David's family is gone, too. Everything is lost.

At such a moment of human sorrow, other emotions come into play. Anger and resentment boil up. When people cannot deal with the agony of the moment, they often turn on those in authority. They can't bear the pain, so they lash out. David's men begin saying, "What were we doing out there, anyway? Whose bright idea was it to go join the Philistine army? We should have been taking care of our families. Let's stone David for this!"

Then comes this wonderful phrase in 1 Samuel 30:6: "But David found strength in the LORD his God." As the bottom was falling out of his life, he must have gone to a quiet place to pray and gather himself before God.

No matter how low you get, no matter what collapses around you, no matter who rejects you or slanders you—God is able to encourage you. He will help you get through. He will strengthen you deep within your heart in a place no one else can reach.

Having gotten back his poise, his spiritual equilibrium, David goes to the priest for a consultation with God about what he should do. Whenever David was walking in grace, he never just shot from the hip; he first sought the Lord. This is the right thing to do for anyone who is uncertain about the next move.

"Should I chase those who marauded our town, and if I do, will I find them?" he asks. A very wise question. (Think of all the terrible consequences we would avoid if we did what David did here!)

God replies, "Yes, go after them—and you will find them."

So they take off. Along the way, riding across the desert, they come upon a half-conscious Egyptian slave. After they revive him with some cool water, the man admits some vital information. "I was with the Amalekites, and we raided the area. We burned down Ziklag—but then I got sick."

"Well, how would you like to help us now—in exchange for your life?!"

The man doesn't have to think too long about that one. He agrees to guide David and his army, so they set out again.

Soon they come over the brow of a ridge to see the Amalekites below, having a big party. Drunken debauchery is the order of the day.

And in the name of the Lord, David leads his men down the hill against them. For a full twenty-four hours—all night and all the next day—they hit the Amalekites hard.

COMING BACK IN A BIG WAY

THIS WAS THE DAY that David found out that God is more than a creator. He is more than a defender. He is more than a rock or a strong tower, as David calls him in some of the Psalms. God is more than a protector from King Saul when you're hiding.

David learned the powerful truth that _God recovers stolen property._ He has a way of getting back what's been ripped off. What the enemy steals, God alone is able to recover.

And here is the best part of all: David discovered that every wife, every son, every daughter was still alive! Amazing! Not even one lamb was gone.

Listen to how the Bible describes the scene. It says that the Egyptian slave

> ... led David down, and there they were, scattered over the countryside, eating, drinking and reveling because of the great amount of plunder they had taken from the land of the Philistines and from Judah. David fought them from dusk until the evening of the next day, and none of them got away, except four hundred young men who rode off on camels and fled. David recovered everything the Amalekites had taken, including his two wives. Nothing was missing: young or old, boy or girl, plunder or anything else they had taken. David brought everything back. He took all the

flocks and herds, and his men drove them ahead of the other livestock, saying, "This is David's plunder" (1 Samuel 30:16–20).

What a victory! In addition to all the recovered goods, David and his army captured an impressive amount of Amalekite goods, so that when they marched back to Ziklag, there was a *surplus*. Everyone was praising God. They were shouting, "Look what God gave us!" They came back with more than they had lost.

Why am I telling you this obscure Old Testament story? To get to this critical point: David and his men came to a moment when they chose to *get up and go after stolen property*.

The moment must come for you and me when we say, "Wait a minute—am I just going to keep sitting here feeling bad for myself? In the name of the Lord, my daughter, my son, my grandchild is going to be reclaimed. In the name of the Lord, I am *not* going to give up on my calling, my potential in life. Satan, you're going to give back that property! I come against you and resist you in the name of Jesus Christ my Lord."

Remember, we are not wrestling against flesh and blood. We are engaged in spiritual warfare. In your life and mine, here at the beginning of the twenty-first century, somebody has to step up and fight for stolen property with the weapons of faith and prayer. You have to say to the devil, "Enough! I'm going to be like David and go after the stolen goods." Get on your horse!

Our enemy Satan has no feelings of sympathy. If you don't resist, he'll rip you off every week, all year long. That's his diabolical work. But Jesus came that we might have life— abundant life. He can revive your marriage. He can bring fire back into your soul. Your spiritual calling can bloom once again.

You can recover the faith that the devil stole. I am not talking here about the mental assent you give to Bible truths you've heard over and over again. I'm talking about vibrant heart-faith and childlike trust in the risen, supernatural Christ—the kind of faith that changes the way you live, talk, and feel.

> **Here at the beginning of the twenty-first century, somebody has to step up and fight for stolen property with the weapons of faith and prayer.** ~

Satan wants to snatch this more than anything else, for he knows "the righteous will live by faith" (Romans 1:17). He knows that "without faith it is impossible to please God" (Hebrews 11: 6). He knows that real faith is our lifeline to God's grace and power. If he can sever the *faith connection*, he has gained a tremendous victory. He knows that without a living faith, prayer as a force in our lives will be extinguished. We will soon be just mechanically going through the outward forms of religion while experiencing nothing of God's power.

But God can revive fresh faith in our souls if we ask him. He will bring faith alive in us through his Word, as Romans 10:17 declares: "Faith comes by hearing, and hearing by the word of God" (NKJV). Nothing is impossible with God. In fact, you will see God recover more than you lost, just as David did. That is what the Bible promises when it says we can be "more than conquerors through him who loved us" (Romans 8:37). The only question is, Do you and I really believe that our God will recover our stolen property? Or do we think our situation is too far gone for him?

That is why I want to tell you the story of a woman named Amalia, who had one of the most amazing recoveries I have ever seen in my life. However badly you've been plundered and ransacked in your personal life, you probably won't be able to match her traumas. But her experience will show how the power of God can turn it all around.

TWO

~

Amalia's Story

THERE'S SOMEONE WHO CAME to church the last two weeks who really needs to talk to you," Pastor Carlo Boekstaaf, my longtime associate, said one Tuesday afternoon in my office. "If it's all right, I invited her for six o'clock this evening, before the prayer meeting starts. I know a little of her story, and it's incredible. But God has definitely begun to work in her life."

Having lived my whole life in New York City and having pastored for a number of years, I figured I was beyond surprise when it came to stories from the wild side. But I must admit that what I heard that evening took my breath away. A tough-looking but attractive young woman walked into my office. She seemed to send out a strange combination of signals; while she had obviously spent time on the "mean streets," there was also a vulnerability and deep sorrow that showed through the tight-fitting clothes and heavily made-up face.

"Hi, Amalia," I said softly, motioning toward a chair. "I'm Pastor Cymbala. They said you wanted to talk to me."

She nodded slightly and sat down, tugging at her hemline.

"Tell me about yourself, if you will. How I can help you?"

In a low, husky voice she began her amazing, utterly dismal story, and for the next hour, this is essentially what I heard. . . .

I GREW UP IN THE Smith Projects on the Lower East Side.* I was the third of seven children packed into an apartment on the sixteenth floor. My father was a kitchen worker in one of the big hotels; he and my mother had both come from Puerto Rico.

The thing I remember most about our home was its fighting and arguing. We never stopped, it seemed. My father was an alcoholic and made our lives miserable. He had a wooden stick that he would swing like a crazy man at any of us who got in his way or irritated him. I never remember the family sitting down to eat a meal together. I felt very confused growing up; I mainly just tried to stay out of trouble.

My parents would argue a lot about money, since it seemed that my father never gave my mother enough to feed and clothe all us kids. Catholic Charities would help us out from time to time. Even though there wasn't enough money for the necessities, there was definitely money for alcohol. And that only made the fights worse, of course. When I would see him hitting her and pushing her around, I would just run to my room and seethe with anger.

I was about nine years old the first time I stood up to him. In the middle of the yelling, I said to him one night, "If you hurt my mother, I'm going to kill you!" How I would actually do that, I had no idea, of course; I was just upset at him.

I turned to my mother and continued, "Look—you go sleep in my bed to get away from him, and I'll sleep in yours." I thought I was helping the situation. She was really a sweet woman, and I wanted to protect her somehow.

But that was the biggest mistake of my life—because there in my parents' bedroom that night, my father began to

---

*The Smith Projects are among the infamous public-housing high-rises that dot New York; this one sits more or less between Chinatown, Little Italy, and Wall Street in lower Manhattan.

molest me. I couldn't understand what he was doing, or why. I didn't know what to say—after all, I was just a fourth-grader.

Somehow I made it through that night, but emotionally I was a wreck.

Soon the next household fight came along—now what was I going to do? I told myself I should try again to protect my mom; maybe it would be different this time.

It was not. An ugly pattern began to be set. The only words I could find were "No, Pop, I don't want to."

"Well, if you don't," he would say, "I'm gonna beat up your mom." So I was trapped; I felt I had to go along with his wishes.

Before long, it started looking as if he was actually *starting* arguments with my mom in order to get us to switch for the night. Or he would just openly call from his room, "Come in here, Amalia. I want you in here with me." In time, I realized to my horror that I was replacing my own mother in some sick kind of way.

"Don't you ever tell your mom about this!" he would order me. "If you say a word, I'm going to kill her." The whole point of my original idea had been to somehow protect my mother, so I kept my mouth shut.

With all of this going on at home, school was an ordeal for me. I couldn't concentrate. I would be sitting in class and, instead of listening to the teacher, I'd be thinking, *Oh, no—in just another two hours I have to go home again.* I was so confused and depressed. I didn't know what to do. I didn't have a chance to grow up normally, playing with dolls and being a happy little girl. I was numb inside.

One time I got to go to a girlfriend's house after school; her name was Jeanette. To my amazement, there was no fighting in this place. It was peaceful and loving, and the family members actually listened to each other and smiled. My heart just welled up within me. *Oh, I wish I could live in a home like this!*

It was so nice being there that I stayed longer than I should have. When I realized the time and stepped outside, my mother was waiting. "Where have you been?" she asked in a worried tone. "Your father is looking for you. He's really mad!"

The minute I set foot back inside our apartment, he grabbed me and pulled me into his room. I caught such a beating that when I came out again, I was covered with blood. My mother took one look at me and immediately got me into the bathtub, where she lovingly washed the blood from my arms, legs, face, and hair.

It came to the point that when I knew I was going to have to spend the night with my father, I would hide a screwdriver or a knife under the mattress, intending to kill him. *Yes, he's my father,* I would tell myself, *but this is absolutely wrong. He is so evil that he needs to die.*

> *"Yes, he's my father,* **I would tell myself,** *but this is absolutely wrong. He is so evil that he needs to die."*—**Amalia** ∼

When it actually came to using my weapon, though . . . I could never muster up the courage. Night after night I would go ahead and submit to him. Of all the girls in the family, I guess I was the most shy and naturally compliant. I just couldn't make myself stand up to him.

This went on for years, until I was sixteen and was eagerly plotting—like my sisters and brothers—to get out of the house as soon as possible. For me, the escape route was a boy named Richard, who lived in the building across from us and was in my grade in school. We started hanging out together—much to my father's displeasure. The only way I knew to get Richard to accept me and love me was to give him my body. Wasn't that what all men wanted?

We soon found a minister to marry us and had a big Puerto Rican reception in the community center of our project. I don't recall that my father even attended; he was always hostile to any of my boyfriends, and certainly my new husband.

We couldn't afford a honeymoon; we just moved into a house a distant relative let us use. This was basically the end of schooling for me. Richard had a job at Metropolitan Hospital, and I figured he would take care of me from now on; I didn't really need to finish high school. Any dreams of what I myself might accomplish in life were left to fade away.

It was hard to have a normal sexual relationship with my teenage husband. Intimacy of any kind always got me thinking about my father again. Our marriage never really had a chance.

Meanwhile, Richard introduced me to drugs, starting with pot. At first I didn't like it, but he kept coaxing me along, and soon I realized it could make me forget all my problems at least for a while. Then came LSD and cocaine. I tried shooting up with some heroin, too—but I didn't like it, because it was a downer. I wanted anything I took to lift me up and make me happy.

The marriage lasted little more than a year. I found myself intrigued with other men, and some women as well. Richard and I split up, and he soon headed off to the army. Meanwhile, I got involved with one man after another, trying to stay high twenty-four hours a day. I got odd jobs as necessary—a shoe factory, a donut shop, whatever I could find with my limited education. But any man who would offer me some sweet talk and a place to stay could have me. And if he would provide drugs as well, so much the better.

I wore crazy outfits to catch attention on the street. I got a sales job at a pretty wild boutique called "Superfly" on Forty-Seventh and Broadway, which kept me up on all the latest fashion. Somehow I earned a reputation for dating boxers. One night I was in an underground disco when a world-famous boxing champion came in. His friend dared me to go ask him for a dance, and I did. By the end of the evening, he had invited me to his hotel.

I was with another guy that particular evening, so I turned the champ down. But a few days later, he showed up in my store, drawing a big crowd of fans on the street. He came around not so much to shop as to ask me out to dinner, and I accepted. That night, after we had been seated at our table in a fancy restaurant, he said, "Here's a pill for you. Take it—it'll make you feel good."

"What is it?" I asked.

"Just trust me. You'll like it," he said.

Whatever he hoped it would do to me—it had the opposite effect. Within minutes I was in the ladies' room throwing up! All through the meal I felt awful. Afterward he took me to his hotel room, but there definitely wasn't going to be any "action" that night—I was too sick to my stomach. I finally told him I really needed to just take a taxi home. I asked him for some cash; he was so disgusted with me that he refused. So I had to pay my own fare.

Another guy I dated in those days was actually a pimp, although I didn't realize it. When we were out, he would park his Cadillac along West Forty-Second Street and watch certain prostitutes, leaving me to wonder, *Why? Isn't he interested in me?* I didn't get it: Those were his girls! Only when he tried to put me into his business, too, did I wake up and stop seeing him.

I was now in my mid-twenties, and all this fast living just wasn't as great as I thought it would be, you know? I decided that maybe I should get a steady line of work. So I signed up to take a bartending course. Why, I don't know, because I hated all alcoholics.

When I finished the course and got my certificate, I had trouble finding a job. A lot of places in those days still weren't too open to the idea of women bartenders. When I applied at a place in Midtown called "Metropole," they said no but offered to hire me as a barmaid instead. With my low self-confidence, I said okay, I'd take the job.

Not until I reported for work did I realize what the tiny stage in the center of the bar was for. This was in fact a top-less go-go bar. *Now what have I gotten myself into?* I said. But a job was a job—and I definitely needed one, so I went to work.

The men who would come there were friendly to me, and sometimes they'd say things like, "Hey, why don't you go up there, too?"

I would glance at the girls on stage . . . and soon I came to realize that that's where the real money was. Here I was, slaving away for $200 a week plus tips, while they got paid a regular salary plus all the twenty- and fifty-dollar bills that customers would tuck into their costumes when they danced. I was afraid . . . but after a while, as the encouragements kept coming, I got the bar owner to switch my job.

My first time on stage was nerve-wracking. In fact, I probably couldn't have done it if I hadn't gotten high to start with. But as minutes went by and the customers started cheering and throwing money my way, I saw the benefits of this line of work.

. . . And that's what I've been doing for the past four years. I'm not wild about it—but what else am I going to do? Sometimes I think to myself, *How did I ever get into all this? I'm degrading myself. This isn't what I really want to do.* I get depressed and just think there's nothing else. My father already destroyed everything I once dreamed of being. I don't care how far I go now ... but then again, I do care, you know?

My finances really took a hit a couple of years ago as the result of meeting this man named Gilbert at the Metropole. I was attracted to him. We started dating. And then one night, right in the middle of a dance, I passed out—collapsed right there on stage.

I figured I had had too many Black Russian drinks that night. But the real cause was, I was pregnant. I'd been pregnant before, several times, and had always just gotten abortions so I could keep working. But this time it was different. For some reason, I wanted to go ahead and see what having a baby would be like.

> **"I'd been pregnant before, several times, and had always just gotten abortions. But this time, for some reason, I wanted to see what having a baby would be like."—Amalia** ~

Gilbert wasn't interested in sticking around for that, though, and promptly took off. I was devastated. I was left all alone—and unable to work due to the pregnancy. Eventually the electricity was cut off because I wasn't able to pay the bill. I really hit bottom. I decided it would probably be best if I just killed myself, either by slashing my wrists or else jumping off a bridge. I took a blade and started making a line on my wrist. I began to bleed. But I couldn't bring myself to cut deep enough to finish the job.

I had to humble myself and ask my mother if I could move back home. (My dad had left her by this time—the police had been called to restrain him so many times that he finally decided he'd better get out of New York City.) She took me in. I admit that I dumped a lot of anger on her. She asked me one day why I couldn't seem to finish a single sentence without using a four-letter word. We got into a big fight. Underneath, I think I was still mad at her for what happened years before.

In time, I gave birth to a healthy baby boy, whom I named Vinny. This was the most beautiful experience of my life. When I looked at him in my arms, I couldn't help feeling grateful to God.

Now I'm asking myself, how am I going to bring him up? What am I going to teach him? I don't know. . . .

In order to support him, I've had to go back to my old work. My mother takes care of the baby while I'm gone each day.

Once, after another argument with my mother, I went up on the roof of our building. Looking down eighteen stories toward the street below, I thought about the lousy job of mothering I was doing—coming home stoned at three in the morning and making my mother do all the real work. Maybe I should just jump. I began shaking and crying.

Somehow I pulled myself away, went downstairs, and went to sit in the quietness of the Catholic church my mother attends. I kept shaking and crying as I said, "God, why am I going through all this? How come you let my life get so out of control? It's all your fault."

Then my latest lover broke off our relationship, and I was devastated and even more confused. I got really serious about making a definite plan for suicide; I would go on one of the bridges and jump into the East River. I was scared to do it, but I was more scared to go on living.

My sister's husband, whose name is Mickey, has done plenty of partying with me in the past. But now he has become a Christian. So has a friend named Carmen. Suddenly she's not interested in getting high with me; now she keeps talking to me about Jesus.

So a couple of weeks ago, Mickey invited my mother and some of the rest of us to come with him here to your church. "All right, I'll go," I said.

We sat in the balcony. I probably wasn't dressed right for church, but—whatever. Mickey seemed so happy, sitting there with a big smile on his face. I couldn't figure out why.

When you got up there to preach and started to speak about God's love, I listened. I remember you saying something about "Jesus loves you no matter what you've done. He will forgive you and take you past whatever has been done to you in your life."

Pretty soon I was going, *How does he know what I'm going through? Did Mickey tell him about my life, or what?* I couldn't believe that God really understood my crazy life. All kinds of questions came to my mind.

Then, without warning, I started to cry. That's not me— I'm pretty tough. But I couldn't hold back the tears. It was ruining my makeup.

When you asked people to come to the front for prayer, I got up and went with the rest. A woman came along and laid her hand on my shoulder. That kind of spooked me— I'm not used to anything like that. But all she was doing was praying for me.

When I went home, I kept thinking about it all. I was still confused about some things. The next day, one of your pastors called to thank me for coming and to ask me how I was doing. At the end, he said, "Are you ready to trust Christ with your life?"

"Well, I don't think I'm ready for that," I answered. After all, I used to laugh at Christian television programs when I'd get high on LSD. But something was happening inside of me. I decided I should come back to your church and at least find out if I'd been "set up," if you all had some kind of plan to get to me.

So I came back this past Sunday. Your message was about the peace of God.

That same pastor caught me again and asked if I wanted to speak to you. I tried to act cool and said, "Well, why should I?" But inside, I knew I needed to.

I looked at this poor woman, so ravaged by sin and Satan, and my heart just broke. She turned to me as if to say, *What next? Am I hopeless?* ~

If something doesn't change soon, then—Pastor, I'm really messed up. I'll be honest with you—I feel really dirty even being here in your office. I don't know if I should have told you all this, but ... anyway ... um, maybe I should stop talking now....

~

THE TEARS HAD BEEN welling up in my eyes as Amalia told her story. A knot in my throat kept me from speaking. We sat there in the silence, both of us thinking deeply. It seemed to me that she had already lived three or four lives—all of them incredibly horrible.

I looked at this poor woman, so ravaged by sin and Satan, and my heart just broke. She turned to me as if to say,

What next? Am I hopeless? Do you want to just kick me out into the street, or what?

I glanced at the clock and realized the prayer meeting would soon be starting. Suddenly, I knew exactly what to do.

"Amalia," I said, "we're going to go into the prayer meeting now and ask God to do a miracle. Jesus Christ can cleanse you and make you into the woman he wants you to be. He brought you here so we could tell you the way out of the mess you're in.

"If you want Christ to save and change you, then come with me right now, and I'll have the whole church pray for you."

She kind of nodded, and we left my office. We walked down the center aisle of the church as people were already praying all around us. We sat down in the front pew.

Later, I took the microphone and announced that God had sent a special visitor to us that night. Soon Amalia was standing in front of the whole congregation. I told them none of her story—only that she had come to a crisis in her life and wanted to receive Christ as Savior. What a wonderful time we had as we prayed together and then worshiped "the Father of compassion and the God of all comfort" (2 Corinthians 1:3)!

Amalia told me later that when she went home that night to her mother, who was baby-sitting young Vinny, she exclaimed, "Mom, guess what I did tonight! I gave my heart to Jesus Christ, and he saved me! He cleansed me! I'm not the same anymore."

Her mother was speechless. Was this troubled daughter of hers finally going to straighten out?

"That night was the best sleep I'd ever had," Amalia reported, "because I felt clean. Jesus did it! No more nightmares, no more drugs, no more self-hatred, no more despair."

Pastor Boekstaaf and his wife, Ingrid, got Amalia into a Monday night discipleship group in their home. We began to see a transformation in her life. She began to look different. Her eyes brightened. Her wardrobe changed. She began to carry herself like a godly young woman instead of what sin had made her become. She found a job as a receptionist in a small law firm, then moved on to a Wall Street insurance company.

Eventually Amalia joined the Brooklyn Tabernacle Choir. A year or two later, when we held a big public concert at Radio City Music Hall, we asked her to share her testimony just before a song my wife, Carol, wrote entitled, "I'm Clean!" After her story, the choir began to sing:

> There is a blood, a cleansing blood that flows
>   from Calvary,
> And in this blood, there's a saving power,
> For it washed me white and made me clean. . . .
> Oh, I stand today with my heart so clean;
> Through the blood that Jesus shed I'm truly free.

While the choir sang, we showed a series of slides on the big screen—one picture after another that Amalia had loaned us. The hardness and degradation kept building until finally the frame dissolved slowly into the beautiful woman she had now become, in a sequined white choir gown. It seemed that all six thousand people broke down in tears together.

A few years after her salvation, Amalia met a dental technician in our church, and they fell in love and were married. The Lord gave them a son together, a half brother to Vinny, and the family moved in 1987 to another state. There they continue today to walk with God, worshiping and serving in a church pastored by a good friend of mine.

I have told Amalia's story at some length here to make the point that no matter how thoroughly the devil messes up a life—no matter how early in childhood he starts, and how frightfully he corrupts the human soul—God can take back this stolen property.

If God could change Amalia, then what are you facing that is "too impossible" for him? If God responded to her cry for mercy and grace, what is stopping you from calling on the Lord right now? God invites you to do that, and there is no better time than today. Listen to his loving invitation: "Call upon me in the day of trouble; I *will* deliver you, and you will honor me" (Psalm 50:15).

> No matter how thoroughly the devil messes up a life—no matter how early in childhood he starts—God can take back this stolen property. ～

You can see Jesus Christ prove himself more powerful than the thief who steals. This very moment is crucial, even as you read these words. Face the reality of your spiritual situation, and go after anything God has shown you to be stolen property that Satan has cleverly taken from you. The zeal and love for Christ you once had *can* be recovered. The calling on your life to serve the Lord in a particular ministry can still be fulfilled.

It's not too late, either, for God to reach that son and daughter, no matter where they are or how they seem to be doing. The family that is falling apart right now is not too hard a case for Jesus Christ if you will just stand and begin to ask in faith that he restore what the thief has tried to steal. God will do it, and you will praise him in a new way.

THREE

~

The Question Nobody Is Asking

Wʜᴇɴ ᴍᴏꜱᴛ ᴏꜰ ᴜꜱ think about how we are doing spiritually, we think about surface things. We zero in on behavior patterns, such as have we been gossiping, have we been staying true to our marriage, have we been reading our Bibles, have we been tithing? We concentrate on outward works while forgetting that they are simply the fruit of a deeper spiritual factor.

In the organized church, too many pastors are interested in attendance alone, which has nothing to do with a church's health. What matters is not how many people are showing up, but how active and vibrant their faith is in the God they serve. You can easily pack a building without pleasing God, because crowds do not equal spirituality.

When Paul sent Timothy to check up on the new Thessalonian church (where he had been able to spend only three weeks before getting run out of town), you think he would have asked first about the church's growth. Did they have a building of their own yet? How many people were attending on Sundays? Were the offerings enough to cover the bills? And what about the individual people: Had they stopped swearing, drinking, carousing? Going to see bad entertainment? Sleeping around?

Not at all! Instead, in 1 Thessalonians 3, the apostle Paul reveals that his primary concern is for the *faith level* of his precious converts. He wants to take a temperature reading of their spiritual health, and faith is what he is looking for. He doesn't just assume that because they are Christians, they are automatically walking in robust faith. Listen to his words and see how unfamiliar his approach is to our modern ears:

- "We sent Timothy . . . to strengthen and encourage you in *your faith*" (v. 2).
- "When I could stand it no longer, I sent to find out about *your faith*" (v. 5).
- "But Timothy has just now come to us from you and has brought good news about *your faith* and love" (v. 6).
- "Therefore, brothers, in all our distress and persecution we were encouraged about you because of *your faith*" (v. 7).
- "Night and day we pray most earnestly that we may see you again and supply what is lacking in *your faith*" (v. 10).

From top to bottom throughout this chapter, Paul is churned up about one simple word. In fact, this is more than a checkup, an inspection. He has sent Timothy to "strengthen and encourage" the people in their faith—in other words, to do what he could to make the report better.

Timothy has brought back a great summary, as quoted above. Nothing is said about the Thessalonian building, you notice. Nothing about the sound system or the lights or the carpet. Instead, a lot of attention to their faith. But even that isn't enough for Paul. In verse 10 he says he wants to make another trip there himself to "see you again and supply what is lacking in your faith." Faith. Faith. Faith. Faith.

Why this emphasis?

WHAT MOVES THE HEART OF GOD

WHAT PAUL KNEW, but what we seem to have forgotten, is that when people break down in their behavior, backslide into sinful living, or grow cold in the Lord, it is because their faith has broken down first. When someone's temper keeps flaring out of control, that is not the real problem; down underneath is a weakness of faith. So it is with all our departures from right living.

My ministry goal in the Brooklyn Tabernacle is not to fill the building. It is to preach the Word of God in such a way that people's faith in Christ is built up. God doesn't need the beautiful music of a church choir. If he wanted great music, he'd have the angels sing! They never miss a word or sing off-key. But what he is really after is a people who show a strong, personal faith in him.

> **God doesn't need the beautiful music of a church choir. If he wanted great music, he'd have the angels sing!** ～

What do you think it would take to amaze Jesus? After all, through him the world and all humanity were created in the first place. He has forever existed in heaven itself. While on earth, was there anything that impressed him to the point of exclaiming, "That's really something! Wow!" Never in any chapter of the four Gospels was Jesus astounded by anybody's righteousness. After all, he was entirely pure and holy himself. Never was he impressed with anyone's wisdom or education. Never did he say, "Boy, Matthew sure is smart, isn't he? I really picked out a financial genius there."

But he *was* amazed by one thing: people's faith.

When he told the Roman centurion he would go to his house to heal his servant, and the centurion said not to bother but just to speak the word of healing, Jesus "was amazed at him, and turning to the crowd following him, he said, 'I tell you, I have not found such *great faith* even in Israel'" (Luke 7:9). The Jewish listeners probably didn't appreciate being outclassed by this Roman, but that is the way it happened, regardless.

> **Never in the four Gospels was Jesus astounded by anybody's righteousness. Never was he impressed with anyone's education. But he *was* amazed by one thing: people's faith. ～**

When another "foreigner," a Canaanite woman, came pleading on behalf of her demon-possessed daughter and wouldn't take no for an answer, Jesus exclaimed at last, "Woman, you have *great faith!* Your request is granted" (Matthew 15:28).

On the other hand, when he went back to his hometown of Nazareth, where he had grown up, "he could not do any miracles there, except lay his hands on a few sick people and heal them. And he was amazed at their *lack of faith*" (Mark 6:5–6). You can be sure that no sickness was too extreme, no demon too powerful for the Son of the living God. But on that particular day in Nazareth, his hands were tied by their unbelief. In fact, he laid down this statement as a first principle: "According to your faith will it be done to you" (Matthew 9:29).

We can't twist the story theologically by saying, "Well, maybe it wasn't God's will for him to heal those folks in

Nazareth." The text gives no indication of that. It clearly says the Son of God was limited that day.

Faith alone is the trigger that releases divine power. As Peter wrote, it is "through *faith* [that we] are shielded by God's power" (1 Peter 1:5). Our trying, struggling, or promising won't work—faith is what God is after. Faith is the key to our relationship with him.

MORE THAN TALK

I AM NOT JUST talking about our words. Faith is far more than talk. Sometimes we are not much better than those in Isaiah's time, of whom the Lord said, "These people come near to me with their mouth and honor me with their lips, but their hearts are far from me" (Isaiah 29:13).

> **In our time, the whole notion of faith has been derailed in some quarters into an emphasis on saying certain words, giving a "positive confession" of health, prosperity, or other blessings.** ∽

In our time, the whole notion of faith has been derailed in some quarters into an emphasis on saying certain words, giving a "positive confession," or announcing a superconfident description of health, prosperity, or other blessings. You know, a kind of spiritual mantra. A mental formula of "how the Bible will work for you" is front and center, while the question of a true heart-faith and communion with the living Christ is rarely emphasized.

This formula is not the spirit or message of the New Testament, and it leads to gross absurdities. It actually has dampened the desire for real prayer meetings all across the land. People cannot call out to the Lord for answers to their problems because, according to their teaching, you shouldn't even say you have a problem. To admit that you're sick or in trouble is supposedly bad; you're using your mouth to say something negative, and that is not "living in faith."

If that is true, why did the apostle James declare, "Is any one of you in trouble? He should pray. . . . Is any one of you sick? He should call the elders of the church to pray over him and anoint him with oil in the name of the Lord" (James 5:13–14). How can we truly pray, or ask others to pray, unless we first admit we're facing some kind of real problem? Believers in the New Testament obviously did this.

A minister once told me that when people come to the altar in his church for individual prayer, he has trained them not to say, "I have a cold" or "I have diabetes" or whatever. Instead, they are to say, "I have *the symptoms of* a cold" or "I have *the symptoms of* diabetes." Otherwise, they would not be walking "in faith." (I guess when someone has stopped breathing for two weeks, they have only "the symptoms of death.")

To me, this is little more than a mind game. The faith God wants for us does not shrink from facing the reality of the problem head-on. When Abraham saw the years going by without a child coming into his home, he didn't say, "My wife and I seem to be having some of the symptoms of infertility." Instead, he was totally straightforward: *"Without weakening in his faith*, he faced the fact that his body was as good as dead— since he was about a hundred years old—and that Sarah's womb was also dead. Yet he did not waver through unbelief regarding the promise of God, but *was strengthened in his faith* and gave glory to God, being fully persuaded that God had power to do what he had promised" (Romans 4:19–21).

Isn't that a powerful Scripture? Realism about the problem was not anti-faith in the slightest. In fact, it made Abraham say, "O God, you are the only one who can change this situation. Come and help us, we pray!"

Paul and the other biblical writers were not promoting "fantasy faith" or "hyper-faith." Nothing in 1 Thessalonians 3 even seems to touch on how the Christians in that city talked or what kind of declarations they made. Paul was looking for something far deeper: true faith.

STRUGGLE ON AND ON?

By contrast, there are many others going to church today in America whose faith has gone dormant. They would never admit that, of course. They would claim to have faith in God and his Word. They stand in church on Sunday morning and recite the Apostles' Creed.

But if you watch carefully, you will see a hybrid Christianity. You will see people who think that the object of Christianity is to read the Bible every day, try to live a good life as best they can, and thus earn God's approval.

> **Whatever happened to the core truth of the Protestant Reformation, namely, that we do not earn our way with God but rather receive his grace by faith?** ~

Their key word in describing the Christian life is "struggle." They say things such as "I'm *struggling* to obey the Lord and do his will. I'm doing the best I can. We all *struggle*, you know." What this reveals is a Christianity focused on our ability rather than God's.

Whatever happened to the core truth of the Protestant Reformation, namely, that we do not earn our way with God but rather receive his grace by faith? Like the Galatians, we have walked away from something vital. No wonder the apostle Paul sent them a stern letter that said, "Are you so foolish? After beginning with the Spirit, are you now trying to attain your goal by human effort?" (Galatians 3:3).

True Christianity is, rather, to know Jesus and trust in him, to rely on him, to admit that all of our strength comes from him. That kind of faith is not only what pleases God, but is also the only channel through which the power of God flows into our lives so we *can* live victoriously for him. It is what Paul meant when he wrote, "I can do everything *through him [Christ] who gives me strength*" (Philippians 4:13).

My coauthor, Dean Merrill, was at a wedding recently in which the bride and groom's responses to the vows were not just the traditional "I do" but rather "I will, with the help of God." The minister who wrote that ceremony knew that human effort alone might not carry the young couple in today's world "until death do you part." He therefore called on them to implore the help of God in building their marriage.

When most people break down in their Christian life, they simply "try harder." Lots of luck! Try harder with what? ∽

This declaration was very much in keeping with what Solomon said at the dedication of the Temple: "May the LORD our God be with us as he was with our fathers; may he never leave us nor forsake us. *May he turn our hearts to him*, to walk in all his ways and to keep the commands, decrees and regulations he gave our fathers" (1 Kings 8:57–58). In that sentence Solomon showed great insight into the fact that God himself must turn our hearts toward him, or else we will stray.

When most people break down in their Christian life, they simply "try harder." Lots of luck! Try harder with what? I've looked inside of me—and stopped looking. There's nothing in there that's good or usable. On the other hand, if I turn the other way and begin "looking unto Jesus, the author and finisher of our faith" (Hebrews 12:2 KJV), I find everything I need.

It does no good to try to control people and get them to behave by giving them only laws and threats about hell. That won't cut it. They won't change. How do the righteous actually live? "By faith."

> **The greatest Christian is not the one who has *achieved* the most but rather the one who has *received* the most.** ∼

When I was growing up, I thought the greatest Christian must be the person who walks around with shoulders thrown back because of tremendous inner strength and power, quoting Scripture and letting everyone know he has arrived. I have since learned that the most mature believer is the one who is bent over, leaning most heavily on the Lord, and admitting his total inability to do anything without Christ. The greatest Christian is not the one who has *achieved* the most but rather the one who has *received* the most. God's grace, love, and mercy flow through him abundantly because he walks in total dependence.

I remember an afternoon many years ago when God made this truth come alive in my heart. While driving down a New Jersey boulevard, I was listening to an elderly minister from Great Britain whose books had blessed me as a young pastor. The radio station was broadcasting a tape of one of his last messages preached at a well-known Bible conference here in America.

The speaker related how, after many years of successful ministry as a teacher and expositor of God's Word, he was forced to stay home due to a lingering illness. This change from his usual busy schedule of speaking, traveling, and writing began to slowly bring on a sense of depression. He struggled to overcome it by fastening his attention on God's Word, but that was difficult due to his ill health.

"Suddenly," he related, "it seemed as if a sewer top had been lifted, and an ugly host of temptations, irritations, and evil thoughts rose up to besiege me." Here he was, a noted Bible teacher and author, fighting against things he had not encountered for many years. His voice broke slightly as he shared his horror at being tempted even to swear, something that had never surfaced in his entire life, even before he became a Christian.

"How can this be?" he cried to the Lord. "After all these years of Christian service and careful study of the Bible, why am I in such a desperate battle?"

As he sought the Lord, God made real to him that his human nature had never really changed. Oh, yes, "if anyone is in Christ, he is a new creation" (2 Corinthians 5:17)—but only because *Christ* is in him as the indwelling Savior and Helper.

I pulled over to the curb that afternoon and wept. One of my heroes in the faith had stunned me with his vulnerability. In the same way, I had to admit that Jim Cymbala the man had never changed—the "old man," the flesh, my sinful nature. Apart from God's grace and power, I too was hopeless.

The truth is that God never works with our "flesh," or old nature—that's how depraved it is. That is why we never stop needing the power of the Holy Spirit during our whole pilgrimage here on earth. We never reach a place where we can live victoriously apart from his daily grace in our lives. Only the Spirit can produce *his* fruit, in and through us, that makes us the people God wants us to be. And God has to show us regularly how needy we are.

The great apostle Paul himself had to learn that seeming contradiction of God's strength coming out of personal weakness. He writes in 2 Corinthians 12:9–10 that the Lord "said to me, 'My grace is sufficient for you, for my power is made perfect in weakness.' Therefore I will boast all the more gladly about my weaknesses, so that Christ's power may rest on me. That is why, for Christ's sake, I delight in weaknesses, in insults, in hardships, in persecutions, in difficulties. For when I am weak, then I am strong."

Paul is not just trying to be overly humble or self-deprecating here. He has found the secret that we were created to be receiving vessels only—not having any strength in ourselves but merely depending on God to fill us hourly with all we need. Paul also knew that God uses trouble and trials of all kinds to heighten that sensitivity so that by faith we can use divine resources.

Don't give up today because you feel weak and overwhelmed—that's the very place where divine power will uphold you if you only believe and call out to the Lord in total dependence. Childlike faith in God is not only what pleases him but is also the secret of our strength and power.

"Help, Lord!"

IF WE ONLY ATTACK the symptoms of unbelief—the various outbreaks of sin in our churches, for example—we will never get to the root cause. That is why legalistic preaching never produces true spirituality. It might seem to do so for the moment, but it cannot last. Christians become strong only by seeing and understanding the grace of God, which is received by faith.

> **If we only attack the symptoms of unbelief—the various outbreaks of sin—we will never get to the root cause. Legalistic preaching never produces true spirituality.** ～

Some years ago I was taking my granddaughter Susie on a walk when a couple of homeless men came walking toward us. Their scruffy appearance made her afraid. In her little mind, she thought she was about to be harmed. She was already holding my hand, but instantly I felt her push her body into mine as she grabbed onto my pant leg. "Papa!" she whispered. Of course, I put my arm around her and said that everything was going to be all right. The men passed us on the sidewalk without incident.

Inside, my heart was brimming. That instantaneous reflex of reaching out for my aid meant that she thought I could handle anything and everything. This was a more precious gift than any sweater she would ever give me for Christmas. She showed that she had a deep faith in me. I would come to her rescue. I would meet her urgent need. I would take care of her.

That is the very thing that delights the heart of God. When we run to him and throw ourselves upon him in believing prayer, he rejoices. He does not want me out on my own, trying to earn merit stars from him. He wants us, rather, to lean into him, walking with him as closely as possible. He is not so much interested in our *doing* as in our *receiving* from him. After all, what can we do or say or conquer without first receiving grace at God's throne to help us in our time of need (Hebrews 4:16)? And all that receiving happens through faith.

Possibly there is a need in your life today to stop all the struggling with your own strength. Let it go, and call out to God in simple faith. Remember that no one has ever been disappointed after putting trust in him. Not one person throughout all of human history has ever depended upon God and found that God let him down. Never! Not once!

Face the obvious fact that the problem or need is far too big for you to handle. Use the very fact of your inadequacy as a springboard to a new, wholehearted trust in God's unfailing promises.

> Therefore let everyone who is godly pray to you
>   while you may be found;
> surely when the mighty waters rise,
>   they will not reach him.
> You are my hiding place;
>   you will protect me from trouble
>   and surround me with songs of deliverance. *Selah*
>
> I will instruct you and teach you in the way you
>   should go;
>   I will counsel you and watch over you.
> Do not be like the horse or the mule,
>   which have no understanding
> but must be controlled by bit and bridle
>   or they will not come to you.
> Many are the woes of the wicked,
>   but the LORD's unfailing love
>   surrounds the man who trusts in him.
>
> Rejoice in the LORD and be glad, you righteous;
>   sing, all you who are upright in heart!
>   (Psalm 32:6–11)

PART 2

Getting Past
the Barricades

FOUR

⁓

Free from a
Hurtful Past

All this talk about faith and God's promises is wonderful, but I've learned that it sometimes falls on deaf ears. Many people carry scars from days gone by. Life has not been kind to them. The idea that God might act powerfully on their behalf strikes them right away as too good to be true. *Maybe somebody else, but not me. Others can get answers to their prayers, but not me. Nothing much can change my life now. Too much has happened, too much has already gone wrong....*

Whenever I meet this kind of person, I always think about a special secret in the life of Joseph. Even if the person has heard his story before, I go through it again, telling how Joseph grew up in what we would call a classic "dysfunctional family." Most circumstances in his boyhood years were beyond his control. After all, he was the eleventh son out of twelve—far down the line.

Joseph's father, Jacob, favors him. For some reason, something about Joseph strikes a tender cord inside of Jacob. The boy has come along late in his life and is the firstborn son of his beloved wife, Rachel.

All this attention turns out to be a curse for Joseph instead of a blessing. The special coat he receives from his father makes him a marked young man. The more Jacob does

53

for him, the more his older brothers hate him. (Siblings have a way of picking up on any little inequity; they notice it right away, and they resent it.)

When Joseph is seventeen years old, he tattles on some of his brothers about something they have done out in the field (see Genesis 37:2). This obviously does not improve the situation. Nobody likes a snitch, especially if he's the father's pet.

On top of all this, God begins to give Joseph dreams about the future. Joseph hasn't asked for this; it just happens. In his youthfulness, he makes the mistake of talking about his dreams—the sheaves of grain that all bow down to his sheaf, and the sun, moon, and stars that bow down to him. With this last one, even his father gets upset. "Get a grip, son!" says Jacob (I'm paraphrasing here). "What are you trying to say— that you're going to run the whole family? That your mother and I and all your brothers are going to bow down to you?"

"I don't know what it means, Dad. I'm just telling you what I saw."

Obviously, this family is not functioning smoothly. For all of us who had rough moments growing up, for all of us who have ever been hurt by a family member, we can understand. Joseph's brothers can see no good in him and never say even one kind word. All of this is taking a toll on Joseph's tender heart.

THE PLOT THICKENS

JOSEPH IS SENT ONE DAY to see how his brothers are getting along with the sheep in the open fields. After a couple of stops, he finds them near Dothan. As he is coming toward them, they look up and see that colorful coat. "Here comes Daddy's boy," someone snarls. Anger boils up anew.

They are all alone on the wide plains. This is a perfect setting for revenge, and a plan takes shape in a matter of minutes. They will not just ignore him, curse him, or even hit him—this time, *they will kill him.*

Within seconds, they grab him and rip off the hated coat. Joseph, being in his late teens, no doubt puts up a vigorous fight. He struggles, but in vain; clearly outnumbered, he is mauled. Several of them intend to kill him immediately, but Reuben, the oldest, suggests shoving him into a cistern, a deep pit in the ground that retains water. Quickly he goes sliding down into the mud hole, his heart pounding with panic, feeling their hatred up close.

Joseph, a sensitive young man, could actually hear his own brothers talk about murdering him. Imagine the emotional trauma of crouching there, helpless, and listening to this from your own siblings. What a jolt to his young mind and heart!

Meanwhile, his brothers coldly sit down to have lunch (Genesis 37:25).

While they are eating, a trading caravan comes along. Older brother Judah suddenly gets a bright idea. "Look, guys, it will be less messy if, instead of killing him, we just sell him as a slave to these traders. That way we can make a little profit on the deal."

Imagine Joseph being pulled back up out of the pit by his brothers, his clothing a muddy mess, if not already torn off. See his eyes wide with shock as his brothers haggle with the traders: "Good-looking kid, don't you think? How much will you pay for him? Only twelve shekels? Ah, come on—he's worth more than that! Twenty-five at least."

Joseph is numb by now. His own brothers are selling him down the river. The bargaining continues. Finally, they settle on twenty shekels. "Sold!"

He watches the silver pieces being counted. Tears well up in his eyes. This can't really be happening, can it? He won't be going back home. Strangers grab him roughly, treat him like a piece of meat, and thrust him toward their caravan.

(It's a good thing Joseph didn't know what his brothers said when they returned home to Jacob: "Look, Dad!—we found Joseph's coat with all this blood on it. It looks like something terrible has happened." And when their father collapsed in tears of grief, they had the gall to pretend to mourn along with him. "God be with you, Dad. It's hard, we know! He was a wonderful brother...." What a charming group of young men.)

A FUTURE AFTER ALL?

BUT THE BIBLE SAYS in Genesis 39:2 that "the LORD was with Joseph." Somehow, standing there on the block in the Egyptian slave market, Joseph ends up getting purchased by Potiphar, a man of prestige and wealth.

An odd thing begins to happen as the weeks and months go by. His master notices that whatever Joseph touches seems to prosper. Potiphar realizes he can trust his young Hebrew slave and gradually gives him more responsibility. In time, he makes him the general manager of his household.

The only trouble is, Potiphar's wife is apparently having other thoughts about Joseph, who is a little too young and handsome for her to ignore. She begins to make a move on him. He turns her down, but she is not easily dissuaded. She keeps flirting with him, until the day comes when her husband is at work, and nobody else is around—just the two of them. Suddenly she reaches for him, grabbing his coat and insisting that he yield to her desires.

But Joseph does not want to disgrace either God or Potiphar, his master, by giving in to this woman. If he loses God's approval, he will lose everything valuable in life. He quickly wrestles his way out of his coat and runs for the exits.

(Funny how Joseph seems to keep having trouble with coats, isn't it?)

Potiphar's wife, humiliated, immediately begins to scream, "Rape! Rape!" The other servants come rushing in, and by that evening Potiphar has heard her whole twisted version of the story. The next day, Joseph's life comes crashing down for the second time. He is promptly arrested and ends up in the slammer.

What is he thinking now? *How could this happen? Why?!* Yet, even in prison, God is with Joseph. His talent and honesty rise like cream to the top. The warden begins to notice the same characteristics that had originally caught Potiphar's attention. Before long, Joseph is put in charge of his cell block. The place is not as plush as Potiphar's house, to be sure, but at least he has some room to maneuver.

Months go by. Joseph lies awake every night thinking about all that has happened to him. The disaster that day in the open field outside Dothan ... the caravan ride to Egypt ... the hopes that got dashed while working for Potiphar. Now he's a convict. His family has no idea where he is, and most of them don't care. There is no legal statute to appeal to, no court-appointed attorney. Where is God in all of this? How will those dreams ever come true?

Joseph lies awake every night thinking about all that has happened to him. Where is God in all of this? ∽

One day a couple of new prisoners show up. Pharaoh has gotten irritated with his baker and his cupbearer, the fellow who had the lucky job of tasting all Pharaoh's wine ahead of time to be sure it wasn't poisoned. (What a great way to make a living!) On the same night both of these prisoners have dreams. The baker's has to do with bakery goods, and the cupbearer's has to do with wine. Both suspect that the dreams have significance, but they can't figure them out.

Joseph then steps in with interpretations from God— one of them a disastrous outcome, the other a happy one. And his predictions come true.

As the cupbearer is dancing out the door to freedom, Joseph says, "Please, friend ... remember me when you get out of this place, okay? I'm doing time for no crime at all. I really don't deserve to be here."

"Sure. Don't worry—you can count on me."

Joseph's heart skips a beat with anticipation. Maybe this will be his big break.

MORE DARKNESS

BUT UNBELIEVABLY, THE CUPBEARER somehow "forgets." And for two more needless years, Joseph rots in his cell.

And we think we have problems? People have forgotten to appreciate us? How would you like to help somebody and have that person promptly forget that you even exist?

After two years, God steps in to overrule human frailty. This time, a vivid dream comes to Pharaoh himself. In fact, it is a "double feature." First he sees seven fats cows coming out of the Nile followed by seven skinny cows, which swallow the fat ones. Then he sees approximately the same thing again, only with heads of grain.

He calls for Egypt's best magicians and occultists—a specialty in Egyptian culture—and asks for the interpretation of what he has dreamed. They are completely baffled.

Off in one corner, the cupbearer is muttering to himself, "Dreams ... dreams ... oh, now I remember! Pharaoh!

There's a young Hebrew in prison I totally forgot about. He's amazing at dream interpretation."

And that is how Joseph ends up before the imperial throne, saying, "I cannot do it, . . . but God will give Pharaoh the answer he desires" (Genesis 41:16). Joseph proceeds to unfold the divine crop forecast for the next fourteen years. The first seven will be years of blessing and plenty, followed by seven years of famine and shortage. Joseph proposes that with good advance planning, Pharaoh can not only prevent mass starvation but also turn his country into the food supplier for the whole region.

That very day Joseph becomes the second-most powerful man in all of Egypt. Pharaoh installs him immediately with authority to prepare the land for the coming famine.

The court officials are stunned to see this thirty-year-old Hebrew, who has come out of nowhere, being given a royal ring of authority, a gold chain around his neck, a government-issued chariot, and a linen robe. (He finally gets a coat *back*, a very expensive one this time!) Within a matter of hours, people on the street are required to kneel down as his chariot roars past.

The bumper crops begin to come as Joseph predicted, and he is very busy managing the abundance. The whole commodities business of the Middle East looks his way. Senior managers wait outside his office; staff members send him monthly reports. The granaries steadily swell with food for the future.

REVENGE AT LAST?

WHAT WOULD YOU have done with all this power? What would you do if you were Joseph now?

I'll tell you what I might have done. I might have said, "Chariot driver, I have a couple of stops I need to make.

Drive me over to Mrs. Potiphar's house, if you will. I have an old score I need to settle. That woman got me sent to the slammer for a big chunk of my life. It's payback time at last!"

Then I would have headed back to the palace and said to Pharaoh, "Excuse me, but I need to take a week off, if you don't mind. I'm leaving with a couple of army squadrons on a run up to Canaan. I've been waiting to visit my brothers up there for a long, long time." Oooh, how sweet it would have been—vengeance at last!

But not Joseph.

The Bible records that "before the years of famine came, two sons were born to Joseph by Asenath daughter of Potiphera, priest of On. Joseph named his firstborn *Manasseh* and said, 'It is because God has made me *forget* all my trouble and all my father's household'" (Genesis 41:50–51).

> When Joseph held the first little baby boy in his arms, he said, "I will name this boy Manasseh, because *God has made me forget* all the evil that has been done to me." ∿

When Joseph held the first little baby boy in his arms, he named him Manasseh, which sounds like the Hebrew word for "forget." Names in those days were not chosen just for their pleasing sound; they always had a meaning.

Joseph could have named his son "Crops" or "Gold" or "Success." He did not. Instead, he focused on the really great thing God had done in his life. As Joseph stood there holding the infant and thinking of all that had happened, he singled out the best of God's blessings as he said, "I will name this boy Manasseh, because *God has made me forget* all the evil that has been done to me."

He didn't say he had learned to forget. He didn't say he had enrolled in a seven-step course or gone to a psychiatrist for help. Instead he said, "God *made me forget.*" God can still touch us supernaturally where no therapist can reach.

Neither was Joseph referring to amnesia. The facts were not erased from his memory. But God took the sting out, so there was no bitterness. The temptation of a mean spirit was conquered. God cleansed Joseph's mind of all the residue that would have naturally festered there from the mistreatment he had suffered. What happiness would his position and wealth have brought if he had been an embittered and angry man?

One of the subtle ways Satan hinders us today is by playing unpleasant tape recordings in our minds over and over and over. People lie in bed at night watching old videos on the inner screen of their hearts. They ride in the car looking out the window but seeing nothing; instead, they daydream about the time someone hurt them, took advantage of them, made them suffer. Hurtful words said by others are heard again and again. Horrible, ugly scenes are repeated hour after hour, day after day, year after year.

> **God can make you forget. He does not obliterate the events, but he can deliver you from the paralysis of the past.** ～

Possibly you are haunted by painful chapters from your past. Some hellish things might have happened to you. Maybe many of them were beyond your control. Whatever the case may be, I want you to know beyond a doubt that God can make you forget. He does not obliterate the events, but he can deliver you from the paralysis of the past.

Earlier I told you about Amalia—but there is more to her story. I remember how, in the early months of her walk with the Lord, I would come onto the platform each Sunday and look up to see her in the same balcony seat. My heart would rejoice as I would notice her with hands raised, praising the Lord and then listening carefully to God's Word.

Every Monday night she was in a home discipleship group. The change in her was dramatic.

Then one Sunday, some months later ... she wasn't there. I was concerned. Silently I prayed, *O God, watch over Amalia!*

The next Sunday, she was back. I saw her in the lobby. "Hi, Pastor Cymbala," she said with a big smile on her face.

"Hello, Amalia. I missed you last Sunday. Is everything okay?"

"Yes, I was away. You know, you preached something about the love of God and forgiveness—so I took the bus upstate to where my father lives."

Her father? I was stunned to hear him even mentioned.

"Yeah—I had to. He lives with his sister up there now, just sitting in a little trailer out in the countryside drinking beer day after day. I forced myself to go see him after all these years."

"How did it go? What did you say?" I asked. It was the last place I expected her to visit.

"I was very nervous. Finally, after the evening meal, I said, 'Pop, I need to talk to you about something. I want you to be serious. You know, I've been remembering the things that happened back when I was a girl. Those years were really hard, and I have to admit that I hated you—'

"'Oh, don't worry about that,' he butted in. 'That was a long time ago; we don't need to talk about that now.'"

Amalia felt the anger well up inside of her again, but she held her composure. She continued, "Yes, we do, Pop. It really hurt me, and I wanted to kill you so many times.... But I came up here this weekend because I want to tell you that I'm a Christian now. I gave my heart to the Lord, and he changed my life.

"You used to be in all of my nightmares. I used to think about you every day. But now, God has made me forget.... Pop, what you did was wrong. But I don't hate you anymore. I forgive you! God can change your life and forgive you, too, Pop. I love you! ..."

The man squirmed in his chair at these words from his grown daughter. He quickly found a way to slide off the topic and lighten up the atmosphere. He never did apologize; it proved to be a one-way conversation, which was a great disappointment to Amalia. The rest of the short visit passed without the hoped-for breakthrough or reconciliation.

But Amalia returned home with a peace in her soul for having done what she knew was right. And the seed of God's Word had been planted.

TIME TO FORGET

THE ONLY REASON AMALIA could do what she did is that God is the God of Manasseh, the God who can make us forget.

If you are paralyzed by your past, if Satan is destroying your gifts and your calling by his incessant replaying of old tapes, you're actually being hit by a double whammy. The original damage in the past is one thing—but now you're letting yourself be hurt and sidetracked again by the memory of what happened.

Think of all the people in the church today who go around with an "edge"—some kind of inner anger or constant irritability. Think of others who seem permanently depressed in spirit because something happened, somewhere, sometime. The ugly memories are like chains around them. We should not be ignorant of Satan's devices, and these ugly memories are one of the main weapons in his arsenal.

God wants to remind you today that the same God who has dealt with every sin and wrong deed you've ever done has the ability to make you forget the negative and hurtful things in your life. The grace of God can overcome their power to haunt you.

> **God's people have found that the most precious fruit often grows in the midst of overwhelming difficulties. Faith grows best on cloudy days.** ∽

When a second son came along for Joseph, he chose another significant name. "The second son he named Ephraim and said, 'It is because God has made me *fruitful in the land of my suffering*'" (Genesis 41:52). God taught Joseph that if you put your life in his hands, the worst damage can be turned to good. You can be spiritually fruitful even in the hardest place. In fact, God's people have found that the most precious fruit often grows in the midst of overwhelming difficulties. Faith grows best on cloudy days. Never forget that name of *Ephraim*—"fruitful *in* the land of my suffering."

Every one of us has had painful experiences in life. If you're alive and breathing, somebody sometime has hurt you! In a city such as mine, nasty behavior is everywhere. But you don't have to live in New York City to be hurt. The pain can come from your own family, your in-laws, or other people you genuinely care for.

If you live in that hurt, if those tapes play over and over, you will be paralyzed by them. Every time the Holy Spirit nudges you to step out in faith and do something God wants you to do, this strange bondage to the past will hold you back from God's best for your life.

Do you believe God can set you free, or are you going to keep being a victim of your past? God is the God of Manasseh. He can make you forget. Approach his throne of grace boldly and ask him for that grace to help you right where you need it.

FIVE

∽

Can I Trust God
to Lead Me?

IT MAY NOT SEEM obvious at first glance, but the way we make decisions in life tells a lot about the kind of faith we have in Jesus Christ. The very process of decision making often reveals our "faith temperature." What does the Bible teach us about this crucial subject?

Some decisions, of course, are about *moral* issues. For example, shall I steal supplies from my employer? We don't need to pray about this one—just read the Bible. There's no need to say, "Lord, is it okay to have this rotten attitude toward my teenager?" The Book already tells us.

Lying is wrong; you don't have to ask God for special insight into the matter. The same thing is true about hating, about prejudice, about marrying a non-Christian. Young women in love will sometimes say to their pastors, "Oh, he's not a believer now, but the Lord showed me he'll come around after the wedding." That cannot be a word from God, for it violates his truth revealed in Scripture. If something is contrary to the Bible, it's wrong. Don't waste your time by praying about it. God gave us a very long "letter" with all kinds of moral instructions. What we need to do is simply read the letter!

Every moral decision, every supposed manifestation of the Spirit, every sermon by a preacher no matter how clever or charismatic—each is to be judged by God's Word. That is what shapes our theology and practice, rather than religious tradition or secular philosophy.

THE FORGOTTEN STANDARD

I AM REPEATEDLY AMAZED as I travel across the country and meet Christians who do not use the Bible as their guide and goal in pursuing spiritual things. Instead, people merely follow the particular spiritual culture into which they were born, never carefully comparing it to the biblical model. In fact, many devote themselves to perpetuating their way of doing things as if they had found it in Scripture itself. Their faith is stale because they are relying on something other than the living God who reveals himself to us through the Bible.

To give an analogy: I was born in a Brooklyn hospital to a Polish mother and a Ukrainian father. I did not ask to have Eastern European parents; I did not ask to be white. That was simply the accident of my birth. To make a big thing about my color or ethnic background is senseless; it just happened to be the way I providentially came into this world. When people get all puffed up about these things, it is really an extension of their own ego. If they had been born a different color or raised in a different country, they would be boasting about that instead.

The same is true about the circumstances of our spiritual birth. The church or denomination where we started out just happened to be where we found ourselves at the time of receiving God's salvation. And as in our natural birth, our initial surroundings gave far-reaching shape to our understanding of things. Our first church atmosphere, with its pastors and teachers, automatically set the definitions for many key words such as *prayer, worship, church, evangelism, God's power, faith*, even *Christian* itself. We didn't first learn those concepts so much from the Scripture as from what we saw around us at church. We unconsciously absorbed a Presbyterian or Baptist or Nazarene or Pentecostal understanding of those important words.

Today those impressions still leap to the forefront of our minds every time we hear the words—whether they are what God intended or not. Thus, instead of coming to the Scriptures like a child, saying, "God, teach me," we go looking for ammunition to back up what we've already embraced. Too often our main goal is to perpetuate the traditions handed down from our elders. We're not really that open to change and growth.

The little church where my parents took me as a boy had some very good qualities to it—but it was also an all-white, mostly Eastern European group in the middle of Bedford-Stuyvesant, one of the best-known black neighborhoods in America! And the church members clearly wanted the church to stay the way it was. They did not seem at all interested in welcoming people who were "different."

> **When we stand before God, we will not be asked, "Were you a good evangelical?" or "Were you a good charismatic?" What will really matter is whether we honestly let God's Word shape our spiritual thinking. ～**

Even though I learned many truths from the Bible there, should I now spend my life trying to replicate that tradition just because it's the place where I started out learning about Jesus? When I stand before God, I will not be asked, "Were you a good evangelical?" or "Were you a good charismatic?" As a matter of fact, God doesn't recognize our divisions. His calling is for us to be Christlike rather than a good member of some man-made denomination.

What will really matter is whether we honestly search God's Word and let it shape our spiritual thinking and values. This is one of the great battles in the Christian life: to approach the Bible without presuppositions, letting it shape us instead of vice versa.

I love what the great John Wesley, catalyst of the Methodist awakening, said in the 1700s: "Would to God that all party names, and unscriptural phrases and forms which have divided the Christian world, were forgot.... I should rejoice ... if the very name [Methodist] might never be mentioned more, but be buried in eternal oblivion."[1] A century later, the equally great Charles Spurgeon, prince of Baptist preachers, said from the pulpit, "I say of the Baptist name, let it perish, but let Christ's name last for ever. I look forward with pleasure to the day when there will not be a Baptist living."[2]

This kind of talk may burst a few bubbles, but here is the truth: Neither your personal background nor mine is the norm! What the Bible teaches is what we should pursue. Whenever any of us encounter something new or different, we should not ask, "Am I used to that when I go to church?" but rather "Do I find this in the Bible?"

What About the Gray Areas?

Some decisions in life are not about moral issues per se, but they simply need *sanctified reasoning*.

For example, the Bible doesn't explicitly say that you should show up for work on time every day. But if you understand God's principles of sowing and reaping, you will be punctual. Also, you are to do your work as if serving the Lord himself.

The Bible doesn't tell you how to respond to your spouse in every situation. But if your husband or wife is upset and discouraged, it's wise for you to be comforting and supportive.

Now, with this foundation, what about the third kind of decision making—those important situations in which we don't have a right-or-wrong element and no Bible passage directly applies? There are many forks in the road where we have to make a choice. What are we to do if we want God's will in everything?

Many people today are making these kinds of decisions without a passing thought of seeking God. They think that as long as they don't lie, kill, steal, or commit adultery, they are in the will of God. They proceed to make other important life decisions based on common sense—or sometimes even less than that. Just "I felt like it!" "My friends are doing it." "My world calls this 'success.'"

When we leave God out of these decisions, we are not really walking in faith. Instead of tapping into God's great resources of wisdom, we rely on mere human ideas.

Isn't it silly to think that the God who gave his own Son for us doesn't also care about the details of our lives?

A faith-filled believer will pray earnestly until he finds God's will for things such as

- Changing jobs
- Dealing with a difficult child
- Choosing a school for your children
- Moving. When you get a job offer in another state, is it just a matter of making more money? Seeing a glossy brochure with lots of green grass? Climbing the ladder of your profession or trade?
- Which believer to marry. (Hint: You're probably not going to find his or her name in the Bible!)

- Buying a home. God has a plan for our lives as detailed as for any person in Scripture. He wants to protect us from being in the wrong place at the wrong time.
- Joining a ministry in the church, such as the choir, the youth ministry, or Christian education.

The all-knowing Creator of the universe *wants* to show us the way in these matters. He has a plan for where we belong and where we don't belong. Therefore we need to seek his direction.

AN INQUIRING HEART — FOR GOD

ONE OF THE BEST Bible examples of a godly person seeking to do God's will is David when he faced a major question at Keilah. The little-known story appears in 1 Samuel 23, during the time David was on the run from King Saul. David had enough trouble of his own trying to protect his modest band of men from the Israelite army—but then word came that this particular town was being threatened by the Philistines.

He began by asking God, "Shall I go and attack these Philistines?" (v. 2). Notice that he didn't assume that just because he had once been anointed by God's prophet, he could win at any time in any place. He knew how important it was to be led by the Lord in every new situation. Not every opportunity for battle meant that he must engage in it.

This is true for us today. Not every Christian cause, not every plea for money—no matter how well intentioned—automatically means that we should respond.

David also knew that if God did lead him into a situation, God's provision would follow. Wherever God leads us, there is an umbrella of protection and supply that stays over our heads. Under that umbrella are the divine resources of wisdom, grace, finance, and all the other things we need to do what God has asked.

That does not mean there won't be problems and difficulties. But wherever the Lord leads, he must then by necessity help us.

However, the umbrella goes only where God leads us to go. If we choose to turn left when God wants us to go right, we cannot expect God to support the plans we made on our own.

Christians today are demonstrating this truth all the time. They are trying to make the umbrella follow them as they make unilateral decisions in life, and it doesn't work. Just because you have declared yourself to be a Christian doesn't mean that God is obligated to supply your needs as you do your own thing.

> **If we choose to turn left when God wants us to go right, we cannot expect God to support the plans we made on our own.** ∾

The Brooklyn Tabernacle Choir has recorded a song based on Psalm 119:133 that says, "Order my steps in Your Word, dear Lord; lead me, guide me every day. . . . / Humbly I ask Thee, teach me Your will; while You are working, help me be still. . . . / Order my steps in Your Word." A minister of music in one church recently told my wife that while the song was a blessing to him personally, his senior pastor had asked him not to use it because "when you have the word of faith, you don't need to ask God to order your steps." In other words, you are so spiritually macho that you can do whatever you choose, and God must go along with you!

This is not in line with the Bible. You cannot tell God what to do and where to go. That is pure spiritual arrogance. How easily we forget that we are not the center of the universe; God is. We must never lose track of the fact that "the world and its desires pass away, but the man *who does the will of God* lives forever" (1 John 2:17).

David was "a man after God's own heart" (see 1 Samuel 13:14; Acts 13:22) because he humbly asked God's direction for his daily life. He knew that if he didn't have the umbrella of God's supply, he had no business tangling with the Philistines outside Keilah. He asked for God's plan, and in this case God said yes—go ahead.

Even then, David came back a second time: "God, my men are not very thrilled about this idea. They say we have enough worries of our own with King Saul chasing us—*so why am I now wanting to take on the Philistines? Should I really do this? Have I truly heard from you?"*

The answer again was yes. "Go down to Keilah, for I am going to give the Philistines into your hand" (1 Samuel 23:4).

This incident reminds us that one of the first rules of spiritual guidance is to assume that we could be wrong. David was humble enough to say to himself, "Possibly I misheard God. I'd better check again." He didn't pretend that he was in constant twenty-four-hour communication with God and above all chance of making a mistake.

> **One of the first rules of spiritual guidance is to assume that we could be wrong.** ～

I remember reading some years ago about a powerful television evangelist who was asked by a reporter from one of the national newsmagazines, "What if you felt God told you to do something, and your whole board of trustees said no?" The preacher quickly boasted, "I'd fire the whole board." It sounded like bold faith, but what he was really saying is that he could never be wrong. Before too long, that man's ministry came crashing down in scandal.

It is not a sign of weakness to look for confirmation. It is often a good idea, in fact, to get a prayer partner, or call a pastor, who can validate your sense of God's will as you inquire of the Lord.

When I first heard about a four-thousand-seat theater in downtown Brooklyn that was for sale and might possibly solve our church's space problems, I got excited. Even though the building was in terrible shape and would require millions of dollars for restoration, I could see the potential for this to become the new Brooklyn Tabernacle.

Very quickly, however, I said to my associate pastors, "You go see it for yourselves and then pray. Unless all six of you feel that God is leading us this way, we won't even present it to the congregation." Would God hide such an important matter from my fellow leaders and reveal it only to me? I don't think so. I also brought other ministers whom I respect, such as David Wilkerson, to see the building. I wanted confirmation that God was leading us this way.

In time, we felt an agreement in our spirits that this step was right. Although the price tag was huge, we moved ahead in faith and confidence.

The story of Keilah shows us that David was firmly convinced in his heart and mind of what he wrote in Psalm 25:9. "He guides the humble in what is right and teaches them his way." In another place, David wrote, "For this God is our God for ever and ever; he will be our guide even to the end" (Psalm 48:14). David triumphed over the Philistines and delivered Keilah, and all of this happened because he inquired of the Lord. David lived by faith, not by sight.

More Decisions

But then King Saul, who was living in the worst kind of spiritual illusion, heard that David was suddenly vulnerable to capture because he had come inside a walled city instead of staying out in rugged terrain. That put a big smile on Saul's face. He was now so deceived in his heart that he even gave the Lord credit for these events! "God has handed him over to me," he said (1 Samuel 23:7).

God had obviously done no such thing. People who are not prayerful and who do not yield to God's will can come to all sorts of wrong conclusions. God was protecting David from Saul, and Saul didn't even have a clue! He immediately called up his army to go capture his nemesis. But David was still inquiring of the Lord. "God, I've heard that Saul is coming, but I'm not sure. Is he really coming?"

Answer: *Yes.*

The next inquiry was "Will these people here in Keilah protect me, since I just saved their necks? Or will they throw me over the wall to Saul?"

Answer: *They'll turn you over.*

So David gathered up his men, and they quickly left town.

Isn't it wonderful that God can even show us who our real friends are and who should not be trusted? He can warn us about what other people are doing behind our backs.

Thus Saul failed to catch David. In other words, success is not by might or power or computers or IQ, but by God's Spirit (Zechariah 4:6). King Saul had better weapons and a far bigger army. But David had the leading of the Holy Spirit. He was in touch with the King of kings.

DOES GOD STILL LEAD?

IN TODAY'S CHURCH, we have a serious shortage of faith in a living, speaking God. Pastors and laity alike do not seem to believe that God really leads and directs. Research by George Barna shows that fewer than 10 percent of churchgoing Christians make important life decisions based on God's Word and seeking his will! In other words, more than 90 percent decide on the basis of their own intelligence, peer opinion, whim, or fancy. They marry people and move to new cities without so much as a ten-minute prayer. Yet every Sunday they sit in church pews singing songs like "Where he leads me, I will follow."

> **Too many church leaders, having been turned off by fanaticism in certain quarters, have stopped believing in an active Holy Spirit at all. The baby has been thrown out with the bathwater. ⌒**

Too many church leaders, having been turned off by overblown claims and fanaticism in certain quarters, have stopped believing in an active Holy Spirit at all. The baby has been thrown out with the bathwater. Mention of the Holy Spirit's leading people is scoffed at. If someone says the same thing that Paul said in Acts 16—namely, that the Spirit wanted him to go to one town rather than another—that person is viewed as eccentric. We are strong in presenting our doctrinal positions as correct, but weak in stressing the daily need of being led by God's Spirit.

I want to affirm that God is not dead; he really does communicate today. He's interested in every part of your life, your home, your finances, every kind of decision—and more than just the moral issues. His eye is always on you. He wants to lead you. But you have to believe that he will indeed speak to you when you wait before him in believing prayer, with a yielded heart to do his will.

I fear that unbiblical excesses done supposedly under the inspiration of the Holy Spirit have frightened people off who should really know better. Pastors today operate church services that are so regimented, there is no place for any spontaneous leading of the Holy Spirit. Events are programmed right down to the minute. Song selections are cast in stone for days in advance. There is no allowance for God to lead anyone in another direction—certainly not during the meeting itself. We aim, rather, at being "smooth" and "slick." What we value most are great organization and "having our act together."

As I've said more than once, if God led the Israelites through forty years in the desert, surely he can lead me through a Sunday service. But God has had to teach me over and over about my own need for sensitivity in this matter.

If God led the Israelites through forty years in the desert, surely he can lead me through a Sunday service. ～

Two summers ago in a Sunday afternoon service, our choir was about to sing. As Carol walked past me toward the podium, I asked what songs she had chosen, knowing that she often changes her mind at the last minute as she senses God's direction in a particular meeting. She named two songs. I then took a seat on the front pew in order to better enjoy the choir's ministry.

The first song was about God's great redeeming love, featuring a solo by Calvin Hunt, a young man who has recorded with our choir and now travels in full-time ministry for the Lord. I closed my eyes and let the words sink in.

Somewhere along about the second verse, I sensed the Holy Spirit saying to me, *Go and preach the gospel—right now. Go up and tell them of God's love.*

At first I thought I was maybe just getting a little emotional about an inspirational song. Or maybe Satan was tempting me into some kind of weird behavior.

Then I thought, *My goodness, we haven't even taken the offering yet! This isn't the time to preach and give an invitation; that comes at the end of a meeting, not this early.* (As if God doesn't know what needs to be done in his own church!)

But the impression would not go away. In another thirty seconds I felt that if I did not respond, I would be grieving the Holy Spirit. I silently prayed, *God, I don't want to fail you by not doing your will. I'm going up there at the end of this song. Somehow stop me if I'm wrong.* I felt I had to obey, but I was still nervous about interrupting the meeting.

As the final chord was resolving, I quickly moved up the steps and onto the platform. Carol glanced at me with a quizzical look on her face. I took the microphone from the soloist and said, "Before you go, Calvin, tell the people briefly what God has done in your life."

He went into his story of terrible addiction to crack cocaine and how God had set him free.* Oddly enough, he didn't stumble for words. It was as if he had been prepared for the moment. He gave a powerful statement of the Lord's redemptive power.

---

*For a fuller account of Calvin Hunt's testimony, see chapter 9.

When he finished, I spoke for about ten minutes about the gospel and proceeded to give an invitation. The organist played softly; the choir stayed quietly in place through all this, just waiting to see what would happen next. From all over the auditorium, dozens of people began coming forward to the altar. The sound of weeping could be heard as people were moved upon by the Spirit and now turned to Christ. We prayed with them all, and it was a blessed time of spiritual harvest. Conviction seemed deep and real as the Holy Spirit blessed the simple gospel message.

Eventually I told them to return to their seats, saying, "Well, we haven't taken the offering yet. Let's do that as the choir sings another song." The meeting continued on to its conclusion.

Sometime that following week, the phone rang in our church offices and was answered by Susan, my daughter, who at that time was working in the music department. A man's voice said, "I would like to get the sheet music for such-and-such a song. You sing it in your church, and I want to pass it along to my church here in Texas."

"Well," Susan replied, "I'm very sorry, but we don't have written music for most of the songs we sing. We just do them by memory. Only if we record a song does the publisher then create a written score to sell."

The man was clearly disappointed. "I just heard you all sing it this past Sunday when I was there, and I really want to get that song somehow."

Susan tried to think of something else to say. "Well, I'll mention it to my mother, and maybe she'll decide to put the song on the choir's next album," she said.

There was silence on the line. "Did you say 'your mother'?" the man asked. "Excuse me, but who are you?"

"Susan Pettrey—I'm one of Pastor and Carol Cymbala's married daughters. I work here at the church."

At that, the man began to get a little emotional. "Would you please tell your dad something for me?"

"Yes."

"My family and I were just on a visit to New York for the weekend. We have a nineteen-year-old son who has totally hardened to the things of the Lord. We brought him up to be a Christian, but he has drifted away in the opposite direction. We've been so concerned about him.

"On this trip, we invited him to come with us. I promised him we would take some time to enjoy the city together, but our real plan was to bring him on Sunday to your church in hopes that God would somehow reach him.

"We enjoyed seeing the city all day Saturday. On Sunday, as we took a cab to your church for the afternoon service, I checked our airline tickets once again and realized I'd made a terrible mistake. We wouldn't be able to stay for the whole thing—or else we'd miss our flight home.

"I was kicking myself for not planning better. My son probably wasn't going to hear the message, which was the point of the whole visit.

"But then early in the service—out of nowhere—your dad walked up onto the platform and started to share the gospel. Suddenly my son was standing up with the others and heading for the altar! He just broke down before the Lord, calling out to God for forgiveness. When he came back to the seat, he was a different person.

"We had to leave a few minutes after that for the airport. . . . Just tell your dad that, all the way back to Texas, we could hardly take our eyes off our son in the next seat. This has been the most incredible transformation that you could ever imagine. My wife and I are overjoyed for the great thing God has done."

God changed the whole meeting that afternoon just for the sake of one nineteen-year-old. He knew the need in his life and the timing of flights and knew that something out of the ordinary schedule should occur. God knows things we have no way of knowing. When we don't inquire of the Lord and ask in faith for guidance, we totally miss what he wants to accomplish.

LET GOD GUIDE

WHAT ABOUT THE SITUATIONS you are facing right now? Are there forks in the road that call for a decision to turn one way or the other? Remember that many seemingly unimportant decisions have consequences far beyond what we could ever imagine. Just think how limited we humans are in really knowing the right thing to do. We "see through a glass, darkly" today (1 Corinthians 13:12 KJV), not understanding so many complexities, so many other things hidden from our view. We know nothing of what tomorrow will bring; we're only guessing about the future and what it will hold. Yet these decisions face us again and again.

But our God knows all things and has all power. Even "the king's heart is in the hand of the LORD" (Proverbs 21:1). God knows exactly the plans he has for you, "plans to prosper you and not to harm you, plans to give you a hope and a future" (Jeremiah 29:11). And his desire as a Father is to share these blessed plans with you.

For that to happen will mean yielding to his will for our lives—that's for sure. Then we will be able to hear his voice and sense his direction. It will also mean learning to wait and listen in his presence. But what blessings will be ours as we join the happy company of those who "will neither hunger nor thirst, nor will the desert heat or the sun beat upon them. He who has compassion on them will guide them and lead them beside springs of water" (Isaiah 49:10).

SIX

∼

The High Cost
of Cleverness

TRUSTING GOD COMPLETELY to lead and guide us sounds good in a book such as this, but let's be honest: It can also be a bit unnerving. Our friends may look sideways at us and think (or sometimes say) that we are going overboard with all this "spiritual" stuff. Seeking direction from God goes against the modern mind's reliance on self. Our culture teaches us to take charge of our lives and call our own shots.

In sharp contrast to the open, inquiring heart of David, the Bible tells about another king less than a hundred years later who had every chance to be as great as David—until he decided to do what seemed smart and clever to his own mind instead of what God had said. David, as you will recall, was followed by his son Solomon, who drifted from God. God had warned Solomon not to take a large number of wives, especially foreign women who would draw him away from the worship of the true God. The mixture with their gods proved to be fatal, because Solomon ended up building temples for his wives' gods right in Jerusalem, the place God had chosen for his presence to dwell.

Near the end of his life, Solomon took notice of a young man with some leadership ability named Jeroboam and, in fact, promoted him in the civil service. One day Jeroboam was innocently walking in a field when a prophet came to him out of the blue, took off his outer garment—and ripped it into twelve pieces! How strange! Giving ten pieces to Jeroboam, the prophet said that God would soon judge Solomon for what he had done and would tear the nation apart—and amazingly, Jeroboam would wind up being king of ten of the twelve tribes. This was followed by some unusual promises from the Lord:

> As for you, I will take you, and you will rule over all that your heart desires; you will be king over Israel. If you do whatever I command you and walk in my ways and do what is right in my eyes by keeping my statutes and commands, as David my servant did, I will be with you. *I will build you a dynasty as enduring as the one I built for David and will give Israel to you* (1 Kings 11:37–38).

Jeroboam must have stood there with his mouth hanging wide open. Why him? He had no claim to anything royal. But out of nowhere, he was selected as God's sovereign choice. Talk about a tremendous "break" at the beginning of your career!

Consider the greatness of these promises to this young man. They are as grand as what the mighty David had received: Control of a nation . . . an ongoing dynasty . . . the promise of God's abiding presence. Jeroboam, we would say, was set for life.

A STINGING REBUKE

NOW FAST-FORWARD the videotape many years to 1 Kings 14. Jeroboam has indeed risen to the throne of the Northern Kingdom (the ten tribes), just as Ahijah the prophet said that day in the field. But by now, Jeroboam has totally drifted away from God. In this chapter we see the powerful king and his wife with a family crisis: Their little boy has fallen seriously ill, and the worried parents are fearing for his life.

Jeroboam says to his wife, "You know, maybe that old prophet could help. He surely was in touch with God the time he prophesied over me. Why don't you go find him and ask him to pray for our son?"

But Jeroboam knows that his lifestyle has been far from godly. His reputation with Ahijah is at its low point. If his wife shows up to visit, the prophet is likely to scold her or give a bad word of some kind. So he tells her to wear a disguise.

Actually, this wasn't necessary, because by this time, Ahijah is so old that he has gone blind. He can't see whether Mrs. Jeroboam looks like a queen or a scrubwoman. On the other hand, Ahijah is still in close communion with God— and you can't disguise yourself from him. You can act like an Academy Award winner, but God will see through the whole thing in an instant. The minute the woman knocks at the prophet's front door, Ahijah calls out, "Hello, Mrs. Jeroboam-dressed-like-somebody-else—come on in!"

Perhaps she nervously chuckled or tried to make small talk with the old prophet. If she did, it didn't last long. Very quickly the conversation got serious. The woman sat there stunned as Ahijah launched into a shocking prophecy:

> I have been sent to you with bad news. Go, tell Jeroboam that this is what the LORD, the God of Israel, says: "I raised you up from among the people and made you a leader over my people Israel. I tore the kingdom away from the house of David and gave it to you, but you have not been like my servant David, who kept my commands and followed me with all his heart, doing only what was right in my eyes. You have done more evil than all who lived before you. You have made for

yourself other gods, idols made of metal; you have provoked me to anger and thrust me behind your back...."

As for you, go back home. When you set foot in
your city, the boy will die. All Israel will mourn for him
and bury him. He is the only one belonging to Jeroboam who will be buried, because he is the only one
in the house of Jeroboam in whom the LORD, the God
of Israel, has found anything good.

The LORD will raise up for himself a king over
Israel who will cut off the family of Jeroboam. This is
the day! What? Yes, even now. And the LORD will
strike Israel, so that it will be like a reed swaying in the
water. He will uproot Israel from this good land that
he gave to their forefathers and scatter them beyond
the River, because they provoked the LORD to anger
by making Asherah poles. And he will give Israel up
because of the sins Jeroboam has committed and has
caused Israel to commit (1 Kings 14:6–9, 12–16).

What a stinging rebuke! By the time the old man finished, Mrs. Jeroboam must have been sobbing. Within hours
she was going to lose her son, and soon afterward her husband's kingship would be history. In fact, the whole nation
would collapse.

We read this kind of story, and we can't help wondering:
How in the world did this happen! What do you have to do
to go from being chosen by God as the next king ... to the
same prophet now telling you that you're cooked meat—
headed for the garbage pail of history, with no hope of salvaging your kingdom or even your life?

God was saying, *Jeroboam, it's all over. You have provoked
my anger. You are now rejected as king. In fact, I'm going to punish your whole nation for what you got them to go along with.*

My goodness, what did this man do!

The Perils of Getting "Smart"

THE ANSWER LIES IN just about eight little verses back in 1 Kings 12, between the first and last meetings with Ahijah. Jeroboam was king, and one day he got to thinking about his strategic position. Yes, he was firmly on the throne—but because of the divided kingdom, God's temple was not in his territory. It was down south in Jerusalem, the capital of the Southern Kingdom. Every holy day (two or three times a year) when his people went to worship, they would have to go down to his rival's turf. God had made himself clear that Israelites could not worship and sacrifice their animals just anywhere and everywhere; they had to go to his one chosen location in Jerusalem. Hmmm . . .

The Bible says:

> Jeroboam thought to himself, "The kingdom will now likely revert to the house of David. If these people go up to offer sacrifices at the temple of the LORD in Jerusalem, they will again give their allegiance to their lord, Rehoboam king of Judah. They will kill me and return to King Rehoboam."
>
> After seeking advice, the king made two golden calves. He said to the people, "It is too much for you to go up to Jerusalem. Here are your gods, O Israel, who brought you up out of Egypt." One he set up in Bethel, and the other in Dan. And this thing became a sin; the people went even as far as Dan to worship the one there (1 Kings 12:26–30).

What poignant tragedy lurks in those four words *Jeroboam thought to himself* (v. 26). His whole downfall began with an attempt at cleverness. He started to strategize. Instead of simply trusting the promises God had given him, he tried to "help things out." Otherwise, it seemed, his power would suffer. That's how this tragedy began: Jeroboam thought to himself and forgot about God and his word of promise.

It is horrible when we use human cleverness instead of faith in God. The old gospel song said it well when it advised us just to "trust and obey, for there's no other way to be happy in Jesus."

What Jeroboam ended up doing here was starting his own religion—an insidious mixture of the true and the false. The following verses tell how he "appointed priests from all sorts of people, even though they were not Levites. He instituted a festival on the fifteenth day of the eighth month, like the festival held in Judah" (vv. 31–32). You didn't have to be called by God to be a leader in the Jeroboam religion; you only had to pay money, and you were installed.

God had clearly said in the Second Commandment never to make anything physical as a representation of himself, but Jeroboam now set up two golden calves to anchor the people's devotion. God, in fact, is spirit, and those who want to worship him "must worship in spirit and in truth," as Jesus said (John 4:24). Anything material would never do justice to the greatness of the invisible God, and even if you make something out of pure gold, it can still be wrong to God. He is not impressed with physical appearance or glitter; instead, he looks at the heart. I once heard Anne Graham Lotz say that gold must not mean much to God, for he uses it as paving material in heaven! The saints will walk all over it throughout eternity.

God put this story of Jeroboam in the Bible as a flashing red light to us. It fairly shouts that when unbelief gets into a leader, or anyone else for that matter, it leads to the first bad decision, which leads to the second, which leads to the third, until the momentum builds out of control. God had said to this man out in the field, "If you do whatever I command you and walk in my ways and do what is right in my eyes . . . , I will be with you." But Jeroboam opted to make up his own game plan, and at the end God thundered against him with words so devastating that they make us shudder to read them.

What Jeroboam did—when you think about it—made excellent logic. Any king would want to carefully monitor the movement of his people, right? Trusting God to build the kingdom as he had promised probably seemed too simple. Jeroboam decided to improvise to secure his position of leadership. In fact, unbelief often clothes itself in "being smart." We use cleverness to cover the tracks of our lack of faith. But who can be wiser than God?

> **Unbelief often clothes itself in "being smart." We use cleverness to cover the tracks of our lack of faith.** ~

As a pastor I sometimes see men in the congregation who are working two or three jobs in order to get ahead financially. They are going to expand their business, make money for a rainy day, or buy a rental property here or a little side business there, and their assets will grow even faster. Yes, it means missing church on Sunday and missing time with their kids, but they use the old saying "Mama didn't raise no fool, you know." In a little while, they tell me, their schedule will lighten up so they can give more attention to the Word and prayer, their service for the Lord, their marriage, their child-raising responsibility . . . soon, but not yet. At the moment, they have to virtually kill themselves for the almighty dollar. These men are sure they can improve on

God's formula: "Seek first [God's] kingdom and his righteousness, and all these things will be given to you as well" (Matthew 6:33).

Jeroboam must have felt *so* smart putting those idolatrous calves in Dan and Bethel—two towns in *his* territory. He told his people he was saving them that long, arduous trip down to Jerusalem. But his new religion was no salvation. It was a dangerous perversion of the true worship of God.

> **In the church today, we are still busy inventing new forms of religion as Jeroboam did. The new models are just as logical and "user-friendly."** ～

In the church today, we are still busy inventing new forms of religion as Jeroboam did. The new models are just as logical and "user-friendly." We must make it *easier on the people*, we say. After all, we need to make church convenient for the busy, modern lifestyle. No one can be expected to sacrifice precious time and energy for the Savior. Subtly, our comfort level becomes the center of the action rather than God. If a weeknight prayer meeting isn't to your particular liking ...well, hey, God's everywhere, you know! Stay home and do your own thing.

In fact, why even have a prayer meeting? That was only for those old Bible days anyway.

At the heart of "Jeroboam religion" is doing *anything* to keep the crowd. Even as Jeroboam's tragic plan altered God's plan for his people, we have church-growth consultants who know how to slickly play the numbers game. They are experts on what will "work." But sadly, they are blind to the fact that only God "works."

No attendance numbers can hide the fact that our new kind of Christianity is foreign to the Bible and grievous to the Holy Spirit. All over America, churchgoers chafe at a Sunday morning service that runs an hour and ten minutes, but have no problem with three-hour football games on television. Where do we find such a mentality in the New Testament?

I am convinced that in many places today, Jeroboam religion has become so institutionalized that even many in leadership have no clue as to what a true, Spirit-filled church would look like.

TALKING TO OURSELVES

UNBELIEF TALKS TO ITSELF instead of talking to God. How much better it would have been if Jeroboam had analyzed his fears and then taken them to the Lord. If only he had prayed, "O God, I didn't ask to be king, but I know you put me here. The way it looks to me, I could lose everything if my people keep trekking down to Jerusalem. But you said you would be with me and establish my dynasty. So tell me what to do."

Jeroboam didn't do this. Instead he talked to himself.

> **If you are headed in the wrong direction, you can always find a few cronies who will pat you on the back and agree with you.** ~

When we talk to ourselves, we're not talking to anyone very smart, because our outlook is very limited. But if we talk to God, we're talking to someone who knows everything. He knows what he promised in the beginning, and he knows exactly how to fulfill those promises no matter the circumstances.

Jeroboam also turned to some advisers (1 Kings 12:28), who reinforced his disobedience. If you are headed in the wrong direction, you can always find a few cronies who will pat you on the back and agree with you. What Jeroboam needed was a godly prayer partner who would have stopped him cold by saying, "Wait a minute—didn't God give you a promise in the beginning? How can doing wrong bring about something good?"

This is not a story about embezzlement, or meeting a woman in a motel, or smoking some illegal drug. This is a story about simply drifting away from God and his Word. *Yes, I'm aware of what God said—but in the present situation, I really feel the need to do such-and-such.* Instead of focusing on the faithfulness of God, we focus on what the circumstances seem to dictate.

But faith enables us to see God on top of all our problems. If we see only the problems, we get depressed and start making wrong decisions. When we have faith, we see God bigger than any mountain, and we know he is going to take care of us.

When you're walking in unbelief, you get out of bed saying, "Oh, no! Is this the day I'm going to lose it all?" The glass is always half-empty. ～

If *God* is for you, it doesn't matter how many demons in hell try to oppose you. If *God* is for you, it doesn't matter what your opponents whisper in the ears of people. Unbelief has a devious way of envisioning negative things. When you're walking in faith, you get out of bed in the morning saying, "Surely goodness and love will follow me all the days of my life, and I will dwell in the house of the LORD forever" (Psalm 23:6). But when you're walking in unbelief, you get out of bed saying, "Oh, no! Is this the day I'm going to lose it all?" The glass is always half-empty.

Those who walk in faith are still realists. They often admit that they don't know how everything is going to work out; but they insist that their God will supply nonetheless.

LISTENING TO THE VOICE OF FAITH

JEROBOAM'S WORRIES EVENTUALLY led to fatalism. Over time he went from imagining the loss of the people's loyalty all the way to fear that "they will kill me" (1 Kings 12:27)! Unbelief loves to paint the bleakest picture it can. It loves to get us mumbling to ourselves, *I'm not going to make it. I just know this is going to turn out terrible. The future is bound to crash on me.*

Let me tell you that God, who began a good work in you, is not about to stop now. After sending his Son to die for your sins, after saving you at such incredible cost, why would he let you fail now?

Let us declare war this very moment on the cleverness that is really a mask for unbelief. Bring your problem to God, as a little child would, in total confidence that he alone can fix whatever is broken. Open your Bible and let the Holy Spirit plant in you the seeds of a fresh faith that will blossom as you wait on the Lord. Don't give up asking, seeking, and knocking—no matter what pressure you feel to "do something."

How can our heavenly Father do anything but respond to our persistent prayer of faith? Jesus said, "Will not God bring about justice for his chosen ones, who cry out to him day and night? Will he keep putting them off? I tell you, he will see that they get justice, and quickly. However, when the Son of Man comes, will he find faith on the earth?" (Luke 18:7–8).

SEVEN

~

Faith Runs on
a Different Clock

REMEMBER THE FATHER from Texas who brought his wayward son to church and was worried about catching a flight? He got an eye-opening lesson that God's timetable is not always the same as ours. The man thought his prayers had gone for naught because of an airline schedule, while God had everything under control to achieve his purposes regardless of how things seemed to be unfolding.

Many of our struggles with faith have to do with timing. We believe, at least in theory, that God will keep his promises— but when? If the answer does not come as soon as we expect, fear begins to assault us, and then soon we are tempted to "throw away [our] confidence," ignoring the fact that "it will be richly rewarded" (Hebrews 10:35). How many times have you prayed for a son's or daughter's salvation? Are you still praying? Do you really believe God is listening?

It would be a good idea if we all just admitted that we need to learn about God's way of doing things. One of the best illustrations of divine pacing in the Bible is the story of Zechariah and Elizabeth, which is laid out in elaborate detail. In fact, the Gospel of Luke has almost as much to say about these two senior citizens as it has about Mary and Joseph. Why didn't Luke write as Mark did in his Gospel and just cut to the chase: "God sent a forerunner, John the Baptist, to tell people to repent and get ready for the great Messiah"—and that would have been enough?

> **Many of our struggles about faith have to do with timing. We believe, at least in theory, that God will keep his promises—but when? ～**

No, God wanted to teach some special lessons through the details of this story.

Zechariah was an elderly priest who had no children. Folks in town naturally assumed he and his wife would never have a family. Not only was Elizabeth barren, but she was now too old to give birth.

Zechariah was simply going about his work in the temple one day when an angel appeared and startled him with a message from God. "Do not be afraid, Zechariah; your prayer has been heard. Your wife Elizabeth will bear you a son, and you are to give him the name John. He will be a joy and delight to you, and many will rejoice because of his birth" (Luke 1:13–14). The boy, in fact, would turn out to be John the Baptist.

God Makes Some Very Odd Choices

Right away this story shows us that God's way of doing things is very different from ours. Even the way he chooses to order events holds specific lessons for us.

If you were God in heaven looking down on the earth, and you could choose any set of parents across the land of Israel to raise this important messenger, whom would you pick? No doubt you or I would select a healthy young woman about twenty-three or twenty-four years old, at the height of her childbearing years, with plenty of energy to get up in the middle of the night with this baby and do all the things a mother must do. We would look for a husband perhaps twenty-four or twenty-five, physically strong, and well established in his career. We would also want this couple to have money and a good education, so the child would have a stimulating environment. They should live in a safe neighborhood in an upscale suburb, with the best schools and all kinds of cultural enrichment nearby.

The couple should also be planning on having one or maybe two more children after this first one, so the boy would not grow up alone. After all, peer companionship is important. Remember, this baby has a divine mission in life.

But what does God do? He casts his eye all across the land of Israel and finds a woman who can't have a baby! While all her friends in the little desert town seem to have gotten pregnant, she has remained childless. Then God waits and waits until she is past childbearing years, so that even if she *could* have conceived a child, it is now too late. She is doubly disqualified as a special mother for this special child.

And the God of heaven says, "That's the one! As the boy grows up, from the time he is nursed to the time he grows into manhood, his mother will be able to tell him over and over the story of his birth, the miracle of his aged parents—all of it reinforcing in his tender mind that 'nothing is impossible with God' (Luke 1:37)."

Many times in life, God waits while a situation goes from bad to worse. He appears to let it slip over the edge, so that you and I say, "There's *no way* now for this ever to work out." But that is the point when the omnipotent God intervenes in our hopelessness and says, "Oh, really? Watch this. . . !"

More than worrying about John the Baptist's schooling or music lessons or anything else, God wanted him to grow up in a godly atmosphere of praise and worship. At least once a day that old, devoted couple must have looked at that little boy and said, or at least thought, "Our God is an awesome God! Blessed be his name!"

So many times when we get into emergencies and the situation seems totally hopeless—it's actually a setup. God wants to do something great. He wants to demonstrate his power, so that his name will be praised in a new and greater way. The next generation will hear all about it. After all, their spiritual nurture is far more important than mere material things. Did you know that parents can feed their children three nutritious meals a day and put the latest $120 sneakers on their feet—and still deprive them spiritually? To withhold from children the knowledge of the wonderful and loving God who created them is the worst kind of parenting. They cannot truly live without Jesus, regardless of the top-drawer education they might receive.

> So many times when we get into emergencies and the situation seems totally hopeless— it's actually a set-up. God wants to do something great. ～

Even beyond our own families, God wants to publish everywhere through our lives the testimony of his mighty power and salvation. Beyond our head knowledge of Bible verses, he wants to demonstrate tangibly that he has never changed. Let's not forget the next time we face the "impossible" that our God is *still* an awesome God.

GOD IS DRAWN TO PRAYER

NOTICE ALSO HOW MUCH of this story is centered around prayer and worship.

Zechariah, the old priest, trudged from his home to Jerusalem to serve his rotation in the temple. His assignment that day, Luke 1:9 says, was to "burn incense"—an act of worship. The placing of spices on the fire on the altar resulted in a sweet scent arising to God. Meanwhile, at that specific hour in the temple courtyard, a large crowd of people "were praying outside" (Luke 1:10). They were all opening their hearts to God as best they knew, reaching out and communing with him—the highest activity that any human being can aspire to.

That was the moment when the angel appeared.

God could have shown up at any time, but over and over in the Bible, he revealed himself when people began to pray.

- Peter went up on a rooftop to pray (Acts 10). There God gave him a vision about reaching out to other ethnic groups with the gospel.
- The early church gathered after some persecution to pray. Suddenly, "the place where they were meeting was shaken. And they were all filled with the Holy Spirit" (Acts 4:31).
- The twelve disciples never asked Jesus to teach them to preach. But they did say, "Lord, teach us to pray" (Luke 11:1). They saw something about his communion with the Father that was so outstanding that they couldn't help saying, "Help us to pray like *that*."

The minute the angel showed up, Zechariah panicked. The first words out of the angel's mouth were "Do not be afraid, Zechariah; your prayer has been heard" (Luke 1:13).

What prayer? Obviously, his many prayers over the years for Elizabeth to have a child.

By this stage in life, Zechariah had probably stopped thinking that fatherhood was even possible for him. *But it didn't matter;* his many years of praying in faith were still on record! When prayer comes from a sincere heart, it rises into God's presence *and stays there.* The more prayers you add, the more they collect in heaven. They don't evaporate like a gas. They remain before God. Remember how another angel said to Cornelius, the Roman centurion, "Your prayers and gifts to the poor have come up as a memorial offering before God" (Acts 10:4). Those prayers didn't just float away. They added up, until the day when God sent a special messenger to this man.

When we seek God for answers, we must persevere in prayer, letting it build up day after day until the force of it becomes a mighty tide pushing over all obstacles. No wonder God says his house is supposed to be known as a house of prayer—not merely a house of preaching or of singing, but especially of prayer. How else will we receive great answers from God unless we persevere in prayer?

How must God feel every Sunday when, all over the nation, so many people gather in churches but do so little actual praying? ∼

How must God feel every Sunday when, all over the nation, so many people gather in churches but do so little actual praying? Congregations make time in the weekly schedule for everything from basketball leagues to weight-loss classes, but they can't seem to find a slot for a prayer meeting. The Lord waits to bless his people with his abundant supply, but we don't take the time to open the channel. What a terrible epitaph: "You do not have, because you do not ask God" (James 4:2).

God is drawn to prayer. He delights in communion with us. Prayer releases his blessing into our lives.

GOD DOES NOT APPRECIATE SECOND-GUESSING

WHEN ZECHARIAH RAISES his objection (Luke 1:18), he betrays the fact that he apparently hasn't been praying for a child recently. In his mind, he pictures Elizabeth back home in the small town. She is certainly no spring chicken.

His question—"How can I be sure of this?"—is logical, I suppose. You might think that Gabriel would reply, "Well, old man, let me tell you: God is going to help you. He will empower you and your wife, and everything will work out fine."

No. The angel has already declared, on God's behalf, what is going to happen—so there's nothing left to discuss. Facts have been stated: Elizabeth *will* have a son, you must give him the name John, he will be great in the sight of the Lord, etc., etc. Case closed.

But Zechariah questions God's ability—and suddenly there is a strong reaction. The angel announces that the old man will lose his speech for nine months! If Gabriel had been from Brooklyn, he might have said, "Yo! What's your problem? I'm Gabriel, the angel God sent to tell you this good news. If you don't want to believe it, then you won't speak at all till you see the baby!"

When God sends his divine promise, he is very grieved and saddened if his people do not believe him. It breaks his father-heart to hear his own children say, "Well, maybe ... I hope so ... but how could that be, really, now? ... Yes, God has said he will bring back my daughter—but, you know, she's so hard...."

Is it not enough that God declared he would do something? He doesn't have to explain any of his methods in advance. "Nothing is impossible," remember?

> **God gets fairly irritated—and rightly so— with Christians who refuse to believe, who question his veracity, who start backpedaling after he has said he's going to do something.** ～

Zechariah's mouth is zipped shut. This response gives potent meaning to the oft-quoted words of Hebrews 11:6: "Without faith it is impossible to please God." God gets fairly irritated—and rightly so—with Christians who refuse to believe, who question his veracity, who start backpedaling after he has said he's going to do something. The Lord wants to shout, "Will you please just *trust me!* Is anything too hard for God?"

One time Jesus said to a woman whose brother had died and who thought it was therefore too late for Jesus to help, "Did I not tell you that if you believed, you would see the glory of God?" (John 11:40). Jesus then proceeded to the cemetery and called Lazarus right up out of his grave.

The great battle of our spiritual lives is "Will you believe?" It is *not* "Will you try harder?" or "Can you make yourself worthy?" It is squarely a matter of believing that God will do what only he can do. That is what God honors. He treasures those who respond and open their hearts to him. He's looking for faith so strong that it will anchor on his

Word and wait for him, the One who makes everything beautiful in its time.

INNOCENCE AT RISK

I SHALL NEVER FORGET the Sunday night we finally persuaded shy, soft-spoken Wendy Alvear to stand in front of our congregation and tell fifteen hundred people her story. She started off hesitantly, telling about her growing-up years in Williamsburg, the Brooklyn neighborhood right at the east end of the Williamsburg Bridge that comes across from lower Manhattan. The people on those streets were a curious but harmonious mixture of Hasidic Jews and Puerto Rican immigrants like her parents. Even the drug addicts, she remembers, were nice to the children on the sidewalk.

> **The great battle of our spiritual lives is "Will you believe?" It is *not* "Will you try harder?" or "Can you make yourself worthy?"** ∼

Growing up the second of four children in the family, Wendy characterized herself as "a romantic," dreaming of the day she would get married to a handsome husband and raise a houseful of children of her own. She loved kids and was an enthusiastic baby-sitter. Her sunny disposition was only partly suppressed by the strict-minded Spanish church she attended with her mother and siblings three or four nights a week. There she learned about Jesus and soon welcomed him into her life—even though they said he had a long list of rules that she had to obey. Wendy's father was not a Christian, but he didn't seem to mind the rest of his family going to church.

One of the rules in that church was that women and girls always wore skirts. When Wendy's ninth-grade class at school went on a field trip to an amusement park, she felt uneasy. A friend said, "I'll bring some pants from home for you to borrow, okay?" And Wendy gladly took her up on it.

"The only trouble was, the trip ran late," Wendy recalls, "and we didn't get back to school at the appointed time. When we finally arrived, my mother was there waiting to pick me up. I was trapped! I could do nothing but get off the bus and face the music."

That was the point when the attractive young adolescent asked to stop going to church. Her father, of course, supported her request. While alone in her room, however, she did feel the need to offer an apology to God: "I'm sorry about this— but I'll go back to church when I get married. I promise."

By her senior year, Wendy's life was taken up with dance clubs, smoking, and drinking—but "no hard drugs," she affirmed to God. Her first real boyfriend, who went by the Hispanic nickname of Papo, was battling to overcome heroin. "I thought I could help him," she admits with a slight smile. "I would plead with him not to do drugs. So as a compromise, we'd drink wine together instead." Papo may have in fact consumed less heroin as a result, but his dark-haired girlfriend became a steady drinker.

One night in McCarren Park, the two of them and a large group of friends were hanging out after midnight, the boys playing basketball and the girls just talking nearby. All had had plenty to drink. Wendy relaxed on a park bench and, in time, fell asleep, while the others gradually drifted away, leaving her alone.

She awoke with a start when she felt the rough hands of a man moving over her body. Her eyes flew open. Papo and the group were nowhere to be seen—just this stranger, intent on having his way with her.

"In my panic, I tried to think what to do. Suddenly an idea came to me. I said to him, 'Okay, okay—this is cool! But you know what? I have to use the ladies room first. . . . I live just a couple of blocks away. Let's go there!' "

Amazingly, the gullible fellow agreed. In fact, the distance was more like fifteen blocks! "Here he was, walking me all the way to my building, where I cheerfully said, 'I'll run upstairs and be right back!' Thank God, he wasn't too swift." Once in her parents' apartment behind locked doors, of course, Wendy promptly went to bed.

The next morning, she soberly said to herself, "Wow!— I was really in danger last night, wasn't I? How come Papo left me there on the park bench, anyway?" The process of finding a nice young man to marry was turning out to be harder than it looked.

MR. RIGHT AT LAST?

THE NEXT BOYFRIEND was better, at least in some ways: He was drug-free and had a job as a shoe salesman. His name was John. Wendy had known him from the beginning of high school, and her family found him to be respectful and polite. There was the complication that he, being four or five years older than Wendy, had already been through a short and turbulent marriage, resulting in a daughter for whom he was now responsible. But the future looked promising.

"I was overjoyed," says Wendy. "Here was the man of my dreams. I had a solid job with New York Life Insurance Company, and he was doing well, too. When we got engaged on Valentine's Day, it was the highlight of my life."

They began planning for a summer wedding. But then, for some inexplicable reason, John's mood began to change. He became less gracious toward Wendy, and then abrupt and demanding. Were the bad memories of his past marriage starting to stir the waters? Wendy couldn't tell. He wanted physical intimacy, and when she declined until the wedding, he grew upset.

Within three months Wendy learned that John was seeking favors elsewhere. She promptly broke the engagement.

"Now I was really lonely," she says. "And I wasn't close enough to God to ask for his help. I sank into more drinking. And it seemed that whenever I would drink, I would become angry and aggressive—which caused me to ruin some parties and alienate my friends. I gradually withdrew into depression, just coming home from work each day and hiding in my room until the next morning."

This unhappy lifestyle continued until Wendy was twenty-five. Her father became suddenly ill and passed away. Shortly before, he had become a Christian, and the two of them had enjoyed some warm conversations. His death was a heavy blow to Wendy.

Two weeks after her father's burial, Wendy was finally ready to listen to the Lord. *Wendy, it's time to come home*, he seemed to say to her—and she responded. A great relief swept over her spirit as the heavenly Father she had long spurned welcomed her back into his arms.

By the next Sunday she was at the Brooklyn Tabernacle. The old legalism was missing—she even saw some women there in pants!—but instead, the love and grace of God pervaded the atmosphere. Wendy started to grow in the Lord, build Christian friendships, join the singles group, and sing in the choir.

Years went by. Wendy was a blessing to us all. Inside, of course, her desire to be married was as strong as ever. She was saying to herself, *Okay, God—where is he?* And God seemed not to give an answer to that heartfelt question. Meanwhile, she watched one friend after another get married in the church.

Wendy's thirtieth birthday came and went . . . then her thirty-fifth. By now she was worrying that maybe God's plan for her life did not include marriage or motherhood. That possibility saddened her greatly. We didn't see quite as many smiles on her face.

One Saturday, alone in her home, she set aside a time to seek the Lord. A couple of her sisters were going through deep waters, and she wanted to intercede for them. But even more, she wanted to talk to God about her singleness. She began to complain. The prayer time "turned into a full-blown pity party," she admits.

In response, the Lord seemed to say to her, "Wendy, you are hurting because you've taken your eyes off of me and put them on the situation. You have forgotten that I am the source of all happiness. Circumstances don't matter. Keep your eyes on me."

A dark cloud lifted as she said in response, "All right, Lord—I will place my desire for a husband 'on the altar,' so to speak. I will give it to you. Go ahead and burn it up like a sacrifice. Consume it! I will stop whining about this."

Peace came back into her soul, and Wendy went on with her life. The only change was that, after seventeen years at New York Life, she quit that job and accepted an invitation to join the Brooklyn Tabernacle staff. What an even greater blessing she became.

Surely Not . . .

About a year later, a man came seeking help from Pastor Michael Durso at Christ Tabernacle, Queens, one of our daughter churches. During an appointment in the pastor's office, he gave his life to Christ. His name was John Alvear—the same John who had been in Wendy's life years before.

Soon John showed up at the Brooklyn Tabernacle, looking for Wendy. A couple of choir members passed the word along to her, which triggered sudden apprehension. She thought, "John wants to come back into my life? Oh, no! I can't handle this. It must be a snare from the Enemy!' People told me he had gotten saved and was serving the Lord now, but still—"

Wendy avoided John for a good while, only agreeing at last to go out with him as part of a large group of friends. John's attitude had indeed changed; he had become a new creation in Christ. He and Wendy began dating, and a warm affection blossomed.

Wendy was still concerned about getting involved with "a babe in Christ," as she puts it. After all, she had now been walking with the Lord as an adult for more than a decade, and John was only four months old in his Christian life. She urged him to talk to Pastor Dan Iampaglia, one of the Brooklyn Tabernacle associates at the time.

John and Dan had lunch together. The next day in the office, Wendy wanted to know how it had gone.

"He seems very nice, very sincere," said Pastor Iampaglia. "I believe his walk with the Lord is genuine."

Even that was not enough. Next, Wendy wanted to talk to me. I told her, "Don't be afraid of what God is doing in your life. John is a very special man."

Wendy still worried about whether she could really be finding God's choice for her life after all this time. Then one day, John called her at work. They began to talk about their relationship. With utmost sincerity, John said, "I am just trying to follow God's plan for me—that's the most important thing in my life. In fact, I never stopped loving you. But I want God's will so badly—even if it doesn't include you." At that, his voice broke as the tears came. Wendy began to cry as well.

And that is how, at the age of thirty-seven, Wendy finally became a bride. Their wedding was an explosion of joy. What a special couple they became in the life of our church!

Wendy feared that she had waited too long to ever become a mother. But by the next year, little Jeniece Rebecca was welcomed into their home. Then, at the age of thiry-nine, Wendy gave birth to John Eric. They were recently able to purchase their own home in the borough of Staten Island, across the harbor from Brooklyn.

As Wendy closed her remarks to the church that night, she said, "Whatever you do, keep seeking God's will for your life. He will do it! Don't settle for anything less. Wait for God—he knows how to give you the best."

LET GOD DO IT HIMSELF

THE HARDEST PART of faith is often simply to wait. And the trouble is, if we don't, then we start to fix the problem ourselves—and that makes it worse. We complicate the situation to the point where it takes God much longer to fix it than if we had quietly waited for his working in the first place.

The timing of God is often a mystery to us, and even sometimes a frustration. But we must not give up. We must not try to arrange our own solutions. Instead, we must keep on believing and waiting for God. We will not be alone as we patiently wait for his answer in his time. We will be joining the great host of saints down through the ages whose faith was tested and purified by waiting for God.

This is what David meant when he testified, "I waited patiently for the LORD" (Psalm 40:1). Instead of taking matters into his own hands, or despairing of God's help at all, David learned to wait for God to work out his plan in his time. But after a while, God proved faithful as always, for David continued his story by adding, "He turned to me and heard my cry. He lifted me out of the slimy pit, out of the mud and mire; he set my feet on a rock and gave me a firm place to stand" (vv. 1–2). What happened was all-glorious, but it came only after a time of waiting in faith.

The timing of God is often a mystery to us, and even sometimes a frustration. But we must not give up. We must not try to arrange our own solutions. ～

Don't give up today, and don't give in to the voices of unbelief and impatience. Remember these words from a beautiful song I have enjoyed so much over the years:

Keep believing in what you know is true;
Keep believing—you know the Lord will
   see you through.
When troubles rise in your life, and you don't
   know what to do,
You'll be fine if you just keep believing.[1]

EIGHT

~

Overcoming Discouragement

WHEN SOMEONE SAYS something outlandish here in New York City, one of the common put-downs is "Get real!" or "Be real!"—in other words, please return to Planet Earth with the rest of us and talk some sense. No matter where you live, I'm sure you've heard the same kind of criticism—that someone is being "unrealistic." That person is not like the rest of us intelligent folks who live happily with both feet firmly planted in the real world.

Let me tell you about a time when a group of very smart folks showed great *realism* based on obvious facts—and the results were disastrous. Moses had brought the Hebrew people out of Egypt in response to God's promise that he would give them a wonderful land. After receiving the Ten Commandments and other instructions from God, Moses sent twelve spies to check out the real estate of Canaan. God had already said he would give it to the Hebrews; in fact, he had begun making that promise several hundred years before, to Abraham.

Moses sent the twelve simply to gather information, not to form opinions. All he assigned them to do was to "see what the land is like and whether the people who live there are strong or weak, few or many. What kind of land do they live in? Is it good or bad? What kind of towns do they live in? Are they unwalled or fortified? How is the soil? Is it fertile or poor? Are there trees on it or not?" (Numbers 13:18–20). Sounds like a fifth-grade geography teacher giving her class a research assignment in the encyclopedia.

Nobody asked the spies to draw conclusions. Nobody asked them to gauge the prospects for military success. God had already guaranteed that.

When they returned from their field trip, however, ten of the spies went far beyond their assignment. They reported the data accurately—and then immediately got "realistic" by adding, "We can't attack those people; they are stronger than we are. . . . The land we explored devours those living in it. All the people we saw there are of great size. . . . We seemed like grasshoppers in our own eyes, and we looked the same to them" (vv. 31–33). This report went against all God had promised, and thus their common-sense realism affected the destiny of a whole generation of Israelites. The people began to panic and murmur against God.

Who could have predicted that these men would cause a historic turning point? Who could have known that this report and the discouragement it triggered would provoke God to the point of saying, "All right—that's it! You will *not* go into Canaan now after all; you will spend another thirty-eight years wandering in this desert instead. In fact, nearly all of you here today will never get to the Promised Land at all. You're going to grow old and die out here on these sands."

What is so amazing is that these people had already seen God do many supernatural things. They had seen the ten remarkable plagues of Egypt. They had walked out into the Red Sea by faith, believing that the miraculous restraint on the water would hold firm until they got across. They had seen God shake a mountain with thunderous force. They had watched Moses bring down the divine law, written by the finger of God on a stone.

But now they chose to believe a human report rather than God's promise. The Bible calls the ten spies' summary "a bad report" (Numbers 13:32). The King James Version is even stronger: "an evil report." What was so wicked about it? After all, its facts were accurate. The Israelites were realistically no match for the fierce tribes of Canaan. But this report of the spies was full of unbelief and spawned deep discouragement among God's people. God was provoked by their distrust.

> **Do we believe what our feelings and circumstances tell us, or do we believe what God has promised to do?** ∼

Thousands of years later, little has changed for God's people: Do we believe what our feelings and circumstances tell us, or do we believe what God has promised to do?

CONQUERING "THE BIG D"

THIS STORY TEACHES us several things:

It's not starting the race that counts; it's finishing. These people, by giving in to discouragement, never saw the fulfillment of God's promise in their lives. Today we sometimes fool ourselves with a theology that mumbles, "Well, God will take care of everything somehow. It doesn't matter what we do; the Lord is sovereign, you know." Not exactly!

The truth is that without faith, it is impossible to please God. We receive things—even the things God has promised us—only if we have faith. As Jesus said to two blind men, "According to your faith will it be done to you" (Matthew

9:29). This means that my life or yours has only as much of God as our faith permits. The promises of God are appropriated only by faith. God is looking for a people who will believe him and take him at his word no matter what the circumstances say or what other people are telling us.

Joshua and Caleb, the "minority" spies, were two such people who took God at his word. "We should go up and take possession of the land," they said, "for we can certainly do it" (Numbers 13:30). Yet they had seen the same enemies the other spies had seen. This is why God gave that wonderful compliment in Numbers 14:24, saying, "My servant Caleb has a different spirit and follows me wholeheartedly." As a result of this willingness to side with God's promise, Caleb and Joshua got to enter the land. The other ten spies, however— and a million or two other people—died along the way.

Pressures are exerted all through life to make us want to lie down and quit. The most spiritual person in the world is tempted to get discouraged. I remember seeing a television interview with Billy Graham and his delightfully honest wife, Ruth. The host, David Frost, said something like, "So you two pray together and read the Bible together on a regular basis. But tell me the truth, Mrs. Graham: In all these years of living with Billy, have you never had problems or disagreements? Have you never even once contemplated divorce?"

"Not once," she fired back. "Murder, a few times—but not divorce!"

Obviously, there are challenges to overcome even in the Billy Graham home. You and I have our share of difficulties, but the most important thing is to finish our lives still trusting God, as the evangelist and his wife are doing.

In fact, the greatest battle on earth has not been fought on the Normandy beaches or on Iwo Jima or in the Persian Gulf. Rather, it has raged inside your heart and mine: the battle to believe. The just not only must begin by faith but continue to live by it as well (Romans 1:17). Faith is as essential to everyday living as it is to initial salvation.

As Athanasius, the early church father, said, "I can do nothing without the help of God, and that from moment to moment; for when, so long as we are on the earth, is there a single instant in which we can say we are safe from temptation or secure from sin?"[1] Only God's grace can keep us, and that grace is activated by faith.

Caleb walked in this attitude of faith his whole life. The book of Joshua shows him as an old man, long after the spying trip, making a rousing speech to his equally elderly partner Joshua, who is now in charge of the nation:

> I was forty years old when Moses the servant of the LORD sent me from Kadesh Barnea to explore the land. And I brought him back a report according to my convictions, but my brothers who went up with me made the hearts of the people melt with fear. I, however, followed the LORD my God wholeheartedly. . . .
>
> Now then, just as the Lord promised, he has kept me alive for forty-five years since the time he said this to Moses, while Israel moved about in the desert. So here I am today, eighty-five years old! I am still as strong today as the day Moses sent me out; I'm just as vigorous to go out to battle now as I was then. Now give me this hill country that the LORD promised me that day. You yourself heard then that the Anakites were there and their cities were large and fortified, but, the LORD helping me, I will drive them out just as he said (Joshua 14:7–8, 10–12).

Caleb never retired! He just kept going, and faith kept him young and strong in heart. To the end, he wanted to fight the Lord's enemies no matter how entrenched they seemed. He knew that God could do anything, and he wanted to be a part of God's action as long as he could. Discouragement never seemed to sap his spiritual vigor.

Now we see the importance of the verse in Hebrews that says, "Let us not give up meeting together, as some are in the habit of doing, but let us *encourage one another*—and all the more as you see the Day approaching" (10:25). Going to church and having Christian fellowship should never leave us discouraged—there's enough of that everywhere around us. Even if God searches our hearts very directly concerning sin, we should still leave the building encouraged, because once the Spirit reveals our disobedience, he will bring cleansing and strength to our hearts. He will cause us to see his promises and his love in a new, clear light.

One of the primary names for the Holy Spirit is "the Comforter." And one of the primary names for the devil, who likes to impersonate the Holy Spirit, is "the Accuser." The Comforter encourages us and builds us up. The Accuser is in the business of tearing us down.

> **One of the primary names for the Holy Spirit is "the Comforter." And one of the primary names for the devil, who likes to impersonate the Holy Spirit, is "the Accuser."** ∼

Wives who are negative and discouraging can sometimes cause more damage in their homes than any drug addiction. Husbands who talk down to their families and go against the promises of God are walking on dangerous ground. They are following in the footsteps of the ten spies! They are once again repeating, "Yes, but . . ." and "It sounds good, but we can't. . . ."

Americans are waging a mighty war against "the Big C"—cancer. The people and the government are investing huge sums to fight this horrible disease that invades millions of people. If only in the spiritual realm we would give equal effort to strike down "the Big D"—discouragement. It kills not the body, but the soul. Its dreadful toll on the people of God is greater than anyone could calculate.

> The only hospital that can treat "the Big D"—discouragement—is the hospital of the Word of God, which is managed by the Holy Spirit. ∼

I have often sat in my office, trying to counsel couples who know that they are in trouble. They are entirely accurate as to the surface facts of their situation. But they are also so negative and pessimistic that you want to scream. There is no faith or expectancy for what God has promised to do for his people.

Try to count all the times in the Bible that God says to us, "Be encouraged," or "Fear not," or "Be not afraid." The battle is always not about giving in to what we see around us, but about holding onto God's promises.

The only hospital that can treat "the Big D" is the hospital of the Word of God, which is managed by the Holy Spirit. Only there can our spirits be lifted.

LOOSE TALK

THE ENEMY USES ordinary people to discourage us. Who caused all the trouble that day in the desert? Not some demon with a pitchfork. Just people talking. People who were part of the

Israelite community, not pagan strangers. People everyone knew and even respected. People chosen by Moses himself.

It is very important for us to watch whom we talk to. Some voices are *not* good for us. Some folks need to be avoided. Those who are negative and don't really believe God will have an effect on your spirit. God has to give you wisdom on how to change the subject or even extract yourself from the situation without offending.

LOOSE EMOTIONS

DISCOURAGEMENT IS AT the heart of other reactions. Numbers 14:1 says, "That night all the people of the community raised their voices and wept aloud." The camp broke down into one massive pity party. While tears before God are usually valued highly in the pages of Scripture, this was a crying produced by unbelief and fear.

I have heard certain people pray with emotion, but their lack of faith made it sound more like the Israelites that day in their tents. They were not really pouring out their souls to God in faith, but rather venting their fear and frustration.

> Let's stop blaming our unbelief on the pastor we once had, on our childhood, on circumstances, or on anything else. There is no excuse for not believing in the Lord. ～

The Israelites' tears soon led to blasphemy. They accused God of bringing them out of Egypt only to die! (v. 3). Think of the blasphemy of that—and yet it all started with simply doubting whether the Lord would do what he promised. Now they had sunk to saying terrible things about the God of Israel.

Then (v. 4) they talked about getting rid of Moses. Discouragement led from emotionalism and blasphemy to rebellion. Things were coming apart at every seam. "It's the leader's fault," they said. How many churches have crumbled because people lost their focus on God's power and, before you could snap your fingers, they were wanting to dump the pastor?

Let's stop blaming our unbelief on the pastor we once had, on our childhood, on circumstances, or on anything else. There is no excuse for us not to believe in the Lord. Christ is still challenging us as he did Peter on the lake one night. Even though Peter was walking on the water, "when he saw the wind, he was afraid and, beginning to sink, cried out, 'Lord, save me!' Immediately Jesus reached out his hand and caught him. 'You of little faith,' he said, 'why did you doubt?'" (Matthew 14:30–31).

FAITH FOR THE LONG HAUL

NOW WE FINALLY SEE why the Bible so many times holds up the great value of *endurance.* That virtue is not often mentioned in our day. We lean more toward spectacular things like great preaching and dynamic spiritual gifts. But the persistent faith that holds onto God, enduring all the various situations of life no matter how difficult—*that* is something we need to ask God for more and more.

Vincent and Daphne Rodriguez are the kind of steady, salt-of-the-earth people whom every pastor loves to have in a congregation. They live in Queens; he has been a reliable letter carrier for the Postal Service his whole life, while she has been a dedicated homemaker for their three children.

While he was volunteering at a children's camp in the Catskill Mountains one summer, Vincent's heart was touched by the boys and girls he met who didn't have fathers. He and Daphne talked about the children's obvious needs for love and care. In time, the Rodriguezes, then in their early forties, applied to the Salvation Army to become foster parents.

They had hardly finished their training when, a few days before Christmas 1988, the phone rang at one o'clock in the morning. A pitiful baby girl in Beth-Israel Hospital—born more than a month prematurely and addicted through her mother to crack cocaine, heroin, and morphine—needed a home. She had finally gotten up to five pounds in weight and could now be released to foster care. Her mother was a young addict who was clearly unfit to care for her, living most of the time in the streets as a prostitute. Would Vincent and Daphne take the baby?

"We didn't know anything about addiction in infants," says Daphne, like her husband a quiet person. "We had assumed we'd probably be getting a healthy child who was perhaps just from a poor economic environment. Without knowing what we were walking into, we said yes."

By ten o'clock the next evening, two social workers were on their doorstep with a bundle in blankets. For the next twenty-four hours, the Rodriguez family did little else but hover in a circle around the child and admire her! When she cried, which was often, they would pass her from one set of arms to the next. "We felt so sorry for her," says Vincent. "She was our surprise gift for Christmas, and we were happy that God had brought her our way."

But the girl didn't quite look like a normal baby, for the stress of drug withdrawal seemed etched upon her tiny face. At the church, she was dedicated to the Lord in a Sunday afternoon service when she was two months old—and weighed six pounds. I broke down as I held her up to the Lord, and the congregation adopted her as their own.

In the Rodriguez home, life was settling into the realities of taking care of a very disturbed newborn. She twitched and jerked and cried out constantly in the pain of withdrawal. Daphne had prepared herself for middle-of-the-night feedings, of course, but she was hardly expecting to be up every two hours, preparing more milk to calm the baby's frazzled nervous system. She would pace the floor, holding the baby tight to give a feeling of security. As the weeks wore on, this was turning into more of an ordeal than Daphne had bargained for. And yet they felt that God had led them to take this child.

"I kept telling myself that God had his hand on her, because he had allowed her to live, even though she was only two-and-a-half pounds at birth," Daphne says. "She hadn't even been given a name. So we chose one ourselves; at our teenage daughter's suggestion, we picked out a beautiful Bible name, Hannah."

Daphne figured out that if she put her teenagers in charge of the baby each afternoon when they came home from school, she could get at least a nap in order to fortify herself for the next night ahead. Otherwise, an hour of sleep at a time was the best she could hope for. Even Vincent's sleep was disrupted.

"But even in the times I was exhausted or didn't feel well myself, I kept going," Daphne remembers. "I tried to soothe her with Christian music through the day. One particular recording—'I Exalt Thee' by Phil Driscoll—seemed to calm her shaking in the bassinet. We played it every day, and the crying would stop."

When I would see them in church and ask how it was going, Daphne would just sort of shrug as she said, "Pastor, it's really hard! She needs me all night long, it seems; I can't get any sleep." I felt concerned for them, and more than once I asked the congregation to continue to bring the Rodriguezes' situation to God at the throne of grace.

In time, Hannah's health improved. She gained weight. At the end of the first year, she finally began sleeping through the night. Her crawling and walking came later than usual, but that was to be expected. So was her hyperactivity.

With a steady diet of love and prayer, Hannah developed into a toddler. Looking ahead toward the school years, however, Daphne saw trouble. Would this child be able to sit still and learn? She had Hannah tested for attention deficit disorder, and that led to placement in a special education program from age three-and-a-half to five. The program had the additional benefit of giving the tired mother a much-needed break from the daily vigil.

When Hannah reached five years of age, Vincent and Daphne formally adopted her. The ink was hardly dry on the adoption decree, making them permanently responsible for Hannah, when a whole new problem erupted. Hannah developed a cold that she couldn't seem to shake; her face became very dry and blotchy. The condition hung on until finally Daphne took her to the doctor and requested a full physical examination. Two days later, a nurse called: "You need to come back for a consultation."

"Why?" Daphne asked. "What's wrong?"

"Well, something is showing here that doesn't look right. The enzymes in her liver are way too high. We need to run these tests again."

Soon the truth came out: The little girl, having already fought off addiction to hard drugs from her birth mother, was also afflicted with hepatitis C—a serious disease that saps energy, sometimes turns the eyes and skin yellow, and wastes away the liver over time.

"Oh, God—how can this be?" Daphne cried. "After all we've been through with Hannah already—why wasn't this discovered back when she was born?"

So many questions, so few answers. Discouragement swept over the besieged family. When they told me the bad news, I realized that a new battle of faith for Hannah had begun for all of us at the church.

We enlisted the efforts of the Brooklyn Tabernacle Prayer Band (a group that intercedes around the clock, seven days a week), the members of the choir, and everyone else we could. We agreed together that God had created this child and had brought her through all the terrors of drug withdrawal, and we now stood united in faith against this latest threat. "God must be planning to use her for something great," we said.

In time, with the help of the Salvation Army, the Rodriguezes secured the help of a chief specialist at Schneider Children's Hospital, part of the Long Island Jewish medical complex, who took on Hannah's case. He put her on a regimen of medication to fight the disease. Vincent even steeled himself to give his daughter injections, which were required three times a week for the next eighteen months. Hannah's condition stabilized.

Throughout the primary grades, Hannah struggled to keep up with her learning. Daphne was a frequent face in the school hallways, working with the teachers to find solutions for her little girl. Performance gradually improved. They never gave up, no matter what new obstacle appeared. They just refused to stop fighting for Hannah.

Today Hannah's hepatitis C is in remission, and her medications have been dropped. She is a beautiful girl with a lovely round face and a shy smile. "We are just trusting in the Lord that he is healing her completely," Vincent says.

"What a testimony she will be able to give in years to come. I sometimes tell my daughter, 'Someday you will get to stand on the highest building in the city and tell everybody!' She always smiles when I say that, and I do, too. The miracle is on its way."

STAY THE COURSE

THE APOSTLE PAUL KNEW that this kind of spiritual endurance was vital for his own spiritual children. He told them that he never stopped praying for them to be "strengthened with all power according to his glorious might so that you may have great endurance and patience, and joyfully giving thanks to the Father" (Colossians 1:11). He brought them tenderly to God in prayer, that they might be able to keep on keeping on, no matter what attacks were made upon their faith.

Many sensational gifts and talents don't mean much over the long haul. The longer I live, the more I treasure people who just keep walking with God. They aren't up or down, left or right; they're always steady on the course, praising God and believing his Word.

> **Many sensational gifts and talents don't mean much over the long haul. The longer I live, the more I treasure people who just keep walking with God.** ～

Just as our bodies need strength in order to keep functioning, our spirits need endurance. When our faith becomes weakened through discouragement, we have trouble standing on God's promises. We struggle to say no to temptation.

It's easy to give in to the devil. "The Big D" threatens to snuff out our spiritual life. But with God, we can have the power to resist discouragement. He can give us the spirit of Caleb and Joshua that triumphs despite the difficulties facing us.

Notice that Paul *prays* for endurance. This was not something he could transmit by verbal teaching to the Colossian believers. This wonderful strength had to come directly from God at the throne of grace.

And it will *keep* coming as we *keep* asking and trusting in our God.

NINE

~

Grace That
Is Greater

Many times at the end of our services, I meet people at the
altar who are so ashamed that they often will not even look
me in the eye. Their shoulders are slumped; their gaze is on
the carpet. I sense no faith in them to ask Christ for mercy.
Praise and worship seem impossible. They are living under
the heavy burden of their own failure, with no hope that their
life can be retrieved. They now feel too unworthy to expect
any blessings from a holy and righteous God.

I am not just talking about people with the stereotypical
inner-city problems of drugs, prostitution, or whatever. These
are average-looking people who have simply given in to a
besetting sin so often that they are convinced they will never
rise above it.

Often, as the congregation is worshiping in the background with a song such as "Grace, grace, God's grace—
grace that will pardon and cleanse within," I notice that the
person before me isn't singing along. It is because the person
isn't sure that the song could really be true for him or her.
Sometimes I will gently try to lift the person's chin or perhaps the hands in upward openness to God.

How I love to remind these people of someone in the
Bible whose life story is often forgotten. You might not think

of him as a failure, because his name, in fact, shows up in very good company. One place is on the very first page of the New Testament, where the opening lines say,

A record of the genealogy of Jesus Christ the son of David, the son of Abraham:

Abraham was the father of Isaac,
  Isaac the father of Jacob,
  Jacob the father of *Judah* and his brothers,
  Judah the father of Perez and Zerah, whose mother was Tamar (Matthew 1:1–3).

How nice and orderly. This passage sets down a clear track from Abraham, the father of the Jewish nation, to Jesus, so that everyone in the first century would know that this Messiah was honest-to-goodness Jewish. Along the way, that track runs straight through Judah and his family.

Then, on one of the last pages of the New Testament, the apostle John writes,

I saw in the right hand of him who sat on the throne a scroll with writing on both sides and sealed with seven seals. And I saw a mighty angel proclaiming in a loud voice, "Who is worthy to break the seals and open the scroll?" But no one in heaven or on earth or under the earth could open the scroll or even look inside it. I wept and wept because no one was found who was worthy to open the scroll or look inside. Then one of the elders said to me, "Do not weep! See, the Lion of the tribe of *Judah*, the Root of David, has triumphed. He is able to open the scroll and its seven seals" (Revelation 5:1–5).

How wonderful that while many others were disqualified, someone who came from the tribe of Judah met the standard to open the mysteries of God. That someone, of course, was Jesus Christ.

This Judah must have been quite a godly man, right? Of all of Jacob's twelve sons, only he is mentioned in the genealogy of Christ. The other eleven were passed over by God. At the climax of history in heaven, it is Judah's offspring who is hailed as worthy when all others fail the test. When we get to heaven someday, we will no doubt continue to hear Judah's name often.

But what do you really know about this man Judah?

A SORDID TALE

JUDAH GETS A WHOLE chapter of the Bible to himself— Genesis 38—and that is the best place to get acquainted with him. If you have the stomach for it, that is. (You might not want to read this chapter aloud to your children in family devotions.)

The story begins with Judah drifting away from the rest of the family and marrying a Canaanite woman (vv. 1–2). That was his first mistake. His uncle, Esau, had already been down that road, getting into a mess by marrying outside of those who served the one true God (see Genesis 26:34–35). As a result, Judah's grandparents had gone to great lengths to make sure their other son, Jacob, didn't make the same error. They told him in no uncertain terms to avoid Canaanite women (Genesis 28:1) and sent him on a long trip to find the right kind of wife.

But Judah disregarded their counsel entirely. He married "the daughter of a Canaanite man named Shua" (Genesis 38:2). The children born to them apparently grew up getting mixed messages about the true God versus Canaan's idols. The bad results showed up quickly in the first son, who turned out to be so wicked that the Lord put him to death in early adulthood (v. 7).

That left behind a young widow named Tamar. Judah asked his second son to marry her, as was the social requirement in those days. But the son selfishly refused. Because of this, God brought destruction on him also.

Judah now procrastinated about giving his third son, Shelah, to Tamar. The years went by, and Tamar kept waiting. She was getting past her prime, and she was lonely. Finally, she heard about a trip her father-in-law, Judah, was going to take. It was sheep-shearing time, which was payday for those in the sheep business. Money flowed and people partied. To Tamar, this seemed like the perfect opportunity to carry out a terrible plan. She covered her face with some kind of shawl and posed along the road as a prostitute.

The Bible records that Judah, "not realizing that she was his daughter-in-law, . . . went over to her by the roadside and said, 'Come now, let me sleep with you'" (v. 16). Judah paid for her services, but it resulted in Tamar's becoming pregnant with twins. Judah went home none the wiser.

When the news came out that Tamar was having a baby, Judah threw a righteous fit. How dare his daughter-in-law cause disgrace on the family! "Bring her out and have her burned to death!" he stormed (v. 24).

As she was being dragged out into the public square, she calmly identified her sexual partner by holding up the personal property Judah had left with her as a down payment for her services. Judah was humiliated before all and had to admit, "She is more righteous than I" (v. 26).

DISQUALIFIED?

YOU JUST WANT TO shield your eyes from this kind of ugliness, don't you? It sounds like something in the *National Enquirer.* If you or I have an ancestor in our families who did something like this, we don't talk about it. We probably leave his picture out of the family album. We don't bring up his name to our children—and hope they never ask. People who so mess up their lives—and others' lives—are best left unmentioned.

Why would God put this seamy story in the Bible? It doesn't seem fit for print. Or, if God had to include the story, why didn't he then say to us, "The stern lesson of this is that the lineage of my holy Son will be Abraham—Isaac—Jacob—*Benjamin*," or one of the other sons? After all, hadn't Judah thoroughly disqualified himself?

Left to our own devices, any of us can self-destruct within an hour, just as Judah did. "There is no one righteous, not even one" (Romans 3:10). "We all, like sheep, have gone astray, each of us has turned to his own way" (Isaiah 53:6). "I know that nothing good lives in me, that is, in my sinful nature"(Romans 7:18). Thus, there is no need for self-righteous snickering as we read Judah's story.

> **We all can be self-righteous and pompous.**
> **If every moment of our past were put on the**
> **big screen at church, who of us would seem**
> **so wonderful?** ～

God has given clear testimony about our moral standing with him. But unfortunately, we are very good at condemning others for the very things we also do. "So-and-so in the church is selfish . . . so-and-so is racist . . . so-and-so is a hypocrite." But somehow, the mirror doesn't work for us.

Like Judah when he was told about his daughter-in-law's pregnancy, we can all be self-righteous and pompous. Not only are we weak, but we are judgmental on top of it! Wouldn't it be better to stop giving opinions about everyone else and do a better job of humbly looking after our own hearts? If every moment of our past were put on the big screen at church, who of us would seem so wonderful?

My main concern today is that we have lost sight of the reason God included Judah's ugly story in the Bible. We are drifting away from the New Testament's message of God's amazing grace to change and redeem soiled people; instead, we are moralizing and expressing self-righteous disdain over the horrible lives others are living around us. Instead of exalting Jesus, who came as a spiritual physician for the sick and unlovely, we are busy rehearsing all the commandments of God, as if that alone would change a single soul. We are giving people only the law, when what they crave is the love and grace of God.

We have forgotten that God specializes in cases such as Judah. We should return to preaching boldly what Paul wrote to the Corinthians—not stopping two-thirds of the way through the paragraph, but continuing on to the glorious end:

> Do you not know that the wicked will not inherit the kingdom of God? Do not be deceived: Neither the sexually immoral nor idolaters nor adulterers nor male prostitutes nor homosexual offenders nor thieves nor the greedy nor drunkards nor slanderers nor swindlers will inherit the kingdom of God. *And that is what some of you were. But you were washed, you were sanctified, you were justified in the name of the Lord Jesus Christ and by the Spirit of our God* (1 Corinthians 6:9–11).

The early Christian church had its own share of "Judahs," but "where sin increased, grace increased all the more" (Romans 5:20).

GRACE BEYOND REASON

THE DEVIL'S SPECIALTY is to swarm in on people and hiss, "You did it! You really messed up! If people only knew. . . . You're not what you seem to be. Do you think you're going to get away with this?" And the devil's victims hardly feel like living. They feel unworthy to go to church. They avoid their Bibles. They see no hope of change.

Satan wants to hide the fact that the mercy of God is for *everyone* who has messed up. As high as the heavens are above the earth, so are God's ways higher than ours (Isaiah 55:9). He delights in mercy. James writes, "Mercy triumphs over judgment" (2:13). God's specialty is forgiving and putting away people's sins from his sight. He delights in taking failures such as Judah and weaving them into the ancestry of his own Son, Jesus Christ.

What is even more remarkable is this: The genealogy of Jesus in Matthew 1:3 continues through Judah and then goes *not* to his legitimate son, Shelah—but to Perez, Tamar's boy, the child of incest. How incredible! It is as if God were saying, "Forever I want my people to know that I not only forgive mess-ups, but I can take them and touch them and heal them—and put them in the line that leads to Christ." What Satan means for evil, God is able to change and work out for good (Genesis 50:20).

To this very day, God delights in hearing Judah's name echo through the heavenly halls. He takes sinners like you and me and makes us right. He takes dirt and pollution and transforms them into holiness. He takes the crooked thing and makes it straight. He takes the tangles of our lives and weaves something new, so that we emerge singing Hallelujah. We love God, not because we've been so good, but because *he* is so good, and his mercy endures forever.

The Lion of the tribe of Judah is about deliverance, not condemnation. He takes our mistakes and wanderings and redeems them for his glory. Greater than his glory as Creator and Sustainer of the universe is the glory of his grace to losers like you and me. No record is so stained, no case so hopeless that he cannot reach down and bring salvation to that person.

> **God takes sinners like you and me and makes us right. He takes dirt and pollution and transforms them into holiness. He takes the crooked thing and makes it straight.** ∼

One of the outstanding gospel singers in America today is a trophy of that kind of divine mercy. When audiences listen to Calvin Hunt's soaring tenor voice, they can hardly imagine that at one time he virtually destroyed his body with crack cocaine—and ravaged the lives of his wife and two stepchildren as well. His story is more than just self-destruction through drugs; it spreads its pain to the single mom he had rescued in the aftermath of her abusive first marriage, and to her innocent daughter and son.

Calvin met the trim, attractive Miriam and her two preschoolers when he was just twenty years old. Miriam lived in the apartment two floors below his mother, and she and Calvin warmed to each other right away. Little Monique and Freddy liked the handsome young construction worker with the hard hat who made them laugh. Calvin was also something of a weekend musician, playing guitar and singing in nightclubs.

Miriam's divorce was not yet final, and Calvin had to comfort her more than once after she had been beaten up by her estranged husband. On one occasion, when the man knocked her out cold, Calvin took Miriam to the emergency room. Their relationship flourished over the next year and then even survived a one-year army stint by Calvin that took him away from New York City.

"When I came back home," Calvin admits, "the easiest thing for me to do was just to move in with her. I went back to working road construction, and we had enough money to party through the weekends." The couple eventually added snorting cocaine to their fairly heavy drinking as they and their friends sought new thrills. Then they added marijuana to the mix, sometimes even sprinkling the joints with cocaine before rolling them in order to experience both drugs at once.

The live-in arrangement continued with little change, until five years later when Miriam told Calvin they ought to get married. And so in 1984, they wed.

SOMETHING NEW

ONE NIGHT THE BEST man from their wedding invited them to a party at his home that featured something new: "freebasing" cocaine, or heating it and smoking it through a glass bottle. Calvin was intrigued; he asked his friend for a hit. But the new drug didn't seem to have much effect, Calvin thought. Miriam gave it a try as well, with minimal results.

Or so they thought. Not until they left the friend's apartment at 7:30 the next morning, having been awake all night and having spent Calvin's entire $720 paycheck for the week, did they realize they had discovered something powerfully attractive—and deadly. They had now joined the world of crack cocaine.

"I remember us going back home, and I just felt horrible the whole weekend," Calvin says. "By the time I went to work on Monday, I was lecturing myself about being more responsible. I had a family to support, and I needed to get back in control.

"Would you believe that by the next Friday night when I cashed my check, I called Miriam and told her to get the kids ready for bed early, because I'd be bringing home 'the stuff'? I showed up with all the new paraphernalia, ready for action. I prepared the crack over the kitchen stove just as I'd seen my friend do it the week before, and again the two of us were up all night. By the time the sun came up Saturday morning, we had gone through another whole paycheck."

This pattern endured for eight months. Meanwhile, household bills went unpaid, the children lacked warm winter clothing, and the rent fell behind. Miriam's brothers, who were Christians, urged her to stop destroying herself, but neither she nor Calvin would listen.

> **If Calvin had any spare cash in his pocket, it went for crack. If he didn't have cash, he would manufacture some by stealing the battery or tires from a parked car to resell.** ～

Calvin's obsession with drugs grew ever stronger, and not just on the weekends. If he had any spare cash in his pocket, it went for crack. If he didn't have cash, he would manufacture some by stealing the tires or the battery from a parked car to resell. Some nights he didn't come home at all.

Obviously, Calvin's job performance suffered. One day his boss pulled Calvin aside for a talk. There were tears in the man's eyes as he said quietly, "You've been one of my most valued employees. I don't know what's happening, and I don't want to know—but whatever it is, you better get it fixed, because you're about to lose your job."

The truth was, Calvin had a new superboss in his life: crack. "I began losing a lot of weight," Calvin says. "I'd be gone three, four, even five days at a time—spending my life in crack dens. Yes, I had a home and a wife and two children—but when I was doing crack, home was the last place I wanted to be.

"The people I did drugs with were actually a pretty scary bunch– violent and heartless. But as long as I was high, I didn't even notice that."

BETRAYED

MIRIAM GREW INCREASINGLY CONCERNED. What was happening to the man she loved, her one-time knight in shining armor? Hadn't she already been through enough chaos with her first husband—and now this? One night she looked at her two children sleeping innocently in bed while Calvin and his friends were in the kitchen getting high. Moral principles once learned long ago seemed to rise up to warn her of where this was all heading. She promptly threw all the guys out – including Calvin.

Miriam began to see that she was being terribly betrayed by a man for the second time in her life. The first one had beaten her physically; the second one was hurting her and her children even more painfully with his addiction. Like Judah of old, he was wreaking tremendous damage on his family through his unbridled thrill-seeking.

"I pleaded with him to stop," says Miriam. "I said, 'Calvin, this is going to kill us! It's going to destroy our marriage.' The arguments got so bad that sometimes I had to have him escorted out of the house. My son began studying ways to add more locks to the apartment so Calvin couldn't get back in."

At the very time Calvin was deserting the family, Miriam put her faith in Christ. Her spiritual life deepened, and her prayer life increased. She found a church and would openly ask for the prayers of others to bring her husband back from the brink. She refused to contemplate the other options: separation, divorce, or his untimely death. She simply believed that God would somehow rescue their family.

She even began to tell Calvin, "God is going to set you free—I just know it!" Of course, that made him furious. He also got irked at the Brooklyn Tabernacle Choir music she had begun to play. She loved it and would respond in worship, sometimes even weeping for joy as she praised the Lord. Calvin would snap back, "If that stuff makes you cry, why don't you turn it off?" He would sometimes fling the cassette out the window, but his wife would quickly replace it.

One day young Monique found a flyer announcing a Friday night showing of the film *A Cry for Freedom*, being sponsored in a high school auditorium by Christ Tabernacle in Queens. The twelve-year-old insisted that Dad go with them to see it. He brushed her off.

Suddenly something rose up within the girl. She said, "Daddy, remember all the neat things we used to do together? We don't do anything anymore. You know what— it's all about you and that drug, whatever it is! Your problem is, you're hooked, and you won't admit it!"

Calvin flared back. "You shut up! Keep talking like that, and I'll give you a whipping!"

"Go ahead, Daddy!" the brave girl responded. "You can beat me and stomp on me if you want—but when you're finished, you'll still be hooked on that stuff." At that, she ran out of the kitchen.

Calvin picked up the flyer from the table. He looked at the sketch of a man inside the bottle that is used for smoking crack, his hands pressed against the glass with a desperate look on his face. Calvin's heart melted enough that he reluctantly agreed to attend the showing.

At the last minute, Calvin tried to back out, but without success. The film's story line turned out to be a shockingly close replica of the Hunts themselves: a husband addicted to crack, and his formerly addicted wife now praying for his deliverance. When the pastor gave an invitation at the end, Calvin was the first one kneeling at the altar. "I didn't actually ask Jesus to come into my heart," he says, "but I was just so guilt-ridden that I had to at least pray and admit the pain I was causing everyone. I started to cry. Miriam and the kids came alongside, and we all cried together."

The next Sunday, the family returned to church, and while Miriam and the children were overjoyed, Calvin still was not willing to get serious about the Lord. *God can't do anything for me*, he told himself. *What am I doing here?* By the next weekend, he was on the run again.

BEARING DOWN

NOW THE CHURCH BODY began to pray harder for Calvin Hunt's salvation. Calvin learned to time his visits back to the apartment during the hours when he knew everyone would be at church. He would sneak in to get a fresh supply of clean clothes and then quickly leave.

"I knew that Calvin was in a prison," says Miriam. "Being an ex-addict myself—I had done heroin before I ever met him—I knew the unbelievable power of this kind of substance. That's why I prayed so hard, crying out to God to set him free, and got all my friends to pray with me. Every mealtime prayer with my kids, every bedtime prayer included, 'O God, please set Daddy free!'"

Another three years went by. Calvin got worse instead of better. At one point he was actually sleeping in a large doghouse in someone's backyard rather than going home to his own bed. He was seriously dehydrated, his cheeks sunken, giving him the wasted look so common among addicts. With no money, Miriam and the children had to apply for food stamps and Medicaid.

Finally, one night—the same night as Christ Tabernacle's weekly prayer meeting—Calvin headed once again for the family apartment after his wife and children had left. In the quietness he found some food in the refrigerator, then took a shower and put on clean clothes. There was still time for a short nap, so he decided to lie down.

But for some reason, he couldn't sleep. Soon he heard a noise. From a closet came the soft sound of someone weeping! He sat up. Maybe Miriam and the children were home after all.

He looked in the children's rooms, under the beds, inside the various closets. No one! But the sobbing continued. He stood in the living room and said out loud, "I know you guys are in here—come on out!" Nobody appeared.

> **Calvin thought of lying down once again,
> but something inside him seemed to say, *If
> you go to sleep tonight, you'll never wake up
> again.* He panicked.** ∼

Now Calvin was spooked. He thought of lying down once again, but something inside him seemed to say, *If you go to sleep tonight, you'll never wake up again.* He panicked. Running out the door, he dashed three blocks to the train station to go see if his wife and children were really at the prayer meeting or not.

He burst into the church and stood at the back of the center aisle, scanning the crowd. Suddenly the same sounds of crying struck his ears—only much louder than back in the apartment. The whole congregation was in earnest prayer, calling out *his* name to God in faith! Calvin was thunderstruck as he slowly moved down the aisle, gazing at the people's upraised hands and their eyes tightly shut in prayer, tears running down their faces. "O God, wherever Calvin Hunt is, bring him to this building!" they pleaded. "Don't let this family go through this horror another day. Lord, you are able! Set him free from his bondage once and for all!"

Soon Calvin found himself at the front, directly before the pulpit. The pastor in charge opened his eyes, took one glance—and then gazed upward toward heaven as he said into the microphone, "Thank you, Lord! Thank you, Jesus! Here he is!"

With that, the congregation went absolutely crazy. They had been calling upon the Lord to bring Calvin to himself, and it was happening right before their very eyes.

Falling to his knees, Calvin burst into uncontrollable sobs. Miriam and the children came from their pew to huddle around him as he prayed, "O God, I've become everything I said I'd never be. I don't want to die this way. Please come into my life and set me free. Oh, Jesus, I need you so much!"

That summer night in 1988 was the turning point for Calvin Hunt. Says Miriam, "It was almost as if he had walked slowly down the center aisle of the church as in a wedding, to be married to Christ. Jesus was patiently waiting for him at the altar. No wonder we all burst into tears!"

ON A NEW KIND OF ROAD

THE OLD LIFE and old patterns put up some resistance for Calvin, to be sure, but the pastors of Christ Tabernacle spoke very straight to him about getting into a Christian residential program in Pennsylvania called Youth Challenge. He agreed to go.

Six months later, Calvin returned to New York City, strong in his faith and ready to live for God. He managed to get his old road construction job back. My wife and I saw him several nights with his crew out working on the Brooklyn-Queens Expressway as we were driving home after church. He was so happy in the Lord! Soon he began turning his singing talent to godly purposes.

Once in a restaurant, Calvin got up to go to the men's room, and there in a stall was someone smoking crack! All of the old desires began to tug at him, but he quickly prayed. *God, I need you to help me right now!* He steadied himself. When the man appeared, Calvin looked him in the eye and said, "Let me tell you something from experience: That stuff is going to destroy your life."

"Whatcha talkin' 'bout, man?"

"I'm serious. It will destroy you—but Jesus can help you overcome it."

The next thing Calvin did was head straight for a telephone to call Miriam and report his victory at overcoming temptation. They rejoiced together in the new strength God had given.

Today Calvin Hunt no longer wields a jackhammer on the highways of New York City. He has recorded two gospel albums and travels full-time, telling audiences nationwide about the road to God's power in their lives. He is also a featured soloist with our choir—the group he once despised—

and a member of the sixteen-voice Brooklyn Tabernacle Singers. Wherever he goes, people's hearts are lifted in praise for God's victory in his life.

Instead of destroying his family, Calvin is now its godly leader—including two new children that the Lord has graciously given to him and Miriam. Doctors had led them to believe that they had both so abused their bodies that conception was unlikely. Then came a daughter named Mia and, a couple of years later, a son named Calvin Jr. From the sin and hopelessness that seemed ready to swallow Calvin and Miriam, God has raised up another monument to the saving power of Jesus Christ, the Lion of the tribe of Judah.

> **May God deliver us from self-righteous judging and make us, instead, merciful carriers of Christ's salvation and freedom everywhere we go. ～**

Let us spread the message far and wide: Jesus Christ is mighty to save! No matter how ruined the life, his blood can erase the darkest stain, and his Spirit can breathe new life into fallen men and women. He is the God of Judah—the man who was a moral failure, a hypocrite, and a disgrace to God and his family. But through Judah we see more clearly the depth of the Lord's love and the incredible richness of his mercy.

May God deliver us from self-righteous judging and make us, instead, merciful carriers of Christ's salvation and freedom everywhere we go. Jesus "came into the world to save sinners," the apostle Paul wrote, even considering himself to be "the worst" of the lot (1 Timothy 1:15). But rejoice in why he was so candid about his condition, for it applies to us also: "For that very reason I was shown mercy so that in me, the worst of sinners, Christ Jesus might display his unlimited patience as an example for those who would believe on him and receive eternal life. Now to the King eternal, immortal, invisible, the only God, be honor and glory for ever and ever. Amen" (vv. 16–17).

PART 3

~

Following the
Divine Channel

TEN

∽

Father of
the Faithful

H AVE YOU EVER READ in Scripture about "Father David"?
Or "Father Moses"?
What about "Father Daniel"?
These were all mighty men of God, to be sure. They
rank among the greatest warriors, kings, prophets, and leaders of sacred history. But none of them achieved the special
honor bestowed upon "the father of all who believe, . . . the
father of [those] who also walk in the footsteps of faith, . . .
our father in the sight of God, in whom he believed, . . . the
father of many nations" (Romans 4:11–12, 17–18). His name
is Abraham.

We know that Jesus once disputed using the title *father*
in reference to any mortal human (see Matthew 23:9). Yet,
when the apostle Paul came to write the fourth chapter of
Romans, it sounds almost as if he couldn't help himself. *Abraham . . . oh, my . . . he's the very symbol of living by faith . . . I have
to set him preeminent above all others . . . he's the spiritual father
of all who believe God's promises.*

This Abraham was obviously the great example when it
comes to faith. How did he ever develop such towering trust
in God?

HE LIVED BY PROMISES, NOT COMMANDS

ON THAT EPIC DAY when God first spoke to Abram (as he was then known), God said,

> Leave your country, your people and your father's household and go to the land I will show you.
>
> I will make you into a great nation
>   and I will bless you;
> I will make your name great,
>   and you will be a blessing.
> I will bless those who bless you,
>   and whoever curses you I will curse;
> and all peoples on earth
>   will be blessed through you (Genesis 12:1–3).

God directed Abram to do only one thing—"Leave"—and in return, God would do eight wonderful things for him. That number alone speaks of the graciousness and goodness of God.

But it did require Abram to leave his country, his people, and his relatives—in other words, his comfort zone. He had to give up the land he knew best, the culture he had grown up in, the familiar sights and sounds. People who walk by faith often hear God's voice telling them, "You need to leave now. It's time to move on to something new."

Sometimes that word has to do with geography, as in Abram's case. We are currently experiencing this at the Brooklyn Tabernacle as we get ready to leave our present building, where we have been since 1979, and head for the larger downtown theater where we believe God is sending us. We have bought this massive shell, built in 1914, even though as I'm writing this we still do not know how we will raise the millions needed for renovation. We are having to walk by faith.

At other times, God directs his people to leave certain work situations, sever pleasant relationships, or make other difficult changes. When you walk by faith, God never lets you settle into some plateau. Just when you reach a certain place spiritually and decide to pitch your tent and relax for the rest of your life, God says, "Leave." This was the story of Abram. In fact, he was never allowed to settle down permanently as long as he lived.

When you walk by faith, God never lets you settle into some plateau. ∼

But we don't have to be afraid. God in the same breath can begin to inundate us with promises, as he did Abram. See the great things the Lord vowed to do:

1. "... the land I will show you." In other words, God will point out the destination.
2. "I will make you into a great nation."
3. "I will bless you."
4. "I will make your name great."
5. "You will be a blessing."
6. "I will bless those who bless you."
7. "Whoever curses you I will curse."
8. "All peoples on earth will be blessed through you."

Thus, Abram's family caravan left town in a mode of *living off the promises of God.* That was their source, and it must be ours as well. We cannot live off the commands of God, but rather the promises. The commands of God reveal his holy character to us, but they hold no accompanying power. Instead, the grace of God flows through the channel of his promises. God must first do for us what he promised, and only then will we be able to walk in obedience to his commands. Remember, he is our Source—everything must start from him.

It is true that God's moral commands teach us where we fall short. That is necessary—but it doesn't bring a solution to our human dilemma. Only the promises bring us hope, if we respond in faith, as Abram did. That is what sustained him throughout his life. By the time Abram arrived in Canaan, God was already adding more promises to the original group. He said, "To your offspring I will give this land" (v. 7). His abundance kept flowing.

But the great majority of us are command-oriented. Every day we wake up conscious of God's moral law and try to do right so he will approve of us at the end of the day. Yet this is a great struggle. We would do far better to wake up thinking about God's wonderful promises—what he has said he will do for us today. Then his power working in us will tenderly direct us in the way of obedience and right living.

> **God's moral commands teach us where we fall short. That is necessary—but only the *promises* bring us hope, if we respond in faith. ～**

The tender love of God toward us, as revealed in his gracious promises, is the only thing that draws us to a closer walk with the Lord. Righteous commands alone, and the judgment always linked to them, can easily frighten us away. Martin Luther was originally repelled by the holy God he saw as only making demands and sentencing people to judgment. Then he saw the truth "the righteous will live by faith" (Romans 1:17). This spoke of grace and mercy to all who simply believe God. Out of this came the whole Protestant Reformation, which turned the world upside down.

Abram felt so close to God that "he built an altar to the LORD and called on the name of the LORD" (Genesis 12:8) there between the towns of Bethel and Ai. Abram's heart reached out to God in worship. This God had been so good to him, so generous, so affirming. Abram had not earned any promise or blessing by previous conduct; it was all because of grace. He could not help lifting up his heart and hands to God in adoration.

HE HAD NO MASTER PLAN

THE BOOK OF HEBREWS tells us that "by faith Abraham . . . obeyed and went, even though he did not know where he was going" (11:8). He had no map, no AAA brochure, no lineup of motel reservations along the way. His caravan simply headed west toward the Mediterranean, and that was that. God had said he would show him where to stop sometime in the future when he got to wherever he was going.

You and I would struggle with this, wouldn't we? Not only in our vacation travel, but in guiding our careers and our churches, we simply have to have a comprehensive plan. I hear pastors say all the time, "Let's see, regarding this or that outreach—will it pay? Is it going to be cost-effective? How can I be sure it will work? Will everyone be pleased?" We do very few things by faith.

Abram didn't have a clue. If you had met up with his caravan at some oasis, the conversation might have gone like this:

"Mr. Abram, where are you going?"

"I don't know."

"Well, how will you know when you get there?"

"I don't know that, either. God only said he would show me."

"You have quite an entourage here. When you do arrive, who will supply all the food you'll need? After all, if you're going to survive in a new place, how are you going to eat"?

"I don't know. He just said he would take care of me."

"You don't seem to have a security force. Who is going to protect you from the Jebusites, the Hittites, the Amorites, and all the rest of the warring tribes?"

Abram would just shake his head and wander away.

Faith is happy to step out not knowing where it's going so long as it knows Who is going along. As long as God's strong hand was holding Abram's, everything was going to work out just fine. The caravan moved ahead in faith.

> **Faith is happy to step out not knowing where it's going so long as it knows Who is going along.** ～

We like to control the map of our life and know everything well in advance. But faith is content just knowing that God's promise cannot fail. This, in fact, is the excitement of walking with God. When we read the book of Acts, we never quite know what's going to happen with the next turn of the page. The Spirit is in control, and that is enough. Paul had no formula as to how he would evangelize; he was simply going by faith. God unveiled the route as he went along.

I was invited to speak at a huge conference of pastors where the entire meeting was plotted out, minute by minute. The man who called me graciously explained, "First there will be an opening song, and then one of our denominational leaders will speak for fourteen minutes on a doctrinal topic. Then will come some additional music, and then we'd like you to speak for twenty minutes. Following your remarks, a choir will present some of your wife's music, and then finally a third speaker will speak for twenty minutes. Then will come the benediction."

This was to occur on a Monday. I thought about the physical drain of leading four services in our own church on Sunday and then right away taking a long plane flight to this conference. Did God want all this travel and expense for such an occasion?

When I hesitated, the man said, "Oh, your book *Fresh Wind, Fresh Fire* has been a great blessing in so many of our churches. We really want you to come."

"Well," I said, "I guess what comes to my mind is this: How many points can an audience remember at one sitting? I mean, you've lined up three speakers, each making important statements. . . . People cannot feel deeply about more than a couple of truths at a time. I think I know the type of speaker you're looking for, but I don't think I'm the man. I'm not really sure that's the best way to minister to thousands of pastors anyway."

"What do you mean?" he replied.

"Well, since you mentioned my book, I have an idea. Why don't you think about scratching some of the program and having a prayer meeting instead? We pastors all need more of God. The general spiritual condition of churches all across America right now is not exactly fervent and prayerful. Divorces are plentiful; young people are falling away; pastors are resigning at record rates—maybe the best thing you could do in your conference is to allocate a block of time just to pray. Why not ask God to open up the heavens and come down? He's the one we really need."

This man graciously replied, "But we don't do those things at our conference."

I said, "I'm not familiar with the traditions of your particular group, but I do see in my Bible where some great promises are given to those who call on the Lord and wait for his blessing."

I finished the call by declining the invitation as politely as I could.

A week later, the phone rang again. "We've decided to adjust the service," the man said. "Why don't you come and bring your wife as well as some others, and you can have plenty of time. You can end the service any way you want."

I felt the Lord opening an important night of ministry. We agreed to make the trip. What a sight it was at the end of that meeting to see thousands of ministers reaching out to the Lord, many of them on their knees, and quite a few with copious tears. "Oh, God, we need you in our churches!" they prayed. "Come and light your fire among us." We were all in the same boat. I wasn't speaking down to them as some outside expert from New York City. I needed to pray the same prayer they were praying. What hope is there for the Brooklyn Tabernacle if we don't pray for God to come by his Spirit and do things we could never do?

The promise at the beginning of the book of Acts is "You will receive power when the Holy Spirit comes upon you" (1:8). No wonder Jesus told the disciples to "wait for the gift my Father promised" (1:4)—just as Abram and his wife Sarai had to wait with expectation for what God had promised them. Having faith in the promise is the key and the only hope for anybody's church, whatever the affiliation.

The great search in too many church circles is not for leaders with the faith of Abram who are willing to trust God wherever he leads, but rather for leaders who are sharp and clever at organizing. We forget that the Christian church was founded in a prayer meeting. It was led in its earliest and most successful years by simple men full of faith and the Holy Spirit. They concentrated not on "the secret of church growth," but on the secret of receiving the power God has promised. Because of their faith, the Lord gave them both power and growth.

We forget that the Christian church was founded in a prayer meeting. ~

Paul was humble enough to admit to the church at Corinth, "When I came to you, brothers, I did not come with eloquence or superior wisdom as I proclaimed to you the testimony about God.... My message and my preaching were not with wise and persuasive words, but with a demonstration of the Spirit's power, *so that your faith might not rest on men's wisdom, but on God's power*" (1 Corinthians 2:1, 4–5). This approach to ministry and igniting faith in God's people is rare today.

In fact, God has a wonderful plan for all his people. But he doesn't have to tell us much about it if he chooses not to. All he asks is that we take his hand and walk along in faith. He will show us soon enough what should be done.

HE FAILED DRAMATICALLY, BUT REBOUNDED

THE CHALLENGE, as we said earlier, is not just to start out in faith, but to continue to walk in faith. The Bible describes the next painful chapter in Abram's life. Although he had started out so wonderfully, he actually failed God by heading down to Egypt because of a famine. He felt the economic pinch, and he reacted. No Scripture shows him receiving any direction from God about this; he just pulled up stakes and moved.

Whenever we stop living by faith, we start unilaterally doing what we think is smart or what circumstances dictate. We soon find ourselves in a weakened position. We get into trouble quickly.

As they neared the Egyptian border, Abram took one look at his beautiful wife and said, "Sarai, I see some problems down the road. Pharaoh and his men will desire you, and they're going to eliminate me in order to have you. So we'd better lie and say you're my sister instead of my wife."

The little scheme only half-worked. Abram avoided losing his life, but poor Sarai was led away to join the royal harem. What an outrageous and low-life thing to do to your own wife! You can be sure the women in the harem didn't get to just sit around there in the palace having Bible studies. Abram saved his own neck, but risked Sarai's virtue and future.

God was watching this whole mess develop and decided to intervene with judgment.

Now, if anyone deserved punishment, it seems it would have been Abram! He was the rascal here. But instead, "the LORD inflicted serious diseases on Pharaoh and his household" (Genesis 12:17), which quickly led Pharaoh to summon Abram.

Pharaoh's wrath exploded in Abram's face: "What is your problem? Why didn't you tell me this was your wife? Take her and get out of my country—now!"

Imagine this great man of faith getting rebuked by a pagan king—justifiably! What a remarkable lesson that in the life of faith, we can wander from the promises and fail so miserably. Nobody yet has walked the perfect faith life. But the important thing is to get back up and back on track. Abram—

"the father of all who believe"—was not quite down for the count.

He and Sarai scurried back again to the land where they belonged, "to the place between Bethel and Ai where his tent had been earlier and where he had first built an altar. There Abram called on the name of the LORD" (Genesis 13:3–4). It seems he could not rest until he got back to the altar where he had once worshiped God—back to the place where he had stood so faithfully on the promises made to him.

> **Whenever we fail God, it is vital to return
> quickly to an altar of consecration and faith.
> God is waiting for us there. ⁓**

Whenever we fail God, it is vital to return quickly to that altar of consecration and faith. God is waiting for us there, like the prodigal's father waiting for his son to return. He looks forward to getting us back on track. The greatness of Abram was not in his moral perfection, but in his getting back to God and believing again.

HE DIDN'T PRESS FOR HIS PRIVILEGES

SOON A QUARREL AROSE between Abram and his nephew Lot, because their cattle and sheep were crowding each other. God had blessed them both (even Abram, after selling his wife down the river!) to the point that a joint livestock operation was no longer practical.

> So Abram said to Lot, "Let's not have any quarreling between you and me, or between your herdsmen and mine, for we are brothers. Is not the whole land before

you? Let's part company. If you go to the left, I'll go to
the right; if you go to the right, I'll go to the left"
(Genesis 13:8–9).

Lot promptly chose the fertile plain—the best the
human eye could see—leaving Abram to try to graze his
sheep on the rocky mountainside.

But Abram did not protest. He could have "pulled
rank"—after all, he was the senior man here, and the younger
fellow had no right to take advantage of him. Instead, Abram
showed that when you have faith in God, you know God will
take care of you no matter what someone else chooses. Faith
lets other people do their thing without getting anxious and
worried. It leaves its case in God's hands.

Too many times we worry about who is forgetting us,
who is not giving us credit, who is reaping benefits at our
expense. We lose touch with the fact that when God "brings
one down, he exalts another" (Psalm 75:7). Both in the secular environment and in church work, we are anxious about
things that are better left in God's hands. Worry always nips
at the heels of faith and tries to drag it down.

> **Faith lets other people do their thing with-
> out getting anxious and worried. It leaves its
> case in God's hands.** ∾

Faith deals with the invisible things of God. It refuses to
be ruled by the physical senses. Faith is able to say, "You can
do what you like, because I know God is going to take care
of me. He has promised to bless me wherever he leads me."
Remember that even when every demon in hell stands
against us, the God of Abraham remains faithful to all his

promises. Jesus Christ can do anything but fail his own people who trust in him.

Why not start afresh today to follow in the footsteps of "Father Abraham"? Begin carefully and prayerfully to search the Scriptures, asking the Holy Spirit to make God's promises come alive to the point where you can live off them, even as Abraham did.

Don't be afraid when you don't know exactly how God will lead and supply for you. Rather, just hold firmly to his hand and walk in faith. There is no need to worry about what the other person might be doing. It really doesn't matter, because God has promised to uphold and defend you.

Finally, if you are someone who has "gone down to Egypt"—walked away from your initial trust and consecration to God—then return right now with all your heart to the Lord. Go back to that altar you once made as a place of worship and surrender to God. He has promised to receive everyone who comes to him through Jesus Christ our Lord. Don't hesitate because of how far away you have strayed or what you did while you were there. Although you cannot see him, the Father watches for you even now, waiting with compassion and love for your return home to him.

ELEVEN

~

God's Deeper Work

W E HAVE SEEN that walking by faith is what brings us into the realm of the supernatural power of God. The Spirit works in us to accomplish things that are impossible to the human understanding. God is indeed omnipotent. He has all power.

Many times, our expectation of that power is slightly misdirected. We are primarily looking for God to show his power in creation, in healing bodies, in supplying employment for his people, in bringing a new baby into the world—and these are all wonderful things. But the Bible declares that the greatest things he does are *internal*, not external. Ephesians 3:20 speaks of God "who is able to do immeasurably more than all we ask or imagine" (we like that part), "according to his power that is at work *within* us."

Only the internal things will go with us into the next world. We won't be dragging along our bodies, our cars, our houses, or our lands. The great church leader Andrew Murray once said, "Your heart is your world, and your world is your heart," and this is the main place where God works in our lives.

What good is it if God heals you and keeps you alive for an extra twenty years if you walk in disobedience for those twenty years? What good is any external blessing without God's peace and joy in your heart? What's the point of receiving a promotion and making a lot of money if your big, fancy house is not a true home, but rather a boxing ring of fussing and fighting?

I have been bothered ever since I was a child by Christian testimonies that neglect the internal to focus only on outside things. "Praise God for the $100 check that came in the mail." "Praise God for sparing me from a traffic accident." While these are definitely blessings, far greater are the things God waits to do within us.

> **Our problems are not merely due to our environment; they are deeply personal. Fixing up the environment doesn't often repair the person.** 〜

God knows that our problems are not merely due to our environment; they are deeply personal. Fixing up the environment doesn't often repair the person. Some people, in fact, grow stronger in the midst of adversity; others have an easy life and still self-destruct.

Soiled on the Inside

No one in the Bible wrote more honestly and eloquently about what God does inside us than David. And perhaps his most difficult piece of writing was Psalm 51.

Like all of us, David was a sinner. He gave in to pressure and temptation more than once. One spring in particular, he stayed home instead of going out with his army, and he got himself into major trouble.

And that is a warning of something I have noticed over the years: It can be dangerous not to go where God sends you, or not to do what he has called you to do. This is true for everyone, not just pastors and missionaries. I have seen choir members sing faithfully and with great effect for a while . . . and then say, "I'm kind of tired; I think I'll go on leave now. Later on, I'll get involved in another ministry of the church." Carol and I have often observed that, if they don't go to the next place of service God planned for them, they eventually drift from the things of God altogether. Satan seizes that moment to reach in and distract them.

People who just hang around churches and "loiter" without getting active in the service God has called them to are in a very treacherous position. There is no difference of reward for preaching the gospel, as I have been called to do, or for serving faithfully as an usher or Christian education worker. If any of us pull back from our calling, we place ourselves at risk.

King David had too much time on his hands, and one night he couldn't sleep. Nighttime brings its own dangers. If you don't sleep well, my advice is that you had better start praising God *quickly*. Otherwise, worry, anxiety, and impure thoughts can easily creep in.

So during the night, David went out on his veranda and saw Bathsheba bathing. The woman was beautiful. He desired her—and being king, he could have anything and anyone he wanted. Everyone knows what happened next.

When Bathsheba's pregnancy became known, this "man of God" acted disgracefully. That's what sin can do to us. David called Bathsheba's husband, Uriah the Hittite, back from the battlefront in order to cover his tracks. It didn't work. So David got the man soused with liquor in a despicable attempt to sway his judgment. Even that failed. Finally, he sent Uriah back to his regiment carrying a letter to General Joab—a letter that was Uriah's own death warrant. David ordered what we New Yorkers call a "hit." He committed murder through other people's hands.

Everything was covered, David thought.

How he ever lived with himself for months and months is hard to understand. The man who had written such wonderful psalms went for most of a year with a wall between himself and God. Then God sent a prophet to confront him.

> **David ordered what we New Yorkers call a "hit." He committed murder through other people's hands.** ～

Only then did David admit his guilt. Finally we hear him come clean in Psalm 51: "Have mercy on me, O God. . . . Wash away all my iniquity and cleanse me from my sin" (vv. 1–2). From the depths of his soul David repents and asks pardon from the merciful God he has offended.

Then, in the middle of the psalm, David spells out three absolutely essential things that he desperately needs from God. He has learned something from his terrible fall. What he desires is impossible for him; the Lord must do it. And the work must be done *inside* him.

When you hear David's words, you will be aware of how seldom, if ever, you hear anyone pray like this in today's churches. Unfortunately, we are not asking God for things along these lines. This isn't the way we usually talk. But these three requests of David lie at the foundation of every victorious Christian life.

1. "Create in Me a Pure Heart"

David asks God to "create in me a pure heart" (v. 10). David is asking for more than having his sin-stained heart washed. He has already asked for cleansing (vv. 2, 7). Now he is going deeper. He wants God to start all over, to *create* a brand-new heart that is pure to the core. He admits that apart from God, he is all twisted inside. He wants to see everything in his world with pure eyes, to hear with holy ears, and to act with godly responses.

His words go far beyond our common language of "vow religion" so prominent today: "O God, I promise to do better in the future. I won't do this ever again." Some of us have turned over more new leaves than Central Park. David has no such hope in his ability to pull this off. He calls on God, instead, to create something entirely new within him. The word *create* here is the same one used in Genesis 1:1, when God created the heavens and the earth. It means a divine act of bringing something wonderful out of nothing. The work is all of God.

> **Some of us have turned over more new leaves than Central Park. David called on God, instead, to create something entirely new within him.** ～

Let me say that receiving a pure heart from God is better than getting healed of cancer. It is better than becoming rich overnight. It is better than preaching marvelous sermons or writing best-selling books. Receiving a pure heart is to be like God at the core of your being.

2. "RENEW A STEADFAST SPIRIT WITHIN ME"

THE SECOND THING David cries out for is God's steadiness in his everyday spiritual living: "Renew a steadfast spirit within me" (v. 10). We all know the feeling of being up one day and down the next ... reading the Scripture every day for a week and then hardly glancing at it the next ... going up and down like an elevator. The Hebrew word for *steadfast* means to be firm, strong, erect, immovable. What David is asking God for is a work of grace within him that will keep him from the kind of rise-and-fall, mountain-and-valley pattern that characterizes far too many of our lives. David wants to resist temptation not just one day, but every day. He knows he cannot do that himself—but with God, all things are possible.

David knows he has been cleansed and forgiven, but he feels he needs something else: a steadfast spirit. He doesn't want to be like Jell-O; he asks to be a *rock*. Isn't that our desire as well? Instead of going up and down in our walk with God, we yearn for God by his grace to do the same work for us that David sought. Do we believe God can do it?

Jesus said to Martha of Bethany, "Did I not tell you that if you believed, you would see the glory of God?" (John 11:40). We must not be content just to hope, or to lament our weak spiritual condition. Instead, we must approach the throne of grace with a bold confidence that what God promised, he will do (Hebrews 4:16). Let us ask him for this steadfast spirit that will hold us through the changing situations of life.

3. "GRANT ME A WILLING SPIRIT, TO SUSTAIN ME"

A THIRD THING that David knows he cannot manufacture on his own is "a willing spirit" (Psalm 51:12). God must grant this spirit, he admits. Beyond being steadfast, he wants to be *willing* to do whatever God asks. When God puts his finger on something in our lives and says, "That's not good for you," or "I want you to do this, or go there," we must be willing to accept his will. We can't go on fighting against God in our spirit.

David realizes that only God's power can make him willing to walk in obedience. In Philippians 2:12–13 Paul urges us to "work out your salvation with fear and trembling, for it is God who works in you *to will and to act* according to his good purpose." God is in the "willing business"—praise his name!

David has recognized that his heart can betray him. His will can consent to the appeals of the world and the flesh, so he cries out for God to give him a willing spirit. This again flies in the face of much of today's Christianity, which bites its lip and tries harder to do what only the Spirit of God can accomplish. In fact, God has to *make* us willing. Salvation is of the Lord—from beginning to end. The sooner we learn that we can stop our futile self-effort and throw ourselves on the strong arms of God, the better off we will be.

We must ask God daily to cleanse us, to hold us, to lift us up and give us a willing spirit so our hearts will "run in the path of your commands" (Psalm 119:32). Then we will actually long to do his will. We will get closer to the attitude of Jesus, who said, "My food ... is to do the will of him who sent me. ... I seek not to please myself but him who sent me" (John 4:34; 5:30). It was a *joy* for Jesus to obey his Father, not a burden.

The Holy Spirit wants to impart this same spirit to us, so that Christianity is not drudgery or burdensome, but instead a life of loving the good and hating the evil.

ARE CERTAIN CHANGES IMPOSSIBLE?

HOW OFTEN HAVE you and I prayed as David did that day? Isn't it about time that we say with new faith, "God, *you* give me a pure heart. God, *you* renew a steadfast spirit within me. God, *you* grant me a willing spirit to sustain me. Don't let me fluctuate, Lord. Keep me strong!"

God is able to do this against the most vicious behavior patterns and the most embedded thoughts. Certain sins have been characterized in Christendom as almost too hard for God to change. Even ministers have said to me, "Jim, come on, tell me the truth—have you ever seen a homosexual really change?"

"What do you mean? Of course, I have!" I reply. "They are all over our church, serving in all kinds of ministries today."

> **Even ministers have said to me, "Jim, come on, tell me the truth—have you ever seen a homosexual really change?"** ∼

One pastor was frank enough to tell me, "The truth is, I don't want those gays even coming to my church. Once they've been in that lifestyle, that impurity just gets engrained. I don't care who says they've been saved—I'm keeping one eye on 'em."

With that kind of unbelief and prejudice, there is little chance of witnessing the amazing grace of God in action.

One Sunday night not long ago, a very polished, intelligent man named Steve shared with our congregation what God has done in his life. Born and raised in the 'hood of southeast Washington, D.C., he nevertheless excelled in school and earned a scholarship to a Pennsylvania prep academy. While living there in his mid-teen years, he confessed to a counselor one day that he felt a vague attraction to other boys and didn't know what to think about that. The counselor answered that this was all very natural and was nothing to worry about. Steve wasn't convinced, but he said nothing more.

Steve's good grades next brought him a scholarship to the prestigious Ivy League campus of Dartmouth University in New Hampshire. His first actual homosexual experience came as a freshman at the invitation, not of an overly effeminate guy, but rather a star athlete and a candidate for the U.S. Olympic team.

"The next morning, I felt so hollow, so empty," Steve remembers. "It had been a reaching out for love, but it didn't satisfy."

Walking across campus that day to his part time job, thinking to himself that he had certainly gotten off track, a voice suddenly said to him, *Get out of it!*

Steve did not heed the warning, however, and without any other spiritual anchor in his life, he yielded to his homosexual impulses again and again. By the time he graduated with honors from Dartmouth, he was experienced in the closet lifestyle—but still not sure if he wanted this for the rest of his life.

The lean young man with the penetrating eyes and electric smile showed talent in the field of dance, and in June 1978 he moved to New York City to accept yet another scholarship, this one at the world-renowned Alvin Ailey American Dance Center. (Eventually he landed a job with the prestigious Martha Graham Dance Company, a position he held for ten years.)

Meanwhile, a cousin challenged him to at least read the Bible, and Steve set about systematically to go through the book, starting with Genesis. It took him a year and a half to reach Revelation. During this time, he was sharing an apartment with four other dance students—all of them gay. A close camaraderie developed in the group.

"They were all very promising dancers, and they warmly took me into their circle," Steve says. "Whenever we would be talking late at night, and I'd say something about a Bible portion I had read that opposed homosexuality, they would reply, 'Oh, don't worry about that—you're reading the wrong parts. Read the Psalms, the Proverbs. God is a God of love, and anything that's loving is fine with him.'

"It made sense to me. I gradually convinced myself that my feelings for other men must be God-ordained."

LOVE OF A DIFFERENT KIND

STEVE WENT FROM ONE liaison to another, until finally a relationship solidified with a very talented artist. The two picked out an apartment to share together—one block from the Brooklyn Tabernacle. On Sundays Steve could not help noticing the crowds on the sidewalk coming in and out of our meetings, and he said to himself that he'd like to visit. In October 1980 he finally did.

"I felt the love of God the minute I came through the door," he says with a touch of amazement. "God's presence was there in a powerful way. Instinctively, I wanted to be there. When I left, I was so full of joy!"

Steve kept coming back. No one sat him down for a lecture on homosexuality. In fact, I don't think any of us knew what he was doing privately. He just kept coming to church, soaking in the Word and the presence of God—and starting to feel more and more convicted about his sin. Although he wanted to be in church, he would run out of the building immediately after the meetings, avoiding contact with other believers.

About that time, a big Gay Pride parade was scheduled in the city, and Steve's friends urged him to go. He knew he didn't want to march in the street, but he did attend the accompanying rally near the waterfront in "the Village," as we call that section of Manhattan.

"I watched the crowds of guys, arm in arm, and listened to the fervent speeches," Steve remembers, "—and I never felt so alone in all my life. Something inside my head asked, *Where will I be ten years from now? Out here 'celebrating' homosexuality in the streets? Surely not!* God was steadily chiseling away at my beliefs."

Not long after that, Steve put himself in a foolish situation one night and exposed himself to a sexually transmitted disease. That meant going to the Gay Men's Health Crisis building for a test. Once again, he felt ill at ease as he looked around the waiting room. *I don't belong here. This isn't my kind of place anymore.*

Soon Steve found himself back at our Tuesday night prayer meeting, crying out to God at a corner of the altar rail. He remembers praying, "O God, I know you love me. And I'm willing to acknowledge that this is a sin in my life. But you have to show me the way out of this. In myself, I just don't have the ability."

The struggle with his emotions continued; there was no quick exit from the gay lifestyle for Steve. He grew depressed at times and lost a lot of weight. But he was determined to believe that God would change him on the inside. In faith he held onto the promise of freedom in Christ. He made the tough decision to stop all gay activity.

Then one cloudy day on his way to work near the end of 1982, he was walking in front of the famous Bloomingdale's department store on East Fifty-Ninth Street, when, for no apparent reason, he felt a release from his bondage. "All of a sudden, I just knew that Jesus had set me free!" he says.

The relationship with his partner dissolved, and the man moved out. Steve joined a men's prayer group, where he found spiritual encouragement, and his life began to overflow with the Holy Spirit. Later he got involved with a Manhattan ministry that worked with gays and lesbians. Such Scriptures as Jeremiah 32:27 came alive to him: "I am the LORD, the God of all mankind. Is anything too hard for me?"

With his articulate speaking ability, Steve soon became a spokesman for the ministry, appearing on college campuses and Christian television shows. He was even invited to the nationally syndicated *Sally Jessie Raphael Show* for the taping of a segment called "Being Gay—Born That Way?" Predictably, he turned out to be the only Christian ex-gay on the show, and the minute he started talking about Jesus' power that had set him free, all chaos broke loose on the set. The audience howled while the other guests vented their anger toward Steve.

"On the way home that day, I was feeling sad about the whole thing. I thought of all the things I should have said that I didn't. I was pretty bummed out.

"But early the next morning, my telephone awakened me. A guy from North Carolina said, 'Were you on TV last night?'

"'Uh, yes, I was.'" (How in the world had he even found my phone number?)

"'Can Jesus really do this for someone?' the young man asked with a voice starting to crack.

"'Yes, he really can!' I replied. I went on to explain the gospel to him. Maybe my words the day before hadn't been for naught after all!"

WHO WOULD HAVE IMAGINED?

IN A FEW YEARS, Steve met a beautiful young Christian woman named Desiree in our church. She also had a desire to minister to people with HIV and AIDS. In time they fell in love and began to talk about marriage.

That presented Steve with an uncomfortable dilemma. "Every partner I had had in years gone by was now dead or at least HIV-positive, I knew. The professional dancing field has been devastated by AIDS. If this thing with Desiree was to go anywhere, I knew I would have to take another test.

"The two-week wait for the results was pure agony for me. Finally the day came. I went to the clinic to hear what had been learned. The verdict was—*negative!* What an act of God's grace that I had not been infected all those years! I left the building weeping for joy."

Steve and Desiree were married June 3, 1989. Desiree knew everything there was to know about Steve—and never flinched. She left a successful sales position and returned to school to earn a master's degree in public health. Soon they started a new ministry in our church, a support group in their home for people with HIV and AIDS. Many were led to the Lord and taught that living for Christ is far more than just gritting your teeth and sitting on your hands. It is walking in faith and joy according to God's plan, which is infinitely better.

Leading the group, of course, also meant coping with loss. In one particular year, fifteen members died with AIDS.

Most recently, Steve and Desiree have moved out of the city a couple of hours away so he could accept an assistant professorship at a well-known East Coast college. Two darling little girls have been born to grace their home as more evidence of God's wonderful love. God's hand is on this couple and their children in a special way.

There is not a doubt in my mind that this wonderful man has been changed by the power of God. He told me once that while attending the National Religious Broadcasters Convention in Washington, D.C., a Christian minister came up to him on the exhibit floor and asked a few things about his work. Then he said to Steve a variation of the same question I mentioned earlier that had been posed to me: "So, you mean to tell me you've been set free from homosexuality?"

"Yes, praise the Lord!" Steve answered with a bright smile. "It's been a tremendous thing that God has done in my life."

The man looked him squarely in the face and dropped his bombshell: *I don't believe it.* With that, he turned on his heels and walked away, leaving Steve speechless.

I am glad I wasn't there at that moment; some of the "Brooklyn" that's still in me might have come out. But a better reply to that pitiful man would have been what the apostle Paul wrote in Romans 3:3–4. "What if some did not have faith? Will their lack of faith nullify God's faithfulness? Not at all! Let God be true, and every man a liar."

No matter how deep and dark the secret, no matter how many times a certain sin has defeated you, God can bring change to your life. ～

God's grace goes further and deeper than we can ever imagine. Steve's life is a reminder that God alone can give us what we really need: a pure heart, a steadfast and willing spirit. No matter how deep and dark the secret, no matter how many times a certain sin has defeated you, God can bring change to your life. But it must be his Holy Spirit working from within and not your weak attempts to "do better the next time." All God asks of you is to bring the whole, sorry mess to him so he can begin the spiritual transformation you need.

Don't attempt to be strong in yourself, for that is the very opposite of what is needed. God is always drawn to weakness. "The sacrifices of God are a broken spirit; a broken and contrite heart, O God, you will not despise" (Psalm 51:17). That verse is from the same psalm with which this chapter started, and if you will join David in his unusual prayer of faith, you will find that God's deeper work will become real in you.

~

TWELVE

Addition by Subtraction

WHEN ANY OF US goes to buy a piece of fine silver jewelry, we walk into an attractive store with aesthetic lighting and well-dressed personnel waiting to show us the various wares inside their glass cases. Everything about the surroundings is clean and sophisticated.

If we were to track that metal back to its origins, however, the opposite would be true. A silver mine is a dark, dirty, dangerous place. Men dreaming of fortunes have lost their lives in mines like Nevada's Comstock Lode during the 1859 silver rush, the Real de Monte y Pachuca in Hidalgo, Mexico (largest silver mine in the world), or the ancient sources of silver in Greece and Armenia during Bible times.

When the ore is brought to the surface, the work is far from over. The crushing, amalgamating, and smelting is still yet to be done. Silver does not melt until it reaches 960.5 degrees Celsius; only then does it start to yield up its impurities. Both King Solomon and the prophet Isaiah had all that in mind when they wrote about God's purging process, the purifying of our hearts and lives:

> Remove the dross from the silver,
>   and out comes material for the silversmith;
> remove the wicked from the king's presence,
>   and his throne will be established through
>   righteousness (Proverbs 25:4–5).

I [God] will turn my hand against you;
    I will thoroughly purge away your dross
    and remove all your impurities (Isaiah 1:25).

While all of us want our fine jewelry to be of high quality, we do not often think about the need for a similar process
in our hearts. In fact, every year it is getting harder to talk
about topics such as this one, because our churches have
become conditioned by the world. "Feel good" and "Keep it
positive" have become the operative slogans. We tend to bris-
tle at the idea of God wanting to make major changes in our
lives. We like it well enough when God says things such as "I
will never leave you or forsake you . . . I will bless your coming in and your going out" and so forth. Yes, God did say all
those things—but the spiritual realities are a little more complex than that.

> **"Feel good" and "Keep it positive" have
> become the operative slogans. We tend to
> bristle at the idea of God wanting to make
> major changes.** ~

God deals with us as a responsible parent deals with a
child. Sometimes you give a compliment or a pat on the back;
however, at other times you do what the apostle Paul told the
young minister Timothy to do: "Correct, rebuke and
encourage—with great patience and careful instruction"
(2 Timothy 4:2). We like certain parts of that verse but are
not so thrilled about the rest; we appreciate the "encourage"
aspect and the part about "great patience," but we are not so
keen about the correcting and rebuking business.

Pastors today are viewed as doing their jobs properly only
when they are giving "a kind word." How many sermons and

counseling sessions contain inspired correcting or rebuking? In too many places, the clergy have been reduced to hirelings—and they will only stay popular (and employed?) if they keep giving messages the people *want* to hear.

LESS IS MORE

BUT GOD'S WAY IN Scripture is far different from the ways of the American church culture. He knows the absolute necessity of removing the dross from our silver, of heating us up to an uncomfortable point where he can, as the New Living Translation puts it, "skim off your slag" (Isaiah 1:25). He is subtracting in order to add. That is strange mathematics, I admit, but it is reality in the spiritual realm. In God's math, you sometimes get more by having less.

I mentioned in my first book that when my wife and I first came to the Brooklyn Tabernacle in 1972, the church was in disarray. Fewer than twenty people came to the services. Within a month or two, I realized that some of the major problems lay within the tiny group itself! A few did whatever popped into their heads during the services. It was both unbiblical and unedifying. There were other problems with racial tension and with people insisting upon lead positions.

I was young and nervous to face this. I guess my predecessor had felt it was best to do nothing; any correction would probably drive someone away, and then the attendance (as well as the offerings) would be even smaller. But I knew in my heart that wouldn't work. I had played enough basketball to know that sometimes in order to win, you have to kick a guy off the team. The problem player may be spoiling the rhythm of the rest. He may have better-than-average talent, but in the locker room and on the floor he is a bad influence and destroys the cohesion of the team. If he won't change, he has to go. Numerous college and professional teams have experienced this. One *fewer* player sometimes means a better team.

I began to pray, "O God, either change people or have them leave." The Lord helped me to accept subtraction in order to start adding. And that is exactly what took place.

If silver is contaminated with dross, it does no good just to add more ore to the pile. The silversmith will not be able to make something beautiful out of it, no matter how large the pile or how much effort is given. Something has to be removed. As long as the impurities remain, the silver will not be shiny or smooth.

We readily accept this truth in many areas, but spiritually we resist it. Imagine someone who is eighty or a hundred pounds overweight going to the doctor and saying, "Please make me feel better. When I wake up in the morning, I'm just dragging. Give me some pills to pep me up."

The doctor would say, "All the pills in the world aren't going to restore your energy. What you need to concentrate on is losing fifty pounds, just for starters."

"What? Hey, I came here to your office to feel better! I can't change my whole lifestyle. Just give me something to help me."

The person *will* be healthier—by subtracting, not adding.

Imagine another patient, with a cancerous growth, who comes in wanting better aspirin to dull the pain. That won't work; the growth has to be cut out. If the patient protests, "Look, I didn't come in here to lose part of my body!" the doctor would reply, "Well, you *need* to lose this particular part of your body. It's cancer; it's got to go."

"You mean you care about me and say you're my friend, and you're going to cut me with a knife?"

"Exactly! If I don't, you're going to die."

TELLING THE TOUGH TRUTH

MANY OF US ARE quick to shout Hallelujah and celebrate God's blessings. Others of us have a sound intellectual grasp of Bible doctrine. That is all good—but we can easily avoid the fact that all the noise and knowledge in the world will take us nowhere if there is unremoved dross in our lives. All the talking in the world won't produce a godly life without the Lord's intimate, ongoing refining process in our hearts.

Some of us are overextended financially. Others of us have a calendar that is way too busy. The only way to get healthy is to reduce the indebtedness, to cut back the busyness. Whatever clutters our walk with God becomes the target of his purging process.

> All the noise and knowledge in the world
> will take us nowhere if there is unremoved
> dross in our lives. ~

So many of us think that the more we do and the more we acquire, the happier we will be. Wrong! This is why so many Christians do not see God's purposes worked out in their lives. They can quote the Bible verse about the peace of God that passes all understanding, but they have little experience of what it means.

Because God loves you, he will always be direct with you. He tells you the truth. He is absolutely ruthless in going after the things that spoil the flow of his grace and blessing into our lives. His process is to subtract in order to add. He will never make a treaty with our secret pockets of sin. "That has to go," he will insist. "You cannot go on with that in your life. I cannot make a beautiful silver vessel with that dross still present."

When Jesus began his public ministry, one of his first stops according to the Gospel of John (see chapter 2) was the cluttered temple. Did Jesus bring new paint colors and expensive furniture to add to the decor? No. He got rid of things that didn't belong there, and he kicked out the profiteering merchants. He showed himself to be a tough refiner that day, because he deeply loved the purpose of the temple as "a house of prayer for all nations," and he wanted it to be restored.

> **Because God loves you, he will always be direct with you. He tells you the truth.** ～

We have to face the fact that in order to be what God wants us to be, he will have to take away things in our life that don't belong. In any life or ministry devoted to him, we must stop and ask, "Are there attitudes here that grieve the Lord? Are there habits that need to be broken? What are the impurities that must go? How about that desire to be seen, that competitiveness, that seeking for glory and acclaim? What about that prejudice or judgmentalism toward others?" We must be absolutely open in inviting God to thoroughly search us and take away anything he sees fit.

One Saturday night I was seeking God in preparation for the next day's meetings, just making a fresh consecration of my life and trying to draw nearer to the Lord, when all of a sudden the names of three people came into my mind. None of them were nearby; they were scattered across the country. In all three cases, my relationship with them was not what it should have been. Nothing on the surface was wrong; I was on speaking terms with all of them. But it wasn't right before the God who is love. I didn't feel I had actually sinned against them, but still. . . .

Jim, the Lord seemed to say, *you know there's a wall between you and each of these people. Something isn't right. Call them up! You need to repair the breach.*

I quickly defended myself: "Look, I'm not the cause of these problems. I honestly feel that they are the ones with wrong attitudes, not me."

But God would not back off: *Call them and repent of any hurt you've caused, whether you meant it or not.*

Within the next week, I made the three phone calls. The humbling was good for me, and I learned new insights into God's ways of dealing in my life. What a blessing it turned out to be as I let God bring that slag to the surface and finally skim it off. Immediately afterward, I studied, prayed, and preached with a new vigor.

UNCOMFORTABLE BUT NECESSARY

LISTEN TO THE PIERCING prophecy by Malachi about Christ: "But who can endure the day of his coming? Who can stand when he appears? For he will be like a refiner's fire or a launderer's soap. He will sit as a refiner and purifier of silver; he will purify the Levites and refine them like gold and silver. Then the LORD will have men who will bring offerings in righteousness, and the offerings of Judah and Jerusalem will be acceptable to the LORD, as in days gone by, as in former years" (3:2–4).

Does your theology include Jesus sitting on a refiner's stool, watching over a cauldron of liquid metal under which the fire is getting hotter and hotter? Can you see him reaching down with a flat ladle from time to time to skim off the impurities that have bubbled to the surface? Is our faith deep enough to yield to the refiner's fire?

Will we always be comfortable in this process? Of course not! Is it pleasant? Not at all! But it is our Savior's method of getting rid of the junk in our lives. And his joy and peace will be felt immediately afterward—far deeper within us than we have ever known.

If you are a parent, you might know what it is to see too much junk food going into your child's mouth and decide to do something about it. Or maybe your child is being affected by some bad influences at school. When you take action, it doesn't exactly make you popular—but you do whatever you can to *subtract* these things from your child's life. You're not trying to rain on your child's parade; you do it because you love him.

The Bible says that "the LORD disciplines those he loves, as a father the son he delights in" (Proverbs 3:12). God's purpose for us is a lot deeper than just how we feel at the moment. He lovingly permits pressures and trials, lets the bottom fall out from time to time, so that our wrong reactions come right to the surface. We see our lack of faith, our lack of love—and that is his aim.

God intentionally places us in situations in which we are beyond our ability to cope. He permits difficulties to come with our children, and we say, "Why, God?" He is refining us. He is teaching us to trust him. He is drawing us away from our strength to his. He knows exactly how much heat to allow in our lives. He will never scorch us, but if we jump out of one cauldron because it's too hot, he has others waiting. The dross *must* be removed.

Do you know how the ancient refiner knew when he was finished, and the heat could finally be turned down? It was when he looked into the cauldron and *saw his own reflection* in the shining silver. As long as the image was muddy and rippled with flecks of slag, he knew he had to keep working. When his face finally showed clearly, the silver had been purified.

This is exactly how it is with our spiritual refining process. God's eternal plan is for us "to be conformed to the likeness of his Son" (Romans 8:29). Jesus Christ continues today as the Refiner and Purifier of his people. As he carefully works on our lives, he keeps looking into us to see his own blessed reflection.

Shall we not trust Christ and surrender to this process, rather than fighting it? Remember that it is a process of love to bring beauty and growth and enlargement in our lives. It is God's way of sanctifying us. And we must never forget that the holier the life, the more true happiness we experience within. It is the spiritual impurities that rob us of God's best.

DON'T FIGHT THE PROCESS

LET US FACE the fact that God will never let us remain the way we are today. That is the reason for this refining process in our lives. We are all "under construction." (Sometimes when I see all the major work still needed in my life, I feel like warning people to put on hard hats around me in case of falling debris.)

> God will never let us remain the way we are today. That is the reason for this refining process in our lives. ∾

We only move ahead by losing some things. God still adds by subtraction. Communion with him is our greatest need—but there are an awful lot of hindrances to that, aren't there? Some folks know more about *Home Improvement* than God's process of spiritual improvement for their lives. They're more up to date on sports teams and heroes than on what the apostles and prophets taught in the name of the Lord. These weights slow us down as we try to run the race of faith. We stagger at God's promises because our hearts are clogged with so many unedifying habits and unnecessary things.

When someone stubbornly fights God's purifying process, things can turn ugly. When the dross and impurities are grasped tightly like some kind of treasure, the future turns dark and foreboding. It is a kind of spiritual self-destruction.

We have had our share of spiritual shipwrecks at the Brooklyn Tabernacle. Many years ago, I lost one of my closest associates who, unknown to me, had begun to spend far too much time with a married woman who was a new Christian. His wife slowly began to sense that something was wrong, but he cleverly justified his actions on spiritual grounds and blamed her for being judgmental. She didn't share her suspicions with anyone else.

The church was much smaller then, and this associate was known and loved by all the congregation. One day in a staff meeting, I asked him to lead us in prayer. He stumbled along for a while and then broke down emotionally. Something was going on—some deep conflict of the soul. I regret to this day that I was not more discerning. I didn't confront him as a friend and brother in Christ.

Within a few months, the spiritual infection grew stronger and more ominous. Suddenly I received a phone call—while on vacation, no less—that I should quickly get back to Brooklyn. My associate had disappeared along with his lady friend, leaving behind her two children and her husband. They had taken $10,000 from the church account. They left behind a pitiful note assuring me that "God understands what we are doing."

What a tragedy! And how mightily sin can deceive.

Because this associate had been so visible, I faced the unenviable task of breaking the news as best I could to the congregation on Sunday. I broke down openly as I spoke. I can still remember the audible groans and anguished weeping throughout the church auditorium.

I have often thought how many times God must have dealt with my friend. How many times must he have been warned by the Holy Spirit? How many nights did he lie in bed fighting off the conviction of sin? We all know how persistent the Holy Spirit is when he tries to save us from the disaster of shipwreck.

I don't care how many millions around the world may have become fascinated with the story of the *Titanic* and the fateful night it sank into the cold waters of the North Atlantic. It was child's play compared with the spiritual tragedy of men and women who shun the purging of the Refiner's fire, only to find themselves in cold and dark places they never imagined.

> *God, I ask you to cleanse and purify our hearts and lives. Melt the dross; remove the impurities—all of it, whether in deed, word, or thought. Save us from ourselves, and establish us in righteousness by your strong right hand. We ask this humbly, depending on you, in Jesus' name. Amen.*

THIRTEEN

~

The Atmosphere
of Faith

THE BATTLE OF THE Christian life has always been not just
to believe, but to *keep on* believing. This is how we will grow
strong in faith and see the actual fulfillment of God's
promises in our lives.

Throughout this book we have seen the biblical primacy
of faith and its vital nature if we are to live in the will of God.
The writer of Hebrews sums this up in a very famous passage:

> So do not throw away your confidence; it will be
> richly rewarded. You need to persevere so that when
> you have done the will of God, you will receive what
> he has promised. For in just a very little while,
>
> "He who is coming will come and will not delay.
>   But my righteous one will live *by faith*.
> And if he shrinks back,
>   I will not be pleased with him."
>
> But we are not of those who shrink back and are
> destroyed, but of those who *believe* and are saved
> (10:35–39).

In other words, the writer is telling us not to be like the
Israelites who believed for a while and then fell away. What

doomed them from ever entering the Promised Land was not the sin of idolatry per se, or immorality, or greed—it was the horrible offense of unbelief. Though God had promised the land to the men and women delivered out of Egypt, they never put one foot in it due to their chronic lack of faith.

> **Faith is like the hand that reaches up to receive what God has freely promised. If the devil can pull your hand back down to your side, then he has succeeded.** ᴥ

Today we tend to soft-pedal unbelief as little more than a common weakness. We say things such as "You know, Mrs. Smith just has a hard time believing that God will help her." God takes no such easygoing approach. He calls it "shrinking back" and lets us know that he is definitely displeased. In fact, to reject his promises to us is far more destructive than the sensational sins we often talk about. The Bible calls it a "sinful, unbelieving heart that turns away from the living God" (Hebrews 3:12). Those are solemn, awesome words!

We see now why the great target of Satan is *to break down our faith*. He knows all too well that the righteous live by faith, so he aims at cutting our lifeline to God. Faith is like the hand that reaches up to receive what God has freely promised. If the devil can pull your hand back down to your side, then he has succeeded. All of God's intended supply will just stay where it is in heaven.

Remember that this faith is not merely a mental assent to certain truths in the Bible. Many people assume, "God said something, and in my mind I affirm that it is true—that's faith." They are wrong. Even the devil can give mental assent to the truth of many biblical facts, yet he remains Satan—our adversary. Real faith is produced when our hearts draw near to God himself and receive his promises deep within us. There, by its own divine power, his Word will work supernaturally.

The minute this kind of heart-faith starts to grow cold, we lose our capacity to receive from God. The chronic disease that afflicts us is not a lack of works or effort; it's a lack of real faith. Many times we are treating the symptom instead of the cause—the outward behavior and not its source.

We are running the race of faith. Those who drop out along the way are people who have stopped trusting the invisible God. None of us want to pull back or make a shipwreck of our lives as we observed in the previous chapter. We desire to receive not only his ultimate promise of salvation in heaven but also the many other promises he has made to us along the way. We want to live in the will of God.

And we don't have much time to accomplish this. As the Hebrews passage says, Jesus Christ is coming soon.

FAITH FOLLOWS PROMISES

IN RUNNING THIS RACE, we must never forget an important principle: Because of the unique place God has given to faith, *his grace flows along the channels of his promises—not his commands.* God's commands do indeed show his holy character and reveal our sinfulness, but that is all. They have no ability in themselves to empower us to obey—which puts us into a dilemma. How many believers worldwide are struggling this very hour with the realization that "I have the desire to do what is good, but I cannot carry it out" (Romans 7:18). It is not that we don't *know* what is right or that we don't *desire* to live that way. Our problem is the spiritual strength to obey, and the commands of God cannot impart that. In fact, it is not in the nature of the "Thou shalts" and "Thou shalt nots" to draw help from God. It is the ministry of his gracious promises to do that.

Saints down through the ages, while lying on their deathbeds, have not so much clung to the holy commands of God and the accompanying judgment to all offenders as they have rather cherished the promises and revelations concerning his great salvation through Christ:

> Therefore, there is now no condemnation for those who are in Christ Jesus.... For what the law was powerless to do in that it was weakened by the sinful nature, God did by sending his own Son in the likeness of sinful man to be a sin offering (Romans 8:1, 3).
>
> If we confess our sins, he is faithful and just and will forgive us our sins and purify us from all unrighteousness (1 John 1:9).
>
> To the man who does not work but trusts God who justifies the wicked, his faith is credited as righteousness (Romans 4:5).

These are the blessed promises of God that, when trusted, release his supernatural grace in and through us.

Listen to a man who often failed while depending upon his own strength, though he knew so well the commands of Christ. The apostle Peter tells us the blessed secret that God "has given us his very great and precious *promises*, so that through *them* [we] may participate in the divine nature and escape the corruption in the world caused by evil desires" (2 Peter 1:4). It is these promises that draw the heart to God in faith. This, in fact, is the great command of the New Covenant—to believe!

Without feeding on the promises of the Word, no faith life will be strong. We will not be able to continue on and persevere without living in the Word. There has never been a great man or woman of faith who was not a man or woman of the Book. My shelves are lined with such biographies as Luther, Wesley, Finney, Spurgeon, Moody—they read the Word, lived in it, meditated on it, and through its divine power working in their hearts, grew strong in faith.

> **There has never been a great man or woman of faith who was not a man or woman of the Book.** ∿

Of course, you will not succeed with only the words on the page. The Israelites who left Egypt came up short with regard to God's promise of possessing that new land for this reason: "The message they heard was of no value to them, because those who heard did not combine it with faith" (Hebrews 4:2). They heard clearly what God promised, but their hearts did not receive it in faith.

Today it is possible to make a living as an esteemed theologian and yet have no more living faith than a slug. Christians can sit in pews listening to the Word preached every Sunday—and even have a devotional life of sorts throughout the week—without rising above the cynicism, depression, and unbelief that are so prevalent in our culture. We can know the Word in some sense, but the Word must find within our hearts an atmosphere in which its divine power can be released.

That kind of dynamic faith fairly oozes from the words of the great Israelite leader Joshua near the end of his life. He was one of only two men who left Egypt as adults and actually *made* it all the way into the Promised Land. Listen to Joshua's parting instructions, which reveal the atmosphere of faith—the environment in which it blossoms and grows.

LOOK BACK WITH THANKSGIVING

JOSHUA BEGINS HIS FAREWELL address with this ringing statement: "You yourselves have seen everything the LORD your
God has done to all these nations for your sake; it was the
LORD your God who fought for you" (Joshua 23:3). In other
words, look back, fellow Israelites, and think about all he has
done.

How about *us* recalling right now all that God has done
for *us* just in the past twelve months? How many hundreds of
mornings did you wake up with strength in your limbs to get
up and function? You didn't manufacture the strength yourself; it was a gift from God. When did you last thank God for
your mental alertness, for a functional memory, or for the
skills to be able to hold a job? "Every good and perfect gift is
from above, coming down from the Father" (James 1:17). We
forget that truth too often. How can we have faith for the
future if we don't often look back and thank God for all he's
given us in the past?

We have become numb to his many benefits. More than
half the persons on this globe have never had the experience
of making a telephone call! What we take for granted as an
everyday convenience is unknown to much of the planet. A
lack of gratitude is, in fact, one of our besetting sins. In most
of our churches, there is no outpouring of vibrant thanksgiving and praise each Sunday because we are too occupied with
our problems. We concentrate on what we don't have rather
than "enter[ing] his gates with thanksgiving and his courts
with praise" (Psalm 100:4).

One day in the lobby of our church, a woman named
Donna said to me with great excitement, "Pastor Cymbala, I
got my first studio apartment—a place of my own! Praise the
Lord!" I began to rejoice with her over the simple blessing

that she now actually had a one-room place to live. You might find that a little strange . . . but then you don't know where Donna was coming from. Several weeks before, the police had gathered outside our church because a "jumper" seemed determined to end her life from a ledge on the building next to ours.

I moved outside with others of our staff and saw Donna high in the air. She had just left the office of her therapist in that building, who obviously had not provided the answer she needed. She was both anguished and frightened at the same time.

I felt God prompt me to enter the building and run up the stairs to where the officers were trying to talk Donna off the ledge. The panicked therapist stood by helplessly. I asked for permission to speak to her, but the cops warned me not to grab for her if I got close, because she might pull me down with her to the pavement.

In about twenty minutes, God helped me to bring her off the ledge into my arms. A staff member went with her in the ambulance for the required examination at a local hospital. We found out later that she had been staying either on a friend's couch or with a man who was abusive to her. Her life had been very sad, but she soon received Christ as her Savior. We helped her find some temporary lodging. When Donna got to the point of being able to rent her own room, believe me, it was a great day to give God a sacrifice of thanksgiving!

Don't you have at least as much to thank God for as Donna does? Then give him praise! Let him know from the depths of your heart how much you appreciate his goodness. Open up your heart and your mouth. Whether it is part of your religious tradition or not, the Bible tells you to express the gratitude of your heart toward the Lord. Get past your self-consciousness and formality to praise the Lord. Refuse to be embarrassed or hindered by anyone.

How pitiful that millions of churchgoers cheer wildly and unashamedly for their favorite sports teams—but are silent as a corpse when it comes to praising God! Read the Bible about the decibel level in heaven. How comfortable will you feel amid the sounds of saints and angels "numbering thousands upon thousands, and ten thousand times ten thousand . . . in a *loud* voice they sang, 'Worthy is the Lamb . . . !'" (Revelation 5:11–12)? Do you have the kind of worshipful, thankful heart that will want to join what John heard as "a great multitude, like the roar of rushing waters and like loud peals of thunder, shouting: 'Hallelujah! For our Lord God Almighty reigns'" (19:6)? May God help us to praise him more!

> **How pitiful that millions of churchgoers cheer wildly and unashamedly for their favorite sports teams—but are silent as a corpse when it comes to praising God!** ∼

Think of the many times we have found ourselves in some kind of a bind and have prayed with desperation, "O God, please—if you'll just help this time, I'll serve you and thank you and honor you forever." If that is your history, then don't forget what God has done. Rather, "through Jesus, therefore, let us continually offer to God a sacrifice of praise— the fruit of lips that confess his name" (Hebrews 13:15).

LOOK AHEAD WITH ANTICIPATION

NEXT JOSHUA TURNS HIS attention to the future. You might think that he would be satisfied, at the end of his years, with his many achievements. The first twenty-two chapters of his book tell how he has led the Israelites in conquering vast sections of Canaan. City after city has already fallen to his troops.

But Joshua is not satisfied. He boldly proclaims, "The LORD your God himself will drive [the remaining Canaanite nations] out of your way. He will push them out before you, and you will take possession of their land, as the LORD your God promised you" (Joshua 23:5). Joshua is still, at this late age, invoking the promises of God and boldly declaring that "the LORD your God *himself*" will do the conquering.

Every one of us, if we are honest, can point to things in our lives today that are not yet the way God wants them to be. There is a good deal of "land" still to be conquered. God wants to make us more like the Savior. He wants to root out things that hinder and mar our Christlikeness. He wants to use us to bless and encourage other people in ways we have never experienced or even dreamed. He wants to destroy the complexes and fears that paralyze us. He wants to revive and bless our local church congregations.

And he *will* do these things himself as we live in this blessed atmosphere of faith!

Among the many definitions of faith, perhaps none is more succinct or important than Hebrews 11:1. "Now faith is being sure of what we hope for and certain of what we do not see."

Notice that faith operates in respect to two special objects:

- Future things ("what we hope for")
- Invisible things ("what we do not see")

Faith is not about the present. It is not about things you could capture right now with a camera. Rather, it is about things in the future promised by God—and faith is certain of them. Faith produces a conviction that those things are going to happen, even though the scientific method and our senses cannot validate that certainty at the moment.

> **Faith is not about the present. It is not about things you could capture right now with a camera. Rather, it is about things in the future promised by God.** ～

Faith is the ability of the human spirit to open up and receive impressions from God that are born from his Word and made alive by the Holy Spirit. This brings about a supernatural conviction of certain facts apart from the senses. Andrew Murray put it this way more than a hundred years ago, "Just as we have our senses, through which we hold communication with the physical universe, so faith is the spiritual sense or organ through which the soul comes into contact with and is affected by the spiritual world."[1] In other words, just as our sense of sight or hearing lies dormant until acted upon by light or sound, so our ability to have faith lies dormant until we open ourselves to receive impressions from the eternal, invisible God.

Then we simply *know* that something is going to happen, for God's Word has been received and has activated this spiritual sense called faith. We now bank our life on it. If somebody says, "Prove it," we cannot—but we still know it is coming.

This is what Moses experienced thousands of years ago. "By faith he left Egypt, not fearing the king's anger; he persevered *because he saw him who is invisible*" (Hebrews 11:27).

How do you see the invisible? Not with the eyes in your head, but with the more powerful eyes of faith.

The senses—touch, taste, smell, sight, hearing—have to do with present and visible things. They can't pick up anything about the future. They have nothing to do with spiritual realities. But faith has to do primarily with these future and invisible things that God has promised us in his Word. Faith makes them more real to us than the headlines of today's newspaper. This other kind of "seeing" is what faith is all about, as the apostle Paul says in 2 Corinthians 4:18: "So we fix our eyes not on what is seen, but on what is unseen. For what is seen is temporary, but what is unseen is eternal."

Faith can be likened to a transistor radio. When you turn the radio on, music pours out. Are there any trumpets or guitars inside that little box? Of course not. Yet the room has sound waves all through it. The human senses can't detect them at all. But the radio can pick them up. The music is not actually in the radio at all. The music is coming *through* the radio from a greater unseen source.

So it is with faith. Faith does not originate within us. It comes from God as we receive his living Word into our hearts. Then a supernatural kind of "music" comes alive in us as the product of this faith. A person filled with faith has an entirely different view of things from the person living merely by the physical senses.

Back in the most difficult days of the Brooklyn Tabernacle, when Carol and I had just come to the little church and were struggling to stay afloat with maybe forty people attending on Sunday mornings, our daughter Chrissy was about two years old. One morning at the breakfast table, we noticed a lump under her eyelid. The next day it seemed bigger. We didn't talk about it, even though the lump grew steadily larger.

"What do you think it is?" Carol finally asked one day with worry in her voice.

"I don't know."

"We'd better take her to a doctor," she said. The trouble was, we had no health insurance.

That night I spent time praying about the problem, and the longer I prayed, the more ominous it seemed. Did my little girl have some kind of tumor that would steal her eyesight? I said the right words to God, but I knew there was no faith in my heart. There was only apprehension.

We scraped up the money, and I took her to a doctor. He confirmed, "Yes, this is a growth—[he gave the technical name]—that shouldn't be there. It's not life-threatening, but we will need to cut it out."

The thought of my little firstborn daughter having a knife only millimeters from her eye immediately frightened me. Additionally, I was concerned how we would ever pay for the surgery.

That night, after Chrissy went to sleep, I returned to her room. I picked her up and held her in my arms. I prayed quietly, "O God, heal my daughter."

As I stood there in the semidarkness, holding my child and staring at the lump under her eye, I was filled with doubt and fear. I needed true, living faith. ～

Once again, although I was saying prayer-words, all I could see was a lump that now seemed as large as a boulder. I knew what God had said in the Bible about healing—I had preached from those texts. A dramatic healing had even played a role long ago in my grandmother coming to Christ.

But as I stood there in the semidarkness, holding my child and staring at the lump under her eye, I was filled with doubt and fear. I needed true, living faith, not theoretical faith.

The following Sunday, after the sermon, we were singing and worshiping together at the end of the service. I led the people in praising God for his goodness, while Carol played the organ. Suddenly my heart was flooded with a kind of divine light that brought a new sense of God powerfully to my soul.

I was overcome with God's awesome greatness, which makes everything on earth seem miniscule. Then suddenly—as God is my witness, I am not embellishing the story—I *saw* my daughter being prayed for at the front of the church. *And I saw her being healed!* It was not emotional or spooky; it was a real and definite picture before the eyes of my heart. God had birthed something within me.

My heart was pounding with joy as I reached for the microphone. "Who is holding my daughter?" I asked. (Our church was far too small back then to have an organized nursery.)

A teenage girl's hand went up in the back.

"Bring her up here quickly," I said. We gathered around her and anointed her with oil, praying together for God to heal her.

Within forty-eight hours, the lump was entirely gone, with no surgery, no doctor, no medical intervention of any kind. The God who longs to do great things for his people was encouraging us once again to believe.

Now what would happen in your church or mine if people came to each meeting with greater faith—a spirit of anticipation, a belief that God was about to do something wonderful? This was the very expectancy that greeted Jesus in many places. People fought just to touch him, for they *knew* something wonderful would happen. What if *we* yielded our hearts to both his Word and his Spirit instead of just mechanically repeating the same old order of service we have been following for the past twenty years? Something tells me things would never be the same.

Unfortunately, I have learned firsthand that many Christians who pound the Bible the hardest and most strongly defend the verbal inspiration of Scripture are the most unbelieving and cynical about God ever doing a new thing in his church. They seem so intent on preserving tradition that any spontaneity is spurned as "emotionalism." My question is: If Jesus is the same today as he was in the Bible we defend, why shouldn't we believe him to do great things among us and through us, so we can touch people's lives in powerful ways as did the first-century apostles? Peter was no perfect saint, as evidenced by his denial of Christ; many churches today would hardly allow such a failure to stand in their pulpits. But God chose him on the Day of Pentecost and used him mightily—and God can do the same with us if we look to him with childlike faith in our hearts.

> **Many Christians who pound the Bible the hardest are the most unbelieving and cynical about God ever doing a new thing in his church.** ～

More than twenty-five years ago, David Wilkerson preached a great sermon called "God Only Uses Failures." Of course, it's true—what else does God have to work with? But if we dare to believe him, we can be valuable instruments in his hand.

LOOK INWARD—BUT CAREFULLY

NEXT, JOSHUA CALLS the people to take stock of their obedience: "Be very strong; be careful to obey all that is written in the Book of the Law of Moses, without turning aside to the right or to the left. Do not associate with these nations that remain among you; do not invoke the names of their gods or swear by them. You must not serve them or bow down to them. But you are to hold fast to the LORD your God, as you have until now" (Joshua 23:6–8).

This separation from ungodly things was for the purpose of the Hebrews' maintaining their strength for battle. Alliance with sinful things—even just questionable practices—saps our strength and leaves us weak before the enemy. If there are some wrong conversations going on, an inappropriate relationship, or some fascination with a questionable topic or thing, we slowly but surely undercut our spiritual vitality. The enemy has subtly stolen our "shield of faith" needed to protect us in "the day of evil" (Ephesians 6:13, 16).

Joshua knew this all too well from what had happened back at Ai (see Joshua 7). After the stirring victory at Jericho, the disobedience of one soldier named Achan clogged up the carburetor of the whole Israelite war engine. The army suffered an unexpected and humiliating defeat—not because God had lost his power, but because something had separated the people from his holy companionship. Joshua had to stop everything and root out the sin before the military campaign took another step.

The apostle John wrote, "Do not love the world or anything in the world. If anyone loves the world, the love of the Father is not in him. For everything in the world—the cravings of sinful man, the lust of his eyes and the boasting of what he has and does—comes not from the Father but from the world" (1 John 2:15–16). Love for the world and preoccupation with its sick value system and enticements will wreck anyone's faith life.

Introspection, of course, is a two-edged sword. If we give long periods of time just to looking inward, we can easily get morose and spiritually depressed. There are special times for focusing on these things—for example, at the receiving of Communion (see 1 Corinthians 11:28–32) and other moments of divine searching within us. But if this process consumes us exclusively, Satan can easily gain the upper hand as our accuser, keeping us preoccupied with *our* failures rather than with Christ's pardon and power.

It is interesting to me that "solemn assemblies"—occasions when Old Testament leaders set aside whole days for confession and repentance and weeping—are not found in the New Testament. Yes, the apostles believed in getting right with God, in dealing with sin—but they did not grovel in it for long periods of time. Instead, it seems that they called people to cleanse their hearts before God and then moved on to faith and the fullness of the Holy Spirit. After all, Jesus left a Great Commission of work for the church to do. How would that be accomplished if his followers were continually looking inward at their own faults and shortcomings?

Look Away to Jesus

Joshua's final instruction is stated very simply: "Be very careful to love the Lord your God" (Joshua 23:11). Our gaze must always be upon him, because he is the one who will perform everything. Only when we are "looking unto Jesus, the author and finisher of our faith" (Hebrews 12:2 kjv) are we truly walking in faith.

Satan wants us to focus on the problem, not the Provider. He constantly points to what *seems* to be rather than to what God has promised to do. If we stop spending time with the Lord in prayer, the concerns of the physical world snatch our attention and dominate us, while the spiritual senses deaden and the promises fade.

> **The number one reason that Christians today don't pray more is because we do not grasp the connection between prayer and the promises of God.** ～

I am absolutely convinced that the number one reason that Christians today don't pray more is because we do not grasp the connection between prayer and the promises of God. We are trying as individuals and churches to pray "because we're supposed to" without a living faith in the promises of God concerning prayer. No prayer life of any significance can be maintained by this "ought-to" approach. There must be faith in God at the bottom.

Time and again I get phone calls and letters from hungry believers throughout the nation saying, "Pastor Cymbala, I am so frustrated—I've been to sixteen churches now in my area, and I can't find one that has a prayer meeting!" It is obvious that while pastors and leaders mentally accept the Bible's teaching on prayer, they don't really *see* its potential power through God. Otherwise, they would be leading their congregations to do it rather than just preaching sermons about it.

When real faith in God arises, a certainty comes that when we call, he will answer . . . that when we ask, we will receive . . . that when we knock, the door will be opened . . .

and soon we find ourselves spending a lot of time in his presence. We seek him for wayward children to be saved, for a greater sense of the Holy Spirit in our church services, for spiritual gifts and power to be released, for the finances we need to do his work.

But I am speaking about more than just presenting a laundry list of requests to God. Faith is especially nurtured when we just wait in God's presence, taking the time to love him and listen for his voice. Strength to keep believing often flows into us as we simply worship the Lord. The promises of Scripture become wonderfully alive as the Spirit applies them to our hearts.

> **Faith is especially nurtured when we just wait in God's presence, taking the time to love him and listen for his voice.** ～

When people come to my office overloaded with problems, not knowing where to turn, I sometimes say, "Here is what I want you to do: Go sit with the Prayer Band upstairs in their special room this Friday night from midnight to two in the morning."

They often react with shock on their faces. "Oh, Pastor Cymbala—I'm so discouraged I can't believe that the sun will come up tomorrow. I could never pray for two hours!"

"I didn't ask you to pray," I reply. "I just asked you to go sit there. The Prayer Band will pray for you. And God will operate on your heart as you just wait in his presence."

How many times have I heard back from these people that while they were sitting in that atmosphere, God brought alive his Word and his promises and lifted their spirits to believe. Thanksgiving began to flow. They began to remember the good things God had done in their past. Faith began to spring anew as they waited on the One who can so easily turn everything around in life.

GOD IS WAITING FOR YOU

WHAT DIFFICULTY ARE YOU now facing in your life that you have not been able to overcome? I wonder what God is waiting to accomplish in your life, your home, your work, your service for him. Why don't you and I face our need in Jesus' name and reach out in fresh faith to the Lord?

Let us not be hesitant or unsure about trusting him after reading all these wonderful stories and encouragements. Let us, rather, "draw near to God with a sincere heart *in full assurance of faith*, having our hearts sprinkled to cleanse us from a guilty conscience and having our bodies washed with pure water. Let us hold unswervingly to the hope we profess, for *he who promised is faithful*" (Hebrews 10:22–23). In the end, that is what really matters—not our efforts or pledges, but the wonderful truth that God is a faithful God.

So now, what will it be for all of us? Will we simply be stirred for a moment, or will we lay hold of God and his promises in a new, life-changing way? After all, it is not what happens externally to people that makes for tragedy in their lives; it is the missed opportunities to see God help them, due to their unbelief. That is the real tragedy.

God will be no different tomorrow than he is today. His love for us is the same. His power to meet our needs is unchanged. Right now his hand reaches out as he says, "Why spend money on what is not bread, and your labor on what does not satisfy?" (Isaiah 55:2). Let us stop the futile search for answers outside of God. Instead, let us arise with hope in our hearts, remembering that this powerful "word of faith" is not far away and difficult, but rather "is near you; it is in your mouth and in your heart" (Romans 10:8). This is the faith that not only saves us from sin but can also keep us victorious over every obstacle that life presents to us. "As the Scripture says, 'Anyone who trusts in him will never be put to shame'" (Romans 10:11).

Joshua must have had God's faithfulness in mind when he finished his speech that day with this great crescendo: "Now I am about to go the way of all the earth. You know with all your heart and soul that not one of all the good promises the LORD your God gave you has failed. Every promise has been fulfilled; not one has failed" (Joshua 23:14). We, too, can finish our race in life with the same powerful declaration, if we will only keep believing in the God whose promises are forever true.

EPILOGUE

~

33 Treasures

MORE VALUABLE THAN anything I could write or preach on the subject of faith are the direct declarations and promises of God's Word. Here are gems from the Bible that have inspired me over the years to believe. They have also formed the foundation for many a sermon.

As you read them, let them penetrate your mind and your spirit. Open your Bible and read the full passages in which they occur. Review them often as you seek to strengthen your own walk of faith.

~

SO THEN FAITH COMES by hearing, and hearing by the word of God.

ROMANS 10:17 NKJV

~

THE ONLY THING that counts is faith expressing itself through love.

GALATIANS 5:6

~

EVERYONE BORN OF GOD overcomes the world. This is the victory that has overcome the world, even our faith.

1 JOHN 5:4

～

THEY ASKED HIM, "What must we do to do the works God requires?"

Jesus answered, "The work of God is this: to believe in the one he has sent."

JOHN 6:28–29

～

IT IS BETTER TO take refuge in the LORD than to trust in man.

PSALM 118:8

～

FAITH IS BEING SURE of what we hope for and certain of what we do not see. This is what the ancients were commended for.

HEBREWS 11:1–2

～

WITHOUT FAITH IT IS impossible to please God, because anyone who comes to him must believe that he exists and that he rewards those who earnestly seek him.

HEBREWS 11:6

～

THE APOSTLES SAID to the Lord, "Increase our faith!"

LUKE 17:5

～

WE DO NOT WANT you to become lazy, but to imitate those who through faith and patience inherit what has been promised.

HEBREWS 6:12

∿

IF ANY OF YOU lacks wisdom, he should ask God, who gives generously to all without finding fault, and it will be given to him. But when he asks, he must believe and not doubt, because he who doubts is like a wave of the sea, blown and tossed by the wind.

JAMES 1:5–6

∿

TRUST IN THE LORD and do good;
    dwell in the land and enjoy safe pasture. . . .
Commit your way to the LORD ;
    trust in him and he will do this. . . .
Be still before the LORD and wait patiently for him;
    do not fret when men succeed in their ways,
    when they carry out their wicked schemes.

PSALM 37:3, 5, 7

∿

CAST YOUR CARES on the LORD
    and he will sustain you;
    he will never let the righteous fall.

PSALM 55:22

∿

TRUST IN HIM at all times, O people;
    pour out your hearts to him,
    for God is our refuge. *Selah*

PSALM 62:8

∿

BUT NOW, THIS IS what the LORD says—
    he who created you, O Jacob,
    he who formed you, O Israel:

"Fear not, for I have redeemed you;
   I have summoned you by name; you are mine.
When you pass through the waters,
   I will be with you;
and when you pass through the rivers,
    they will not sweep over you.
When you walk through the fire,
   you will not be burned;
    the flames will not set you ablaze."

ISAIAH 43:1–2

〜

I AM THE LORD, your God,
   who takes hold of your right hand
and says to you, Do not fear;
   I will help you.

ISAIAH 41:13

〜

TRUST IN THE LORD with all your heart
   and lean not on your own understanding.

PROVERBS 3:5

〜

WHO AMONG YOU fears the LORD
   and obeys the word of his servant?
Let him who walks in the dark,
   who has no light,
trust in the name of the LORD
   and rely on his God.

ISAIAH 50:10

～

MY EYES ARE EVER on the LORD,
for only he will release my feet from the snare.
PSALM 25:15

～

TO ALL WHO received him, to those who believed in his
name, he gave the right to become children of God.
JOHN 1:12

～

"WHOEVER BELIEVES IN ME, as the Scripture has said,
streams of living water will flow from within him."
JOHN 7:38

～

"HE MADE NO DISTINCTION between us and them, for he
purified their hearts by faith."
ACTS 15:9

～

WHAT THEN SHALL we say that Abraham, our forefather, discovered in this matter? If, in fact, Abraham was justified by
works, he had something to boast about—but not before
God. What does the Scripture say? "Abraham believed God,
and it was credited to him as righteousness."

Now when a man works, his wages are not credited to
him as a gift, but as an obligation. However, to the man who
does not work but trusts God who justifies the wicked, his
faith is credited as righteousness.
ROMANS 4:1–5

～

Against all hope, Abraham in hope believed and so became the father of many nations, just as it had been said to him, "So shall your offspring be."

Romans 4:18

～

Christ is the end of the law so that there may be righteousness for everyone who believes.

Romans 10:4

～

They were broken off because of unbelief, and you stand by faith. Do not be arrogant, but be afraid.

Romans 11:20

～

. . . so that your faith might not rest on men's wisdom, but on God's power.

1 Corinthians 2:5

～

In Scripture it says:
"See, I lay a stone in Zion,
a chosen and precious cornerstone,
and the one who trusts in him
will never be put to shame."

1 Peter 2:6

～

Not that we lord it over your faith, but we work with you for your joy, because it is by faith you stand firm.

2 Corinthians 1:24

∼

IN ADDITION TO ALL THIS, take up the shield of faith, with which you can extinguish all the flaming arrows of the evil one.

EPHESIANS 6:16

∼

LET US DRAW NEAR to God with a sincere heart in full assurance of faith, having our hearts sprinkled to cleanse us from a guilty conscience and having our bodies washed with pure water.

HEBREWS 10:22

∼

"MY RIGHTEOUS ONE will live by faith.
And if he shrinks back,
    I will not be pleased with him."

But we are not of those who shrink back and are destroyed, but of those who believe and are saved.

HEBREWS 10:38–39

∼

WHEN HE HAD gone indoors, the blind men came to him, and he asked them, "Do you believe that I am able to do this?"

"Yes, Lord," they replied.

MATTHEW 9:28

∼

IMMEDIATELY THE BOY'S FATHER exclaimed, "I do believe; help me overcome my unbelief!"

MARK 9:24

Notes

Chapter Five—Can I Trust God to Lead Me?

1. *The Works of John Wesley*—CD (Franklin, Tenn.: Providence House, 1995); see also "The Character of a Methodist," *The Works of John Wesley*, 3d ed., vol. 8, p. 339 (London: Wesleyan Methodist Book Room, 1872; reprinted Grand Rapids: Baker, 1996).

2. Sermon entitled "The Eternal Name," preached on the evening of May 27, 1855, at Exeter Hall, London.

Chapter Seven—Faith Runs on a Different Clock

1. "Keep Believing" by Tim Pedigo (Nashville: Meadowgreen Music, copyright © 1985).

Chapter Eight—Overcoming Discouragement

1. Cited in *Words Old and New*, compiled by Horatius Bonar (reprint Edinburgh: Banner of Truth Trust, 1994), pp. 16–17.

Chapter Thirteen—The Atmosphere of Faith

1. Andrew Murray, *The Holiest of All* (1894; reprint Grand Rapids: Revell, 1993), pp. 441–42.

FRESH FAITH STUDY GUIDE

CHAPTER ONE: STOLEN PROPERTY

Pastor Cymbala points out that *Satan steals spiritual, eternally significant treasures* that God values. What types of things does Satan do to steal our sense of purpose in life, to cause our zeal and passion for God to wane?

Personal Reflection

Jesus said to the Ephesian church in Revelation 2, "I know your deeds, your hard work and your perseverance. . . . Yet I hold this against you: You have forsaken your first love." What do you notice when you compare your love for the following today to the love you had when you first became a Christian?

- Your love for Jesus?
- Your love of and desire to know the Scriptures?
- Your energy and passion for the church?

Pastor Cymbala writes about the "unique calling that rests on every Christian's life—the gifting to serve others in the name of the Lord."

- What are some ways in which Satan has sidetracked you from your God-given calling—or hindered you from accomplishing what God wants you to do for him? Did you recognize them as Satan's effort to sidetrack you? How did you respond? What would you have done differently if you had recognized Satan's efforts to steal, kill, or destroy?

Pastor Cymbala emphasized that Satan intends to destroy our marriages, credibility, and effectiveness. What are some evidences of his "successes" in our society today? Among Christians?

A Time to Share

Break into groups of two or three and discuss the following questions:

- What is faith?
- Which specific events or thoughts cause people to stop trusting God, to stop expecting him to answer their prayers?
- What do you think will happen if we go after specific problems in the name of the Lord?

Pastor Cymbala used the story of the time when David and his men recovered their families and all their possessions from the marauding Amalekites to illustrate that "what the enemy steals, God alone is able to recover."

- Why is it important for us to recognize that we aren't wrestling against flesh and blood but are engaged in spiritual warfare?

- Why is it important for us to use the spiritual weapons of faith and prayer to resist Satan and in the power of God "get up" and recover what Satan has stolen from us?
- Why do some of us refuse to battle Satan and seek the abundant life Jesus promises—in our marriages, in our spiritual calling, in our desire to have a vibrant heart-faith and childlike trust in the risen, supernatural Christ?

Personal Reflection

In what ways do you tend to respond toward God when bad things happen in your life? Do you angrily blame him? Do you, as the psalmist David did, "find strength" in the Lord your God? Do you ask God for guidance and encourage-ment? What do your responses reveal about your faith?

Romans 1:17 reveals that "the righteous will live by faith," and Hebrews 11:6 reads, "Without faith it is impossible to please God." What must we do to keep our "faith connection" to God fresh and vibrant?

CHAPTER TWO: AMALIA'S STORY

Remember the story Pastor Cymbala told concerning Amalia—her wretched home life, the sexual abuse, drugs, exotic dancing, plans for suicide?

- What things in our lives seem "too impossible" for God to change?

- In light of what God changed in Amalia's life, how might he change the "impossibilities" of our lives if we will in faith ask him to help us reclaim what Satan has stolen from us?

A Time to Share

Pastor Cymbala writes, "You can see Jesus Christ prove himself more powerful than the thief who steals [Satan]. This very moment is critical, even as you read these words. Face the reality of your spiritual situation, and go after anything God has shown you to be stolen property that Satan has cleverly taken from you. The zeal and love for Christ you once had *can* be recovered."

- In what ways would your life change if you were to recover what Satan has stolen from you?
- What might the consequences be if we continue to allow Satan to steal the treasures God has for us—our children, our marriages, our churches?

Personal Reflection

Psalm 50:15 reads, "Call upon me in the day of trouble; I will deliver you, and you will honor me."

- What prevents you from calling on God right now for mercy and grace?
- Think of an area in your life in which you need to ask in faith that Jesus will restore what Satan has stolen. Be honest! Then take some time to ask God for help. Instead of allowing Satan to keep ripping you off, begin to ask Jesus in faith for the abundant life he offers you. Ask him to restore what Satan has tried to steal. (And when God does it, be sure to praise him in a new way!)

CHAPTER THREE:
THE QUESTION NOBODY IS ASKING

Why do you think Christians tend to measure how they are doing spiritually by focusing on what Pastor Cymbala calls "surface things" instead of answering the question: *How active and vibrant is our faith in God?* What is the difference?

Pastor Cymbala writes, "What [the apostle] Paul knew, but what we seem to have forgotten, is that when people break down in their behavior, backslide into sinful living, or grow cold in the Lord, it is because their faith has broken down first."

- Do you agree or disagree with this? Why?
- What specific things cause our personal faith in God to "break down"?

Personal Reflection

We read in the New Testament that Jesus was amazed by some people's faith—for example, the Roman centurion (Luke 7) and the Canaanite woman (Matthew 15). If Jesus were sitting across from you in a restaurant or in your home, what do you think he would say about your faith in him?

The Bible clearly states that our faith is the key to our relationship with God. Pastor Cymbala calls it "the trigger that releases divine power." Jesus said, "According to your faith will it be done to you" (Matthew 9:29).

- How does this truth match what you have learned about God's supreme power and what he will do for you?
- In what way(s) does this truth support or contradict what you have heard about what it means to walk "in faith"?

- If people realize this truth, how might they act and respond differently—toward God? Toward the Bible? Toward prayer?

What happens to our walk with God when we focus on our human efforts and abilities rather than on God's, meaning that we focus on earning God's approval by doing certain things (daily Bible reading, trying to live a good life, etc.) rather than receiving his grace by faith?

Paul writes, "I can do everything through him [Christ] who gives me strength" (Philippians 4:13). What does it mean, in practical terms, to receive "strength" from Christ?

God, on one hand, calls us to live "by faith." Yet Jesus is "the author and finisher of our faith" (Hebrews 12:2 KJV). How would you describe the balance between what we do and what God does in and through us?

In the following verses written by Paul, what might seem contradictory to people who don't yet know Jesus? "The Lord ... said to me, 'My grace is sufficient for you, for my power is made perfect in weakness.' ... That is why, for Christ's sake, I delight in weaknesses, in insults, in hardships, in persecutions, in difficulties. For when I am weak, then I am strong" (2 Corinthians 12:9–10).

Describe a time in your life when, as Pastor Cymbala says, "God used trouble and trials of all kinds" to remind you that you need him to fill you constantly so that you had the faith to use divine resources. What did the troubles and trials teach you about your need for God? Your need for faith?

"Childlike faith in God," writes Pastor Cymbala, "is not only what pleases him but is also the secret of our strength and power."

- What does Pastor Cymbala mean by childlike faith?
- Why is childlike faith so important to our spiritual growth and effectiveness?

A Time to Share

Pastor Cymbala writes, "When we run to him [God] and throw ourselves upon him in believing prayer, he rejoices . . . He is not so much interested in our *doing* as in our *receiving* from him."

- What is "believing prayer"?
- Why does God desire us to be in a mode of receiving from him?

As a group, read Psalm 32:6–11 aloud. Then discuss each of these verses, exploring how they relate to faith and trust in God's character. You may use the following questions as a springboard.

- In what way(s) is God our "hiding place"?
- What does God promise to do for us?
- What, according to God, surrounds a person who trusts in him?

CHAPTER FOUR: FREE FROM A HURTFUL PAST

Pastor Cymbala points out that Joseph named his first son Manasseh because God had made him forget all the evil things people had done to him.

- Why is it important for us, when we've been hurt by others, to seek God's help in delivering us from the paralysis of the past?
- What was accomplished when Amalia, who was greatly abused, visited her father and told him that she had forgiven him and loved him?
- What is Satan able to accomplish when he uses the hurts and ugly memories of our past to steal our callings, our peace, and our joy?

Personal Reflection

Think about a time when you or someone you know stopped struggling in his/her own strength and called out to God in simple faith. What happened? Are you fully depending on God today and trusting him to help meet a particular problem or need? Why or why not?

Personal Reflection

Do you believe that, as Pastor Cymbala puts it, "Faith grows best on cloudy days"? Do you believe that God can set you free from painful experiences and hurt? Will you ask him to make you spiritually fruitful even when you face the hardest challenges? Why not approach his throne of grace boldly right now and ask him for the grace to help you right where you need it!

CHAPTER FIVE: CAN I TRUST GOD TO LEAD ME?

Pastor Cymbala writes, "It may not seem obvious at first glance, but the way we make decisions in life tells a lot about the kind of faith we have in Jesus Christ." To what extent do you base your decisions on feelings? On the advice of godly family members and/or friends? On what the living God who reveals himself through the Bible says?

A Time to Share

Pastor Cymbala points out that some Christians follow the spiritual culture into which they were born—such as a particular church, denomination, or religious tradition—rather than using the Bible as their guide and model. Instead of coming to the Scriptures and asking God to teach them, these people hold on to what they have already embraced and are not really open to change and growth.

- How does this "closed" approach to the Christian life influence people's understanding of these words: *prayer, worship, church, evangelism, God's power, faith, Christian?*
- Why is it important, as Pastor Cymbala writes, to "honestly search God's Word and let it shape our spiritual thinking and values"?
- What are some of the dangers of letting our personal background, rather than God's Word, be the main force that shapes our spiritual thinking and values?

What are the consequences of making decisions without seeking God and tapping into his great resources of wisdom? Of doing just about everything *except* praying earnestly until we find God's will for our lives?

A Time to Share

Pastor Cymbala writes, "Wherever God leads us, there is an umbrella of protection and supply that stays over our heads.

Under that umbrella are the divine resources of wisdom, grace, finance, and all the other things we need to do that God has asked. That does not mean there won't be problems and difficulties. But wherever the Lord leads, he must then by necessity help us." Break up into twos and threes and talk about times when you have seen in your lives or in the lives of others how God has provided for people who have obeyed God and gone where he wanted them to go.

When Pastor Cymbala heard about a four-thousand-seat theater in Brooklyn for sale, he asked the associate pastors to look at it and pray about buying it. Unless all of them felt God was leading them, they wouldn't present the option to the congregation.

- In what ways can we seek God's confirmation for decisions we must make?
- Why is it important for us to receive confirmation from God concerning our decisions?
- What role does humility play as we seek God's guidance?

A Time to Share

Pastor Cymbala points out research showing that fewer than 10 percent of churchgoing Christians make important life decisions "based on God's Word and seeking his will." We don't think God really cares about us, are too proud to admit we need God's help, or simply continue the same decision-making habits.

- To what extent does our understanding of God's character influence the degree to which we will seek his leading?

According to Pastor Cymbala, "Too many church leaders, having been turned off by overblown claims and fanaticism in certain quarters, have stopped believing in an active Holy Spirit at all." Discuss your opinions on this and the consequences this may be having in your church today.

Personal Reflection

Do you believe God is interested in every part of your life? That he watches you and wants to lead you? How does your belief affect your life—and people around you?

What situations are you or someone you love facing right now in which you need God's guidance? Have you yielded to his will for your life so you can hear his voice? Why or why not? What will you do in coming days in order to wait and listen in God's presence?

During one Sunday afternoon service, Pastor Cymbala sensed God telling him to preach the gospel right away. So, after giving Calvin Hunt, the soloist, time to speak, Pastor Cymbala interrupted the schedule and preached. As a result, a wayward young man heard and responded to the gospel.

- Why is it important for us to listen to the Holy Spirit's leading—even during our preplanned church services?

CHAPTER SIX: THE HIGH COST OF CLEVERNESS

A Time to Share

Pastor Cymbala writes, "Our culture teaches us to take charge of our lives and call our own shots." In what ways does this view conflict with trusting God completely to lead and guide us?

Selected by God to become king of Israel, Jeroboam received wonderful promises that were conditional on his obedience to God. Instead of having faith in God, obeying God, and trusting in God's promises, he "thought to himself" (1 Kings 12:26) and depended on human cleverness.

- What are some situations in which we do this same thing today?
- How does our unbelief affect our relationship with God?
- What makes it easier to trust in ourselves rather than in God?

King Jeroboam built golden calves in his territory so people would worship in Israel rather than in the southern kingdom. Pastor Cymbala points out, "In the church today, we are still busy inventing new forms of religion as Jeroboam did." In what ways might our new, "user-friendly" kind of Christianity be quite different from a Spirit-filled Christianity?

Why is it important for us to pray honestly to God, tell him our fears, and trust in his faithfulness rather than "talking to ourselves" and trying to figure out all the details?

In what way(s) might each of us benefit from a godly prayer partner who can help us remain focused on God's faithfulness?

CHAPTER SEVEN:
FAITH RUNS ON A DIFFERENT CLOCK

Personal Reflection

When you experience problems, do you believe that God is really "for you" and will supply what you need—or do you believe that you have to face everything on your own? Are you still asking and seeking God—even when you feel pressure to "do something" in your own strength? What are some specific ways in which you can trust God to keep his promises?

A Time to Share

As the story of Zechariah and Elizabeth in Luke 1 illustrates, God accomplishes his will according to his timetable. Let's recall their story and explore a few truths together.

- How do you think Zechariah felt when the angel announced Elizabeth would bear a son?
- The angel said to Mary, who would be the mother of Jesus, "For nothing is impossible with God" (Luke 1:37). How does this relate to us today?
- What does God reveal about himself and our relationship with him when he intervenes in the seemingly hopeless situations in our lives?
- Describe a time when God intervened on your behalf, perhaps when a situation seemed too awful to be fixed.
- What impact did God's action have on you? On others close to you?
- After Elizabeth gave birth, Zechariah praised God. Why is it important for us to praise God after he demonstrates his mighty power and salvation in our lives?

Why, according to Pastor Cymbala, must we "persevere in prayer"—as individuals and as a body of believers? Relate your answer to James 4:2: "You do not have, because you do not ask God."

Personal Reflection

When do you, as Zechariah did, find it hard to believe God's promises? Are you persevering in prayer, or are you trying to get by on your own? What may be keeping you from completely trusting God, who can accomplish so much when you have faith in him? " Do you believe what your feelings and circumstances tell you or what God has promised to do?

When you read the following lyrics, what do you *feel?*

> Keep believing what you know is true;
> Keep believing—you know the Lord will see you
>   through.
> When troubles arise in your life, and you don't know
>   what to do,
> You'll be fine if you just keep believing.[1]

In *Fresh Faith*, Pastor Cymbala describes Wendy Alvear's search for a husband and good marriage and how she learned to keep her eyes on God rather than on her situation. "Wait for God," she later shared with the Brooklyn Tabernacle congregation, "he knows how to give you the best."

- What does it mean, in practical terms, to "keep on believing and waiting for God"?

---

[1]"Keep Believing" by Tim Pedigo (Nashville: Meadowgreen Music, copyright © 1985).

CHAPTER EIGHT: OVERCOMING DISCOURAGEMENT

"The promises of God," Pastor Cymbala writes, "are appropriated only by faith. God is looking for a people who will believe him and take him at his word no matter what the circumstances say or what other people are telling us."

- Why is it more difficult for us to place our faith in God and what he has promised to do than to believe what our feelings and circumstances tell us?
- Why do you think God values our faith in him so highly?

A Time to Share

Pastor Cymbala writes, "The battle is always not about giving in to what we see around us, but about holding on to God's promises." Do you agree or disagree? Why? Share some experiences you have had relating to trusting God with important issues. Describe how you fought the battle.

Colossians 1:10–12 reads, "And we pray this in order that you may live a life worthy of the Lord ..., being strengthened with all power according to his glorious might so that you may have great endurance and patience, and joyfully giving thanks to the Father, who has qualified you to share in the inheritance of the saints in the kingdom of light." Which parts of these verses are especially meaningful and encourage you to live a life that is worthy? Why?

Satan, according to Pastor Cymbala, uses loose talk and loose emotions to discourage us.

- What are some signals that reveal we should try to limit our time with a particular person because of his or her negative effect on our spirit?

- What are some ways to deal with a person who discourages us?
- Describe what Pastor Cymbala calls "loose emotions" and identify their causes.
- What is the biblical antidote to loose talk and loose emotions?

What are some differences between Christians who are able to endure life's challenges and other Christians who become discouraged in the face of attacks on their faith?

"The longer I live, the more I treasure people who just keep walking with God," Pastor Cymbala writes. "They aren't up or down, left or right; they're always steady on the course, praising God and believing his Word." Why is praise important in our walk with God?

CHAPTER NINE: GRACE THAT IS GREATER

Judah, the Old Testament patriarch, wasn't exactly a model of godly obedience. He married a pagan, lost two evil sons to God's judgment, and had sex with a woman he believed to be a prostitute. He was a moral failure, hypocrite, and a disgrace to God and his family.

- Why do you think God included Judah's ugly story in the Bible and included Perez—Tamar's son from her union with Judah—in the genealogy of Jesus? What does his story reveal about God's view of sin and forgiveness in light of our own sins and feelings of unworthiness?

- What is the difference between proclaiming God's grace in changing and redeeming sinful people on one hand and emphasizing God's commandments and expressing self-righteous disdain over other people's sinful lives?

"God's specialty," Pastor Cymbala writes, "is forgiving and putting away people's sins from his sight." In what ways could we better emphasize the mercy God has for every person who messes up?

Personal Reflection

When you read the story of Calvin Hunt's addiction to crack cocaine, how does what God did in his life and in the life of his family relate to your life? To the life of someone you know? To what our powerful God can do?

In what way(s) does what the apostle Paul says in the following verse, 1 Timothy 1:16, relate to each of us today? "But for that very reason I was shown mercy so that in me, the worst of sinners, Christ Jesus might display his unlimited patience as an example for those who would believe on him and receive eternal life."

Chapter Ten: Father of the Faithful

Pastor Cymbala writes, "When you walk by faith, God never lets you settle into some plateau." In what ways have you found this to be true in your life?

A Time to Share

Break into small groups and discuss these questions:

- What happens when we try to live off God's commands rather than God's promises?
- If we woke up every morning thinking about God's wonderful promises—what he has said he will do for us today—how might our lives be different?
- What price do we pay when we don't step out in faith and believe God's promises?

What are the dangers of concentrating on external evidences of God's work, such as "the secret of church growth," rather than receiving the power God has promised to give his people as they walk in faith?

Just as Abraham headed to Egypt without consulting God because of a famine, trouble ensues when we stop living by faith and do what we think is smart or what circumstances dictate. How will God respond to anyone who turns back to him, to what Pastor Cymbala calls "an altar of consecration and faith"?

Personal Reflection

"Jesus Christ," writes Pastor Cymbala, "can do anything but fail his own people who trust in him." Why is it so important to trust in God—in his care for you and those you love—rather than worrying? Do you find it hard to trust God sometimes, even though you know God's promises? Set aside time this week to carefully and prayerfully search the Scriptures, asking God to make his promises come alive to you and also reviewing his promises included at the back of *Fresh Faith*.

Regardless of whether you have strayed from God, he is waiting to receive you.

CHAPTER ELEVEN: GOD'S DEEPER WORK

Over and over, Pastor Cymbala emphasizes that walking by faith brings us into the realm of God's supernatural power. Often we expect God to work in external areas, such as healing our bodies and supplying jobs. But where, according to Ephesians 3:20, does God often exhibit his great power? What does he want to accomplish?

"God," Pastor Cymbala writes, "knows that our problems are not merely due to our environment; they are deeply personal." What does he mean by this statement? In what way(s) does this statement go against current perspectives concerning our problems?

A Time to Share

Nearly a year after David's affair with Bathsheba, he admitted his guilt and came clean. In the middle of Psalm 51, he spelled out three essential things he needed from God. Break into groups of two or three and discuss these three things.

1. "Create in me a pure heart" (Psalm 51:10)
   - What did David admit here about himself?
   - Why did David want a brand-new heart?
   - If this prayer were the cry of our hearts, how might our lives be different?

2. "Renew a steadfast spirit within me" (Psalm 51:10).

- Why is "steadfastness" in everyday spiritual living important?

- What causes many Christians to have a "rise-and-fall, mountain-and-valley" relationship with God?

- What keeps us from boldly asking God to make our faith firm and do what he has promised?

3. "Grant me a willing spirit, to sustain me" (Psalm 51:12).

- According to this verse, how do we obtain "a willing spirit" that will do whatever God asks us to do?

- What happens when we try to do God's will on our own rather than depending on his Holy Spirit to work from within us?

- What has happened to Christians who view Christianity as drudgery and burdensome rather than a joyous life of loving the good and pleasing God?

God, according to Pastor Cymbala, will give *anyone* a pure heart, renew a steadfast spirit, and grant a willing spirit. It doesn't matter how deeply evil thoughts are embedded or how vicious a person's behavioral patterns have become. Jeremiah 32:27 reads, "I am the LORD, the God of all mankind. Is anything too hard for me?"

- What, then, do Christians who are unwilling to realize that God can fully redeem anyone and change even the "worst" behaviors believe?

- What conclusions do we come to when we believe that God's power isn't effective for all sins, that he can't completely change anyone from the inside out? What are the consequences of such beliefs?

Personal Reflection

Is your Christian walk all you want it to be? What might be keeping you from walking in faith and joy according to God's plan? What, in practical terms, happens when you believe your faithful God has the power to completely change your life—and the life of anyone else no matter how deeply rooted sin may be in his or her life?

Psalm 51:17 says, "The sacrifices of God are a broken spirit; a broken and contrite heart, O God, you will not despise." Why is God always drawn to weakness?

CHAPTER TWELVE: ADDITION BY SUBTRACTION

In which area(s) of your life are there "secret pockets of sin"? Is your faith deep enough to yield to God's refining fire and allow him to purify your life and take away anything he sees fit that hinders your communion with him?

A Time to Share

God clearly expressed his desire to remove our impurities through a purging process, yet many of us don't like to think that God wants to make major changes in our lives—including correcting and rebuking us.

- What is the intent of pastors who focus only on kind, "feel good" topics that people want to hear?
- What consequences does this focus create for individual Christians listening to their sermons? For the church as a whole?

- What might God want to accomplish when we become uncomfortable as we recognize our impurities and how they are affecting our relationship with him?
- Pastor Cymbala writes, "He [God] will never make a treaty with our secret pockets of sin." What is God seeking to accomplish as he ruthlessly goes after things—attitudes, habits, actions—that spoil the flow of his grace and blessing into our lives? What does this process of spiritual refinement reveal about who God is and why he will never allow us to remain the way we are today?

Why do some Christians hold on to their impurities and fight God's purifying process despite the Holy Spirit's persistent warnings and conviction of sin? If you feel comfortable sharing, describe times when you resisted God's purifying process and share what happened as a result.

CHAPTER THIRTEEN: THE ATMOSPHERE OF FAITH

Do you agree or disagree with this quotation from Pastor Cymbala: "The battle of the Christian life has always been not just to believe, but to *keep on* believing"? Why? What kinds of things can cause us to believe for a while and then fall away?

What is the difference between giving mental assent to a biblical truth on one hand and drawing near to God?

Why does God consider our chronic lack of faith to be such a serious sin rather than just a weakness?

Why does Satan work so hard, in Pastor Cymbala's words, to "break down our faith"?

A Time to Share

Pastor Cymbala points out that many believers struggle with this realization: "I have the desire to do what is good, but I cannot carry it out" (Romans 7:18).

- Why don't the commands of God make us strong enough to obey him?
- What tends to happen to believers who know what is right and desire to live that way yet can't seem to do it?
- Why must we understand that God "has given us his very great and precious promises, so that through them ... [we] may participate in the divine nature and escape the corruption in the world caused by evil desires" (2 Peter 1:4)?
- If we don't feed on God's promises of the Word, what will happen to us? Why?

Personal Reflection

The Israelite leader Joshua encouraged people to look back and see what the Lord had done for them. What has God done for you within the past year? Which "good and perfect gift" has he given you? (See James 1:17.) Do you "enter his gates with thanksgiving and his courts with praise" (Psalm 100:4)? Are you opening up your heart *and* your mouth to express the gratitude of your heart toward the Lord?

Think of several things in your life that are not yet the way God wants them to be. What is keeping you from invoking his promises and letting him do his work in these areas of your life?

Pastor Cymbala writes, "How pitiful that millions of church-goers cheer wildly and unashamedly for their favorite sports teams—but are silent as a corpse when it comes to praising God." Why do you think this occurs? What compels us to praise God?

We read in Hebrews 11:27, "By faith he [Moses] left Egypt, not fearing the king's anger; he persevered because he saw him who is invisible." Note how it was possible for Moses to persevere. What does it mean to see "him who is invisible"?

Faith "comes from God as we receive his living Word into our hearts," writes Pastor Cymbala. What is involved in receiving God's Word into our hearts?

Personal Reflection

Pastor Cymbala shares a story of how God miraculously removed a growth from under his daughter's eyelid. What great thing(s) has God done for you or someone you know that he may be using to encourage you to once again believe in him? What may be keeping you from believing that God is about to do something new and wonderful in your life? In your church? In your community? What will happen, if you haven't already done so, if you yield your heart to God's Word and his Spirit?

When we ally ourselves with sinful things or questionable practices, our spiritual strength and vitality are weakened. Thus the "shield of faith" that we need to protect us has been stolen by the enemy. Without dwelling on your failures so much that you lose focus on Christ's pardon and power, think about your life. What sin in your life is separating you from God's holy companionship? Which steps will you take to cleanse your heart before God and then, as Pastor Cymbala expresses, move on "to faith and the fullness of the Holy

Spirit"? What seemingly insurmountable difficulty are you facing that you need to bring before God in fresh faith?

"I am absolutely convinced that the number one reason that Christians today don't pray more," writes Pastor Cymbala, "is because we do not grasp the connection between prayer and the promises of God." What is this connection, and how is it established?

What is the difference between waiting in God's presence, taking time to love him and listen to his voice, and simply presenting him with a list of requests?

Hebrews 10:23 tells us to "hold unswervingly to the hope we profess, for he who promised is faithful." In what ways do our lives change when we embrace this truth?

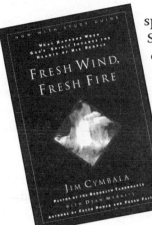

FRESH POWER
Experiencing the Vast Resources of the Spirit of God
Jim Cymbala with Dean Merrill

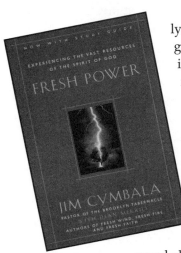

Pastor Jim Cymbala of the Brooklyn Tabernacle has taught his congregation how God's mighty power can infuse their present-day lives and the mission of their church. He continued that teaching nationally in his best-selling books *Fresh Wind, Fresh Fire* and *Fresh Faith*, which tell about the transforming power of God's love to convert prostitutes, addicts, the homeless, and people of all races and stations in life.

Now in *Fresh Power* Cymbala continues to spread the word about the power of God's Holy Spirit in the lives of those who seek him. Fresh power, Cymbala says, is available to us as we desire the Holy Spirit's constant infilling and learn what it means to be Spirit filled, both as individuals and as the church. With the book of Acts as the basis for his study, Cymbala shows how the daily lives of first-century Christians were defined by their belief in God's Word, in the constant infilling of his Spirit, and in the clear and direct responses of obedience to Scripture. He shows that that same life in Christ through the power of the Holy Spirit is available today for pastors, leaders, and laypeople who are longing for revival.

Hardcover 0-310-23008-X
Softcover 0-310-25154-0
Audio Pages® Abridged Cassettes 0-310-23467-X
Audio Pages® Unabridged CD 0-310-24200-2

Pick up a copy today at your favorite bookstore!

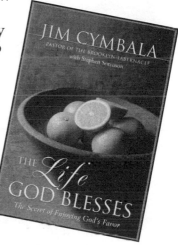

HE'S BEEN FAITHFUL
Trusting God to Do What Only He Can Do
Carol Cymbala with Ann Spangler

Carol Cymbala's ministry in a tough inner-city neighborhood in New York can be summed up in one word: unlikely. She is the director and songwriter for a Grammy Award-winning choir—yet she doesn't read music. She is the pastor's wife in a six-thousand-member congregation filled with people of color—and she is white. A shy girl who struggled to get through school, she is the last person you'd expect to stand before a packed house at Radio City Music Hall, confidently directing the Brooklyn Tabernacle Choir.

But Carol's God is the God of the unlikely. *He's Been Faithful* is an honest story about the struggles we all face and the power of God to help us. It is told through Carol's eyes as well as through the eyes of various members of the Brooklyn Tabernacle Choir, who have experienced the grace of Christ in remarkable ways. *He's Been Faithful* tells the story of the way God works despite—or maybe because of—our many inadequacies.

But Carol's faith hasn't always come easily. There have been times of wavering and challenge, like the time a man walked down the aisle of the church pointing a gun at her husband, Jim. Or like the time she was assaulted outside the church. Or like the time she wanted to pack up her children and run away from the city for good because of what was happening to her family.

Whether you are a pastor, a choir director, or someone who is seeking a deeper experience of God, *He's Been Faithful* will renew your faith and increase your understanding that only Jesus can fill that deep, deep longing we all have for something more in life.

Hardcover 0-310-23652-5
Audio Pages® Abridged Cassettes 0-310-23668-1

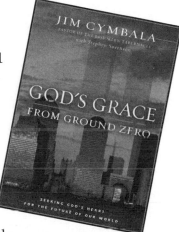

THE CHURCH GOD BLESSES
Jim Cymbala with Stephen Sorenson

God wants to transform his church into a people of power, joy, and peace. Jim Cymbala reminds us that Christianity is only as strong as the local church and that God wants to bless our churches in ways we can't possibly imagine. It doesn't matter whether a church is alive and growing or barely surviving on life support. God has a plan for it. It doesn't matter whether a church is facing financial challenges, internal divisions, or strife among its leaders. God has a plan for it. God is able to deal with any problem a church will ever face—as long as his people earnestly seek him.

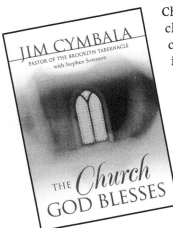

As the pastor of the Brooklyn Tabernacle, Cymbala knows that God's blessing and grace is available to us today just as much as it was in the early church. Then, as now, God chose the church to manifest his presence to the world.

Hardcover: 0-310-24203-7
Unabridged Audio Pages® Cassette 0-310-24801-9
Unabridged Audio Pages® CD 0-310-24800-0

Pick up a copy today at your favorite bookstore!

ZONDERVAN

GRAND RAPIDS, MICHIGAN 49530
www.zondervan.com